THE RISE AND FALL OF BECKY SHARP

Beautiful, brilliant, ruthless — nothing can stop Becky Sharp. She has big dreams, and no connections to pull her down. Determined to swap the gutters of Soho for the glamorous, exclusive world behind the velvet rope, she will do anything to achieve fame, riches and status. Whether it's seducing society's most eligible bachelors, or befriending silly debutantes and rich old ladies, Becky Sharp is destined for great things. Because it might be tough at the top, but it's worse at the bottom. From London to Paris and beyond, Becky Sharp is going places — so get the hell out of her way. . .

SARRA MANNING

◆

THE RISE AND FALL OF BECKY SHARP

Complete and Unabridged

CHARNWOOD
Leicester

First published in Great Britain in 2018 by
HarperCollins*Publishers*
London

First Charnwood Edition
published 2019
by arrangement with
HarperCollins*Publishers*
London

*A catalogue record for this book is available
from the British Library.*

ISBN 978–1–4448–4090–2

Published by
F. A. Thorpe (Publishing)
Anstey, Leicestershire

Set by Words & Graphics Ltd.
Anstey, Leicestershire
Printed and bound in Great Britain by
T. J. International Ltd., Padstow, Cornwall

This book is printed on acid-free paper

Dedicated to William Makepeace Thackeray
who created these wonderful characters
that I got to play with.
I hope that he would approve.

'All is vanity. Nothing is fair.'
Vanity Fair, W. M. Thackeray

1

BATTLE OF THE BIG BROTHER BEAUTIES! Will It Be Amelia Or Becky Who Wins Tonight's Final? Place Your Bets!

In one corner we have blonde banker's daughter, Amelia Sedley, 22, the posh totty who's been unlucky in love but has become princess of the nation's hearts. And in the other corner we have red-headed stunner Becky Sharp, 20, a care assistant with a big heart and a wicked sense of humour.

Ahead of tonight's final, bookies have slashed odds on either of them to win and are saying it's too close to call. One thing's for certain, this year's *Big Brother* has had a massive ratings boost thanks to these two babes.

Who can forget Poolgate? Or Becky's rousing 'chicks before dicks' speech? The double eviction of house villains, Leanne and Johnny? Or just how fabulous Amelia and Becky look in their bikinis?

So *The Globe* would like to wish both girls best of luck tonight and thanks for all the mammaries!

★ ★ ★

'*Big Brother* house! You are live on Channel Five, please do not swear.'

Even though they'd been expecting the announcement, the two young women jumped as the excited tones of the TV announcer were broadcast into the house on a studio set in Elstree where they'd spent the last two months.

'Are you all right?' Becky Sharp mouthed to Amelia, her BFF, who was clutching her white acrylic wine glass for dear life.

The roar of the crowd gathered outside was audible even in the hermetically sealed house. It didn't sound like a good roar but more like the last thing the Christian martyrs heard before they were ripped to shreds by lions in a Roman amphitheatre.

Although it was a warm August night, Becky couldn't help the shiver that ran through her. Her eyes widened and she bit her bottom lip, making sure that her slightly furrowed brow was shown to its best advantage by the camera to her left, positioned high up in the corner. You couldn't spend eight weeks in a house with eighty cameras in it without knowing exactly where those cameras were. Anyone who said that after a while you forgot their presence and showed your real self — like, say, the ten other contestants who'd already been kicked out of the house — were either liars or idiots. Or both. Yes, definitely both.

'I'm so nervous,' Amelia said, her wispy voice catching at the same time as her soft, pretty features began to wobble. Becky recognised the signs, Lord knows she'd seen them often enough to recognise when Amelia Sedley was about to burst into tears. On average, at least three times a day. On the day that Amelia had been cruelly cast aside by Gav, an ex-Marine, now personal trainer, from Wigan so he could fall into bed with Chloe, a glamour model from Braintree, she'd cried an unprecedented ten times. 'Anyway, I won't win. I don't want to win. *You* deserve to win, Becky.'

'Oh, Emmy, if anyone deserves to win, it's *you*,' Becky said, even as the possibility of winning sent a thrill through her.

'So, the votes have been counted and verified and I can reveal that the winner of *Big Brother* is . . . '

Amelia grabbed hold of Becky's arm so that Becky could feel the tremors running through the other girl. Amelia was entirely lacking in any inner reserves of strength. In fact, after Gavgate, she'd been planning to walk, but it was Becky who'd persuaded her to stay. 'Chicks before dicks every single time. And if you leave, then I'll leave too. We made a promise that we were in this together, Emmy, because together, nothing can stop us. So, come on! Stay! Stay in the name of sisterhood.' Becky had spent *hours* locked in the toilet rehearsing that speech, so Amelia was right: if anyone deserved to win, it was Becky Sharp.

'Amelia Sedley!'

You have got to be fucking kidding me!

It took everything she had not to screech it out loud, instead Becky bit her tongue so hard that it brought tears to her eyes, even as she hugged

Amelia, who also had tears in her eyes, because she was gearing up for her biggest, ugliest cry of the summer.

'I'm so happy for you, Emmy! Of course it had to be you!' Becky said loudly enough that her words could be picked up over the chanting of the crowd.

Amelia was sobbing too hard to reply so Becky rubbed soothing circles on her back and murmured inanities into the other girl's blonde hair.

'Congratulations, Amelia, you're our winner!' the presenter bellowed and Amelia raised her head from where it had been nestled on Becky's shoulder and showed her red, blotchy face to the world. 'Now hold tight, Becky, I'm coming to get you!'

It was very hard to keep her face from contorting into a snarl of rage but somehow Becky managed it. It was going to be even harder to exit the *Big Brother* house with Amelia, still sobbing, clinging to her like a limpet on steroids.

'Becky, this is Big Brother! Becky, you have been evicted. You have two minutes to say your goodbyes and leave the house.'

'We should go out together,' Amelia insisted phlegmily as Becky patted her back and prepared to disengage. 'Really, we're both winners.'

'No, don't be silly! This is your moment and I'm not going to spoil it for you.' Becky would rather die than be accused of stealing Amelia's thunder. As it was, because she was the runner-up, she'd get a rushed exit interview before they came back to get Amelia. Then

4

there'd be fireworks and cheering and Amelia would cry *again* as she watched the winner's prize of £70,000 hit her bank account. Like Amelia even needed the money. Becky eyed Amelia's tight, black, designer bodycon dress and then looked down at her own ASOS knock-off. At least she could take some small comfort from the fact that Amelia had put on at least half a stone since she'd entered the *Big Brother* house and her expensive Herve Leger dress now resembled sausage casing.

'Becky, this is Big Brother! You have been evicted. You have one minute to leave the house.'

'Emmy, please, I have to go,' Becky said firmly, disentangling Amelia's arms from her neck. 'Drink some water. Go and repair your make-up so you look beautiful for your big exit and I'll see you on the flipside.'

Then she gently pushed Amelia to one side. Took a moment to straighten the skirt of her white dress, which was tight but not too tight, short but not too short, and slightly off the shoulder but not low cut because only the wrong sort of girl did legs *and* cleavage. Then she straightened her spine and, in time-honoured tradition, took a second with the mirror by the door. Fluffed her red hair, ran a finger under one eye to check that her mascara hadn't run and mouthed very clearly for the benefit of the viewing public, 'Come on, Becky, you got this.'

She pulled open the door, took a deep breath and began to climb the stairs.

'Becky! You have been evicted! Please leave the *Big Brother* house!'

She was climbing towards freedom after being trapped for weeks in a state-of-the-art prison. OK, a prison with a huge gold sofa, a swimming pool full of unicorn and flamingo inflatables and copious amounts of alcohol as a reward each time the housemates completed an asinine task designed solely to humiliate them, but a prison nevertheless.

Outside was unknown. Becky had played a clever game but the general public were fickle. Who knew how she'd come across or how she'd been edited?

'Becky! You have been evicted! Please leave the *Big Brother* house!'

There was only one way to find out.

The doors swung open and the almighty wall of noise that greeted Becky made her rock back on her spindly silver heels. All those people cheering *her*? Not one single, solitary boo. She put an unsteady hand to her heart.

You like me. You really like me.

Ha! Suckers!

2

It was a blur of light and heat and noise as Becky's hand was firmly taken by the excitable Emma Willis and she was pulled through the crowd, a camera in front of her, brazenly in her face this time.

There was a gratifying amount of poorly made banners with her name on them or proclaiming 'Chicks before dicks'. Hands thrust at her. People screaming. Then up another flight of stairs on to a stage and past her former housemates sitting in two rows. Becky hadn't even made contact with the chair before everyone's attention was focused on the big screen above them which showed Amelia sitting on the big gold sofa in the *Big Brother* house with her head between her knees as she tried not to pass out.

Considering that Amelia was a posh girl, proper posh, who'd been torn from the bosom of her loving family and sent off to boarding school at the tender age of ten, Becky had been astounded that she wasn't made of sterner stuff. In a year out from university, she'd even spent two weeks in Niger working in an orphanage, which had done absolutely nothing to toughen her up.

Maybe the joke was on Becky and Amelia was playing the longest of cons herself. But then Emma tapped Becky on the knee and a producer counted them back from a commercial break and she needed to focus on her own long con.

'So, hello, Becky Sharp,' Emma said by way of introduction. 'The housemate whose shoulder everyone cried on, who had more girl power than all the Spice Girls combined, and who might not have found love in the *Big Brother* house, but found her way into your hearts with 37.4 per cent of the final vote. It was very close, Becky. Amelia just pipped you to the post with 39.1 per cent of the vote.'

Becky shook her head and smiled. 'The best girl won,' she said to approving cheers, because what else could she say?

'And you had quite the chequered love life while you were in the house,' Emma continued cheerfully. 'You seemed fated to never get your man.'

'Well, I went into the house to find myself rather than find love, though love would have been nice too,' Becky said, and she caught the eye of Carlo who she'd enjoyed a brief flirtation with, safe in the knowledge that he'd be evicted in week two because he had all the personality of damp cardboard. Carlo smiled and waved back. 'Even better than love, I made friends that I know I'll have for the rest of my life.'

The script just wrote itself, really.

'You even let one of those friends come between you and what we all hoped was going to be a *Big Brother* romance,' Emma said, as footage appeared on the big screen of Becky watching Johnny (who called himself an entrepreneur though he was hard pressed to explain what he actually entrepreneured) and Leanne, PR girl (which really meant that she handed out free, flavoured vodka shots in Cheshire nightclubs), frolicking in the hot tub. One single, solitary tear rolled down Becky's alabaster cheek, because one tear was far more effective than sobbing all your make-up off at least twice a day.

'Well, I realised that if Johnny and Leanne really cared for each other, then I shouldn't stand in the way of their happiness,' Becky explained with another glance over to the housemates. 'I just never imagined that they'd be put up for eviction because of it or that there'd be a double eviction that week. You guys are still together, right?'

Of course they weren't. They were seated as far away from each other as possible and, judging from the skin-stripping looks that Leanne was sending Johnny's way as a muscle pounded in his cheek, they now hated each other with a passion. Even more passion than when Leanne had given him a blow job in the *Big Brother* toilet.

'You might have been one of our most popular housemates but you still managed to land yourself in hot water, Becky,' Emma said urgently, putting one hand on Becky's knee again. 'We need to talk about Poolgate.'

Becky made sure her green eyes were especially wide. 'Poolgate?' she echoed breathily.

Another scene was beamed up on the screen. Becky and Marie curled up on the big swan inflatable in the swimming pool. It was odd that they were curled up so amicably when Marie had earlier accused Becky of stealing a Chanel lipstick from her, though Becky, with trembling dignity, had insisted that the Chanel lipstick in question was hers and that maybe Marie had simply lost her own one.

'Now you weren't miked up here because you were in the pool but Marie swears that you whispered in her ear, 'You chat shit about me again and I will wipe you off the face of the earth, bitch.''

Becky put her hands to her cheeks as if they were burning. She couldn't even look at Marie and the inevitably outraged expression on the other girl's porcine and pugnacious face. If she did, she might laugh.

'Really? She *swears* that I said that? Wow! Maybe I had a strange reaction to the chlorine in the swimming pool and it gave me a complete personality change and amnesia too.' Becky shrugged and shook her head. 'Because I have no memory of that happening.'

Emma went on to mention 'Slag-gate' (it had felt like the right thing to do to tell Leanne that Marie had called her a slag), 'Pubegate' (and who could blame Becky for nominating Carlo for eviction because of the shocking state he left the shower in each morning?) and 'Gavgate' (of course Becky was going to take Amelia's side when Gav had done her wrong, even though it was Becky who'd told Gav that Chloe fancied him).

'More gates than a garden centre,' Becky noted to the approval of the audience, and anyway, she hadn't been *directly* involved in any of the incidents. The fact that Primark were now apparently selling 'Chicks Before Dicks' T-shirts and the *Guardian* had labelled Becky as 'this summer's most unlikely feminist icon' was completely beyond her control.

There was just time for Emma to remind the viewers that when Becky had won a task and been rewarded with a phone call home, she'd given her prize to Amelia.

Again, there was Becky's face on the screen — she really did look so much better from her left side — telling a sobbing Amelia that 'I don't have a home or a mum and dad, but you do, so I want you to have the call.'

There wasn't a dry eye in the house. 'Is that true?' Emma gently probed even as Becky could hear the producer telling her to wrap things up. 'That you don't have a family?'

If she concentrated really hard, Becky could always get that single, solitary tear to start its slow descent down her cheek. She'd just recall the sting of her father's hand across that same cheek as he coached her on how to cry on cue. Rich tourist or DWP case worker, no one could resist a whey-faced little moppet crying so prettily.

She felt the tear begin its journey now, let it get level with her mouth before she brushed it away with an impatient hand. 'My mum and dad died so long ago that it hardly even hurts any more. Anyway, friends are the new family, isn't that what they say?'

Emma reached forward and gathered Becky

11

into a motherly hug until they both heard the producer snap in their ears, 'We're due an ad break, cue her best bits.'

'Becky, you've been one of our favourite housemates of all time and here are your best bits!'

What if the two minutes that comprised Becky's highlight reel were the sum total of her life's work? How she'd always be remembered? A slender girl in a white bikini with green eyes, riotous red curls, fair skin and what *The Sun* called 'the best boobs in *Big Brother*' schooling another girl in a bikini about the 'most basic rule of feminism. Chicks Before Dicks.'

Was this it? In years to come when Becky was standing in a queue in the Post Office or the supermarket, would someone tap her on the shoulder and say, 'Excuse me? You are, aren't you? *Big Brother?* Chicks Before Dicks? Sorry, I can't remember your name.'

She'd had a taste of it now: the applause of the crowd, the flash of a hundred cameras. She knew how easy it was to win the slavish adoration of the public and her fellow housemates (apart from Marie, and Marie could just go and fuck herself). But just one taste was never going to be enough.

No, Becky intended to gorge on it all: fame, power, success, as if she was standing in Nando's with a tapeworm and a black card.

By the time she was done, everyone was going to remember her name.

3

But first she had to stand down stage, take her place with the other former housemates and watch Amelia be crowned the winner, then fluff and weep her way through her exit interview.

The only gratifying part was when she said, 'The best bit of my *Big Brother* experience was meeting Becky, because I know I have a friend for life. More than a friend. She's my sister from another mister.'

After the cameras stopped rolling Becky and the other losers were herded like cattle into a people carrier to be ferried to an Elstree hotel, while Amelia was whisked off in a limo, as befitted her winner's status. She was the best of them all and Becky was left to mill about the after party nursing a lukewarm white wine that was all the production budget would stretch to.

Her fellow housemates were surrounded by their families. Not that Becky felt even one pang on that score, having lost her mother when she was eight and her father seven years later.

Poor Becky. Not only had she come from the most broken of homes, but at fifteen she was an actual bona fide orphan, like some poor creature from a Victorian novel waiting to be sent either to the workhouse or to live with a kindly guardian and benefactor.

In the end, her father's old Soho drinking buddy, Barbara Pinkerton, agent to the stars of stage and screen, had fallen somewhere between the two, and even now was bearing down on her in the same hotel bar they'd waited in before Becky had entered the *Big Brother* house.

'Becky!' Babs boomed once she was within booming distance. 'My little Becky Sharp.'

She descended in a cloud of Opium to place lips slick with shocking-pink lipstick in the vicinity of Becky's cheek.

'I'm surprised a devious little cow like you didn't go all the way,' she murmured as she sat down on the leather-look banquette next to Becky. 'You played a blinder, even had my stony-cold heart stirring when you gave that insipid little debutante your phone call home. But turns out insipid little debutantes trump sparky orphans. Who knew?'

'I couldn't be happier for Emmy,' Becky said, as she'd been saying at regular intervals to whoever drifted into her orbit. 'It really couldn't have happened to a lovelier person.'

'Bet she has a trust fund the size of the Guatemalan national debt. What does she need the prize money for?' Barbara wondered. 'It shouldn't be allowed.'

'Too fucking right.'

Their eyes met. Pupil and master, though for the first time Babs Pinkerton couldn't tell which was which.

'I promised your poor, dear old Pa that I'd look after you like you were my own,' she'd said when she'd shown up at the council-run children's home in Tower Hamlets where Becky had been assigned a bed and a case worker, after six different foster placements had returned her to sender.

Compared to the horrors of the home, Babs Pinkerton was definitely the lesser of two evils, but she was still fairly evil. Becky had known Babs all her life. The Sharp family had lived in a series of rooms in Soho, usually reached through a street door with a tatty handmade sign — 'Model 2nd floor' — invariably pinned to it. Her father didn't have far to stagger to The Coach and Horses, and when that shut, on to The Colony Rooms, where he'd often take a snifter with Babs.

Sometimes he'd think it amusing to bring Becky along so she could mimic the regulars. More often she'd be sent by her mother to bring her father home or ask for five quid to feed the meter and buy a can of beans. Babs Pinkerton was like an honorary aunt, or so she claimed as she sat with Frank Sharp, a large gin and tonic always within reach, and always dressed in pink because that was her thing, as if she was a frilly, feminine, frivolous little thing when actually she was a shark in lipstick. In a show of affection, she'd pinch Becky's cheek, her fingers hard and unforgiving, and it was a point of pride to Becky never to make a sound.

So when Babs turned up in Tower Hamlets, Becky didn't hope for the best. Just expected the worst.

For the first two weeks or so, the worst wasn't that bad. Despite spending so long in The Colony Rooms each night that the next day she seeped noxious gin fumes through her pores,

Babs did have a roster of clients in work, albeit strictly D-list. Comedians still hankering after their glory days in the seventies when they could get a primetime slot on Saturday-night TV telling mother-in-law jokes and making racist jibes. Superannuated dollybirds hoping to resurrect their careers with a slot on *Celebrity Masterchef* or in a gritty TV drama on Channel 4. More recently, Babs had started to mine a lucrative seam of reality-TV contestants determined to cling on to their fifteen minutes of fame like it was the last lifebelt on the *Titanic*.

Babs had done well enough for herself that she had a house in a little mews in Paddington where she installed Becky in a spare room along with boxes of glossy ten-by-fours of former clients and left her alone every day with ten quid to buy herself snacks and a big TV with all the satellite channels.

Becky knew it couldn't last because nothing ever did.

The worst, when it came, was far worse than Becky had ever imagined: Babs shipped her off to *Bournemouth* to act as a companion to her ageing aunt, Jemima Pinkerton, once the queen of British soaps, and now a septuagenarian with atrial defibrillation, two artificial hips and a recent dementia diagnosis.

'I've been so worried about poor Auntie Jemima,' Babs told Becky as they travelled down to poor Auntie Jemima's well-appointed bungalow in the exclusive enclave of Southbourne, under the guise of a little daytrip to the seaside. 'She hasn't got a soul in the world — fame is a fickle, heartless bitch. And then I thought, well, poor, dear Becky doesn't have a soul in the world either. You'll be the granddaughter she never had.'

'You want me to spend my days wiping the shitty arse of some senile old has-been?' Becky had spluttered.

'She's not senile. Not yet. Just a bit forgetful, and the years might not have been kind — neither was her third husband, an absolute brute — but Jemima's a sweetheart . . . '

'I don't care if she's the queen of fucking everything,' Becky had interrupted. 'I'm not doing it.'

Then Babs had taken Becky's cheek between thumb and forefinger as she'd used to do, and this time when she finally let go, she'd left a bruise. 'Listen to me, you ungrateful little wretch, you'll do this or we'll turn round and I'll take you to the nearest police station so I can turn you in for stealing three pieces out of my jewellery box and four blank cheques.'

'They're not worth anything. Just glass and paste,' Becky muttered, but she subsided.

'Also, once you're sixteen you can claim a carer's allowance, which is something because it's not like I could even get you a walk-on in a crisps commercial,' Babs had pointed out because in those days, Becky had been small, wan and her perfectly pert breasts had yet to put in an appearance. It also explained why Babs had left her to rot in care when Frank Sharp had first been sent down four years ago. At nearly sixteen, Becky was useful in a way that she hadn't been

17

when she was nearly twelve. 'Besides, you owe me for two weeks bed and board, plus your expenses. Take you *months* to work off that debt.'

It had taken months, but by then Becky and Jemima Pinkerton were firm friends. Jemima trusted Becky implicitly ('You might as well have my pin number, because God knows, I won't be able to remember it before too long') and Becky made herself indispensable to the old lady. After all, you didn't bite the hand that fed you and in her way, Becky supposed that she was quite *fond* of Jemima.

Certainly, Becky had learned more from Jemima than she'd ever learned on the infrequent occasions when she'd somehow found herself in a classroom. Becky had listened transfixed to all of Jemima's stories. From her ingenue days as a contracted player at Gainsborough Studios, the blink-and-you'll-miss-it scene that had earned her the title Bond Girl, through stints as a series regular on cop shows and medical dramas, a short season with the Royal Shakespeare Company and a dry spell ('drier than the bloody Sahara in a heatwave') that had lasted five years and had seen Jemima working the Christian Dior counter at Harvey Nicks. Then fame had beckoned again as the matriarch of an East End gangland family in a new soap opera, which had put a sizeable sum in Jemima's pension pot and had led to all kinds of lucrative voiceover work.

Yet it wasn't life treading the boards or working on a big sound stage at Shepperton that had enthralled Becky. On the contrary, that seemed to involve a lot of hanging about and knitting, and she wasn't ever going to be the type to knit one purl one. No lessons to be learned there.

But Becky was fascinated by Jemima's tales of the casting couch, amorous directors and handsy casting agents; of ambitious starlets nobbling the competition with a tube of greasepaint carelessly left on the dressing-room stairs; of young juvenile male leads seeing to the needs of rich, older ladies; and of that other, shadow world of gangsters and dealers, kingmakers and hookers . . . Well, all of human life was there.

Again, it couldn't last for ever. But it lasted long enough. Besides, her father had always said that the longer the con, the bigger the reward. Nearly four and a half years, by which time Becky had blossomed like a dewy young rose, petals slowly unfurling. And Jemima, bless her, had withered. Her limbs clawed with arthritis and her mind slowly eaten away by the ravages of time.

In the end, Jemima had gone in her sleep. The ink was barely dry on the death certificate (natural causes) before Babs Pinkerton descended in a cerise power suit ('Auntie Jemima wouldn't have wanted me to wear black') clutching a will that predated the newer will that Jemima had drawn up from a will-making kit that Becky had purchased in WHSmith.

'It will never stand up in a court of law,' Babs had said, when Becky had presented her with the evidence that she, Becky Sharp, loyal companion to Jemima Pinkerton during her twilight years, was the late and much-loved actress's sole heir and beneficiary. 'Everyone knew that Jemima's mind was so addled that she didn't know her arse from her elbow, God rest her soul.'

It had got nasty enough, even without Becky daring to seek legal counsel. It seemed that there were items of jewellery missing, large sums gone from Jemima's bank account, her fur coat currently in the window of the local pawn shop. But as Becky sweetly pointed out, 'Like you just said, poor Jemima was very confused towards the end. We may never know where she hid her jewellery or what she spent all that money on.'

While Babs was gasping like a landlocked fish at that sheer audacity, Becky happened to mention that the press might be quite interested to know that a large standing order on Jemima's account was paid to Babs every month. 'Though it's not like you've been busy finding her work. And Jemima was beloved of so many that I think people might get quite cross if they thought that she was being taken advantage of by her niece, who also happened to be her agent.'

'Or by the common little tart that's been living off Jemima for the last four years,' Babs countered, and Becky was old enough and big enough now that when Babs' hand crept up to take hold of her cheek in a bruising grip, she knocked her hand away.

'I'm *not* a common little tart,' she corrected. 'I'm a poor little orphan devoted to Jemima. The granddaughter she never had, that's what Reverend Squills used to say when he invited us over for Sunday lunch. Towards the end, you see, Jemima found God . . . '

Babs Pinkerton snorted in derision at such a notion.

' . . . Anyway, we were quite regular churchgoers so I'm sure the Reverend would be happy to defend me. He's got quite a taste for publicity. It's hard to keep him out of the local paper banging on about the gangs of feckless youths hanging about on the seafront. I can't even *imagine* his reaction if the nationals started sniffing about . . . '

'What do you want?' Babs had asked thinly.

A modest sum from the eventual sale of the bungalow, the right to keep any mementos — for instance, any jewellery that Becky might just happen to find when she was clearing out the bungalow — and some insurance against the future.

'I've been stagnating in Southbourne for the last four years, so what now?' she demanded of Babs who'd taken command of Jemima's favourite easy chair and a very large gin, easy on the tonic. 'I don't have a qualification to my name and I can't really see the point of toiling away at evening classes just so I can end up working in a call centre.'

Barbara had raised one over-plucked eyebrow. 'The world needs people to work in call centres. Natural selection and all that.'

'We can do better than a call centre. These . . . ' Becky gestured at her breasts, 'her famous frontal development', as they were described by the good Reverend, who wasn't as godly as his venerated

21

status suggested. Not when he was chasing Becky around the vestry with an avaricious gleam in his eyes. 'And this . . . ' she pointed at her pretty face, her slanting green eyes and defined cheek-bones giving her an almost feline, feral look, 'and this . . . ' she tapped her head, 'would be wasted on people wanting to change their internet service provider. You have contacts and connections. You can make me famous!'

Although Becky couldn't sing or dance, her dramatic talents clearly weren't in any doubt. If Babs could turn the girl into a meal ticket rather than a thorn in her side and collect her 20 per cent commission, then it would be win/win. Babs knew a producer at a production company who owed her a rather large favour and so eight weeks ago, Becky had entered the *Big Brother* house.

'The rest is up to you,' Babs had said.

Now, Babs placed a consoling, pink-taloned hand on Becky's arm. 'Even though technically you're a loser, there's still some serious money to be made before your meter runs out,' she said. 'We have a golden window right now. I'd make the most of all those personal-appearance fees to press the flesh at suburban nightclubs. Then we can get you at least ten thousand to appear in one of the Sunday tabs in your undies to spin, some sob story about your dear departed ma and pa. We might even be able to bag you a footballer. Not Premier League but definitely First Division.'

What was that unpleasant sound in Becky's ear? Ah yes, the bottom of the barrel being scraped.

'I didn't spend eight weeks locked in a house with a bunch of vacuous morons to get my tits out for the *Sunday People* and then disappear. Have you any idea what I've been through, Babs? There were times when I had to lock myself in the toilet and bite my hand towel to stop myself from screaming.'

'They were a particularly sorry bunch this year.' Babs' eyes narrowed. 'But if you were to get your knockers out, I could probably get you a few more thousand.'

There was a commotion at the other end of the bar as the more worthy, though far less deserving winner, entered the room. Amelia was with her mother and father, both of them tall and rangy, fair of hair and face. Amelia had told Becky that her father managed a hedge fund, and that her mother was the daughter of a man who'd made his fortune in plumbing supplies. Rich enough that home was a six-bedroom town-house in Kensington *and* a pretty, ivy-strewn manor house in Oxfordshire. Rich enough that Mr and Mrs Sedley both had a set expression as if they were clenching their jaws and trying not to breathe in the smell of fried food, air freshener and cheap white wine that permeated the bar of the Elstree hotel.

There was no sign of Amelia's Eton-educated brother who did something lucrative with energy drinks but there were a man and woman bringing up the rear, the man clamped to his mobile phone, the woman clamped to *two* mobile phones. It was clear that Amelia's agent and publicist were cut from a very different cloth to Babs Pinkerton.

'I don't just want 'a few more thousand'. I want more,' Becky said to Babs Pinkerton, as she caught Amelia's eye. The other girl smiled, waved enthusiastically and beckoned Becky over: but she wasn't going to hurry to Amelia, like an obedient little pet dog.

'More what? More money? Your boobs aren't that great, Becky,' Babs said witheringly. 'And don't start thinking that another agent will get you more cash — they won't. They'd tell you the exact same thing and anyway, you signed an exclusive contract with me.'

That was a lesson learned the hard way: never sign anything. And no, it wasn't just more money. Or more time in the spotlight.

It was more *everything*.

Amelia detached herself from the adoring throng that had congregated around her and hurried over to the corner where Becky and Babs were still in their unhappy huddle, followed by her anxious-looking Mama and publicist.

'Becky!' Amelia seized her hands and hauled her up. 'I can't wait for you to meet Mummy! I know you two are going to be best friends.'

From the pained and furrowed brow of Mrs Sedley, Becky very much doubted it. 'It's so lovely to meet you, Mrs Sedley,' she said politely and as Mrs Sedley unwillingly leaned forward a scant five degrees for an air kiss, Becky held out her hand instead, to the other woman's evident surprise and gratitude.

Then Becky made sure the handshake was

brisk, firm but not *too* firm.

'Rebecca, congratulations on doing so well in the house,' Mrs Sedley said tightly.

'I wouldn't have lasted five minutes in there without Emmy,' Becky said, resting her head on Amelia's shoulder. 'She was an absolute lifesaver.'

'I think you have that the wrong way round,' Amelia said, putting her arm round Becky's waist. 'Come and sit with us.'

'No, you must have so many people wanting to talk to you, I don't want to intrude,' Becky said, as she heard another one of Barbara Pinkerton's snorts from behind her as her erstwhile mentor levered herself off the banquette.

'When you've stopped having notions, you know where to find me,' Babs muttered as she pushed past Becky who was giving her full attention to Amelia and Mrs Sedley, so that even in the muted lighting of the bar, they'd be able to see the slightly forlorn expression on her face before she gave them a brilliant smile that drooped ever so slightly at the edges.

'Honestly, Emmy, after eight weeks you must be sick to death of me,' Becky said with a self-deprecating little laugh. 'I know how close you are to your mother, how much you must have to catch up on.' She ended on a wistful little sigh.

'Oh, Becky! And you don't have anybody,' Amelia exclaimed, the arm round Becky's waist tightening. 'You don't even have anywhere to call home now we're out of the house.'

'Is that true?' Mrs Sedley asked. 'Are you homeless?'

'Homeless' had all sorts of unpleasant connotations even if technically it was true. 'I was a live-in care assistant before *Big Brother* but the lovely lady I was looking after — she was like a grandmother to me — well, she died.'

Becky had mentioned this on the show. Just the once. To Carlo and Amelia (and three million viewers) but Amelia's eyes filled with tears. 'Oh, Becky . . . '

'I'll be all right,' Becky insisted, squaring her shoulders and raising her chin but it was just a momentary act of bravado and then she drooped again. 'Babs, my agent, says I can make some money if I agree to pose topless but I don't think that I want to do that. I'm sure something else will turn up and in the meantime, I just have to look on the bright side. Like, I can't be homeless because I'm booked in here for the night.' Becky caught her bottom lip between her teeth and looked off to the side. 'I'm sure I could extend my stay. It can't be that expensive. It's not a particularly grand hotel, is it?'

'It's an *awful* hotel. They have pot-pourri in the ladies' bathrooms,' Mrs Sedley said from between gritted teeth, as if, of all the indignities heaped on her by her daughter appearing on a reality TV show, pot pourri in the ladies' loos was the very final straw. 'I'm sure Emmy would never forgive me if I didn't insist that you come and stay with us, for a week or so, until you've made other arrangements.'

'I really wouldn't want to impose.' Becky lifted her chin again, even as her bottom lip trembled. 'I can look after myself.'

'Only because you've never had any other option,' Amelia said, tucking her arm through Becky's. 'You haven't even met Rhoda, my publicist, yet,' she added, gesturing at the woman hovering next to them, who was in a sleek black suit with a sleek black bob to match and looked as if she had all sorts of useful contacts and strategies to ensure that her clients (and potential clients) could forge long, successful careers without having to flash their breasts to the readers of a downmarket Sunday tabloid. 'She wants me to do all sorts of things. TV and radio interviews. Photo shoots. It all sounds terrifying but it wouldn't be so terrifying if we did them together.'

'Well, I suppose . . . If I could help out . . . then I wouldn't feel quite so bad about imposing,' Becky decided. 'And as soon as I've outstayed my welcome, you're to let me know and I'll pack my bags. I mean, I hardly have anything in the way of bags, but you know what I mean.'

'You can stay as long as you want,' Amelia promised rashly. 'Now, let's get out of here. The smell of fried food is making me feel nauseous.'

4

The Sedleys' London residence (because any
house with a staff annexe and its own sauna and
steam room counted as a residence) was in
Kensington. On the wrong side of the park,
because no matter how many millions Mr Sedley
had made from hedging funds and gilt-edging
futures, the family weren't old money. Only old
money and the very newest money could afford
the right side of the park.

But as Becky was shown into a pretty
guestroom, decorated in white and a delicate
pale green, with its own en suite bathroom, she
decided that it would do very nicely indeed.

She hadn't been exaggerating for dramatic
effect when she'd told Amelia that she didn't
have much in the way of bags. Baggage, perhaps,
but that was another matter. All her worldly
possessions fitted into her *Big Brother* suitcase, a
shabby black holdall and a checked laundry bag.

Amelia swept into the guest room the next day
to be confronted by the sorry state of Becky's
goods and chattels and the even sorrier state of
Becky's wardrobe. There hadn't been much call

28

for anything other than jeans and a jumper when she was tending to Jemima Pinkerton and the only man she regularly came into contact with was Reverend Squills. No wonder Amelia's mouth and china-blue eyes had become three perfect circles of horror.

'Oh dear,' she said. 'Oh, Becky. Oh no.' Then she swept out again.

She was back not even ten minutes later, her arms full of clothes. 'No, Emmy, absolutely not!' Becky said, from the doorway of the en suite. She was swathed in a fluffy white towelling robe, her hair hidden by another towel so that she looked all eyes and cheekbones. 'I have my own clothes. They're not as nice as yours, but they'll do.'

'These are all too small for me,' Amelia insisted, having spent a lot of time in the *Big Brother* house comfort eating. Mrs Sedley had remarked on the way home last night that Amelia would have to go on a juice fast immediately.

'It goes straight to your face, Emmy,' she'd said with some concern. 'We were quite shocked at how puffy you looked in the last week on that show.'

Now Amelia held up a floral dress. 'I bought this after I came back from Niger. It fitted me for two weeks and now it's just taking up wardrobe space.' Then a pair of designer jeans. 'I've never been able to get into these. Bought them online from Net-a-Porter and never got round to returning them.' Next a grey cashmere jumper was lifted up for Becky's inspection. 'Grey completely washes me out but you can wear pretty much anything.'

'Not anything,' Becky disagreed, creeping forward to touch the luxurious soft pile of the grey cashmere as if she couldn't help herself. 'Oh, I've never felt anything so soft.'

'And Jos — my brother, Jos, you'll meet him soon — sent over some workout gear. He's booked me a personal trainer too. Said he can't have a lardy sister . . . '

'It must be delightful to have a brother like that,' Becky murmured as she held up a navy-blue designer dress which would be perfect for her TV appearance that morning.

'He *is* delightful,' Amelia agreed, because she never had a bad word to say about anyone. It grew quite tiresome after a while. 'Except, I feel as if I hardly know him. He's ten years older than I am so he was at school when I was growing up and then he went to LA after university . . . LA is so far away and he has rather taken to the lifestyle.'

'Oh? Is his wife from LA too?' Becky asked as she wriggled into the navy-blue dress.

'No, Jos isn't married,' Amelia assured her. 'He says that there's no way he could have built up the second-largest protein ball business on the West Coast if he'd prioritised relationships. He also said that he wasn't going to get married until he was thirty-five so we tease him that he's only got three years left to find a wife. Oh, Becky! That dress looks so much better on you than it ever did on me.'

'I'm sure it doesn't,' Becky said automatically

30

but later on, in front of the TV cameras, Becky's navy-blue hand-me-down really made her skin and hair pop whereas the cream blouse Amelia wore put at least ten pounds on her and, despite the best efforts of the make-up department, seemed to blend into her skin tone in the most unflattering way.

The day passed in a blur of TV-studio and radio-station green rooms. Nobody was pleased that Becky was there too, like a free gift with the booking of the latest *Big Brother* winner. Amelia's publicist, Rhoda, even suggested that Becky wait in the car and Becky really didn't want to get in anyone's way ('honestly I don't, but Emmy, you're shaking. Shall I come and sit with you while you wait to go on?').

When it quickly became clear that Amelia only made good TV when she was crying, Becky was no longer the spectre at the feast. On the contrary, she soon had joint billing and it turned out she was a natural for live TV and radio, with an endless supply of amusing anecdotes about life in the house, all good to go. 'No one could get to sleep for the smell, could we, Emmy?' she recalled as she sat side by side with Amelia on the *This Morning* sofa.

'No. It was a very bad smell.'

'Finally we tracked it down to a rancid mug of soup that Johnny had left under his bed that had attracted maggots, and they made us stay in the garden while the fumigators dealt with it.'

'And it was raining,' Amelia added timidly.

'Pouring with rain,' Becky elaborated. 'And that's why I'm never going to eat mushroom soup for as long as I live.' She paused. 'At least Johnny swore it was mushroom soup but we all had our suspicions, didn't we?'

'Did we? But what else could it have been?' Amelia's face was absolutely without guile as Phil and Holly hooted with laughter.

They ended the day at a shoot and interview for *Hello* magazine shot in a location house in Clapham, because Mrs Sedley absolutely wasn't going to have people tramping in and out of her house with equipment when she'd just had the parquet flooring redone. (She was also quite terrified that her choice of soft furnishings wouldn't pass muster because she'd insisted on doing the decorating herself even though Mr Sedley had begged her to hire an interior designer.)

The journalist was blonde and perky and cut from the same cloth as Amelia who happily reeled off her list of achievements to date. The Chelsea prep school where she graduated, being able to speak German and Mandarin (though neither of them had stuck). She'd then attended the same boarding school as the Duchess of Cambridge where she failed to excel academically but had won a trophy for tennis. Only two hardships had blighted Amelia's life to date: her sluggish metabolism which meant that the only way she could maintain a size-ten figure was by eating twelve hundred calories a day and working out for an hour, and the three years she'd spent sleeping in a back brace to improve her posture.

'Daddy and Jos always used to joke that it was

because I had no backbone,' she admitted with a nervous giggle. And of course there was the measly two weeks that Amelia had spent doing volunteer work in Niger.

'Like Princess Diana,' the journalist, Emily, noted dryly. 'Were you worried about catching something awful like yellow fever or malaria?'

'Not quite like Princess Diana. I mean, there were no landmines and we had WiFi,' Amelia said. 'But I did have to have a lot of jabs before I went. My arm was sore for days afterwards.'

On the other hand, Becky's biography was quite sparse. It was also quite hard to remember what she'd told people in the *Big Brother* house. Another lesson learnt: come up with a story then stick to it as if your life depended on it.

'My father was an artist,' she recalled with a misty look to her eye, because to be fair, some of his scams really had possessed quite a lot of artistry. The judge who'd sent him down had described him as 'a curious mixture of criminal genius and petty thief with poor impulse control.' 'Everyone said that he was destined for greatness but he died before greatness came.'

'And, I understand how hard this must be for you, but how did he die?'

Becky cast her eyes down. 'He had a brief but brave fight against a cruel disease.' When she said that people always assumed that it was cancer and that she'd been at her father's side as he was carried away by the angels. The ugly truth of the matter was that it had been cirrhosis of the liver and the only person at his side had been a prison chaplain, as Francis Henry Sharp had been serving seven years at Her Majesty's Pleasure for five counts of fraud and one count of ABH for breaking the nose of the arresting officer.

Next to her, Amelia snivelled a little and the journalist leaned closer. 'And your mother died when you were still quite young?'

Becky did her best brave face. Downcast eyes, a little half-smile, a sudden intake of breath as if she was fighting to control herself. 'Yes, by the time I was eight, it was just Daddy and me. I'm sorry, can I have a moment?'

'It's very painful for Becky to talk about,' Amelia whispered, taking hold of Becky's hand as if she could loan her friend some of her own meagre courage. 'Are you OK to carry on? Do you want some water?'

An intern was despatched to bring Becky water. Sparkling water in a cut-glass tumbler with crushed ice and a big chunk of lime.

Who could blame a girl for not wanting to go back to a life where there was only tap water in any receptacle that was vaguely clean?

'Your mother?' Emily prompted. 'You said in the house that she was French.'

'*Mais oui, maman etait francaise*. She came from a very old family, the Mortmerencys, and she was a model. No! You wouldn't have heard of her. She did a little catwalk, but mostly fit work,' Becky explained, though the closest her mother had come to the catwalk was draping herself over the bonnet of a Ford Fiesta at a motoring exhibition at Olympia. She had been quite pretty before the booze and the pills and the putting up with Frank Sharp had taken their toll on her.

'Her passing was very sudden.'

Hurling yourself in front of the 7.08 District Line train pulling into Fulham Broadway station didn't lend itself to a long, lingering death.

'Oh, Becky,' both Amelia and Emily exclaimed.

'Sorry, it's just that it's painful to talk about.'

Had it been painful at the time? Becky could hardly remember. Sidonie had barely fulfilled her job description. She swung from high to low, as Mr Sharp had vacillated from sweet to mean, so from a very young age, Becky had learned to keep her head down, stay out of the line of fire, especially when her parents had fought, which they did with intense ferocity. If that was love, then you could shove it.

'So, Becky, let's switch it up, shall we?' Emily asked.

Becky clapped her hands together. 'God, yes, please, let's!'

Where had she gone to school?

School of hard knocks.

Had she had many boyfriends?

Only if you count a Bournemouth vicar who used to try to put his hand up my skirt when I was helping with the church jumble sale.

Who were her celebrity crushes?

What would be the point of having a crush on some distant celebrity who would be of absolutely no use to me?

Dear, sweet Emily and her voice recorder would probably both short circuit if Becky told them a few home truths, so she settled for the current truth and put her arm around Amelia.

'I'm just here for moral support. Emmy's the

star and so she's the one you should be asking about boyfriends and crushes.' Becky nudged Amelia who giggled obligingly.

'There is someone,' Emmy confided, because it never occurred to her that she could fudge the details, hint, or stretch, bend and pull the truth this way and that, so it hardly even resembled the truth any more. 'I've known him all my life, he was at school with my brother Jos, so I'm sure he thinks I'm still the silly little girl that he always teased.'

Such a cliché. The haughty older boy who . . .

' . . . used to pull my pigtails.'

Even Emily was starting to look as if her back teeth were aching from Amelia's brand of simpering, saccharine sweetness.

'And does this someone have a name?' Emily asked with the weary air of a woman who had an Oxbridge degree and a childhood ambition to be a lady war correspondent, but was currently interviewing the winner (and runner-up!) of a reality TV show.

Amelia ducked her hair. 'George,' she said on a gasp, as if even saying his name out loud was tempting fate. 'His name is George.'

5

'He's very good looking,' Becky whispered loudly to Amelia as they stood in the doorway of the Sedleys' drawing room later that evening and she caught sight of the man sitting on an antique loveseat, his gaze fixed on his iPad. 'You might have thought to mention it!'

Amelia frowned. 'Really? Do you think so?' The frown was replaced by a mischievous smile. 'Shall I tell him?'

'I'll hate you for ever if you do,' Becky said, noting the way the man began to stab frantically at his touch screen, as if he'd actually heard every word of their conversation.

It was no wonder that Jos Sedley — the object of Becky's affection, Amelia's own brother, and both the brains *and* the brawn behind A Load Of Balls, the second-largest protein ball company on the West Coast (soon to make major inroads into the East Coast market too) — had caught Becky's attention.

He truly was a sight to behold. A cross-fit addict who could bench press his own weight (two hundred and ten pounds) and a man who hadn't knowingly eaten a carb in five years, Jos Sedley was triangular in shape. His over-muscled top half, bulging biceps, pecs even perter than Becky's, strained the seams of his tight T-shirt, which was daringly low cut to show off his stunning he-vage. His spindly, skinny, jeans-clad legs didn't look able to support all that complex musculature.

It took a while for Becky's eye to take it all in and travel adoringly up Jos's physique, past his thick neck to a face still resolutely fixed on his iPad screen. It wasn't a distinguished face. If it weren't for his extraordinary physique, it would be hard to pick Jos out in a police line-up. The only remarkable thing about it was that, like the rest of him, it was somewhere between teak and mahogany on the fake-tan colour spectrum.

'Jos! Nothing on your iPad could be as interesting as my Becky,' Amelia said and finally Jos looked up from where he'd been studying a new pull-up technique that his personal trainer had devised for him.

Becky had been gazing down at the Aubusson rug because it would have been rude to keep staring at Jos even though he really was a *fascinating* sight, but now she looked up too in time to see Jos blush fiercely as their eyes collided.

'Any friend of Emmy's and all that . . . ' He muttered awkwardly as he stood up, trying desperately to remember the most appropriate way to greet his sister's friends. He'd spent his formative years in all-male boarding schools and he'd been a fat kid. A fat, *shy* kid. Even when there'd been dances with the neighbouring girls' boarding schools, Jos had stayed on the sidelines, never daring to try and steal a kiss or cop a feel during the last dance. Since moving to LA after an equally unhappy three years at Keele University, Jos had turned his bulk from blubber to muscle but he was still shy. What's more, he knew he was shy and awkward, so he was instantly suspicious of any woman who showed an interest in him.

Becky noted the blush, which highlighted Jos's terracotta face. It seemed to Jos that she could see deep into his soul and evidently what she found wasn't at all repulsive to her, because she stepped forward and suddenly threw her arms around him.

There was so much softness pressed against Jos that he hardly knew what to do with himself but all too soon, it was gone. Becky stepped back, hands to her own cheeks, as if she were blushing too, though her blush owed more to the Benefit cheek tint she'd taken from Amelia's make-up bag that morning. The last thing that Amelia needed was blusher so really Becky had been doing her a favour.

'I'm sorry,' she apologised to Jos, who was staring at her like a cartoon character who'd just had an anvil dropped on his head. 'I don't know what came over me. I'm not normally a hugger, am I, Emmy?'

'Becky's mother died very young so she has cuddle deficiency syndrome,' Amelia said, even though Becky had told her that in the strictest confidence in the *Big Brother* house as eighty cameras filmed their every move.

'But as soon as I saw you, I wanted to hug you,' Becky said, shrugging helplessly. 'I've behaved like a total idiot, haven't I?'

'No, no! Not at all. I'm very honoured to have been, er, hugged. You're a very good hugger. It was a good hug. Best hug I've had in a long time.' Jos held up his hand in despair. 'Hug. Never realised what a strange word it is before. Hug.'

'A very strange word,' Becky agreed. 'But such a nice thing to do.' She turned to Amelia who had her hands clasped to her chest, her mouth wide in wordless delight that the first meeting of her beloved brother and her BFF had gone far better than she could ever have hoped for. 'Emmy, do you think you might hug Gorgeous George when you see him again?'

'Gorgeous George? Hug him?' Jos echoed. His massive chest shook with mirth at the idea. 'I'd love to see his face if you did, Emmy.'

Jos's laugh was infectious. Deep, braying and loud, like the mating cry of an amorous water buffalo. Becky couldn't help but laugh at the sound of it. Amelia pouted but she could never stay angry for very long and also George *would* be very surprised if she did suddenly hug him, so she ended up giggling too.

When Amelia saw George Wylie later that night, it was true that she felt a strong impulse to hug him. But what she secretly wished was that George would be so overcome by the sight of her that he'd be the one to stride over and take her in his arms, kiss her on the forehead and murmur throatily, 'I've missed you, Emmy. Missed you more than I can say.'

It wasn't to be. Instead, George slightly inclined his head when Amelia waved frantically at him from across the room, then went back to talking to his friends.

'He'll probably come over in a bit,' she said to Becky who had wanted Gorgeous George pointed out to her as soon as Amelia clapped eyes on him. 'He looks quite busy.'

'And then *you'll* be too busy to talk to him,' Becky said firmly, because although she was many things, most of them not at all good, in times of adversity she could be a great comfort. 'After all, this is your party.'

The party was being thrown by Mr and Mrs Sedley in Amelia's honour, less because she was the winner of a ghastly, low-rent, reality-TV show and more because she was their doted-on only daughter who'd soon be leaving London to return to Durham University for her final year where she might actually scrape through her degree in Art History with a 2.2.

An army of flunkies had spent most of the day transforming a restaurant in Chelsea into a distressed fairy grotto. There was ivy and other trailing green plants liberally strewn about, along with hundreds upon hundreds of tealights in glass holders. Adorning the rooftop bar was yet more artfully scattered foliage and paper lanterns, and it was there that George Wylie didn't quite cut Amelia but made it clear that she could wait.

Amelia was very good at waiting for George. It was a running joke between their two families, that when Amelia Charlotte Louise Sedley was born, she'd marry George Wylie, eldest son of Sir John and Lavinia Wylie. Sir John's great-great-great-great-great-grandfather had been a self-made man who made his money in the slave trade and bought his baronetcy, a fact which never failed to enrage his great-great-great-great-great grandson who longed to be aristocracy rather than merely landed gentry. The family fortune, built on the backs of men, women and children torn from their homes, had all but gone, most of it sunk into an ancestral pile that had almost killed Sir John's father when a piece of decayed ornamental masonry had fallen inches away from him.

Sir John had had to do the unthinkable and restore the family's failing fortunes by going into trade.

Trade had been very good to the Wylies, as had Mr Sedley, who'd initially provided capital and investment advice to young Sir John. Now, some thirty years later, George would never have to work a day in his life and could pootle about the estate killing any poor beast that flew across his land, scampered through his forests or swam in his streams.

However, George wasn't content with a life of leisure. His years at Eton, then at Oxford (where he'd been a member of an infamous drinking club whose membership initiation involved setting a tramp on fire), were the perfect training for a bright young man from a good family who wanted to go into politics.

George currently worked at a right-wing think-tank while he and his backers waited for a safe Conservative seat to fall vacant. There was no rush. George wasn't even thirty, though just as Amelia yearned for him, he yearned to make the *Evening Standard* Thirty Power Players

Under the Age of Thirty' list.

In good time, Mr Sedley would make the perfect, political father-in-law, happy to bank-roll his son-in-law's campaigns with his many millions of pounds, but for now, Amelia held very little interest for him. George watched her visibly droop in the face of his casual indifference. She was easily one of the silliest girls he had ever met so he was quite happy to bide his time. He'd wait for Amelia to finish university and have her heart broken by someone who'd make George seem like quite the white knight when he finally made his move.

Her friend, on the other hand, wasn't the sort of girl a man waited for. She was strictly right here, right now, don't let the door catch you on your pretty little arse when you leave. George would swear on a thousand bibles that he didn't watch reality TV but he'd somehow seen enough of *Big Brother* to get the measure of Amelia's new friend.

The calculating glint in her downcast eyes. The steely determination behind that quivering bottom lip. Though she had a cracking pair of tits, he'd say that for her.

George smiled to himself, and, catching sight of his reflection in the mirrored wall behind the bar, couldn't help but admire the jut of his own cheekbones. As he did, he caught the gaze of Amelia's little friend, who had her eye fixed keenly on him. As if it were *she* who had his measure and not the other way round.

'So what do you think of George?' whispered

Emmy, noticing Becky's intent focus on her one true love.

'You can do much better than him,' Becky said to Amelia who immediately gasped in disbelief that anyone could find fault with George Wylie.

'I couldn't,' Amelia declared. 'He's so handsome.'

Handsome was pushing it. George had a pale, interesting face, which reflected centuries of good breeding with the odd exotic import to keep the family line free of hereditary disease. His patrician features looked better in profile, though his body was sleek and supple, especially compared to Jos Sedley who had now lumbered over to George to reminisce about their time together at Eton.

'Not that handsome,' Becky said flatly, because she'd seen the dismissive way he looked at Amelia. It wasn't with the tenderness of a man who'd treat her like the precious bauble that her family had raised her to be. There was no good reason for George to be so careless with Amelia's affection when it was so unselfishly given. 'Oh, don't pout at me, Emmy! You should be pleased that the sight of Gorgeous George leaves me cold. You don't have to worry that I'd steal him out from under your nose.'

'I know that you would never do that!' Amelia's misguided belief in the goodness of Becky's heart was interrupted by a Chelsea show pony who shouldered Becky out of the way so she could fall on Amelia.

'Emmy! Oh my God! So glad you're back from slumming it with the chavs!' she cried and that was the cue for a whole pack of them — all with indentikit buttery, long limbs and sleek, shiny hair — to surround Amelia and squeal at a pitch that had every dog in the neighbourhood in a frenzy.

Becky had no choice but to step to the side or be mown down by a sharpened elbow or this season's must-have heel.

'How could you have kissed that awful Gav? He dropped his aitches more often than he dropped his trousers.'

'You wouldn't think they'd let people like that in the Marines.'

'Was it very awful? The food looked terrible. And all that prosecco. Didn't even give you decent bubbles.'

'And as for that Becca girl. Common as the proverbial. What did she really say in that swimming pool? Go on! You can tell us.'

Amelia cast agonised glances between her *Made in Chelsea* crew and her new, common-as-the-proverbial BFF.

As it was a special occasion, Becky took pity on her. 'It's Becky, actually, and what I said in that swimming pool was, 'If you chat shit about me again, I'll wipe you off the face of the earth, bitch,'' she recalled with the same menace that had made Leanne fall off the swan inflatable in fear.

The posh girls all took a synchronised step back, which was the first sensible thing they'd done.

'Joke. That was a joke.' Becky laughed lightly and stepped back into the circle so she could take a proprietorial hold of Emmy's arm. 'As if I would say something like that! And I wouldn't say I was common. I mean, *I* don't drop *my* aitches.'

'You're Bohemian,' Amelia squeaked. 'Becky's parents were very artsy.' The girls all sniffed: 'Bohemian' was secret code for 'working class'. 'Anyway, Becky, I want you to meet everyone. I know they're going to love you as much as I do.'

It was doubtful that Minty, Muffin, Molly, Milly and Maddy would ever find it in their cold, solid-platinum hearts to love her. They each leaned in gingerly to kiss the air above Becky's cheek as if she were covered in grime and smelt of body spray from Poundland, when actually she was freshly showered and doused in Mrs Sedley's bottle of Coco by Chanel, which was far too young a scent for someone thundering through her fifties.

Becky might have been wearing another of Amelia's old dresses and a pair of shoes with loo roll stuffed into the toes because they were a size too large, her pale skin unloved by the Mediterranean sun, but she refused to lower her eyes away from their collective, condemning gaze.

She was just as pretty as them, if not prettier. Besides, her beauty hadn't been helped along by the attentions of a favoured plastic surgeon in Harley Street who'd given them all the same nose. Becky's beauty had flourished in the harshest conditions, like a winter primrose fighting its way through frost to flower. Who knows what she might she have been with the advantages that these girls took for granted?

The Montessori nursery, the nannies, the private schools and personal tutors. The wholesome food, free of additives and E numbers, grown on the country estate or purchased by the housekeeper from London's finest grocers. The tennis and ballet lessons. The holidays on exotic beaches and snowy ski slopes. The trips to art galleries and the theatre, Glyndebourne for the opera, Ascot for the racing.

If Becky had been born into that kind of privilege, there was no telling what she might have become.

'You all look so glamorous,' Becky said at last, so grateful to Jemima Pinkerton for ironing out her vowels so they were a lot less cockney and a bit more cut-glass. 'I bet you've all been lounging somewhere lovely while poor Emmy and I were holed up in Elstree.'

'Saint Tropez,' Miffy admitted and Becky widened her eyes.

'When my mother was alive, we used to summer in Cap d'Antibes. She was French, one of the Mortmerency family,' she said a little wistfully. 'We'd stay at La Belle Plage.'

It was the truth. Kind of. If you squinted at it and were already severely short-sighted. Her parents had met in Cap d'Antibes. Her mother and her mother's mother had been chambermaids at La Belle Plage while her grandfather, pushing sixty, had never been promoted past busboy.

Her father had rolled into town one summer

with a card-counting scam that had him thrown out of every casino within a fifty-mile radius. He also had three of his ribs broken and a mild concussion when he was roughed up by some casino heavies in the alleyway at the back of La Belle Plage, which was where Becky's mother first laid eyes on him when she was rifling through one of the bins to find a pair of diamond earrings that she'd earlier thrown from a fifth-floor window.

It wasn't so much love at first sight as like recognising like. 'A girl after my own heart,' her father would say when he was the good kind of drunk, pulling Sidonie on to his lap so he could kiss the top of her head.

When he was the bad kind of drunk, Sidonie was the one most likely to end up with broken bones and a mild concussion but still, it hadn't all been bad.

There had been that one summer when the Sharps had slummed it on the Cap d'Antibes, staying on a nearby camp-site and getting all gussied up to visit the family elders at La Belle Plage. Becky could remember being taken to the kitchens and treated like a visiting royal dignitary. There'd been a concoction of ice cream as big as she was and she'd sung an absolutely filthy song in French that her mother had taught her, much to the delight of the kitchen staff.

'Good times,' Becky sighed and now the show-ponies were looking at her as if maybe, just maybe, she wasn't an irredeemable little chav.

'Now you really must meet George,' Amelia

said urgently as if engineering an introduction between Becky and George was the only excuse she had for going to talk to him.

It was hot in the bar. The tealights had all but melted, the foliage had wilted and Amelia was ruddy-faced as she edged herself and Becky through the open doors that led out on to the roof terrace.

'I'm pretty sure that I saw him slip out here when we were talking to the girls,' she murmured as her eyes darted around the terrace, lit by paper lanterns and yet hundreds more tealights. Mrs Sedley had obviously sent a lackey to the nearest IKEA to buy out their entire stock. 'Maybe he's gone downstairs.'

'Maybe George should chase *you* and not the other way round,' Becky suggested because desperation was never a good look, but Amelia had her wrist in a surprisingly firm grip as she pulled Becky along.

There was a champagne bar in one corner and an oyster station in the other though Becky couldn't think of anything more vile than sliding slimy, snotty oyster guts down her throat. Waiters circulated with canapés — an amusing affectation of tiny hamburgers, miniature newspaper cones of fish and chips, and hot dogs that could be eaten in one bite.

'You haven't eaten a thing all evening,' Becky reminded Amelia, who was still gazing over people's heads to catch a glimpse of the lesser-spotted George Wylie. 'And you've already had two glasses of champagne.'

'I'm really not hungry and I put so much

weight on in the house,' Amelia protested. She had let Becky, against her better judgement, persuade her into the black bodycon dress she'd worn for her *Big Brother* exit, its seams straining against all the flesh which didn't want to be contained.

'What rubbish! You look stunning,' Becky insisted as she beckoned a canapé-bearing server over with an imperious finger. 'I wish I had some curves. It doesn't matter how much I eat, I can't seem to put any weight on. Can you even imagine what that's like?'

Amelia shook her head sadly. 'No, I can't.'

'Apart from these beasts.' Becky looked down at her breasts with some satisfaction, their upper curves just visible against the black silk of her borrowed frock. 'Anyway, your parents will be cross if you get drunk on an empty stomach, so, here, have a burger!'

In one deft move, she plucked a mini burger off the tray that appeared in front of them and popped it into Amelia's mouth, which had opened to say that she really, really didn't want a burger. It was a little too big to be eaten in one bite and Amelia could feel her cheeks puff out as she frantically chewed and, of course, it was at that moment that George arrived at her side.

Almost as if Becky had planned the whole thing.

'Emmy,' he said coolly. Amelia felt a slight brush of his lips against her cheek, could feel the heat of his lean, tall body against hers, smell the faint hint of limes from his aftershave, but, still masticating furiously, she could take no pleasure from George's attention.

It was left to Jos, bringing up the rear, to make the introductions.

'George, this is Emmy's friend — lovely girl, staying with us — lucky us!' he stuttered, his face turning as red as his sister's.

'Does this lovely girl have a name?' George said, his coolness turning chilly, because he knew exactly who Becky was from all the times when he absolutely did not watch *Big Brother* while he was waiting for *News at Ten* to start.

Amelia swallowed the last morsel of dead cow and bread, almost choking in her haste to be done with it and then, in an act of great daring, placed her hand on George's arm. Her hand was as hot as her face, and as it rested there uncertainly on the white cotton of his Huntsman of Savile Row bespoke shirt, his left eyebrow quirked almost imperceptibly. Unless you were watching him as intently as Becky was.

'George, this is Becky. I do hope you two are going to be friends. And Becky, this is George.'

Their eyes met, green clashing with black. 'Darling Emmy has told me so much about you,' Becky said sweetly, pulling her hand back as soon as she could: there was something quite reptilian about George's touch, the cool disregard on his face, as if he didn't like being in such close proximity to the lower orders.

'I've heard absolutely nothing about *you*,' George said flatly.

There was something about her that he didn't trust; a knowing look in her eyes before she cast them down, a pretty smile that was a millimetre

51

away from a smirk. It was as if the fox had disguised himself as a chicken to trick his way into the henhouse. She was clearly going to be a bad influence on his Emmy if she wasn't quickly despatched back to whatever council estate she'd come from.

'Oh, there isn't much to tell,' Becky said and then in one graceful movement, George was presented with the sleek line of her spine, her skin milk-bottle white against the black of her dress, as she curved herself into the considerable bulk of Jos Sedley. 'Is there, Jos?'

Jos's face lit up as though all his Christmases and birthdays, and even Easter and the day every month when his trust fund was paid into his Drummonds bank account, had come at once.

'No, there isn't,' he agreed. 'No, I mean, there is! I'm sure you could tell me lots of things.'

'I'm sure I couldn't,' Becky said as she snuggled closer to Jos as if the temperature on the terrace on a balmy August night wasn't positively roasting. 'I haven't done anything, been anywhere. Not like you!'

'It's so lovely to see you, George,' Amelia said a little desperately, because he had eyes only for Becky, as she quizzed Jos about bench pressing, though surely Becky had already asked him all about that when they'd sat side by side on the loveseat back in the Sedleys' drawing room. 'It feels like ages since we were in the same room.'

George turned to her. 'Though we're not actually in the same room now. We're on a terrace, looking up at the stars.'

Becky was forgotten. When George smiled at

her like that, so that even his coal-dark eyes warmed, it was hard for Amelia to remember her own name.

'Mummy had planned to do a marquee in the back garden.' She giggled. 'But then she realised that all the marquees were too big and would play havoc with her herbaceous borders. She was very cross about it.'

'And I'm very cross with you,' George said, though he still had that lovely smile, which completely transformed his face. He was still handsome, but now he looked kind and caring too, even as he pretended to cuff Amelia's chin. 'That awful show, Emmy. And that even more awful personal trainer who you let paw you.'

'He hardly pawed me!' Amelia protested. The turn the conversation had taken was thrilling: George was jealous! 'Gav . . . '

'Gav!' George all but moaned the name as if it caused him great pain. 'Emmy, you cried over some cretin called Gav.'

'So, you watched the show, then?' Amelia asked, her every nerve alight at this paltry show of attention. If it were possible to die from being thrilled, then they'd have to carry her home in a coffin.

'Never!' George smiled loftily. 'Though I might have caught a few seconds every now and again. Enough to know that some horrible oik called Gav made you cry. I don't believe he was in the Marines either. Dobbin said he's going to check and see if he can be court-martialled.'

'Oh, is Dobbin here?' Amelia looked around for George's best friend, who'd gone straight from Oxford into Her Majesty's Royal Regiment and had already been promoted to captain. He was an absolute darling. Not a patch on her absolute *absolute* darling George, but still.

'No, he's at some dreary regimental dinner. You'll see him soon enough,' George said dismissively, because when Dobbin wasn't on active duty and in some war-torn hellhole in danger of being blown to smithereens, George wasn't exactly sure what Dobbin did. 'Honestly, Emmy, it's been five minutes and all we've talked about is Dobbin and Gav the Chav. Any more men you want to taunt me with?'

'Oh, no!' Amelia put a hand to her heart at the very suggestion, her face as round and as red as an autumn apple. 'I wasn't taunting.' She seized every last atom of courage she possessed. 'I have missed you, George.'

George sighed to himself. Hopefully, once she'd done with university and a few more unsuitable men like Gav, Amelia would toughen up a bit. She was a sweet girl but you got sick of sweet after a while; started to crave something tart, acidic . . .

Amelia plucked at George's sleeve again, her expression pleading. 'Have you missed me too? Even a little bit?'

George patted Amelia's hand and gently removed it from his arm. 'Of course I have,' he said, but his smile wasn't as warm as it had been and his eyes were fixed on a point across the terrace. 'Come on. We should really go and rescue poor Jos before your friend Rebecca eats him alive.'

'She's not like that and her name's Becky,' Amelia insisted, but she didn't protest too much because then George's arm was around her waist (she sucked in her butterfly-filled stomach) and he was steering her over to where Becky was daring Jos to eat a mini doughnut, even though everyone knew perfectly well that he hadn't eaten a carb in five years.

6

While Amelia and Becky's former housemates made the most of what time they had left to get paid for nightclub appearances and sponsored posts on Instagram, the odd appearance in the tabloids and a few kiss-and-tell-everything stories, the Sedleys had decided that enough was enough.

Despite her desperate pleas, Rhoda, Amelia's publicist, was dismissed because, while *Big Brother* had been an amusing diversion, Mrs Sedley was still being ostracised at the tennis club and Mr Sedley had had to fire one of his underlings at the bank when he discovered a picture of his darling Emmy in a bikini as the man's screensaver.

Amelia couldn't hide her relief that she no longer had to stammer her way through any more exclusive interviews. Instead she could go back to her normal life of beauty treatments and shopping and coffee dates and lunch dates, all the while complaining that she'd hardly had a holiday this summer at all, what with being in Niger then in the *Big Brother* house, and having to go back to university in a few short weeks.

Becky was less relieved. She'd been hoping that Rhoda might overlook the fact that she was already signed with Babs Pinkerton and find her some lucrative media opportunities. But now Rhoda wasn't returning Becky's calls and

Becky's position in the Sedley household was starting to feel quite precarious.

Mrs Sedley had even asked via Mrs Blenkinsop, the housekeeper, what Becky's plans were and just how much longer she intended to stay. But Becky had learned from Jemima Pinkerton that to be rude to the help was unforgivable, and Mrs Blenkinsop was not Mrs Sedley's biggest fan anyway (she micro-managed Mrs Blenkinsop beyond all measure and insisted she use a solution of white-wine vinegar and baking soda to clean everything when Cillit Bang did the job much better). So she and Becky were already firm friends and when Mrs Blenkinsop said that Mrs Sedley wanted her gone, Becky had burst into pitiful, anguished tears.

Mrs Blenkinsop had marched downstairs, shot Mrs Sedley (who, for all the micro-managing, was secretly more terrified of Mrs Blenkinsop than she was of any of the women at the tennis club) a black look and then taken out her fury on the Miele vacuum cleaner and Mrs Sedley's new floors.

Nothing more was asked about Becky's future plans, but Becky knew that she needed a plan B, and fast. Once Amelia had resumed her studies at Durham University, it would leave Becky without a friend in all the world and with nothing in the way of an income — when she'd phoned Babs Pinkerton to ask for her cut from the sale of Jemima's bungalow, Babs had just laughed and hung up. Becky was left with no choice but to make hay, and other things, while the sun still shone.

So, while Amelia was still in bed, Becky spent her mornings in Kensington Gardens with Jos Sedley. He had been planning to go back to LA and his protein balls weeks before, but if he'd done that, then he wouldn't have been able to devise a fitness programme for Becky.

'But you're perfect,' he gasped when Becky had descended the stairs on that first morning in the Lululemon workout gear he'd bought for Amelia, which his sister couldn't squeeze into. 'You are fit. I mean, you don't need to get fit.'

'But I'm not firm. Everything wobbles. Look!' Becky had done a shimmy, which had made everything wobble, including Jos. Becky had looked down at her chest and shimmied again. 'Particularly these.'

Jos had clung on to the banister for dear life. 'I . . . I see what you mean.'

'You naughty boy,' Becky had purred in a low voice and Jos's torture wasn't over, because she turned around and stuck out her Lycra-encased bottom. 'This jiggles too.'

'Dear Lord . . . '

'I bet the women in LA are firm,' Becky had lamented, taking a step closer to Jos, who thought that he might be having a relapse back to his childhood asthma. 'Taut. Supple.'

She was face to face with Jos now, who swallowed convulsively — was he in heaven or hell or some heady combination of both?

'Feel my thighs, Jos,' Becky had commanded and she'd taken his hand and placed it just above her left knee. 'They're so fleshy. Can you do something about it?'

'Water!' Jos choked. 'We need water!' And he'd snatched his hand away and hobbled in the direction of the kitchen as if he was in great pain.

He'd then devised a programme for her that involved a lot of squats and lunges while he stood behind her with a sports bag clutched to his groin. Then there were a lot of exercises that thrust her chest forward, by which time Jos was standing in front of her, and though she said that she should probably work on her triceps too, Jos said that it was best to concentrate on her glutes and her pectorals for now.

Afterwards he'd help her stretch in a secluded spot.

'I can't help but groan when you're manhandling me, Jos. Especially when you have my legs hooked over your shoulders. It burns but it's the good kind of burn, do you know what I mean?'

'No pain, no gain, eh?' Jos would say every time. He'd grown a lot more comfortable in Becky's presence, though after her stretches, he could often hardly talk on their walk back to the house.

In the afternoons, Becky would spend time with Amelia and whichever combination of the M's, usually Minty and Muffin, she'd made plans with. Usually they'd have a mani/ pedi or a facial, maybe even a stress-busting massage at the fancy spa on Kensington Church Street where Amelia had an account.

Then it was out in the evenings. To dinner, then to a bar or club with some more M's and their dreary, chinless, floppy-haired boyfriends.

'We should ask Jos to come,' Becky would say

each evening as she and Amelia were getting ready to go out. 'It's so lovely to see the two of you becoming closer. I wish I had an elder brother.'

'And it's lovely to see the two of you becoming closer as well,' Amelia would sigh and she'd insist that Jos should come with them, and the upshot of it was that Jos hadn't been to a Crossfit session in weeks and he could now say whole sentences to Becky without breaking into a sweat and his face changing colour.

Amelia watched the courtship with barely concealed delight. Her Jos and her dear Becky, who might actually become a real sister.

Mr and Mrs Sedley could conceal their delight only too well. 'Why is that girl still living with us?' Mrs Sedley asked after they'd waved off their offspring and the ubiquitous Becky to deepest, darkest Fulham to celebrate the birthday of one of the M's' floppy-haired beaux. 'Do you see the way she cosies up to Jos? I'd have her out of the house tomorrow but Mrs Blenkinsop says she'll hand in her notice if I do and I don't trust anyone else with my new floors.'

Mr Sedley glanced at his wife with exasperated fondness. How many sleepless nights had she had over those bloody floors? Which meant Mr Sedley had had many sleepless nights too, which wasn't very helpful when he was dealing with so many figures. One decimal point in the wrong place or one extra nought subtracted when it should have been added and they'd be ruined.

He patted her hand. 'That Becky will do as

well as any other,' he said mildly. 'Let him marry who he likes.'

Mrs Sedley turned to him aghast. She could feel one of her heads coming on. 'Who said anything about them getting married?' she exclaimed in horror. 'We hardly know a thing about her!' A muscle was spasming painfully between her eyebrows. 'Although I do worry that he works so much and he's never once had a girlfriend, but does it have to be *her?*'

'She's pretty enough,' Mr Sedley said diffidently as if he'd never once caught his breath at the sight of Becky in her workout gear.

'There's something about her that I don't like. She reminds me of a ginger cat we had when I was a girl,' Mrs Sedley remembered with a shudder. 'It would bring in these half-dead animals — mice, baby birds, that sort of thing — then toy with them for *hours* instead of putting them out of their misery.'

'Maybe you should take one of your pills,' Mr Sedley advised because his wife had turned a mottled red colour, which never boded well; such a pity that Emmy and Jos had inherited her high colouring. This conversation about Emmy's little friend was getting tedious. 'Jos is big enough and ugly enough to do as he pleases, and that's the end of the matter.' And then he stalked off in the direction of his study to have a glass of whisky and she went off to take a pill and have a lie down, and they were still at odds with each other the next day and Mrs Sedley couldn't help but feel that Becky Sharp was to blame.

61

7

'I have that horrible back-to-school feeling,' Amelia said with a sigh. Mid September had rolled around all too soon, and Amelia was about to return to Durham.

No wonder Becky felt as if something were about to change. Something big and monumental.

She stared down at the third finger on her left hand and wondered how it would bear up under the weight of a huge rock.

Jos wasn't at all subtle so he'd probably go for something that was at least ten carats. Becky had never thought about getting married and she was only twenty and who got married at only twenty, unless they were dull religious types? But Becky needed a plan B and Jos had his successful protein balls and his huge trust fund, and embracing the LA lifestyle wouldn't exactly be a hardship. If she stuck it out for a little while then she could have at least half his balls in the divorce settlement.

'Don't you think, Becky?'

Becky blinked at Amelia as she was torn away from her little fantasy of a big house in the Hollywood Hills with its own swimming pool. She'd hardly ever gone to school so she'd never really known the Sunday-evening gloom of finishing homework that had been left to the last minute, then bath and an early night. Her childhood gloom had lasted for years and encompassed far more than a little angst about a half-finished essay on the Spanish Armada.

'Actually, I have quite a good feeling about the future,' Becky insisted to Amelia's reflection as her friend put the last touches to her make-up. 'New beginnings, new adventures, and all that. By the way, I'd go easy on that blusher if I were you, Emmy. You're so lucky having naturally rosy cheeks. I wish I did. I'll just have to settle for being pale and interesting, I guess.'

Amelia cast aside her blusher as if it had scalded her and started dabbing at her face with powder instead.

'I think you look beautiful, Becky,' she said a little enviously. Becky was wearing another one of her cast-offs, a gauzy grey little dress with tiny crystals sewn into it, which made Becky look like an ethereal wood nymph. When Amelia had worn it, she'd looked like a dumpy rain cloud.

'You look lovely too,' Becky said a little more perfunctorily than Amelia would have liked. She hadn't been sure about her new dress; it was very pink and puffy, like a gigantic marsh-mallow, but Becky had persuaded her otherwise. 'You look so sweet. Gorgeous George won't know what to do with himself when he sees you. He'll want to eat you up!'

'I wish!' Since her party, Amelia hadn't seen George at all unless she was stalking him on all forms of social media, which wasn't that rewarding. George was so focused on his political ambitions that he wouldn't risk a careless meme or a whimsical picture of a sunset on Instagram.

Instead, he tended to tweet links to leader articles in the *Daily Telegraph* and *Financial Times* and it was hard for even the most besotted young woman to feign an enthusiasm about cuts to farm subsidies.

'Honestly, Emmy, he'll take one look at you in that dress and lure you away to some dark corner and ravish your poor, defenceless, young body,' Becky said and she snatched up the pillow from Amelia's bed and gathered it to her in a passionate embrace. 'I'd put money on it!'

Amelia flushed with painful hope but unless George had undergone a personality transplant since their first meeting, the poofy marshmallow dress was hardly going to cut it.

They were going to an End Of Summer party at an exclusive Mayfair nightclub. There was rumoured to be a brace of young royals attending, as well as *everyone*. When you and all your friends lived in one postal code, had all attended one of several boarding schools and your mothers all sat on the same committees, then your *everyone* was actually quite small.

There were paparazzi outside when Jos gallantly handed Amelia and Becky out of the car and for once Amelia was happy to pose for photos. The hope of . . . (not being ravished because, try as she might, Amelia knew that George wasn't the ravishing sort) . . . George's face lighting up when he saw her put a sparkle in Amelia's eyes, gave her a giddiness and an allure that she didn't normally have. And when she saw

Becky's hand tucked into Jos's meaty paw, saw the way that Becky leaned into her brother and whispered in his ear, Amelia felt nothing but happiness for them. Maybe one day, let it be soon, she'd know that same kind of happiness. With George.

But the first person she saw, when they found the table that Jos had reserved for them, wasn't George at all.

One sweet pang of regret pierced Amelia's heart to be replaced by a genuine pleasure as the man who'd been sitting there got to his feet and promptly knocked over his drink.

'Dobbin!' she cried as Becky stared in amazement at Captain William Dobbin of Her Majesty's Royal Regiment. She'd heard his name in passing from Amelia because when she wasn't mooning over Gorgeous George, her conversation still revolved around him, and this Dobbin was his best friend. Dobbin had distinguished himself with honours several times in war-strewn, dusty places and so Becky had expected some dashing and glamorous war hero.

Not this tall, ungainly man with large hands and feet and even larger ears, shown in all their massive glory by his close-cropped black hair, while the rest of him was poured into a hideously tight suit. Perhaps he shared the same tailor as Jos.

In fact, Dobbin might have been a good back-up plan (a plan C), but one look at those ears — so big they had to be a hazard on the front line . . . A world of no. She'd asked Amelia why everyone called him Dobbin instead of

William and now she knew; he was like a great big carthorse in a world full of sleek thorough-breds.

'Emmy!' Dobbin said in a rusty voice full of wonder. 'How long has it been?'

He took Amelia's hand, realised his own was wet after spilling his drink and pulled out a voluminous white handkerchief to mop at both of them.

Becky hid her smile in Jos's shoulder. Jos was quite the heart-throb next to the hapless Dobbin.

'Dobs, it's fine. I'm hardly damp at all,' Amelia said, taking pity on him. 'And yes, it's been ages. A couple of years. You were just shipping off to Helmand Province.' She put her hand on his arm without any of the agony she experienced when she dared to put her hands anywhere near George. 'Was it very awful?'

'Quite awful,' Dobbin conceded. Amelia eyes filled with tears at the thought of anything being quite awful and he hurriedly corrected himself: 'But it wasn't so bad. The *Big Brother* house looked a jolly sight worse.'

Dobbin had never seen anyone blush so prettily as Amelia Sedley when she covered her hands with her face. 'Oh, Dobbin, you didn't watch it, did you?'

'I did and I'm looking into having that Gav fellow court-martialled,' he said and he wasn't joking — he barely knew how to — but Amelia giggled and his heart melted.

'I'm pretty sure that you can't have somebody court-martialled if they've already left the forces,' she gulped, tears forgotten.

'*If* he was ever in the forces. If that's the calibre of soldier the Marines are taking on, then God help us if there's a war,' Dobbin declared to more giggles from Amelia until the saccharine display was interrupted by George, deftly threading his way through the throng to break up their little tête-à-tête.

'Sorry, Emmy,' he said. 'Is this oik bothering you?'

'Never!' Emmy said with another giggle that made Becky grind down on her back molars.

'Shall we order some champagne?' she asked Jos as she sat down. Amelia appeared to have no plans to introduce her to Dobbin the talking horse and anyway, what was the point of being introduced to him?

'Is it table service, do you know?' Jos asked, peering about the room.

For someone so rich, Jos was absolutely lacking in panache and suaveness and all the other qualities that Becky imagined they gave out on the first day at Eton, along with those funny top hats and tailcoats.

'I'm parched,' she said. 'But if you don't want any . . . Look! It is table service. There's a waiter! Oh, he doesn't seem to have noticed you.'

'I'll run after him,' Jos promised and he was gone, his shoulders looking especially wide in his white dinner jacket. Unfortunately, the wait staff were also in white jackets which meant that on his way to the bar Jos was stopped by three different groups of people who tried to order drinks from him.

Becky settled back in her chair to watch the rich and entitled at play. Amelia was caught between George and Dobbin and over the chatter of the party and the DJ dropping slow beats, she could still be heard giggling in the same inane fashion.

Jos was at the bar now and when he turned round he was bearing aloft a huge bottle of champagne with a sparkler stuck in it so that on his journey through the club, he was given a wide berth. It was a very romantic gesture but when Jos reached their table and proudly placed the bottle in front of Becky, she heard George murmur to Dobbin, 'God, how common.'

Becky was sure that she was meant to have heard because when she gave George a reproachful look — the faintest puckering of her forehead, a little pout — he raised his glass in what could only have been a mocking salute.

Well, Amelia was welcome to him, for all the good it would do to love a man who thought he was superior to everyone around him. No wonder he had political ambitions. Becky turned starry eyes to Jos.

'This is the loveliest thing that anyone has ever done for me,' she informed Jos with the adoring gaze that always made him put a finger in his shirt collar like it was suddenly choking him. 'I know you don't drink, but could you have one glass of champagne? For me?'

'No carbs plus alcohol are a dreadful combination,' Jos protested. 'And anyway, this stuff is pure sugar.'

'I think it's mostly bubbles,' Becky said as she

hefted up the bottle, tilted one of the empty glass flutes on the table and expertly poured. 'Anyway, aren't we celebrating?'

'Are we? What are we celebrating?' Jos asked, as dense as the pads he strapped on when he and Becky were boxercising in the park.

'Well, we've known each other three weeks,' Becky said with a heavy-lidded glance that made Jos adjust himself when he thought she wasn't looking.

'Th . . . three weeks,' he gulped. 'Only three weeks? It seems longer.'

'Doesn't it?' Becky agreed, holding out a glass. 'It feels like I've known you all my life. Here, have just one drink so we can toast our . . . *friendship*. Though I suppose all good things come to an end.'

'It's coming to an end?' Jos echoed, his brow furrowing as he took the glass in his meaty paw and manoeuvred it with some difficulty to his lips. He didn't really have the right build for drinking from delicate champagne flutes.

'Yes, that's why we're here, silly!' Amelia said, sitting down next to them and leaning across Becky to help herself to a glass. 'To celebrate the end of summer. I expect you'll be going back to LA soon, Jos.'

No one had ever treated Becky with as much kindness and sweetness and without any kind of expectation, but in that moment, Becky could quite happily have throttled Amelia Sedley. She wouldn't even have bothered to make it look like an accident.

'I suppose,' Jos sighed, as if the thought of

going back to a place where it was sunny all the time and he had a beautiful, architect-designed house in Malibu with three different kinds of pool in its landscaped grounds, was about as appealing as a fortnight in Scunthorpe.

'Becky's never been to LA, have you?' Amelia said, nudging Becky's arm. 'You'd love it.'

Maybe she wouldn't kill Amelia. Not just yet. After all, Amelia was the only person who wanted Jos to make an honest woman of her as much as Becky did.

'I've always wanted to go to LA,' she said wistfully. 'Do you know lots of famous people, Jos? I bet you do.'

Jos gulped down the rest of his champagne and puffed out his chest. 'Well, I'm very good friends with Ryan Gosling's personal trainer.' He didn't even notice when Becky refilled his glass. 'We sent him some protein balls and apparently he loved them.'

'Wow! Ryan Gosling,' Amelia gasped. 'Who else?'

More stars than there were in the heavens. An Oscar-winning actress next door who was always having loud parties with no consideration for the fact that Jos got up at five to do his first workout of the day. A legendary film director lived up the hill who was obsessed with shooting coyotes and had accidentally killed two of his own bichon frises. And all manner of rap artists, hotly tipped young actors and even a couple of *Real Housewives*' husbands, who all worked out at Jos's gym.

Jos polished off most of the bottle of

champagne as he got into his stride; namedropping all the celebrities he'd seen as he queued for his collagen berry lattes or hiked in the Hollywood hills.

'You're so well connected. I suppose you have lots of friends. Lots of very glamorous, very beautiful friends who are girls. Girlfriends,' Becky said, with just a hint of a quiver of her bottom lip. 'No wonder you can't wait to go back to LA. We must seem so dull by comparison.'

'Never. You're the most beautiful of them all,' Jos declared rashly and loudly so that George Wylie, who was still hanging around like a bad smell, smiled thinly. 'They're all stuffed full of silicon and Botox and actually they're not friends at all because they're very unfriendly.'

'They sound awful,' Amelia said but then her attention was caught by one of the M's and with a coy flutter of her lashes at Becky, she slipped out from between them. 'Must go and say hello to Muffin.'

'It sounds to me as if you don't like LA as much as everyone thinks you do,' Becky commented. Although this was said gently, she was the daughter of Frank Sharp, con artist, hustler and trickster, so there was something hardwired into her DNA that gave her the ability to sniff out a person's weaknesses. Once she'd identified what made them tick — the dark, secret heart of them — then of course she was going to use that knowledge for her own advantage. Anyone with any sense would do the same.

'It's good for the protein ball business. I don't

71

think there's a single person in the 90210 zipcode who's eaten gluten since Obama became president but, Becky . . . ' Deep set within his roughly hewn face, Jos's eyes were troubled.

Becky placed her hand on his knee. 'You can tell me anything,' she whispered, leaning forward so that Jos could tell all his fears and worries to her breasts. 'I would never judge you.'

'Oh, Becky, I'm so lonely,' he confessed. He'd never told this sad truth to anyone. 'Also, and I . . . I know you might find this hard to believe, but . . . but . . . well, I'm shy. Very shy. Always have been.'

Becky shook her head then turned her face away, then sighed, and the hand that was on Jos's knee slid up a few centimetres, not enough to cause alarm or raise eyebrows, but Jos's heart was thundering away as if he'd just done thirty minutes of high-impact cardio. 'There is a way that you wouldn't ever have to be lonely again,' she said, leaning up to whisper in his ear so that her breasts almost brushed his chin and Jos had to close his eyes and practise mindful deep breathing. 'And, a secret for a secret: I'm shy too. The whole reason I went on *Big Brother* was to build up my confidence.' Her hand, almost of its own accord, moved up another inch or so. 'It's like we're kindred spirits, isn't it?'

'Soulmates,' Jos agreed and Becky's face was still tilted up towards his own and he licked his lips nervously and . . . and . . . and . . .

'For fuck's sake!'

'What the hell?'

Their romantic moment was cut short by a

sudden dousing of cold champagne from the bottle Dobbin had attempted to pour into Jos's empty flute.

'Sorry, sorry,' he muttered. 'Didn't want to interrupt you, thought I'd be all stealthy like, but the bottle slipped.'

'I'm soaked!' Becky snapped, furious both at the interruption and that she'd been taken unawares and sworn, when nice, shy, orphaned young ladies didn't go round dropping the f-bomb. 'You should be more careful.'

Dobbin actually dared to try and mop at her with a napkin held in his huge hands, then caught his cufflink on one of the crystals sewn on to Becky's borrowed dress, which tore. Not enough to do much damage, to the dress at least, but enough that he apologised again, profusely, and Jos subsided back on his chair with a hopeless look, and the moment was ruined. Completely ruined.

'Bad luck!' said a silky voice and Becky looked up to see George Wylie standing over her, with a smug expression that made her curl her hands into fists, her nails digging into her palms so hard that she'd still have little half-moon marks the next day.

It was a lost cause after that. Jos drowned his sorrows not just with champagne but with whisky chasers, even though Dobbin warned him that he shouldn't mix grape with grain.

'I'll drink what I bloody well like,' he bellowed belligerently, swaying back from the bar with yet another round. Becky felt her heart sink, knowing only too well that how a man behaved when he was hammered revealed his true nature.

'I'm going to find Emmy.' She extricated herself from Jos's clutches: he had also become very handsy, trying to touch what he wouldn't dare go near when he was sober.

By the time Becky returned with a predictably agitated Amelia in tow, a large crowd had gathered around Jos who'd attempted to run after Becky but had slipped in the spilt champagne and toppled over on to his back.

He pitched one way then another like an upended turtle while the crowd of braying posh types roared their approval and held up their next-gen iPhones to record the moment for posterity.

'Up you get, fatso!' cried one young wag.

'I'm not fat, I'm big boned and heavily muscled,' Jos panted to even more hoots and jeers.

'We have to help him,' Amelia cried but Becky held her back. That was a sure way to end up in a video that could well go viral by the next morning.

'We can't manage him on our own,' she pointed out reasonably. 'Where's your George?'

George Wylie, of course, had slunk off at the first sign of trouble, as he didn't want to end up in a viral clip any more than Becky did, so it was left to Dobbin to valiantly step in and hoist Jos to his feet, to a helpful commentary from the peanut gallery.

'Heave! Heave! Heave ho!' they shouted as Jos was finally levered upright so that he could then lurch unsteadily against their table and send all the glassware flying.

'More champagne!' Jos shouted, trying to click his fingers to summon a waiter and almost blinding poor Dobbin. 'Champagne for my real friends, real pain for my sham friends!'

'Jos, I am cutting you off!' Dobbin said very sternly, clamping his arm round Jos's shoulders and steering him out of the club, with Amelia and Becky bringing up the rear.

Becky would much rather have stayed. She was sure she'd spotted a couple of young royals at the bar, but Amelia was crying. Much as the missed opportunity stung, she had no option but to leave with their sad, humiliated little party.

Once they were in the club foyer, George joined them. 'There you are!' he said. 'I've been looking for you everywhere.'

'You couldn't have been looking very hard, then, as you were at our table until poor Jos fell over and then you disappeared,' Becky pointed out.

Amelia stopped crying for long enough to gaze damply and disappointedly at George. 'You didn't do that, did you?'

'Of course I didn't. Your little friend must be confused,' he said firmly as if nothing could be further from the truth. 'Fell over, did he? But no bones broken? Well, let's get him and you girls home.'

Then he took Jos's other side and the three men lumbered out of the club like some mythical three-headed beast, only to run into a pack of paparazzi who sprang into action in the hope that one of them might be a rat-arsed young royal.

The popping flashbulbs had a disastrous effect on Jos's centre of gravity. Or it might have been because George took one look at the cameras and abruptly let Jos go so he could slither back into the shadows. He was a prospective Member of Parliament, after all.

It was left to Amelia to take up the slack and help Dobbin to support the considerable weight of her brother, to the delight of the smudges. Two posh boys weren't worth the effort but a *Big Brother* winner might do for a page-seven lead.

Then the drunk young Hooray lurched around towards the pretty redhead who'd come second in *Big Brother*, trailing a few steps behind as if she had nothing to do with the unfortunate trio in front of her, and he broke free of his captors so he could take her in a very enthusiastic embrace. This could be a front-page story after all.

NEW BALLS PLEASE!
Big Brother Becky Caught In Clinch With
Protein Ball Millionaire!
Friends say he wants to put a ring on it!

She might have only come second in this year's *Big Brother*, but beautiful Becky Sharp, 20, looked like a winner last night as she was caught canoodling with Jos Sedley, 33, brother of Amelia Sedley, who snatched the title from her best friend.

Jos, the brains behind a health-and-fitness lifestyle brand which makes a successful range of protein balls, divides his time between London and LA. But judging by the way he locked lips with Becky, to the delight of the crowd, he's thinking of making London his permanent base.

'It's been a whirlwind romance,' a close friend of the couple reports. 'They might only have known each other a few weeks but they're already talking about marriage.'

Three people who would be delighted to hear wedding bells are *Big Brother* winner Amelia, 22, who regards Becky as a sister, and her parents Charles and Caroline Sedley, who invited Becky to live with them in their Chelsea townhouse worth £15 million, and have apparently given the young couple their blessing.

'They adore Becky as if she was their own daughter,' said a source close to the Sedleys. 'Caroline is already planning the engagement party.'

It will be quite the rags-to-riches story for Becky. She entered the *Big Brother* house a penniless orphan who'd been working as a care assistant and may now be walking down the aisle with Jos, who is a millionaire in his own right and also inherited millions from his maternal grandfather.

Who said fairy tales never come true?

8

'This is bad. This is very, very bad.' Jos Sedley groaned the next morning from his horizontal position on the sofa in Dobbin's Ladbroke Grove flat. 'It's the worst.'

Dobbin and George didn't know if he was talking about his hangover (he'd spent most of the night throwing up and now his face was the colour and texture of elephant hide) or the front page of the *Sun*. Though the front pages of the *Daily Mirror*, the *Daily Star*, the *Daily Mail* and the *Daily Express* had all gone with similar stories.

'It's not so bad, Jos,' Dobbin said stoutly, because while his patience was infinite he couldn't stand malingerers. Especially when the malingering was self-inflicted. 'You'll feel much better with a pot of tea and some toast inside you.'

'No caffeine. No carbs!'

'It's a pity you didn't stick to no alcohol last night,' George said cheerfully. He threw a copy of the *Daily Mirror* at Jos's head. 'What a gigantic idiot you are! I have absolutely no sympathy for you.'

'Steady on,' Dobbin murmured, but George was not to be swayed.

'I saw you last night,' he reminded Jos, tapping the other man's pounding head with the now rolled-up newspaper. 'Even caught some of the tender things you were murmuring at each other. No wonder she went to the papers and told them that your intentions were honourable!'

'Rebecca would never go to the papers,' Dobbin said because surely no friend of dear, sweet Emmy would act in such an underhand way. It simply wasn't how things were done.

'I'd bet money on it,' George insisted. 'Girls like that, you don't need to promise them marriage to get their knickers off, Sedley. You just buy them a bottle of something bubbly, shag them, then put them in an Uber and send them on their way.'

Later, as George and Dobbin strolled through Holland Park on their way to Kensington, Dobbin wondered aloud if George hadn't been too harsh on their friend.

'Not harsh enough,' George said without a shred of pity. 'I did him a huge favour. He spends far too much time pumping iron and guzzling protein shakes, not that it's made him any more attractive to the opposite sex. If it had, then he might have a bit more experience, might know when he's being taken for a ride by some jumped-up little tart with ideas far above her station.'

Dobbin didn't reply at first and they walked through the sun-dappled paths of the park in silence. It was a glorious September morning, the sky impossibly blue, the leaves fluttering in a slight breeze as dogs chased each other round and round in circles, barking joyfully. Mothers, but mostly nannies, clutched hold of toddlers intent on feeding the ducks and not waiting their turn for the swings. On the lush, green grass couples lounged and a group of taut young men and women contorted themselves on yoga mats.

Surely, if Becky Sharp had gone to the papers in order to force a shy young millionaire's hand, she'd have asked them to photograph she and Jos as they exercised together? When they'd both looked their best in flattering black workout clothes, the photos playful and flirty. Not when they were falling out of a nightclub, Becky in a torn dress, Jos lumbering and drunk.

It was almost as if the photos of last night were the work of someone who'd disappeared at a crucial point during the night. Someone well versed in the art of spin, working, as they did, in politics. But why would someone be so invested in tearing apart two young souls who each believed they'd found their match?

Captain Dobbin certainly wouldn't have ever imagined that George Wylie, his friend since they were tiny boys starting prep school together in knee-length shorts, red blazers and adorable little caps, might act in such an underhand, cavalier fashion.

True, George had been a member of the infamous Rakehell drinking club at Oxford, which Dobbin had never been invited to join, but George had always kept his hands and nose clean. He was more likely to be trouble-adjacent than in the thick of it.

'But why should you care?' Dobbin asked, then cursed under his breath as two small dogs came barrelling through his legs and almost upended him. 'If she makes Jos happy, then that's a good thing, isn't it?'

'You know why I care, you fool. I'm going to marry Amelia,' George stated calmly. The shock was so great that Dobbin stumbled over his own size-fourteen feet and had to grab hold of a lamppost to stop himself falling to his knees.

'I didn't actually,' Dobbin managed to say, gasping out the words though his throat had closed up, his heart had stopped beating, his world suddenly turned ashen and grey. 'I thought you were seeing that little blonde researcher, Polly Somebody.'

'Well, obviously, I'm not going to marry Amelia any time *soon*,' George said with an impatient edge. 'At the moment, she bursts into tears if you even look at her funny. And she's twenty-two — no one gets married that young, it's unspeakably common.'

'I hadn't thought about it like that,' Dobbin choked out, because all he had thought about was how Amelia Sedley — beautiful, sweet, kind little Emmy — was perfect in every way. Far too perfect for the likes of him and, for as long as Dobbin had known Amelia, she'd fancied herself in love with George . . . 'So, you're not seeing that Polly Somebody, then?'

'I haven't taken a vow of chastity until Amelia acquires some backbone and a little sophistication,' George snapped.

Being friends with George wasn't always easy and at this particular moment, it was especially hard because Dobbin wished that he was in uniform and fully kitted out so he could Taser the living daylights out of his dear friend.

'These girls,' continued George, 'the junior researchers and the likes, the Pollies and Bellas, they're all gagging for it but they're fabulously discreet so as not to jeopardise their own careers, so it's win/win really.'

Dobbin glanced over at George. The dark curls framing that exquisitely patrician face, the beautifully cut grey suit, which clung to his lean frame. On this sunny day, there was something of the night about him.

'I still don't see what any of this has to do with Jos Sedley and Amelia's friend,' he said and George came to a halt, all the better to roll his eyes.

'Must I spell it out? I'm going to marry Amelia, I'm really quite *fond* of her and she should shape up quite nicely, but the family's not exactly top drawer.'

'Then again, they're not exactly bottom of the ladder,' Dobbin pointed out, because he liked to think that he was egalitarian in his outlook. Though he himself came from a distinguished military family, his father was only the third son of an earl, so he'd pretty much had to make his own way in life.

'Dobbin, I'm the heir to a baronetcy,' George said, even though *everyone* knew that the Wylies had bought the baronetcy. 'The Sedleys might be rich but they come from very humble stock and there is absolutely no way that I can have a sister-in-law who's a nothing. A nobody. The sooner she scuttles back to whatever hole she crawled out of, the better. Like I said to Sedley, it's just as well she was holding out for marriage because otherwise, she's the sort to either make an incriminating sex tape or get knocked up — either way, she'd have had his balls in a vice and his millions in her bank account.'

'I suppose you know best,' Dobbin said dubiously. 'Though do you always have to see the worst in people?'

George grinned, though Dobbin hadn't meant it as a compliment. 'I'm sure Miss Sharp will need some consoling. She might even let you go where Jos didn't manage to break ground. Why don't you come with me as I give her the bad news?'

Dobbin declined: the bad news that George was about to deliver so gleefully was sure to make Amelia cry, and to see Amelia cry would break his heart. Though it wasn't true that she cried all the time. Whenever he saw Amelia, she always looked delighted; a smile on her face that had to be the reason that the sun came up and flowers grew and birds tweeted.

9

The Sedley house was in an uproar that morning. Mrs Sedley had cast one look at the *Daily Mail* and her heart had started to beat so furiously that she thought she might be having a stroke. She wasn't but she'd had to take to her bed with one of her heads, hissing to Amelia as she went, '*I want that girl out of the house by the end of the day, Emmy.*'

Becky was already packing or, rather, she'd told Amelia that she was packing. 'I can't stay here,' she said to Amelia after Mrs Sedley had been tucked up with two Valium and a hot-water bottle. 'What must your poor parents think of me? What must Jos think of me? You do know that it wasn't me who went to the papers?'

'Of course I do,' Amelia gasped, because her sweet young mind wasn't capable of such a calculated thought. 'I'm sure it's not that bad. You'll feel much better after you've had some breakfast.'

'I can't eat. Food would choke me,' Becky declared, a trembling hand to her throat as if she was already finding it hard to breathe. She stood at her bedroom door, her body barring Amelia from the room, not just for full dramatic effect but because there were a few items that had found their way into Becky's possession that she hadn't had a chance to squirrel away yet. 'I'm going to pack. I'll be gone in a few hours.'

But Becky wasn't packing at all. She was leaning out of the window of the second-floor guest room as she waited for the first sight of Jos lumbering into the square. He'd have a terrible hangover, which was his own fault, as nobody had forced him to drink all that champagne, and he'd be sweating profusely. Becky would let him stammer and stutter his way through a series of abject apologies for humiliating her.

After a tense two minutes — no, make it three — she'd forgive Jos, which would make him feel even worse, even more ashamed. Then with some gentle nudging, and that thing she did with her eyes, he'd admit that he'd wanted to kiss her ever since he first saw her. He'd then go on to confess that the kiss in front of the paparazzi, despite its sordid circumstances, had been the happiest moment of his life.

'We could have more happy moments like that, Jos,' she'd say, her voice catching, then she'd look away. Though sometimes, actually all the time, it was hard work trying to tunnel through Jos's thick skull, so perhaps she'd have to be a lot less subtle. 'Our whole life would be a series of happy moments. Of kisses . . . '

Of course, Jos would ask her to come back to LA with him. Once they were in LA, away from the annoying presence of his mother and father, and the bad influence of George Wylie, then Becky wouldn't let Jos do anything more than kiss her and paw her over her clothes, and a proposal would be inevitable.

So, all was not lost. Far from it. Though Becky hadn't gone to the papers (and no one could prove it either way), there was no reason why this had to end in tragedy.

Becky leaned out a little further, just in time to see George Wylie come striding around the corner. She beat a frantic retreat, banging her head so hard on the sash window that it brought tears to her eyes, especially as it had all been in vain because that smug little fucker waved cheerfully up at her.

'Ha! Caught you!' he cried.

Still, Becky's tears were no match for the flood of eye-water and snot that Amelia had been producing ever since Becky had shut the bedroom door in her face. She cried even harder as George described, with particular relish, what a sorry state he'd left Jos in.

'Been chundering for six hours straight. I left him prostrate on Dobbin's sofa. And it's just as well we did take him to Dobbin's last night, as he's the only man in London whose dressing gown would fit round your brother. Pity that he puked down it,' George finished with an appreciative chuckle. The whole episode reminded him of similar japes at Oxford.

Also, the fact that they'd taken Sedley to Dobbin's and not to George's own flat in Victoria, had made him quite light-headed with relief.

'I never thought you could be so mean,' Amelia sobbed.

'Then you haven't been paying attention,' Becky said from the doorway, because staying upstairs and sulking would achieve absolutely nothing. Not when there was no sign of a suitably contrite Jos and in his place was George Wylie, who might just explode from sheer malicious delight. Here's hoping. 'Where's Jos?'

George turned around, eyes gleaming, his delight magnified now that Becky had joined them. 'I'm afraid Jos sends his regrets but he's otherwise engaged. Oh! Sorry! Bad choice of words. Otherwise detained, shall we say?'

Becky's innate distrust and dislike of George Wylie, in that moment, crystallised and hardened into anger; a stinging, corrosive fury that this arrogant, odious prick had the nerve to mock her, laugh at her. It was only through a sheer accident of birth that the whole world was his for the taking and that she had nothing — not even the clothes she stood up in, because they were borrowed from Amelia.

There was an edge to George Wylie this morning, a febrile glitter in his eyes, high on his own triumph. He must have said something to Jos about her which had frightened Jos off, and Becky knew then that Jos wasn't going to turn up and beg for her forgiveness. It wasn't all going to come good in the end.

Oh, but she would make George Wylie pay. She would ruin him, destroy everything that he'd worked so hard for.

Not that she was going to tell him that, like some second-rate Scarlett O'Hara.

'You're always joking,' she noted with a quiet dignity that made George falter. 'It's not nice to be the punchline of a joke, especially when there's no one here to defend me.'

Then she walked away and George was left

with Amelia, who had stopped crying and was now looking at him with a furrowed brow and jutting bottom lip. It was almost as if . . . as if she, silly little Amelia Sedley, was disappointed in him. 'That wasn't very kind of you,' she said quietly and George immediately felt the need to squirm, even though kindness wasn't a quality that he thought much of.

'Amelia, you are too good for me.' It was the most sincere thing he'd ever said. 'Look, I know you've hugged orphans in the Third World and spent a few weeks with a bunch of chavs, but you don't understand the world the way that I do. That Sharp girl overplayed her hand and Jos has had a lucky escape.'

Amelia's heart gave a sad little flutter. 'So, he's really not coming, then?'

'He's not,' George confirmed. 'Believe me, it's for the best. I volunteered to fetch his things because, actually, I can be kind, Emmy. This whole business with that Sharp girl — I was only looking out for Jos because he's your brother and well, I do rather care about you, you know.'

The sad little flutter transformed into a rapturous symphony when George took Amelia in his arms.

He smelt delicious — a heady mix of citrus and spices from the cologne that he favoured. But though Amelia raised her face to his, her lips slightly pursed, he kissed her forehead.

'I'm . . . well, I rather care about you too, George,' she dared to say and the smile he gave her then was kindness personified.

'I know.'

After George left, it took quite a bit of time and some dawdling, before Amelia felt brave enough to face her friend.

Becky was perched on the window seat on the first-floor landing, her gaze fixed morosely on the square outside, the *Daily Mail* a crumpled, torn heap of paper at her feet.

'You never know, he might still come,' Amelia said consolingly.

'Really? Have you spoken to him?' Becky asked and even though it was hopeless, she couldn't help the eager note in her voice.

'I could speak to him,' Amelia offered just as her phone chimed. She pulled it out of the pocket of her jeans. 'I don't need to! He's just texted me. Let's see . . . oh . . . '

Ems 2 ill 2 say gdbye. Hv 2 go back 2 LA due 2 protein ball emergency. Will b gon v.long time. Pls send bst wishes 2 Becky. I was v.drunk 1st nite & she shld 4get everything I said. ☹ Luv Jos xxx

10

Of course, Amelia made it all about her. Crying over and on top of Becky so Becky could hardly think straight.

'I can't believe he didn't say goodbye,' Amelia wailed at such length, and there was no time to process, recover, regroup.

In fact, Becky was still reeling when there was an imperious peal on the doorbell, and who should be standing on the other side of the door but Babs Pinkerton, summoned by Mrs Sedley, who hadn't been zonked out on Valium in the master bedroom suite but actually plotting Becky's immediate departure.

'Pack your bags, sweetie, you're being thrown out,' Babs said by way of greeting when a fuming Mrs Blenkinsop showed her into the drawing room where Becky was still being wept on by Amelia.

Amelia protested, tearfully, to her mother who pointed out that Amelia would be leaving for Durham at the end of the week.

'So, you see, she had to leave sooner or later, and it was only ever meant to be a temporary arrangement,' Mrs Sedley explained as she stroked her daughter's hair and wished that she hadn't just taken her Valium, because she really didn't have the energy to deal with this. 'I understand that Barbara, who says she's always been like a mother to Rebecca, has found her a lovely little job as a nanny with a charming family. In the country. Deep in the country. Miles and miles away from here. She'll be fine.'

Becky had been with the Sedleys for almost a month but it would take no more than twenty minutes to remove all traces of her from their house. It wasn't as if she had any choice when Sam, Mrs Sedley's driver, was pointedly lingering in the hall with 'strict instructions to take you to the station'.

He didn't come into Becky's room — no, not her room, not any more, it was the guest room — while she packed, which was just as well. Becky tucked away several of Amelia's dresses, which looked much better on her, a few pieces of jewellery that Amelia wouldn't even miss, an iPad that Amelia had thought she'd lost and had already replaced, and several other items that technically didn't belong to Becky. All the while Babs Pinkerton, in her trademark cerise which did absolutely nothing for her gin-raddled complexion, lounged on the bed enjoying Becky's impending banishment far too much.

'A nanny?' Becky spat in disbelief when Babs told her where she was going. 'In some place in the back of beyond? I went to the country once and it stunk of cow shit.'

'You should feel right at home then,' Babs said with a delighted smile. 'Actually, it's a country estate. Beautiful big house, set in acres of land, horses, duck pond, and all that jazz. And you'll be looking after the children of Sir Pitt Crawley,' she added like she was presenting Becky with a winning scratchcard.

'Pitt who? Never heard of him,' Becky muttered savagely as she stuffed a Rolex watch, which had been a silver anniversary present from Mr Sedley to his wife, into one of her trainers.

'The Crawleys! One of Britain's premier acting dynasties, you little imbecile,' Babs drawled. 'Sir Pitt was quite the sex symbol back in the day.'

'When was back in the day?' Becky asked, pausing her suitcase-stuffing. Working for some famous actor might not be so bad.

'Before you were born. In the seventies,' Babs said, which might just as well have been the Dark Ages. Yet he was still famous and he had a house, a very big house, in the country. He was bound to have his celebrity friends constantly dropping by and if he was very famous, then he was very rich too. There'd obviously be an indoor swimming pool, one of those fancy screening rooms and the children would be at school for most of the day, so it wasn't as if Becky would have to do much nannying.

It might be the perfect opportunity to reassess things. Maybe even catch the eye of one of those celebrity friends that dropped by . . . but still the country wasn't London, and London was the most likely place where a girl with no prospects but a hell of a lot of ambition could find fame, fortune and fools ready to give them to her.

'No. It's not happening, Babs. I came second in *Big Brother* . . .'

'What you mean is that you didn't win *Big Brother* . . .'

'Whatever! Come on! You could find me some

other job. Something more exciting, better paid.' Becky zipped up her tatty holdall. 'You know, I could do a kiss-and-tell on how Jos Sedley did me wrong.' No, that wasn't enough. 'How he turned out to be a complete love rat after I'd given him . . . '

'Boring!' Babs yawned exaggeratedly. 'The photos of him tumbling out of that club with his hand down your dress were one thing, but you wouldn't get more than a couple of hundred quid for a follow-up.' She examined her neon-pink talons. 'The problem, my darling, is that you missed your window. I hate to be the one to say I told you so, but I told you so. Couldn't even get you a thousand if you dropped your knickers for the *Sunday Sport*. Are you done packing, 'cause you do have a train to catch?'

Mrs Sedley had gone back to bed so it was left to Amelia to say a fitting goodbye. She clung on to Becky and Becky clung back, in the vain hope that if she attached herself barnacle-like to Amelia, then she might never have to leave.

'We have to go now,' Sam said implacably and firmly from behind them, and Babs sighed impatiently and Amelia was persuaded to release Becky from her Vulcan clutches.

'This is from Mummy,' she murmured brokenly, tucking an envelope, which at least felt like it contained a wad of banknotes, into Becky's hand. 'And you're still my sister from another mister. I'm going to text you before you've even got in the car, and I get really long holidays so I'll see you soon.'

'I probably won't be allowed the time off,' Becky said with a pathetic little sniff that tore at Amelia's soul, though Becky wouldn't be taken for a fool twice and she was going to get time off and sick pay and whatever the going rate was for nannying the children of a famous actor. 'You know how people exploit their domestic staff. I bet I won't even get minimum wage with the hours they'll expect me to work.'

'Oh, Becky, I wish there was something I could do,' Amelia cried imploringly.

'It's all right,' Becky said as Babs took her arm in an uncompromising grip and began walking her towards the door. 'I don't blame you.'

No, Amelia was the one person that she didn't blame. She blamed George Wylie, above all others. Next came Barbara Pinkerton, who could easily have found something exciting and well paid for Becky to do, and also Becky was pretty sure that Jemima's bungalow had already been sold and that Babs would make sure she'd never see a penny of the £250,000 it was worth when Becky had had a valuation done before Jemima had died. She also blamed Jos Sedley for being weak and foolish and easily influenced but alas, not easily influenced by her. And though Mrs Sedley had sent her on her way with £500, Becky added her name to the list of people who'd done her wrong: one day she'd be in a position to pay them all back.

But right now, as she sat in a second-class carriage on her way to Southampton where she had to change on to a branch line, Becky wasn't in any position but to take the job that Barbara

Pinkerton had grudgingly found for her.

She was twenty, without any family. It wasn't just a line she spun for sympathy; those were the facts. There wasn't a parent or a grandparent, not even a stray aunt or uncle who'd take her in. Apart from the few trinkets she'd acquired from the Sedleys to go with the trinkets that Jemima Pinkerton would have wanted her to have, Becky had no assets. She didn't even have a bank account.

If she threw herself on the mercy of the state, she might be found a bed in a hostel and if she was really, really lucky she'd be given a zero-hours contract on minimum wage stacking shelves or working in a call centre. Which was fine. The world needed people to stack shelves and work in call centres, but Becky wasn't one of those people. Just as George Wylie and Amelia and the five M's had been born into wealth and privilege, Becky had been born with beauty and a native cunning. She was meant for more than a bed in a hostel and a zero-hours contract. Maybe she was meant for gracious country living. Wafting about a huge mansion, being spoiled by a very famous actor in his dotage. As soon as she could get a decent WiFi signal, Becky would google the hell out of Sir Pitt Crawley, she decided, and she straightened her posture and put her shoulders back. Down but not out. If she didn't make the most of this opportunity that fate had thrown at her, then she deserved to be stacking shelves.

★ ★ ★

It was raining when Becky finally reached her destination: Mudbury. The light was fading and everything was grey as she came out of the station to find herself in a dismal little backwater, rather than a charming and bucolic village. It boasted a convenience store, which was closed, a pub, which was less of a charming country inn and more like a glorified Portakabin, and a bus-shelter covered in graffiti.

Only one other person had got off the train and they had already got into a car that had been waiting outside the station and driven off.

Babs had told her that someone would pick her up at the station but there were no signs of life. She squinted left, then right for the welcoming glow of a pair of headlights coming towards her, but all she could see was sheeting rain in all directions.

Becky hurried over to the bus shelter but there was no timetable and from the barrenness of her surroundings, it was clear that Mudbury was the type of place where the bus only came once on market days and market days only happened every other week. She shivered inside her jacket. When she had left London, it had been late summer, the sun still shining, the weather warm enough that most days she didn't even need a jacket. But in the course of four hours and two trains, winter had come.

She debated waiting inside the pub. It might be quite cosy once she was inside — or she could be raped and murdered by a bunch of inbred villagers. Just when Becky had decided that at least she'd be dry even if she did have to fight them off with a pool cue, she heard the rumbling of an engine over the persistent drumming of the rain on the roof of the bus shelter. When she peered out, there were the headlights she was longing to see. She didn't even care if it was her lift. She ran into the road to wave whoever it was down and beg them to take her back to civilisation. Or to the nearest mainline station, at least.

The battered, ancient Land Rover came to a juddering halt and Becky scrabbled at the door handle, which swung open with help from inside.

'You be the young lady coming up t' Big House?'

There was no light inside the vehicle, just two shadowy figures, one of which had just spoken to her in such a rough, local dialect that Becky had trouble understanding him.

'I'm Becky Sharp and you're late!' she snapped. 'Does Sir Crawley know that you've kept me waiting in the pouring rain?'

There was a diffident grunt. Then, 'Just light drizzle, lassie. Jump in. Don't mind old Hodson. Wouldn't hurt a fly.'

It turned out that the shadowy figure closest to her was a dog; a big, hairy, foul-smelling beast that growled at Becky as she hefted her bags and herself into the Land Rover. The back of the Sedleys' chauffeur-driven, air-conditioned Bentley already seemed as if it belonged to another world, another life, as the man sped off with a crunching of gears. The suspension was shot and the vehicle, and Becky, shook every time they hit a bump or a hole in the road.

It was pitch black outside, but there didn't seem to be anything to look at out of the windows, which were streaming with condensation. It was just country. Fields and hedges, and when they turned off on to a smaller road, more of a rugged track really, the branches from the overhanging trees skittered across the roof of the car and Becky stole a glance at the man driving.

Her eyes had adjusted to the gloom by now and she could see that her saviour was a grizzled old man, though the grizzle was probably dirt, because he didn't smell that fresh. In fact, she wasn't sure which one of them was the most malodorous — the old man or Hodson, who kept wiping his slobbery snout on Becky's shoulder. Most of the man's face was obscured by a filthy trucker's cap that was pulled down so she could only make out his mouth and chin, which didn't look like it had seen a razor in months. His clothes looked and smelt filthy too: a pair of ragged trousers and an old jumper full of holes.

He could be anyone. Maybe he'd lured many a young woman to a grisly end by picking them up outside the station. Maybe that was why the Crawleys needed a new nanny, because each new nanny was intercepted before she could start her new job.

'Do you work for Sir Crawley, then?' she asked, striving hard to keep the belligerence out of her voice. 'Is it far to the house?'

'Far enough.'

Becky settled back with a tiny but discontent huff. She had done all that boxing with Jos, so if worst came to worst, she could whack him around the head followed up by a swift knee to his bollocks, then she'd run for her life.

They rounded a bend at breakneck speed, which threw Becky against the door, and just as she righted herself, she could see that they were travelling up a drive lined by trees, and in the distance there was a big house, the warm glow of electric light at some of its many windows. They were crunching over gravel now as they drove around a big ornamental pond then veered left. Maybe her dreams of gracious country living were about to come true after all. Or maybe not.

'This is Queen's Crawley, is it?' Becky asked as they whisked past the grand front door. She thought she might cry if they kept going, disappearing back into the darkness until they reached this man's hovel and whatever terrible fate awaited her.

They took a sharp right, just past the house, under an arch and Becky let out a shaky breath as they came to a jerky halt inside a yard, which must have been the old stable block.

'Front door ain't for the likes of us, is it?' The man opened his door so he could cough then spit on to the gravel.

Becky clenched her fists, felt Hodson's hot breath on her neck again.

Enough!

'How dare you!' she hissed, turning to the man so he could get the full benefit of her fury. She was so angry she could hardly force the words out. 'Just wait until Sir Pitt Crawley hears about the way you've treated me.' Even in the midst of her rage, she wasn't going to admit that she'd been scared half to death. Wouldn't give this . . . this . . . dim-witted yokel the satisfaction. 'You're rude and you're inconsiderate and you smell like a rubbish tip!'

She expected him to spit on the ground again. Or worse, spit on her, but he did neither, just took off his cap so Becky could see that his greasy hair was as neglected as the rest of him. He looked at her and grinned — she was surprised to see that his teeth weren't blackened pegs but actually were even and gleamed white in the gloom — and there was an expectant air about him, as if he was waiting for Becky to say that she wouldn't really go to Sir Pitt Crawley and do everything in her power to have him fired.

In that case, he was going to be disappointed.

'I might only be the nanny but I'm not some silly little girl who's only used to dealing with naughty toddlers.' She drew herself up. 'You try something like this again, and I will make you sorry you were ever fucking born,' she finished with a determined sniff.

There was a moment's silence as they both stared at each other, weighing up their enemy, then the man smiled again. He ran his fingers, nails black with dirt, through his hair, then offered his hand to Becky who looked at it in much the same way that she'd look at Hodson if he suddenly took a dump on her bag.

'Are we clear?' she asked.

'Clear as crystal,' he said, not in a guttural drawl but in plummy tones that had delighted

101

both theatre-goers and film critics alike. 'I'm Sir Pitt Crawley, delighted to make your acquaintance, Miss Sharp. May I welcome you to Queen's Crawley, and I hope that your stay here will be a long and happy one.'

11

Sir Pitt Crawley, knighted by the Queen for his ground-breaking contribution to British film and theatre, had woken up one morning, taken stock of his life and decided that it was shallow and empty.

He was in LA at the time and had been woken up by the sound of his girlfriend (the second Lady Crawley turned a blind and grateful eye to Pitt's peccadillos) on the phone to her therapist. Or he might have been pulled out of sleep by the sound of his gardening crew trimming the hedges that had been trimmed only the day before. Or awoken by his personal trainer calling him on his cellphone because Sir Pitt was currently meant to be doing lunges, squats, burpees and other undignified exercises in his basement gym.

Later he would spend two hours in make-up before emoting in front of a green screen so CGI effects could be added in later. And later still, he was due to have dinner and drinks with a producer who he hated and the producer's wife, who he'd slept with and who now also hated him.

It was all bullshit, Pitt thought. He thought it again. Then he said the words out loud: 'It's all bullshit!' He scrambled out of bed, naked as the day he was born, flung open the windows so he could stand out on the balcony that overlooked the Olympic-sized swimming pool and shout, 'IT'S ALL BULLSHIT!' to the heavens and the bemusement of his gardening crew. And it was at that moment that he had an epiphany, and a few hours after that he was at LAX waiting to fly back to England to find his true, authentic self.

WHAT A PITT-Y!
Legendary luvvie Sir Pitt Crawley retires from acting to become a blacksmith

The papers had been full of incredulous headlines, passing it off as pretentious nonsense, but Pitt had retired to the crumbling estate that had been in his family for generations (the original Pitt Crawley made his fortune in the brewing of beer for none other than Queen Elizabeth I) to strip away the trappings of fame and adulation and get back to nature.

And yes, he had the old forge on his land restored and got the only blacksmith in the county to give him lessons. It transpired that blacksmithing was very strenuous work and Pitt was knocking on for sixty-five (but a very distinguished sixty-five), so when the only horse he ever shod promptly went lame, he gave up his Lawrentian dreams of hewing metal, if not his dreams of a more authentic life.

It turned out that living authentically also meant eschewing soap and water so Pitt could retain the earthy scent that was entirely masculine, striding about his grounds doing the odd bit of scything (though he had a ride-on lawnmower that did the job far more effectively) and working on his memoirs.

Every now and again his accountant would ring with bad news. Then Pitt would manage to wash, shave and fly to Japan to do a lucrative advertising campaign. He had also appeared in a very successful film franchise of a much-loved series of children's books, but the director was an old, old, *old* friend 'and the books are much beloved by my own dear children,' as Pitt explained to the journalist from the *Sunday Times* who'd dared to suggest that Pitt wasn't really that retired.

Pitt had many children, and it wasn't as if he could let them starve, which would be quite likely if he'd persevered with his dreams of becoming a blacksmith.

He had two sons, Pitt Junior and Rawdon, from his marriage to his first wife, who he'd met at RADA, falling in love with her haughty, antagonistic performance as Kat in *The Taming of the Shrew*. Pitt had endured ten long, haughty and antagonistic years with Francesca before she'd been involved in a car crash, lingered in ICU for a bit and then died.

'It was a merciful release,' Pitt had said with much feeling during Francesca's eulogy. Not a dry eye in the house, he'd been pleased to note as he'd hugged his two young sons to him in the Actor's Church in Covent Garden. He couldn't help but think what a wonderful picture they'd make on the front pages of the newspapers the next day.

Pitt hadn't intended to marry again; not when he could shag lots of beautiful women, then end things with a heartfelt 'I just can't love again since Frankie's death' when he got bored with them. Alas, eight years ago, he'd made the mistake of shagging Rosa, the pretty daughter of the landlord of Mudbury's only pub, The Pig's Ear, and when the stupid girl got pregnant, said landlord had come after Pitt with his shotgun and a journalist from *The Sun*.

Still, it wasn't all bad. Pitt had always said that if he got married again, he'd choose a simple woman and Rosa, bless her, was as simple as any woman he'd found. She popped out a child every couple of years (never could remember to take her pill) and now they had at least four young children (maybe even five) running around, though neither he nor Rosa could be relied upon to feed them regularly or get them enrolled in school, hence the need for a nanny. Not that they could keep a nanny for long, being as isolated as they were, with patchy WiFi, and Rosa having very funny ideas about raising children. She'd never been the same after an immersive yoga retreat in Mykonos to relieve a bout of post-natal depression following the birth of their second child. Or was it the third? What with all the yoga, when Rosa did pop out yet more sprogs, her figure snapped right back and it also made her very bendy, so Sir Pitt managed to overlook her other shortcomings.

The other reason that they couldn't hold on to a nanny was that each girl objected to Pitt's true, authentic self and his true, authentic smell. Back in the day, he'd been fighting them off but now they fought him off, and the last one had actually

106

gagged when he'd tried to steal a kiss, and she'd then threatened to go to the papers.

But the latest one, pretty little Becky, was shaping up quite nicely. She'd claimed not to know who he was but Pitt knew that was just the dance of courtship. And the children seemed to adore her, Pitt thought as he watched the new nanny cavort with a horde of children on the ragged lawn he could spy from his study window. What a charming picture they all made, he thought to himself indulgently.

Like Diana frolicking with her nymphs. Little Pitt wouldn't mind a spot of frolicking himself . . .

*   *   *

'If you call your brother a see you next Tuesday again, then it's nothing but vegan food for the rest of the week, you horrible child,' pretty little Becky shouted at Calliope Crawley. 'At least say it in French like I taught you.'

'I'm sorry,' Calliope said and immediately stopped trying to throttle her younger brother. 'Please don't take away our chicken nuggets. I'd rather that you beat us instead.'

'Don't push me any further then,' Becky said warningly, because the merest hint of a threat worked wonders on the brats under her tender, not really that loving, care.

They were many little Crawleys. Becky wasn't even sure that all of them belonged to Sir and Lady Crawley but suspected some of them came up from the village each day. Though she couldn't imagine why, because being the offspring of the famous actor and his hippy-dippy wife was awful.

During her childhood, Becky had known real deprivation. Many times she'd had to sleep on the floor of assorted doss-houses, council B&Bs riddled with mould and mildew, once even a crack den. There had been many times when she'd gone to bed hungry. Her clothes came from charity shops and not a week went by without her being slapped so hard by one of her parents that she saw stars. But that was nothing compared to the torture that the poor Crawley children were put through on a daily basis.

For one thing there was no TV. Or rather, there was a TV in the drawing room but Sir Pitt was adamant that it would rot their young minds and also, he expected the children to spend most of their time outside, in the fresh air. Or the freezing cold. Or the pouring rain.

There was no WiFi either. Or rather, there was WiFi, but hardly any signal and Lady Crawley couldn't remember the password and Sir Pitt wouldn't tell Becky what it was because she was meant to be schooling his children in how to find their true, authentic selves.

Then there was the food. The little Crawleys had never once experienced the joy of a McDonalds Happy Meal. Not once. It was enough to make even Becky cry. The only chocolate they'd ever known was raw cacao. Sir Pitt was full Paleo and would only eat food that his primitive ancestors might have eaten, which involved a lot of meat and nuts and leafy vegetables. Becky didn't know much about primitive man but she was pretty sure that he'd had a life expectancy of about twenty-five. Still, it had to be better than the radical vegan diet adopted by Lady Crawley. No wonder Mrs Tinker, the cook, was in a permanent foul mood as she tried to feed the children a balanced diet approved by both their parents.

'Gluten-free, dairy-free, taste-free,' she'd mutter every morning as she banged around the kitchen making a truly disgusting porridge flavoured with soy milk and whatever berries the children had foraged the day before.

Babs Pinkerton hadn't thought to mention it but Becky was also expected to home school the children, though she'd rarely gone to school herself. They longed to go to school, Becky longed for them to go to school too — getting the crap kicked out of them a couple of times would be the making of them.

Not that Becky was softening. Her heart was still a hard little thing but she knew what it was like to have parents who were indifferent to anything but their own needs and desires.

Also, she'd learned an important lesson from her stay with the Sedleys. She'd spent all her time and energy on cultivating Amelia and Jos, when if she'd made herself indispensable to Mr and Mrs Sedley too, she'd probably still be enjoying the luxury of their six-bedroom Kensington house. So, this time round, she made sure that every member of the household could barely function without her.

It had been easy to win Rosa Crawley over.

Anyone who did that much yoga and meditation and hadn't eaten a bag of crisps in eight years was obviously desperately unhappy. Rosa had no friends because what passed for society in the back of beyond looked down on her for being a publican's daughter, and her old friends were jealous of her new-found status and comforted themselves with the opinion that 'Rosa's really up herself now.'

Also, she wasn't very bright and Becky had always found that stupid people tended towards unhappiness, since they lacked the inner reserves to entertain themselves. Still, Rosa was clever enough that she'd actually managed to pass her driving test, though she needed someone to navigate as she always got her left and right mixed up.

On Wednesday mornings, Becky would dump the children on Mrs Tinker and Rosa would drive them both to Portsmouth while she poured her heart out about how difficult it was to be married to a reclusive celebrity. 'It weren't so bad when he was in that there Hollywood half the time, but now he int, and he's on me all the time, the randy bugger.' She'd turn mournful eyes on Becky. 'Rooting around like a pig going after truffles.'

'Poor Rosa. You really deserve some me-time.' This was all the encouragement Rosa needed to go off to be manipulated and palpated by a Brazilian masseur called Javier, and Becky would head off into town with Rosa's credit card.

But it was when Becky suggested that Rosa get an IUD fitted that their bond was well and truly cemented: no more little Crawleys crawling about ever again.

With the children, it was easy to find out what they wanted most in the world, give it to them, then withhold it whenever they were being badly behaved bastards who should have been drowned at birth, which was quite a lot of the time.

What they wanted most in the world was everything that their parents denied them. Becky downloaded several Disney films on to the iPad she'd liberated from Amelia Sedley, and *Frozen*, in particular, transfixed them as if they were witnessing the opening of the Ark of the Covenant.

While Rosa was having her weekly massage, Becky would buy all the food that the children were usually forbidden: chicken nuggets, oven chips, Haribo and Heinz tomato ketchup. Pitt and Rosa never sat down with the children at meal times to know exactly what they were eating and Mrs Tinker would much rather shove some fish fingers under the grill than have to spend the best part of a day soaking mung beans and activating almonds.

Sir Pitt Crawley, on the other hand, was harder to crack; hard in the sense that he was perpetually horny.

Queen's Crawley was a crumbling, draughty old house with antiquated plumbing, holes in the roof and a mouse infestation. There was barely a radiator to be seen, never mind the swimming pool Becky had once imagined. As she bedded down for yet another freezing night, swaddled in tracksuit, thick socks and several musty, hairy blankets, Becky would think longingly of the Sedleys' house and in particular, the under-floor heating. She even missed the dour, monosyllabic Mr Sedley who'd hardly seemed to notice her at all, a welcome change from Sir Pitt who would burst into her room most evenings, commanding her to turn out the light.

'I'm not made of money, little Becky, my residuals barely cover the day-to-day running of the estate. You keep burning electricity like this, we'll all become destitute.' Then he'd run his eyes over her blanket-clad form speculatively. 'You know, if you're cold . . . in the Army Cadets at school, when we went camping we'd huddle together . . . '

'I'm not cold,' Becky would say every time, her jaw clenched to stop her teeth from chattering. 'I'm positively toasty.'

In spite of her nightly rejection of his advances, Sir Pitt was slowly falling under her spell. Like most actors, he loved to talk. Or rather he loved to talk at Becky and he was convinced that she loved to help him write his memoirs.

By now, Sir Pitt had quite forgotten that he'd seen Becky's true, authentic self that first night. He much preferred her cow-eyed, mouth slightly parted, as she made sure his Dictaphone was recording as he orated about his transcendent performance in the Scottish play and 'Did I ever tell you about the time I nearly worked with Scorsese? I didn't? Oh, good! You'll like this story, Becky, is that thing recording?' And Becky much preferred to spend her evenings in Pitt's study where there was a roaring fire even though sometimes he came and sat right next to her on a cracked leather Chesterfield and begged her to stroke Little Pitt. But when Sir Pitt had his back to her as he paced about the room and performed, there were all sorts of interesting pieces of paper in full view, from bank statements and credit-card bills to the Post-it note with the WiFi password scrawled on it.

Becky had arrived at Queen's Crawley halfway through September and by November, the children adored her almost as much as they feared her. Lady Crawley treated Becky as a trusted confidante, Mrs Tinker regarded her as an ally and Sir Pitt wanted nothing more than 'to become better acquainted, my dear', so he'd started to wash more regularly.

It wasn't the bright lights and the riches that Becky craved, but she was biding her time. Waiting. Sir Pitt was only semi-retired and he was still a famous actor. Sooner or later, he'd have to take another job, if only to pay the colossal tax bill that Becky had come across, and it wouldn't be such a leap for Becky to make the move from nanny to PA. To swap nursery for film set where she could forge all sorts of useful friendships. Or maybe. Rawdon Crawley might visit, Pitt's youngest son from his first marriage, who Becky had on a google alert. He had brooding good looks and a successful film career, which was sure to become even more successful once he stopped gambling, drinking and partying hard with the young Hollywood set.

He just needed the love of a good woman to steer him right.

In the meantime, the days passed in a quiet kind of monotony until Becky thought she might go mad with the boredom of it all. And just when she was trying desperately to come up with an exit strategy because she was twenty and she was wasting her best days and all her best assets in muddy Mudbury, Dame Matilda Crawley came to stay for Christmas.

12

On a freezing-cold December afternoon, the Pitt
Crawley branch of the Crawleys lined up outside
Queen's Crawley to greet their imperious
matriarch. As an ancient Rolls Royce, driven
sedately by a beloved factotum named Briggs
— an exquisitely turned-out, plump gay man of
a certain age — came to a graceful stop directly
opposite the steps that led up to the house,
nobody moved, apart from a few shivers from
the waiting Crawley offspring. After a suitably
dramatic pause, Briggs alighted and, with some
ceremony, opened a rear door.

A slight figure dressed all in black took the
hand Briggs offered, stepped out of the car, and
cast a baleful glance over the assembled
company as she sighed loudly.

'Pitt, good of you to make the acquaintance of
soap and water,' Dame Matilda Crawley said as
her younger brother stepped forward. 'Really,
I'm honoured. And the second wife is still
around, I see,' she added, sweeping a disapproving eye over Rosa, who visibly wilted. Then she
turned her attention on the children.

Calliope, the eldest, stepped forward. '*Bon-
jour, ma chère tante*,' she parroted in a passable
French accent, as Becky had made it clear that if
any of them screwed this up, there'd be no iPad,
no Haribo, no fucking tomato ketchup, until well
into the New Year.

'*C'est tres gentil de vous voir encore*,' trilled the next in line, Orion, and one by one the children, five of them in all, spoke a line of French to greet their venerable aunt.

'*Oh! Oh! Incroyable*,' Dame Crawley said and she and Briggs shared a delighted smile. 'Such a transformation. Last time I was here, you were all practically feral.'

'The ringworm,' Briggs recalled faintly with a little shudder as Matilda Crawley's eye fell on Becky. She raised an enquiring eyebrow.

'Just the nanny,' Pitt said, taking his sister's arm to lead her away. One might try to shag the help, but one didn't want one's elder sister to know that, so it was best to keep help and sister far, far apart.

'Stop manhandling me, Pitt, you know I have osteoporosis,' Matilda snapped, tugging her arm free and giving Becky a once-over far more comprehensively than Sir Pitt ever had. 'Have you actually managed to teach these brats some French? They used to barely be able to speak English.'

'Becky's a wonder,' gasped Rosa, then shrank back when Briggs glared at her.

It was up to Pitt to reluctantly make the introductions. 'Mattie, this is Becky Sharp, who came to us by way of Babs Pinkerton. Becky, this is my *dear* sister, Dame Matilda Crawley.'

'Babs Pinkerton! Hah! That old lush,' Matilda snorted.

'Runs on gin,' Briggs added, *sotto voce*.

'Becky Sharp,' the dame continued, as Becky stood there and tried to look demure in the plain

116

grey dress and white pinny that Mrs Tinker had told her to wear to get in Matilda's good graces. 'Becky Sharp. Briggs, where do we know Becky Sharp from?'

Briggs stepped forward to peer intently at Becky, who looked Briggs in the eye and pinned on a pleasant smile even as she waited for the truth to come out. Briggs had the whiff of backstage about him so had no doubt encountered her father in various Soho drinking dens and might remember a pre-pubescent Becky turning up to fetch him home or ask for some fifty-pence pieces for the meter.

'It's her,' Briggs announced with some satisfaction. 'You know, Mattie. That girl from *Big Brother*.' He leaned forward again. 'We had a tenner on you to win.'

'So it is!' Matilda said gleefully. 'How thrilling! What on *earth* are you doing running around after these appalling children? Probably running away from my brother's wandering hands too. No! Don't tell me now.' She linked arms with Becky. Despite the *froideur* of her *grande dame* demeanour, she was frail and bird-like to the touch. There were still echoes of her famous refined beauty in the jut of her cheekbones, the mischievous smile that curved her lips, but she was an old lady (some fifteen years older than Pitt) who'd already overcome two bouts of cancer and her heart fluttered alarmingly if she drank too much champagne. 'It's far too cold to stand around outside, though I expect it's not much warmer inside. You shall sit next to me at dinner and keep me entertained with tales of the

Big Brother house. I'm dying to know what Gav was really like.'

★　★　★

The Crawleys wouldn't have been much of an acting dynasty if its only paid-up members of Equity were Sir Pitt and the annoyingly absent Rawdon. It pained Sir Pitt, more than he'd ever admit even to himself, that his own sister, Matilda, had one more Oscar than him, two more Olivier awards and had been awarded her dameship long, long before he'd been made a knight of the realm. As she never failed to remind him.

A starlet in the sixties, with a talent for picking good roles and even better lovers, in the seventies she'd metamorphosed into a serious actress and had done three seasons with the Royal Shakespeare Company. People still talked of her Lady Macbeth in hushed, reverent tones. In the eighties, she'd done a big glitzy Hollywood primetime soap opera. She'd done Merchant Ivory films, she'd done art house. Her performance as Rose Kovick in a revival of *Gypsy* had gone down in legend, as had her three husbands, each one richer than the last. Now, Dame Matilda was a happily widowed national treasure and ensconced in a Sunday-night period drama where she played the indomitable matriarch of a titled family. Her own family, she found sadly wanting.

'They're all waiting for me to die,' Dame Matilda explained to Becky later that night at dinner. 'I married well, all three of them, I invested well and I have no children. That's why Pitt's so intent on sucking up to me. Wants to tap me for funds.'

'Nonsense,' Pitt declared stoutly, on Matilda's left. 'We're family. You know I *adore* you.'

'Adores my loot, more like,' Matilda said with a sniff. 'Not that he'll spend it on something useful like a new boiler. Those radiators are positively antique, aren't they, Becky?'

'I don't actually have a radiator in my room,' Becky said while Pitt's attention was diverted by Rosa who was staring at the dishes on the table with horror. 'Thank God for hot-water bottles.'

'Tight-fisted old git,' Matilda said. 'And I won't put up with any of that raw food or vegan nonsense either, so we either eat my Ocado delivery or I'll spend Christmas in Palm Beach.'

The table was heaped with food the likes of which Becky hadn't seen since she'd arrived at Queen's Crawley. Instead of the meagre vegan fare they usually had while Sir Pitt dined on grilled slabs of dead animal, Mrs Tinker had whipped up a delicately seasoned chicken stew with dumplings, freshly made bread positively groaning with gluten, and all manner of side dishes full of cream, butter and other usually *verboten* ingredients.

'Why does the second wife keep looking at the stew like it's about to bite her?' Matilda asked Becky.

'She probably does think it's going to bite her. 'Oh, Becky, I can't bear to eat no food what

119

comes with a face',' Becky said in a tremulous, breathy, note-perfect impersonation of Rosa Crawley.

'Oh! Oh!' Matilda Crawley clapped her hands together in sheer pleasure, though thankfully Sir Pitt hadn't heard, as he was too busy hissing at poor Rosa that she wasn't going to die just from sitting adjacent to a chicken stew. 'You are a wicked girl. I said to Briggs at the time, that Becky Sharp is a minx if ever there was one. I bet you did say something vile to that horrible girl in the swimming pool when you both had your mikes off, didn't you? Didn't you?'

Becky folded her hands in her lap and smiled primly. 'I'm sure I don't know what you mean.'

Matilda hooted again. 'Thank God for you! I didn't know how I was going to get through Christmas, especially when the rest of the creeping Crawleys descend on us, but I have a feeling that you'll keep me entertained, at least until Rawdon gets here.'

'Rawdon?' Becky queried innocently. As if she never read the sidebar of shame assiduously each morning to keep up to date with which leggy model Rawdon was currently dating. As if Sir Pitt never once poured scorn on his second son's latest antics or acting job. 'Of course, by the time I was his age, I'd been arrested twice *and* I'd already played *Hamlet* and been awarded an Oscar,' he'd tell Becky every time Rawdon's name came up. Every. Bloody. Time.

'You know full well who Rawdon is, you little baggage.' Matilda Crawley tapped Becky on the arm with an arthritic finger. 'My darling boy.

He's the only one of them I can stand, but you'll do very well in the meantime.'

★   ★   ★

The rest of the Crawleys soon descended in short order, and by the night before Christmas Eve, they were all gathered in Queen's Crawley, preparing for the first festive meal en *famille*.

'We're only here to see Aunt Matilda,' Pitt Junior informed his father as they gathered for pre-dinner drinks. 'Otherwise we'd have spent Christmas with Jane's parents. They've just had solar panels and triple glazing installed. Not to mention some decent grub. Last time we were here, the chick peas gave me indigestion for days.'

'Oh, do pipe down, boy,' Sir Pitt scowled and Pitt Junior scowled right back at him. Poor Pitt Junior was an inferior tenth-generation copy of his father. As if someone had scanned Sir Pitt's face so many times that only traces of him could be glimpsed on his son's fleshy face, while the rest of Pitt Junior was blurry and indistinct. Even the famous, luxuriant Crawley hair that Sir Pitt loved to sweep back from his face had missed Pitt Junior, whose hairline was receding quicker than the English coastline. Pitt the Younger was thirty-five and had quickly realised that the acting life was not for him. Nor was holding down any kind of a regular job, so he styled himself as a writer and every now and again managed to persuade *The Spectator* or *The New Statesman* to publish one of his long, meandering pieces on the division between church and state or male feminism. He'd also managed to persuade a very dull young woman called Jane to date him and the pair of them now lived in a flat in Finchley, and apart from the annual Christmas visit they had very little to do with Sir Pitt.

Pitt Junior retreated to a corner to lick his wounds and gaze around the drawing room, looking for any darker spots on the walls, which signalled that his father had sold another painting. His mother, God rest her soul, had collected art and instead of handing her collection over to her two sons, her father had kept it while it increased in value, then would sell a painting off whenever he was short of ready funds.

Pitt Junior would probably have stayed in the corner sulking if it weren't for a young woman with red hair, mesmerising green eyes and a shy smile approaching him. 'I'm Becky, the nanny,' she said, twisting her hands in front of her as if she were nervous. 'Hope you don't mind consorting with the help.'

As the help was employed to look after the five cuckoos who had thrown him out of the Crawley nest and had drastically decreased his inheritance, Pitt Junior did mind a little. 'Not at all,' he said stiffly.

'It's just . . . I bet you get this all the time . . . ' Downcast eyes and a hesitant manner wouldn't have worked on Matilda Crawley but they had quite the opposite effect on her nephew, who felt something stirring in his chest. 'Well, I'm a big fan of your writing. *Huge* fan. Loved the piece you wrote last week for the *Observer Review* on the death of the novel. *You* should write a novel,' Becky added, eyes now wide as if she was slightly shocked by her own audacity.

And with those four sentences Pitt Junior became a big fan of Becky Sharp. 'Oh, that's very kind. But I'm just a humble wordsmith, a jobbing hack, at the mercy of my muse. Though, well . . . can I let you into a little secret?'

Becky sidled closer so Pitt Junior could smell the apple scent of her shampoo. 'I'll take it to the grave,' she breathed in his ear and he closed his eyes for a scant second just to gather himself. He was very fond of Jane but she'd never caused Pitt Junior to have to take a second to gather himself.

'I am working on a novel,' Pitt Junior revealed in a hushed tone and then he wished he hadn't said anything, because he'd been working on his novel for years and all he had to show for it were three very inferior drafts and expulsion from his writers' group after an argument with a Faber Academy graduate who had called it 'post-colonial porn'.

'Oh goodness. I'd love to read it,' Becky assured him and she was so close now that not even one of Mrs Tinker's cheese straws could have passed between them.

'You really wouldn't,' Pitt Junior said a little sadly and he wished that he could be more like his father, or like Rawdon, who believed absolutely in their own greatness and wouldn't countenance anyone who didn't.

The little nanny she really was a sweet thing,

lightly touched his hand. 'I probably shouldn't be telling you this but Sir Pitt is so proud of you. He reads every single piece of yours and then we discuss them together.'

'He does?'

'Oh yes, absolutely.' It wasn't a lie. When Sir Pitt wasn't orating his memoirs he'd often read out his second son's latest piece in a mincing voice for Becky's amusement, with added commentary. ('I don't have a bloody clue what the silly boy is wittering on about.')

'Thank you,' Pitt Junior said fervently and Becky's little hand was still resting on his, so he gently squeezed her fingers. 'Goodness, I never imagined that he showed any interest in me or my ridiculous scribbles.'

'They're not ridiculous, Pitty,' said a shocked voice from behind them and they turned to see Jane, Pitt's long-term, long-suffering girlfriend standing there with a bright, brittle smile to mask her hurt that Pitt Junior still wouldn't put a ring on it, even though it had been *years*, and now here he was, holding hands with a very pretty, very young woman. 'Your articles are well-written and astute. We've been through this. I'm Jane, by the way, and you are . . . ?'

Becky summed up the decidedly average Jane Sheepshanks in one swift, sweeping glance that took in her mousy hair, round face and size-twelve figure, right down to her Russell & Bromley dress flats in black patent leather, topped off with a contrasting red velvet bow. If you cut Jane's head off then the words 'Home Counties' would run through her like a stick of rock. She was pleasant, sturdy, middle-class stock, her parents were doctors or solicitors and she'd gone to the local grammar school where she'd worked diligently for a steady B grade and excelled at sports. She had probably gone to a fairly decent university to study something that would get her a fairly decent job on a fairly decent income, but she yearned to be wild and Bohemian. Yet living with Pitt Junior ('Oh yes, he's related to *those* Crawleys, Sir Pitt is actually his father but we try to keep that on the downlow') and supplementing his freelance wages with her salary as Head of Marketing at a company that specialised in green energy was as free-spirited as Jane got. She did try to have a creative side, but it was hard work.

Becky, however, spotted it right away.

'I'm Becky, I'm just the nanny,' she said vaguely, her eyes fixed on the knitted corsage pinned to Jane's little black dress, which had left a residue of red fluff on her bodice. 'That flower you're wearing. It's so pretty. Did you make it yourself?'

Jane felt the same stirrings as Pitt had in her heart, which swelled with pride that someone in this house, even if it were just the nanny, had said something kind to her. Saw her as more than 'that horribly plebeian girlfriend of Pitt Junior's. She's so jolly hockey-sticks. Reminds me of my old games mistress' — which was how she'd just heard Matilda Crawley describe her to Briggs.

'I did make it,' Jane squeaked. 'I love to knit. I think everyone should have a creative outlet.'

125

'I don't have a creative bone in my body,' Becky said with a wistful sigh, because telling outrageous lies didn't really count. 'You're so clever.'

'I could teach you to knit, it's very easy. If I can do it, anyone can,' Jane offered eagerly and Becky nodded a lot less eagerly, but was then saved by Sir Pitt who wasn't at all happy that his little Becky was looking at young Pitt and his dreary girlfriend with the same rapt attention she usually gave him.

It was quite the happy family as the Crawleys sat down to dinner that night. That is, apart from poor Rosa, who was terrified to open her mouth because Matilda and Briggs would roll their eyes at everything she said, and Bute and Martha Crawley, who were positively vibrating with silent yet deep rage at one end of the table.

Bute Crawley, next in line between Matilda and Sir Pitt, would forever be furious that while his older sister and younger brother had been garnished with stardust, he'd had to languish in obscurity as a character actor. The pinnacle of his career was playing a Gestapo officer, Herr Shirt, in a BBC WW2 comedy sitcom about the Resistance in occupied Belgium, *Good Moaning*, which had run for several years during the eighties. He was now reduced to bit parts in police procedurals (he'd been in *Midsomer Murders* an unprecedented eight times) and teaching the glorious art of acting to A-level performance art students who all called him Herr Shirt, because *Good Moaning* was endlessly repeated on UK Gold.

His wife, Martha, was even more furious than her husband. She'd thought she was marrying into one of Britain's premier acting families and ended up with the runt of the litter. Yet, in her way, she was devoted to Bute. His disappointments were her disappointments. His rejections cut her to the very quick. The bitterness might have been jollied out of him if he'd married a more agreeable sort of woman, but under Martha's tender ministrations it had been left to fester and simmer.

Although Becky had vowed to make herself indispensable to every Crawley and Crawley dependent that crossed her path, one glance told her she could do nothing with Bute and Martha. They were perfectly content to be a malcontent presence in the house. They glowered and seethed and muttered furiously at each other and Becky decided that in their own vicious, miserable way they were happy and it was best to steer clear of them.

The gathering hadn't even finished with the soup course or Matilda's amusing account of how she landed the lead in the play that transformed her from Hollywood superstar to the greatest actress of her generation ('and then I said to my agent, 'Get Alan on the phone. No, not Bennett, Ayckbourn''), when they all heard a commotion in the hall outside.

The sound of something heavy falling to the floor, the crash of china, a squeal from one of the girls who'd come up from the village to help out, then the dining-room door crashed back on its hinges and a figure appeared in the doorway.

He was tall and lean, dressed in tight jeans, a tight black T-shirt and a black leather jacket. The exquisite yet rugged beauty of his face was obscured by a large pair of shades, even though he was indoors and it was past eight thirty on a winter's night. He ran long fingers through his thick, unruly mane of dark hair, in a manner that was very familiar to the assembled company.

Becky knew who it was even before Dame Matilda said with quiet joy, 'My darling boy's come home.'

Rawdon Crawley, for it couldn't be anyone else, finally removed his sunglasses to reveal brilliant-blue but bloodshot eyes. It was as if he came with an electrical charge, which sparked with every movement he made, no matter how slight, so that when he was on stage or even playing second lead in a movie, all eyes were on him. As they were now.

He smiled a perfectly crooked smile and threw open his arms. 'Happy fucking Christmas, everyone!'

13

The next morning, Christmas Eve, Becky lay on the floor of the nursery, which was stuck at the end of a long hallway on the second floor where no one of any interest ever ventured, and tried really hard not to scream.

All her threats, all her bribes, even promises of violence were having no effect on the five little Crawleys who had reached peak Christmas hysteria even though they were still a day away from the main event. Even the very littlest one, Artemis, who was usually quite well behaved, had perfected an ear-perforating shriek this morning that was working Becky's last nerve.

'Shut up! Shut up! Shut up!' she growled but none of them paid her any attention apart from the middle one, Thisbe, who hurled himself at Becky's chest, and once he'd landed decided to bounce on her. 'Get off me, you little shit.'

'Santa won't bring you any presents if you say shit,' he informed her while his two eldest siblings ran in circles around them singing 'Let It Go' at the very top of their vocal register.

'Newsflash, Santa doesn't even exist,' Becky hissed and she looked little Thisbe right in the eye as his mouth fell open. 'Yup, not real. I mean, how stupid do you have to be to think some fat bloke is going to be able to break into every person's house in the whole country in the space of a few hours?'

'But ... but ... magic?' Thisbe offered hopefully.

'No such thing,' Becky said and his bottom lip began to wobble alarmingly and at least he'd stopped bouncing, but if he was going to start crying and add to the already deafening racket, then it wasn't really a win. 'If you cry, I'm going to tell Tinker that you're only to have gluten-free toast and soy spread for lunch. No fish fingers for you.'

It was no use. The first fat tears were leaking out of his eyes and as Thisbe opened his mouth to unleash hell, the nursery door crashed back on its hinges. A figure stood poised in the doorway.

'Hello, brats! Come and give your big brother some loving!'

Rawdon Crawley lived to make an entrance and rarely was his audience as adoring as his five little half-siblings, who gawped at him for one blissfully silent moment then erupted into a series of squeaks, squeals and squawks as they moved like one many-limbed creature to swarm all over him.

Who would have thought that Hollywood's hottest hell-raiser would have the softest and sweetest spots for the five children of his father's second wife? Becky watched in amazement as Rawdon crouched down to their level so he could scoop them all up in a hug, laughing as his hair was tugged in all directions and Artemis wiped her very snotty nose on the sleeve of his tracksuit top.

For Hollywood's hottest hell-raiser was wearing a baggy grey tracksuit that was too baggy and too grey to even count as post-ironic fashion.

'Nice outfit,' Becky said when the children's volume knob had come down from eleven to about six. 'I think I saw something similar on the Paris runways.'

Last night, it had seemed as if Rawdon had looked everywhere but at her. Mostly he'd had eyes only for his aunt Matilda, who'd tersely ordered Sir Pitt out of his chair so she could seat her beloved next to her.

So now when he looked at Becky, it was as if they were meeting for the first time. Their eyes locked, both of them determined not to blink. Becky was still lying on the threadbare rug in the centre of the room but she raised herself up on her elbows, which did wonderful things to her breasts, and wouldn't drop her gaze.

Or couldn't.

Compared to Jos Sedley or even Sir Pitt, who when he was suited and booted was handsome in a distinguished sort of way, Rawdon was like the rarest of fillet steaks after first trying a meat substitute, then a tough old piece of rump that was more gristle than anything else.

'I'm going incognito,' Rawdon said in reply. Becky had already forgotten what she'd said, she was so riveted by the sight of six feet two inches of box-office bad boy in the nursery.

'You what?' she muttered.

'I'm taking the brats out to buy their Christmas presents,' Rawdon said, scooping up two of them and holding them by their ankles

131

while they whooped with delight. 'You're coming too. I can't wrangle all five of them on my own.'

Becky gave him her best gimlet gaze. Not even Sir Pitt dared to order her around like that. 'Say please.'

Rawdon batted his ludicrously long eyelashes at Becky. 'Please,' he drawled.

They piled into Matilda Crawley's stately Rolls Royce Silver Phantom, despite Briggs' protests, and drove off with an awful crunching of the gears.

It would have been perfect if there hadn't been five children crammed into the back seat, all talking at once, and if Rawdon Crawley hadn't ignored Becky entirely and addressed all his remarks to his brattish half-siblings.

Which was fine. If that was the game that Rawdon wanted to play, then Becky would ignore him too. They ignored each other all the way to Southampton and the big toy superstore on the outskirts of town.

'Isn't this exciting?' Becky exclaimed to the children as they tumbled out of the car. 'And it's so kind of Santa to ask your big brother to help him with your presents. Apparently, Santa's been so busy this year that the elves in the workshop went on strike over their bad working conditions.'

Thisbe pulled his finger out of his nose. 'You said Santa didn't exist.'

'I did not,' Becky said, digging her fingers into Thisbe's shoulder as she marshalled them through the car park, painfully aware of Rawdon, slouching behind them with a baseball cap pulled down low over his face. Becky put an extra little swing in her hips just in case he wasn't *completely* ignoring her. 'What I said was that little children who tell lies don't get any presents.'

'That's not what you — '

'Look, Thisbe, I don't make the rules.' Becky pulled them through the automatic doors into the ninth layer of hell: the biggest toy superstore on the south coast at eleven forty-five on the morning of Christmas Eve.

Two hours, five meltdowns and one awkward moment (when Artemis pulled down her pants and decided to do a wee right in the middle of aisle seventeen) later, they were camped out in McDonalds.

The children were hopped up on full-fat Coke and involved in very tense negotiations about swapping their Happy Meal toys with each other. Every time Artemis emitted her new high-pitched shriek, Rawdon would flinch and huddle deeper into his hoodie.

'Artemis, I swear, if you make that noise again, you're going to wake every bat within a fifty-mile radius,' Rawdon said at last as the negotiations hit a wall and Thisbe hit Phaedra over the head with an empty Happy Meal box.

'All those toys we just bought are going back if you don't pack it in right now,' Becky growled, her temper now frayed to the very edge. She glanced surreptitiously at Rawdon, but he didn't so much as blink at her sudden change in tone. In fact, for just the merest microsecond, she could swear she saw the faintest glimmer of a smile quirk his lips.

'You wouldn't,' Calliope stated doubtfully.

Becky pointed at her own grim expression. 'Look at my face. Does this look like the face of someone who's joking?'

It didn't. It looked like the face of someone who had shown the five Crawley children, time and time again, that she could give with one hand and snatch back with the other if they dared to displease her.

Like someone had pressed a cosmic mute button, the five of them settled back in their seats with some low-level grumbling. Rawdon shrugged and turned to look out of the window at the non-moving row of cars trying to leave the retail park.

Becky sighed. He would be back in LA the first chance he got, so she might as well take this little opportunity to appreciate him on a purely aesthetic level. Because even in grey marl cotton with a Manchester United baseball cap obscuring a lot of his face, including his piercing, blue eyes, Rawdon Crawley was an absolute joy to behold.

But a little opportunity was *still* an opportunity. Rawdon Crawley was a new plan B and far more pleasing to the eye and entertaining company than Jos Sedley had ever been. If he was planning on disappearing at the earliest opportunity, which would be Boxing Day, then Becky would have to make her play sooner rather than later, even though she much preferred a long con. She absolutely could not screw this up.

Did she play the feisty reality-TV runner-up?

The angelic nanny? The acerbic Becky Sharp who'd survived on her wits ever since she could remember?

Becky decided to go with (d) all of the above.

'I never showed you what I got Matilda,' Rawdon suddenly said as Becky was still deciding on her first move. He hefted up one of the carrier bags and delved inside. 'Do you think she'll like this?'

This was a toy pug, wearing a pink jumper and a malevolent expression.

'That is one of the creepiest things I've ever seen,' Becky said honestly. There was no way to put a positive spin on the hideous beast. 'It's not too late to take it back.'

'I would rather have rectal surgery without an anaesthetic than step back in that fucking shop,' Rawdon said cheerfully, though Calliope gave him a stern look.

'Don't say fucking,' she said primly. 'It's rude.'

'It is,' Rawdon agreed, then he picked up the pug and waggled one of its paws at Becky, who stared back at him, eyebrows raised. 'Trust me, she'll love this. When I was a kid, she had a pug called Stanley, who was completely lacking in any kind of charisma. He'd just wheeze and fart a lot. Matilda always said that she'd have got more companionship if she'd killed him and had him stuffed. This will put a smile on her face.'

'Really? Are you sure that it won't just send her over the edge?' Becky peered at Rawdon over the rim of her coffee cup.

'Matilda loves a tacky gag gift and she needs cheering up . . . ' Rawdon tailed off, then leaned in close. 'Can I trust you with a secret?'

'I'll take it to the grave,' she promised, her eyes wide, her face solemn.

Rawdon leaned even closer so that Becky could see that where his face wasn't obscured by baseball cap or stubble, he had perfect, unblemished skin. Not a single open pore. 'They're killing her off in the *Lyndon Place* Christmas Special.'

Interesting. 'Oh?'

'If we end up watching it tomorrow, will you act surprised when it happens but also don't make too much fuss about it? There's no way that Matilda would let herself be killed off unless the part was too demanding for her, and she'd hate for people to think that she wasn't well.' When Rawdon talked about Matilda, his face, even his voice, softened like someone had taken a rubber and smoothed out all his hard edges. 'She did a whole fortnight as Desdemona with walking pneumonia.'

That was interesting too. Next to her, Thisbe had started swinging his legs, kicking Becky on each backstroke, which she quelled with just one look, then turned back to Rawdon — he didn't have a ring of encrusted snot around each nostril, for one thing.

'You know, Hollywood hell-raisers aren't meant to be like this. Kind, caring . . . '

Rawdon smiled the crooked, lazy smile that had launched a thousand teenage dreams. 'You obviously haven't met many Hollywood hell-raisers.'

'Well, no, they are quite thin on the ground in

Mudbury,' Becky conceded.

'It might not be 'cool' to admit it, but I love Matilda. When Mum died and it was obvious that Pitt wasn't going to step up, she took care of me. Paid for me to go to Eton . . . '

Becky nearly snorted in weary derision. Why was it that every man she'd met since she'd left the *Big Brother* house had been to Eton? It was a cabal. A conspiracy. An exclusive club that Becky could never hope to enter. Not even because she'd dragged herself up from the gutters of Soho, but because, last time she checked, Eton didn't admit girls as pupils.

Meanwhile Rawdon was still misty-eyed about his favourite aunt.

' . . . She also put me through RADA, because Pitt wasn't going to pay for anything that might mean that I'd one day take the spotlight off him.' Rawdon smiled in a deprecating fashion. 'My therapist says that I have unresolved daddy issues.'

Becky rolled her eyes. 'Don't we all?'

Rawdon dipped his head in acknowledgement of this universal truth. 'My therapist also says that I'm an unapologetic narcissist and that I shouldn't always talk about myself, especially when I'm on a date with a beautiful woman.' And then in case Becky hadn't got the hint, Rawdon's knee nudged against hers.

Becky moved her leg away. These rich boys spent their whole lives having whatever they wanted handed to them on a plate. If Rawdon Crawley put in some time and effort, then he might appreciate his prize a little more than Jos

Sedley had done. 'If your idea of a date is a McDonalds in a retail park, then talking about yourself is the very least of your problems.' She gave Thisbe a shove so he'd get to his feet and she could slide out from the table. 'Come on, Crawleys, time to go. Who needs wees?'

14

Christmas at Queen's Crawley was not like any Christmas Becky had known before. It didn't involve one or both of her parents passing out drunk, for example, or Jemima Pinkerton wandering the streets of Southbourne in her nightie trying to find the Angel Gabriel.

Still, Becky wasn't too fond of being woken up at the ungodly hour of five thirty in the morning, when it was still pitch black outside, by Artemis and Thisbe jumping on her bed and screaming that Father Christmas had left them stockings.

The stockings were from Rosa. They couldn't have been from anyone else because they contained wooden toys made by amputee orphans in some godforsaken Third World country and organic, Fair Trade trail mix.

Becky shoved the iPad at them, *Frozen* already cued up and ready to go, then put the pillow over her head and managed another couple of hours of sleep.

At a more reasonable hour, she brought all five children, washed and dressed and vibrating with anticipation, downstairs to a proper breakfast. Sir Pitt had ordered one of his prize sows to be slaughtered, so there was bacon, eggs laid by the vicious chickens that ruled the kitchen garden with beaks of iron, and fresh bread.

Even better, Bute and Martha were intent on going to church, mainly so they could sit in the family pew with martyred but lofty expressions. Once they'd left to walk to church through the estate, as no Crawley had done for at least two generations, everyone else became quite giddy with relief.

After a long, leisurely breakfast, and the first bottles of champagne had been opened, there were presents for everyone, even Becky. Rosa had bought her a lump of rose quartz suspended on a silver chain, and Jane had stayed up half the night to knit Becky her very own moulting red corsage.

She hadn't been left off Sir Pitt's list either. He cornered her in the scullery before lunch. In honour of the most sacred of all days, the heating was cranked up full blast and Sir Pitt was swanning around in silk pyjamas and an ornate dressing gown, like some posh, English version of Hugh Hefner.

'Little Becky,' he crooned, closing the door softly behind him. 'Have you been naughty or nice?'

'Depends who's asking,' Becky said with a resigned note. Sir Pitt came up behind her so he could ghost hot breath over her neck and rest one of his hands on her waist, high up enough that the tips of his fingers grazed the underside of her breast. She let him have that much, because it was Christmas, then wriggled away from him. 'No need to ask you whether you've been naughty or nice. You're *always* a very naughty, naughty man.'

He chuckled appreciatively. 'I have a very special present for you, but you have to turn around.'

Becky treated the scullery window to an exasperated grimace then turned round. 'I can't see any present,' she said, because Sir Pitt was empty handed.

'It's in my pocket. No, I'm not going to tell you which one. You'll have to have a feel for yourself.' He smiled wolfishly then raised his hands above his head. 'I'm entirely at your mercy.'

If the only present he was hiding turned out to be his ageing cock, then Becky was going to give it such a squeeze that he'd be bent double for the rest of the day. But after gifting him a few fleeting gropes as she investigated his dressing-gown pocket, she found something in the pocket of his pyjama bottoms that was also hard to the touch.

'A family heirloom,' he explained as Becky held up an art-deco-style diamond brooch, by which he meant that it had belonged to his first wife's great-grandmother.

Becky didn't know that but she did know that Sir Pitt was a cheap bastard, so she bit down on the brooch to test if the gold was real, then scraped the big central diamond against the scullery window where it left a pleasing scratch. She'd have to have it valued properly but it seemed that it was legit, so she gave him another grope and swirled her tongue lasciviously around the brooch.

Sir Pitt's eyes darkened and he tried to put her hand back on his crotch. 'Be kind to Little Pitt, Becky. He's got all sorts of treats planned for you.'

This was starting to become a problem and one that Becky really didn't want to deal with. It was a very delicate game that she was playing. One little hand job could upset the balance but maybe another gentle tug would keep him happy for a couple of hours.

'Becky! Those brussels sprouts aren't going to top and tail themselves! Oh, Sir Pitt, whatever are you doing in the scullery in your fancy dressing gown?' Mrs Tinker asked, bursting into the small room and rescuing Becky in her hour of need.

'It's not a dressing gown, it's a smoking jacket,' Sir Pitt said sulkily and Becky, with a sigh of relief, vowed to avoid him for the rest of the day.

Mostly she helped Mrs Tinker in the kitchen while happily bitching about Bute and Martha, but she was expected to join the Crawleys for Christmas Dinner. It was served at five, by which time the whole Crawley clan was past pissed and heading for hammered. Even Jane was squiffy on the Baileys; only Bute, Martha and Becky abstained. Technically, Becky was working and not so technically, she was the child of two alcoholics and had so many balls in play that if she were to lose control of her mental faculties, then the whole lot could come crashing to the ground.

After dinner, the children, fractious from too much sugar and being awake since five thirty, were sent to bed. Becky gathered them up, hissed at them to sing a couple of verses of 'Silent Night' in French, then took them upstairs, little Artemis slung over her shoulder like a sack of spuds. Rosa dabbed a tear from her eye, Jane sighed and looked at Pitt Junior hopefully, and even Martha Crawley looked a little less boot-faced. It was as if Becky were a modern-day Maria Von Trapp, but beautiful, and without the least inclination to take holy orders or 'Climb Ev'ry Mountain' with the head of the family.

When Becky came back downstairs after a protracted bedtime during which she had threatened to tie Thisbe (always Thisbe) to his bed, it was to find that the Crawleys had now relocated to what the family called The Den.

It wasn't particularly den-like, more a dark and gloomy cave. The walls were hung with heavy brocade paper and paintings, not by Old Masters, but by well-regarded pupils of Old Masters. The room was furnished with thread-bare Aubusson carpets and uncomfortable chairs and sofas upholstered in the slipperiest fabric known to man. The one TV set in Queen's Crawley was kept here in a cabinet, which Sir Pitt was unlocking with some ceremony and unsteady fingers, because he'd been drinking all day.

'What time does your programme start, Mattie?' he bellowed, his face red from all the alcohol and his exertions with a lock and key.

Dame Matilda was uncomfortably perched on the slipperiest sofa, Briggs on one side, Rawdon on the other. All three of them had their feet planted firmly on the floor to stop themselves sliding off. Maybe that was why the old lady had such a peevish expression. She waved the hand that wasn't clutching a large gin and tonic dismissively, 'Let's not, Pitt. Nobody needs to see me making a fool of myself in period costume.'

Pitt grunted in triumph as he managed to wrench open the cabinet doors. 'Well, you force us to watch it every other year, so why should today be any different? Anyway, my house, my rules!'

Matilda and Briggs exchanged their seventeenth eye roll of the day as the television came to life and the familiar theme tune rang out. Becky had never seen *Lyndon Place* before, but it seemed fairly accurate from her experience of the strange hinterland between below stairs and above stairs. She was currently perched uncomfortably on an old footstool, out of range of the cosy, roaring fire and on the fringes. Among them but not of them. If it wasn't for the way that Rawdon would occasionally glance her way, his gaze as smouldering as the logs in the grate, then Becky might just as well be invisible.

She pointedly looked away from Rawdon with a tiny, disapproving shake of her head; she'd pointedly avoided him all day and if she wasn't mistaken, his interest was piqued. She turned her attention back to the television. There was a complicated storyline about the Earl's hunting boots, which had gone missing, the chinless suitors of the daughters of the house all looked the same, and just as Becky was thinking that she might slip below stairs for more gossiping with Mrs Tinker, events took a dramatic turn.

On screen the family gathered for a grand festive dinner. The table was dressed with spotless white linen, sparkling glassware and much gilt-bedazzled china, very different from the yellowed tablecloths and napkins, cloudy glasses and mismatched crockery for the Crawleys' Christmas meal.

Still, in art as well as in life, there were different factions within the family, all with their own agenda, and ruling over all of them, an iron fist in black-lace evening mittens, was the Dowager Countess. It was quite obvious that Dame Matilda had been typecast because there was absolutely no difference between her on-screen and off-screen personas. She gave the Earl's second eldest and most whiny daughter a quite spectacular dressing down, which echoed the quite spectacular dressing down she'd given Rosa earlier when she'd asked not to be seated so close to the pigs in blankets.

The Dowager Countess banged her ornate cane on the floor as Dame Matilda muttered something to Briggs, who shook his head and could be heard to murmur, 'I know. *Unbelievable.*'

Then the cane fell to the ground with a clatter as the Dowager Countess gripped her chest, slumped to one side and began to projectile-vomit blood all over the snowy-white tablecloth.

And that was the end of her.

Back in the den at Queen's Crawley, there was a moment of shocked silence.

'Well, I said to the director, 'Nigel, dear,' I said, 'please let me die with dignity.' But no,'

Matilda sniffed. 'Now, shall we turn over to the BBC? Have we missed the *Strictly* Christmas special?'

But Sir Pitt was determined to have his pound of flesh. 'Poor Mattie,' he proclaimed with such a lack of sincerity that it was hard to believe that he'd ever won an Oscar. 'From Lady Macbeth to *that*. Quite the letdown.'

He'd barely finished his gloating when he was interrupted by Martha rising to her feet to fling herself at a grim-faced Dame Matilda. Becky sat up straighter on her footstool: this was much more entertaining than watching the Dowager Countess spray blood all over the cheese plate.

'Auntie! I can't believe they've killed you off,' she cried.

'Absolutely appalling,' Bute echoed, wringing his hands in faux agitation.

'Get. Off. Me,' Dame Matilda snapped. 'Briggs, please . . . '

'Get off her.' Briggs jumped up to tug at Martha's sleeve with a pained expression on his face, as if he couldn't bear to touch something that had started off life in the Per Una department of M&S. 'You don't ever touch Dame Matilda. Really!'

'Martha's just upset on your behalf, we all are,' Bute said, his cold grey eyes positively gleaming.

'I'm sure you'll be a shoo-in for a BAFTA,' Pitt Junior piped up as Jane mopped at her streaming eyes. Her tears and the subsequent snotty blowing of her nose were the only display of genuine emotion in the room. Only two

146

people in the room were unaffected by all the dramatics: Rosa, who was glued to her phone, lips moving soundlessly as she read a text message; and Rawdon, who was slouched so far down in his seat that it was a wonder that he didn't slide to the floor.

To think that she'd almost excused herself to gossip with Tinker. Becky wouldn't have missed this for the world, especially not when Dame Matilda struggled to her feet with Briggs' assistance and cast a gnarled, trembling finger at the assembled company. 'I'm sorry to disappoint you all, but I have no intention of dying in real life, so stop toadying to me,' she said icily. 'It won't do you any good because I'm leaving everything to Rawdon, as you all know very well, so enough! Rawdon, can you take my other arm?'

Rawdon unfolded himself from the couch and said something in a whisper to his aunt, which made her face soften and her hand come up to stroke his cheek. 'Horrible boy,' she said fondly, as the three of them began a slow journey to the door, Briggs hissing a warning as Martha darted towards them again.

Becky was quite sorry to see them go, especially as Sir Pitt was now casting his lusty, drunken gaze in her direction.

'Becky, a pot of tea, you can bring it up to my room,' Dame Matilda demanded. Becky didn't appreciate her peremptory tone, not even a please or thank you, but she did appreciate the rescue from Sir Pitt's clammy hands and even clammier breath.

When Becky knocked on the door of the

Queen Anne suite where Matilda had been installed, it sounded as if the mood had lightened because she could hear the dame laughing and Briggs saying, 'Oh, stop it! I can't breathe.'

She pushed open the door and almost choked on the fug of cannabis-scented smoke from the huge joint that Rawdon was passing to his esteemed aunt, while proclaiming in a not-too-shabby impersonation of his equally esteemed papa, 'Dear Mattie, your death scene couldn't hope to compare to my *Hamlet*. Did I mention that I played *Hamlet?* Several critics believe that my performance as the Danish prince was far, *far* superior to Sir Larry's.'

Briggs clutched his sides and rocked with silent mirth while Matilda cackled and, if Becky hadn't been lightning quick to set the tea tray down and whip out a saucer, Matilda would have dropped ash on the imported Italian silk bedspread, which she'd brought with her from London because, quite wisely, she didn't trust that the bedding at Queen's Crawley was regularly laundered.

'Ah, Miss Sharp, and what did you think of my death scene?' Matilda enquired, taking custody of the saucer so Becky could move the tea tray to her bedside table. 'Don't tell me a sharp-tongued little thing like you is shy.'

Becky looked up from pouring tea, caught Rawdon's eye as he raised his eyebrows. She could rarely resist a challenge and she wasn't going to resist Rawdon either. Not now she knew he was going to inherit all of Matilda's millions.

'You know, you're quite a good actress,' she said and felt the lightness of the mood puncture as if she'd disappointed them all with yet more toadying. 'Have you been in anything else?'

Briggs sucked in a shocked breath, Rawdon turned away to hide his smile and Dame Matilda looked positively evil for one second until she threw her head back and laughed so hard that she burned a hole in her £5,000 coverlet with the joint.

'You are a wicked, wicked girl,' she pronounced a little while later, after Becky had shown her own acting prowess by impersonating Martha at her most shrill and obsequious. 'And you have more brains than all of them stewing downstairs. If life was fair, they'd be waiting on you and not the other way round, but alas, life isn't fair. You'll come back to London with me, Becky. Can't have you mouldering away down here and fighting off that randy old goat of a brother of mine every night. Rawdon's shooting a film in town, so I'll have my two favourite people with me.'

Becky dared to steal a glance at Rawdon from under her lashes. He was dealing out cards so the four of them could play poker for Quality Street. He returned her glance with such intensity, it was a wonder that the good dame's bedspread didn't burst into flames.

'What about me?' Briggs called indignantly from the en suite where he was brushing out Matilda's wig.

'Don't be silly,' Matilda said crushingly. 'You're not people, you're Briggs.'

'Bartha'
13 Torrington Road
Tooting
London
Pinkerton's Talent Agency
Dean Street
Soho
London
29th December

Dear Ms Pinkerton,

I'm not sure if you remember me, but my husband Bute Crawley (a character actor of some repute) and I met you at a benefit for the Distressed Actors' Benevolent Fund at the Wyndham Theatre a couple of years ago.

I've recently discovered that we have a mutual acquaintance, one Rebecca Sharp, employed by my dear brother-in-law, Sir Pitt Crawley, as nanny to his five children by his second wife. In fact, I understand that it was through your auspices that Rebecca came to work for Sir Pitt.

Rebecca has now left poor Sir Pitt in the lurch by decamping to London with my darling sister-in-law Dame Matilda Crawley. It transpires that we know nothing of Rebecca, Sir Pitt had no references from you, and so I'm writing to ask for some background on Miss Sharp.

It would be very helpful to ascertain how you first came to know her, her family background and previous employment. A quick Google search would suggest that she recently appeared on a reality-TV show (Bute and I are not at all familiar with this dreadful genre) where she spent eight weeks gallivanting about in a bikini with the most appalling people.

Dame Matilda, as I'm sure you know, is getting on and, strictly *entre nous*, appears to be suffering from the early symptoms of dementia, so I would hate to think that she might be taken advantage of by anyone unscrupulous.

I'm sure you understand my concerns and hope that you can allay my fears. I also hope that you will treat this delicate matter with the utmost discretion.

I look forward to hearing from you.

Kind regards

Martha Crawley (Mrs)

15

The Crawley children cried when Becky left on Boxing Day. All apart from Thisbe (always Thisbe) who said that he wouldn't miss her at all.

'Oh, Thisbe,' Becky laughed because all the Crawleys had gathered to watch, in stunned disbelief, as she departed without even giving a week's notice. She crouched down in the grand entrance hall of Queen's Crawley to pull his stiff, resistant body in for a hug. 'And I won't miss you either, you little shit,' she hissed in his ear.

And then she was climbing into the back of Dame Matilda's Rolls Royce Silver Phantom and barely had a chance to wave and laugh at the forlorn expressions on the faces of Sir Pitt and Rosa, before Briggs drove off.

'Can't wait to get back to civilisation,' he said, sending up a cloud of gravel. 'I'm sure one of the children has given me head lice.'

'We'll get you a treatment,' Dame Matilda promised. 'I'm sure Becky is a whizz with a nit-comb. Now, I'm going to have a nap, wake me up when we're back in London.'

London! Becky couldn't wait to be hurled back into the grimy, fleshy arms of London. London was a hard, unfriendly place full of hard, unfriendly people, all of them on the hustle, so no wonder she felt so at home there. But for now, home was a huge Victorian villa on a pretty tree-lined Primrose Hill street and her new neighbours included a Man Booker Prize-winning novelist, four pop stars who'd been big in the nineties, Britain's highest-paid comedian and two Labour MPs.

Matilda's four-storey house was a migraine-inducing clash of different styles and themes. The kitchen was Victorian farmhouse chic, the front room was a mini Versailles with swathes of chintz and ormolu, and Becky's room had a seventies shag-palace feel with mirrors everywhere and a carpet so deep that she sank down into it rather than walked. Even the downstairs cloakroom was like having a wee on the Orient Express.

On every floor, in every room, there were pictures of Matilda. A Warhol screen-print done when she'd visited The Factory in the sixties, a Hockney portrait painted by the swimming pool of the house in Palm Springs she and her first husband had owned in the seventies. In the eighties, she posed for a heavily stylised illustration by Patrick Nagel. There were also her two *Vogue* covers shot by David Bailey, the Annie Leibovitz portrait which had graced the cover of *Vanity Fair*, and a black-and-white head-and-shoulders crop by Mario Testino, which would have been the cover of *The Sunday Times* magazine if the Princess of Wales hadn't had the bad manners to die the week it was due to come out.

Becky had never seen a house like it but once again, she was living indefinitely in someone else's home. Being entirely dependent on their

153

good graces was a very familiar feeling and while Dame Matilda was a hoot, she was also far more capricious than Mrs Sedley. There was also another ubiquitous housekeeper, Firkin, who said very little but always seemed to pop up when Becky least expected it, silent and judgemental.

Becky didn't doubt that if she happened to borrow some little trifles of Matilda's, a necklace here, a pair of earrings there, then she'd come back to her room to find them laid out on the bed along with a neat pile of laundry, rather than wherever she'd hidden them. So she didn't. She would be on her best behaviour, beyond reproach, though that wasn't hard: her duties, such as they were, were hardly onerous compared with ensuring that none of the five Crawley brats had come to any harm on her watch.

Matilda wasn't fit for human company until at least eleven most mornings. Then Firkin would admit Becky to her inner sanctum, where Matilda would be arranged on a pink velvet chaise longue, and while Briggs would begin dressing her hair, she and Becky would go through the newspapers.

'To see what those bastards are saying about my dear friends,' Matilda would say crossly, because she knew everyone, from politicians to pop stars, writers and aristocrats.

Matilda actually quite enjoyed it when those bastards wrote horrible things about her dear friends. She also liked to critique their outfits with acid-tipped commentary. 'A deep slit with *those* thighs? Interesting.'

On one frost-tipped February morning, five weeks into Becky's residency, she was surprised to see one of her own acquaintances staring back at her from a double-page spread in the *Daily Mail:*

The Blue Party's golden boy — meet 'gorgeous' George Wylie, the new breed of Conservative

Old Etonian, heir to a baronetcy, and prospective Tory candidate for the safe seat of Squashmore, George Wylie is tipped for the top by everyone who knows him.

'He's not tipped for the top by me,' Becky said, her face curdling. 'Arrogant wanker. Look at that smirk!'

She waved the paper at Matilda who squinted at the photograph of George in suit, tie and supercilious smile posing outside the Houses of Parliament.

'I think I did cocaine with his mother at a party in Biarritz in the eighties,' she murmured.

'What a pity that the cocaine didn't make her infertile,' Becky said, much to Matilda's amusement. 'Listen to this! 'At Eton, he excelled in academic pursuits as well as on the cricket field, the best batter and bowler the school had seen in a generation. He was popular with all his classmates and even more popular with their sisters.' Those sisters must have had cotton wool for brains,' Becky commented sourly. 'It gets worse.

' 'At Oxford, 'gorgeous' George, as he was quickly known, caused quite a stir about the female student body, there were even rumours that he'd enjoyed a brief romance with a Princess from the Luxembourg royal family as well as a couple of dates with a member of girl band, St Amour, after they played one of the Oxford May balls.

' 'George was such a hit with the ladies that one of his party tricks was to light a cigar with the love letters they would send to his rooms at Magdalen College, much to the delight of his drinking chums. His pyrotechnic skills also came in handy as a member of the notorious Rakehell drinking club where one of the initiation rites was to set a homeless person on fire.' '

'He sounds positively vile,' Briggs remarked as he laid out a heather-blue Jaeger suit for Matilda's inspection. 'Will this do for lunch?'

'Do you think I still have the complexion for that shade of blue? I don't want to look like a cadaver,' Matilda said with a little sigh. Becky couldn't help but notice these days that before Briggs started on her make-up, her skin did have a certain waxy pallor.

'Oh no, dear,' Briggs shushed her anxiously and nudged Becky.

'Stop fishing for compliments, Mattie, you know you look gorgeous,' Becky said so she could get back to reading about George Wylie, even though reading about him made her furious. 'God, this is such bullshit! 'Of course, such youthful indiscretions are a thing of the past and since leaving Oxford, George has lived in a manner more fitting for a prospective Tory MP.

''After a brief stint at *The Daily Globe*, where he interned on the political desk, George has worked for the centre-right think-tank, The Way Ahead, funded by media mogul and Conservative Party donor, Lord Steyne, the perfect launch-pad for an ambitious young man who wants to succeed in politics.

''His private life is also a good deal more private. Though George is said to be quite the heart-throb with the junior researchers and assistants at Conservative HQ, according to his best friend since prep school, Captain William Dobbin of Her Majesty's Royal Regiment, George is already taken.

'' 'George only has eyes for Amelia Sedley, a charming young woman, who he intends to marry one day.' Yes, that would be the same Amelia Sedley, the posh totty with curves for days who won last year's *Big Brother* and whose 'father founded Sedley's Bank and would surely be happy to fund his future son-in-law's political campaign.

''Let's hope Mr Sedley has deep pockets, as political pundits believe that Gorgeous George could well be Prime Minister one day.''

Becky threw the newspaper on the floor in her fury. 'If that over-entitled bell-end ever becomes Prime Minister, I'm emigrating. And if Amelia Sedley does marry him, then she's a bigger idiot than I thought, which is really saying something. Though she deserves him. After saying that we were practically sisters, she can hardly be

157

bothered to even text me.' Becky scowled ferociously as she recalled Amelia's empty promises. 'I hope she gets a third in her poxy degree.'

'Rebecca, I do adore it when you're being viperous. You're like the daughter I never had,' Matilda said approvingly. 'If only you'd take my Rawdon in hand. You'd be much better for him than those ditzy models he's so fascinated with. He needs a woman to take him down a peg or two. Are we seeing him tonight, Briggs, dear?'

As well as hair, face and wardrobe, Briggs was also in charge of Matilda's diary, which, as she was currently 'resting', involved a lot of lunches and at least one evening event per day, sometimes two, though she was usually home at a very respectable hour.

'It's the premiere of the new Working Title film tonight, so, yes. He's coming here first.'

'I shall be very rude to him then,' Becky promised, and Matilda gave a delighted chuckle. 'I might even make him cry.'

'I'd like to see that,' Matilda said as she rose from the chaise longue slowly, her hand clutching Briggs' arm in a death grip. 'I'd also like to see the faces of all those silly, pouty girls when you snatch him out from under their noses.'

So would Becky, but when Rawdon arrived at the house promptly at six thirty, she greeted him with a cool, polite smile as he was shown into the drawing room.

'You look pretty,' he said as he slouched nonchalantly against the door jamb as if he were physically incapable of standing up straight without some kind of lumbar support.

She was artfully perched on a velvet navy sofa, wearing a silver-sequinned slip of a dress that Matilda had once worn to Studio 54 and had now donated to Becky, as she said that her 'disco days are, alas, over.'

'You could have made an effort,' Becky said with a sniff. Rawdon was wearing his usual jeans and leather jacket, which made him look deliciously mean and moody, not that she would ever let him know that. 'And I don't know why you're wearing sunglasses when it's been dark for a couple of hours now.'

'I'm wearing shades so you won't be able to see how your words wound me,' Rawdon drawled and he put a hand to his heart, pulling at his T-shirt so Becky couldn't help but notice how taut and muscular his chest was underneath the tight, well-worn black cotton.

'Hah! You'll live,' she said, and now they'd got the usual pleasantries out of the way, she patted the sofa. 'Come and sit down next to me.'

Rawdon walked over with feline grace and sat down next to Becky, close enough that his leg brushed against hers. But then he took off his sunglasses and took Becky's hand, and she let him.

'So, how is she today?' he asked, with an anxious look towards the ceiling as if he expected Matilda to suddenly bang on the floor and demand to know why they were talking about her.

'She was an awful colour this morning and quite wobbly on her feet, but she insisted on going out to lunch and managed to eat a little grilled salmon and some asparagus,' Becky dutifully reported. 'Then she had a nap this afternoon and she's on pretty good form now. Though Briggs and I have made her promise that she's only to have a couple of glasses of champagne.'

'Yeah, she shouldn't be mixing all those pills with too much alcohol,' Rawdon noted. Becky now knew first hand that he was an expert at mixing pills with a lot of alcohol. But he wasn't a mean drunk and the pills and other substances that he liked to sniff and snort clouded his judgement rather than his temper. Otherwise she wouldn't be pursuing him with such studied indifference that it hardly looked as if she were pursuing him at all. Rawdon was still holding Becky's hand, his thumbs absent-mindedly caressing the backs of her fingers. 'And we'll make sure she's on her way home by ten?'

'Yup, and tucked up in bed,' Becky agreed, then looked down at their joined hands in feigned surprise. 'Oh!' She pulled free. 'OK, so we're done here, then?'

Rawdon looked upwards again like their little tete-a-tete might be interrupted at any minute. 'Yeah, I guess . . . except, well, I got you something.'

'You did? I don't know why,' Becky said dismissively, though her heart knew exactly why and pounded triumphantly. 'I'm just your aunt's companion. Like something out of a boring old novel.'

'You're so much more than that,' Rawdon said

and Becky still couldn't tell if that throaty inflection to his voice, the way he gazed down at her with such tenderness, was something he'd picked up at RADA, or if he really meant it. She supposed the tenderness worked on Rawdon's other conquests — the pouty models and junior starlets — but Becky wouldn't let herself succumb. She needed a lot more than tenderness from Rawdon. 'Anyway, I got you this.'

He pulled something out of the pocket of his jacket. His father had given her diamonds and yet Rawdon was giving her . . . 'Another toy from a McDonalds Happy Meal,' Becky said, holding the miniature polar bear between her thumb and forefinger like she was going to burn it the first chance she got. 'I really don't know why you keep giving me these.'

'You know why,' Rawdon said, staring at her with a deep and soulful look.

Becky shook her head. 'If you say so.'

'You know what, Becky? You can be a real bitch.'

She smiled then. The first genuine smile she'd given him since he'd walked through the door; he'd earned that smile. Becky leaned close, so she could smell the leather of his jacket, the cigarette he'd smoked outside, the faint whiff of Ponds cold cream, which he'd used to take off his make-up after he'd finished shooting. It was quite the heady combination.

'Oh Rawdon,' she whispered into his ear and felt him shudder before he could check himself. 'You have no idea what I can be, but wouldn't you love to find out?'

161

★ ★ ★

Before today, Becky had barely thought about George Wylie for months (though occasionally she'd flashback to that morning at the Sedleys' when he'd laughed right in her face and she'd have to force herself not to punch the nearest wall), and then in the space of a few hours, he was spread all over pages six and seven of the *Daily Mail* and now he was right in front of her as she waited for Dame Matilda and Rawdon to be done with the red carpet.

One day, quite soon hopefully, she'd be on the red carpet herself, rather than acting as a glorified pack mule, charged with looking after Matilda's handbag and fur coat while she posed for the assembled photographers.

George was with another man, a standard-issue chinless wonder with slicked-back hair and red braces, and was looking inordinately pleased with himself.

One day, I will make him suffer horribly, Becky promised as she always did whenever George Wylie crossed her mind.

Becky was standing in the little patch of no-man's-land between the red carpet and the entrance to the restored Victorian cinema at the northernmost tip of Regent Street. She was almost obscured from view by the bank of photographers and publicists wrangling celebrities on and off the carpet, and anyway, George Wylie and his friend were far too busy gawping at any model/actress/whatever who wandered their way to pay any attention to Becky, so she

162

was free to glare at him and wish that she could shoot laser death-rays out of her eyes.

'Becky? Becky! It is you! Gosh, you look very cross. Is it because you're cold? You must be cold with no coat and no tights on, but I love your dress!'

Then before Becky could summon up a response to the sight of Amelia Sedley suddenly standing before her, Amelia threw her arms around the girl who she'd said was like a sister to her. And yet somehow, that sister had been all but forgotten as soon as they were parted and only worthy of the occasional text message, which was low in text and very high in emojis.

Becky managed to extricate herself from Amelia's clutches. Unlike everyone else in attendance, Amelia was dressed for the freezing February weather in a huge silver Puffa jacket over a black woolly dress, thick tights and were . . . were those . . . Ugg boots? Was Amelia Sedley actually wearing Ugg boots to a film premiere?

'Interesting outfit,' Becky noted then shivered. 'I wish I'd dressed for comfort rather than style. Don't frown, Emmy. You look adorable. Cuddly.'

'It's just so cold,' Amelia confided. 'George didn't say it would be red carpet. He just asked if I wanted to come to the cinema with him.'

'You're here with George?'

'Yes, isn't it wonderful?' Amelia's eyes gleamed with the sheer bliss of being somewhere with George Wylie.

'So, you're not at university?'

'Gosh, Becky, this is starting to feel a bit like a

police interrogation.' Amelia giggled nervously. 'I hope you're not going to shine a bright light in my eyes to get me to talk.'

Becky folded her arms and looked as sorrowful as a girl could when she was wearing a silver-sequinned dress. 'It's just I thought you must be dead in a ditch somewhere. Though I can't say I blame you for not wanting to stay in touch with someone who's just a lowly nanny on minimum wage. I was obviously dragging you down and that's why you stopped calling and emailing me . . . '

'University is so much more intense now I'm in my final year. I've had so many essays to write.' Amelia's bottom lip wobbled alarmingly and she clasped her hands together as if she were praying for forgiveness. 'And also, I don't know how, but someone got hold of that old iPad that I lost, and I forgot to have it taken off my tariff and they've chomped through my entire data allowance and then some. When Daddy saw the bill, he hit the roof. Things at home have been quite . . . well, they've been quite difficult . . . Anyway, he actually confiscated my phone. Can you believe it?' She widened her eyes.

'No, I can't believe it,' Becky said. Everyone knew Mr Sedley thought sunbeams shot out of his daughter's fulsome arse.

'But it's the truth! He said I had to learn how to manage a monthly budget and that I needed to become financially mature.' Amelia's eyes were now glassy with the threat of tears. 'Like I said, things are very odd at the moment, which is why it was so lovely of George to try and cheer me up.'

'Taking my name in vain, Emmy?' said the sneering voice that made Becky's hands curl into fists. She felt someone come up behind her and Amelia's face transformed from crestfallen to ecstatic.

'George, look who I found!' Amelia cried and Becky turned her head in time to catch George's astonishment that the redhead he'd been eyeing up was none other than . . .

'Becky Sharp!' he exclaimed, mouth agape.

'George,' Becky said thinly, then she looked past him to the far more agreeable sight of Rawdon Crawley loping towards her. 'Rawdon! There you are!'

'Here I am,' Rawdon agreed and because Becky was smiling delightedly at him for once, he dared to put his arm around her shoulders. 'You're like a block of ice. Here, take my jacket.'

How Amelia goggled as Rawdon slipped off his leather jacket and placed it around Becky who tucked her arm into his.

'Then you'll be cold,' she purred. 'Let's cuddle together for warmth.' She glanced over at Amelia whose mouth was still hanging open. It wouldn't do any harm to throw her a few Crawley crumbs. 'Rawdon, this is my friend, Amelia Sedley, though she hasn't spoken to me in months.'

'I really am sorry about that, Becky . . . '

'And, Emmy, this is Rawdon Crawley. Would you say we're friends, Rawdon?'

Rawdon put his hand on Becky's chin to tip her face towards him. 'I hope so,' he drawled and it was a cheesy gesture and a cheesy line but Amelia sighed and now clasped her hands together in wordless rapture.

While these introductions were being made, George was being soundly ignored: he couldn't bear it any longer. 'Crawley,' he said in a clipped voice. 'Haven't seen you since you got expelled from school.'

'Wylie, haven't seen you since you were thrashing one of the younger boys for not cleaning your rugby boots to your liking,' Rawdon recalled. As they glowered at each other, it was clear that there was absolutely no love lost between them, but there were still the bonds of the old school tie and all that, so they shook hands like they were trying to break each other's bones. 'What have you been up to lately?'

George flushed. How could Rawdon have possibly missed his mostly flattering profile in the *Daily Mail* that very morning? 'Well . . . ' he began.

'He's standing for Parliament,' Becky interrupted. 'Some old duffer has died and George hopes to take his safe Conservative seat.'

'Conservative?' Rawdon's lip curled even though he'd never voted and if he had, then tax breaks trumped social reform every time.

'Yes, well . . . '

'It's *fascinating*, isn't it?' Becky butted in again before George could get even three complete words out. 'Let's imagine young George with all the education and privilege that anyone could ever want, making an informed choice about his future. He looked around at what was going on

166

in the world of politics: the stripping back of essential services, more children living in poverty, families reliant on foodbanks and thought yes, I want to be a Conservative MP, because these are my people.' She gave George a dazzling smile, which made him see stars even though he hated this chippy young woman like he'd never hated anyone else before. 'So, good luck in the by-election, George, and God help us all if you ever have a say in the running of this country.'

Then she swept away as she could see Dame Matilda and Briggs waving impatiently at her.

'She's one hell of a girl,' Rawdon murmured as he watched Becky reunite his aunt with her fur coat and help her into it.

'She's lovely,' Amelia agreed. 'One of the sweetest, kindest people I know. And gosh, you probably don't remember him, but you were at Eton with my brother Jos, too.'

'Oh for God's sake, Emmy, nobody cares,' George snapped. He wagged a reproving finger at Rawdon who looked at him in amusement. 'I'm warning you, Crawley, you want to watch out for that Sharp girl.'

'Thank you, boy,' Rawdon said, with a look of peculiar gratitude. 'I can see you've got her number.'

Then George, pleased that Crawley wasn't a complete fool, and Amelia, unhappy because her love for George didn't blind her to all his many faults, went to find their seats.

Pinkerton's Talent Agency
Dean Street
Soho
London

'Bartha'
13 Torrington Road
Tooting
London
27th February

Dear Martha

Thank you so much for your letter and apologies for not replying sooner. Such are the demands of the business called show, as I'm sure you're aware!

So, Rebecca Sharp. Where to even start with that one? A very common-looking girl, though I'm sure she can't help her appearance, given her rocky start in life — I don't think she'd ever seen a vegetable, much less eaten one, until I took her in after the death of her father, who was a business acquaintance of mine.

I say 'business' but the man never did an honest day's work in all the time I knew him. He was a card counter, confidence trickster and crook who ended up dying in the infirmary of Wormwood Scrubs.

Her mother was no better, either. She insisted that she was descended from a noble French family, the Mortmerencys, but when I knew her she was a *glamour* model, though there wasn't much glamour about any of the magazines she appeared in. She had substance abuse issues, mental health issues, her issues had issues, quite frankly. I hope you'll forgive me for saying that it was a mercy when she decided to jump in front of a tube train when Rebecca was eight.

Of course, I did my best for the girl. She was in a council home for children who were too awful to be fostered when I took her into my home. I did *everything* for that girl. Loved her like she was my very own and I really thought that I'd lifted her up when she went to live with my beloved Aunt Jemima in Bournemouth.

Instead, she preyed on a weak, elderly lady, demanding a salary even though she was welcomed into a kind, loving home. When my aunt died, supposedly of natural causes though I have my suspicions, the girl had the audacity to suggest that Jemima had left her a bequest. Also, there were several items of jewellery, including my late mother's wedding ring, which went missing.

But once again, I felt sorry for the girl, given her tragic start in life, and when I pulled strings to get her on the reality-TV show, I really hoped it would be an opportunity for her to better herself. But when she came out of the *Big Brother* house, she spurned all my kind offers of representation, claiming that she knew best. Of course, within weeks she was down on her luck and desperate for my help again.

Now, you may ask why I sent her to

Queen's Crawley to look after five impressionable children? I acted with the best of intentions, believing that Rebecca could only benefit from being in the loving home environment of the dear Sir Pitt and Lady Crawley. I also thought the sweet souls of those five dear, innocent children would act as a balm to Rebecca's own troubled nature.

So I was very alarmed to hear that, once again, Rebecca Sharp had inveigled herself into the home and graces of another fragile old lady. Once I'd received your letter, I got in touch with the ungrateful girl, as I really didn't want to think the worst of her. I was sure that there was a simple explanation, which showed Rebecca in a better light. Also, I have considerable experience of managing such *grande dames* as Dame Matilda and I couldn't help but feel that Rebecca would benefit from my assistance. Well, I was wrong! Once again, Rebecca thinks she's an expert in things she knows absolutely nothing about, and has very rudely rejected my countless sincere overtures to help her and your dear aunt.

I even popped round to Dame Matilda's house to see Rebecca in person and she had the audacity to slam the door in my face after using such foul language that it shocked me to the core. I've come to the sad realisation that Rebecca Sharp is utterly irredeemable and I urge you to pluck out this thorn as soon as you are able, or you may live to regret it. She can't be trusted.

And though one could say that I am in some small way responsible, I can only put the blame on my soft, tender heart, which has only ever wanted to do right by the girl.

Give my regards to Bute and do remember me to Sir Pitt, handsome old rogue that he is!

All best, etc.

Barbara Pinkerton

16

As the harshness of winter softened and green buds began to appear on the trees, Dame Matilda Crawley began to fade like the crocuses that adorned the flower beds of Primrose Hill.

And as she wilted, staying in bed later and later each day, often cancelling her lunch plans, and complaining of new aches and pains, Briggs wilted with her.

Becky had no choice but to banish him from Dame Matilda's bedroom suite because he quite obviously and tearfully cracked under any kind of pressure.

'I know you think you're helping, but you're not,' she told him softly. That April morning, he'd gazed down at Matilda, propped up on her Pratesi pillow with an eye mask on because she said the light hurt her eyes, and quoted, 'I can't live if living is without you,' as if it were Shakespeare and not a soft-rock anthem by Badfinger made famous by Mariah Carey.

'I used to be a care assistant, so I'm happy to do the heavy lifting. No disrespect, Briggs, but you aren't exactly a spring chicken and I can handle the sleepless nights much better than you can. Honestly, it would be a way to repay all the kindness that Mattie has shown me.'

'You are a dear, dear girl,' Briggs said, clasping her hands. 'But nobody could be devoted to Mattie like I am. I've been her slave for the last twenty years. Her happy, happy slave.'

'And now you won't even let me die in peace,' came the wavering cry from behind the door, because although Dame Matilda was quite ill, there was nothing wrong with her hearing. 'I can't take any more fussing.'

For the next few days Briggs hung around outside his beloved Mattie's suite like a faithful, ageing dog, hounding Becky and the three doctors who attended regularly for updates. Eventually he was banished downstairs where Firkin listened impassively as he fretted and speculated on what form Dame Matilda's tragic demise would take. 'I can only hope that she goes peacefully in her sleep and that Becky lets me in her room so I can at least hold her hand while she shuffles off this mortal coil.'

Not even Briggs at his most diligent was as devoted as Becky. She cheerfully dealt with the incessant moaning of a very difficult patient. When Dame Matilda was awake, she read her choice snippets from the *Mail Online's* Sidebar of Shame and when Dame Matilda was asleep, she made sure nothing and no one disturbed her. Becky slept on the pink chaise longue, which wasn't designed to be slept on, and even Firkin was so moved by her care of Dame Matilda that, without asking or comment, she presented Becky with tiger balm-infused heat pads for her bad back.

In fact, the only time Becky could be persuaded to take a proper break from her vigil was when Rawdon Crawley popped round most evenings to check on his aunt. Rawdon, and only

Rawdon, was able to get Becky to eat something, especially if he popped into Nando's on his way to Primrose Hill for a chicken burger to go. He'd spend an hour with Becky in her room and if one were to listen closely at the door — someone like, say, Briggs — then they'd hear the low murmur of conversation.

'You don't really mean that, do you?' the eavesdropper might hear Becky say as they pressed their ear right to the door. 'I wouldn't expect you to do that.'

'That's because you have such low expectations of me,' Rawdon might reply in a voice that, helpfully, had been trained to carry. 'But I won't let you down. Not ever. I promise.'

There might be a pause, then muffled sounds, and sometimes Becky even laughed, though the poor girl had had precious little to laugh about with her dear friend and mentor so ill. So it was wonderful that by the time Rawdon left Becky's room each evening, she no longer looked pale and wraith-like from her nursing duties, but positively radiant and glowing.

'Oh . . . Rawdon offered to pick up Mattie's prescription,' Becky explained vaguely when Briggs dared to wonder what they got up to behind closed doors. 'It took a while for him to persuade me. You know how irresponsible he can be.'

'Probably wants to get his hands on her Tramadol,' Briggs said archly, expecting Becky to throw in an acid remark of her own, but instead she shot Briggs a reproachful look which made him quake in his loafers.

'Rawdon's sworn off all that. He's not even drinking, he promised me,' Becky said, and though this was surprising news to Briggs, he was beginning to realise that Becky Sharp's powers of persuasion were not to be underestimated.

And though everyone expected the worst, the worst never happened. Due to Becky's tender care and because Dame Matilda had only had a chest infection but had acted like she had pleural pneumonia, she rallied.

By the time May came into bloom along with the pink blossoms on the trees outside, there really wasn't that much wrong with Dame Matilda. She was still staying in bed until midday but that was mostly due to her own sloth rather than ill health.

'I was at death's door,' Dame Matilda insisted once she was up to receiving visitors again. 'Darling Becky pulled me back from the brink. I don't know what I'd have done without her.'

At all hours of the day, the great and good of London's thespian community came to call or sent round huge bouquets of flowers and bottles of Matilda's favourite Ruinart champagne. So, it wasn't really that much of a surprise when Sir Pitt Crawley himself turned up on the doorstep.

Although it was quite a surprise that he was in a smart suit and had even been to his barber in Jermyn Street for a shave and a haircut.

'Is Mattie expecting you?' Becky asked when Firkin silently indicated that there was someone waiting for her in the morning room, and she found Sir Pitt posing by the fireplace, hand on

175

the mantelpiece, his face in profile to show off his left, and best, side. 'I hope you haven't come to tap her for a loan and send her into a relapse?'

'My little Becky would *never* have dared to talk to her Pitt like that when she was at Queen's Crawley,' Sir Pitt noted sadly.

'Yes, but we're not at Queen's Crawley.' Becky spread her arms. 'That's why the heating's still on even though it's May and there's not a single cobweb or spider to be found.'

'So, you're not missing us then?' Pitt flung himself down on to a primrose-yellow sofa so he could put his hand to his forehead as if he were suffering some deep, existential angst. 'Because I haven't come to see Mattie. I've come to see *you*. To take you home.'

Becky pulled a face. It was either that or burst out laughing. 'Back to muddy Mudbury? No, thank you!'

'Come and sit next to Sir Pitt,' he cajoled, patting the seat next to him in an inviting manner.

'Again, no thank you.' Becky took a step back. 'Was there anything else? Because I've got things to do.'

'Where is that soft, yielding creature that I used to know? That I used to hold?'

'You mean, when you used to take advantage of me because I was entirely at your mercy in that wreck of a house in the back of beyond?' Becky asked sweetly. 'I think you'll find that was sexual harassment, actually.'

'Such harsh words for the tender moments we shared,' Sir Pitt declared in shocked tones and cast another mournful glance at Becky. Then at last he realised that he was on a hiding to nothing, and sat up straight. 'Rosa's left me. Run off with her Brazilian masseur and didn't bother taking the children with her, so you have to come back, Becky. We need you.'

Becky did burst out laughing then. 'Rosa ran off with Javier? Good on her! Though, obviously, not from your perspective,' she added as Pitt glared at her.

'Indeed,' he said. 'So you can see my predicament.'

'I can, but it's not *my* predicament. I'm not coming back to take care of your children,' Becky scoffed.

'But it'll be different! You won't have Rosa interfering and having conniptions each time they eat a chicken nugget or want to watch a cartoon.' Pitt smiled in what he thought was a winning manner. Becky wasn't entirely sure but it was almost as if he were fluttering his eyelashes at her. 'You'll have sole charge of the children.'

'That's really not the incentive that you seem to think it is. The answer's no,' Becky said firmly and with a grim finality that made Sir Pitt huff like a wolf demanding entry.

'Oh, for God's sake, Rebecca, I'll marry you then. You'd like that, wouldn't you?' he added knowingly. 'Rosa and I were never officially married, you see. Got some tinpot shaman in the Mojave Desert to do the honours, so now I can make an honest woman of my little Becky.' He stroked a hand down his chest and left it to linger suggestively at his crotch. 'Little Pitt and little Becky reunited. What fun we shall have.'

'No. No way. Not going to happen.' Becky was implacable to the demands of both Sir Pitt and Little Pitt.

He pouted. 'But I miss you. The children miss you. Even the middle one. Theodor? Thaddeus? What is the little bugger's name?'

'Thisbe, and it's still no. It's always going to be no,' Becky said.

'But I'll wash and shave every day; we can have it written into the wedding vows if you like,' Pitt offered and Becky, though she'd never, ever imagined that he'd propose to her, couldn't believe that he was being so dogged about them being joined in matrimony.

'Tempting an offer as it is, it's still no,' she said a little desperately now, because Sir Pitt just didn't seem to be getting the message and she'd just heard a noise outside the door — a little gasp, which could only be Briggs.

A coy look came over Sir Pitt's distinguished features. 'Now, I think I know what's behind all this playing hard to get, not that I don't enjoy the dance.' He was definitely fluttering his eyelashes now. 'I may have led you to believe that I was one step away from abject penury but actually, well, that's not *altogether* true. In layman's terms, I suppose I could be considered *quite* wealthy.' He smiled winningly. 'Wealthy enough to have a new central heating system installed in Queen's Crawley, if that would seal the deal.'

'Of course you're wealthy,' Becky said wearily. 'You get at least two million quid every time you pop off to Japan to shoot those coffee ads, but I still can't marry you.' For the first time, a note of real regret crept into her voice. 'I'm sorry, but I just can't.'

He was back to huffing like a wolf with a house that he had to blow down. 'Give me one good reason why not.'

Becky strained her ears. There didn't seem to be anyone still lingering outside the door but to be on the safe side, she walked over to where Sir Pitt was sitting and leaned over, a hand on either side of his head, which was the closest that he'd ever get to her breasts again. He closed his eyes in near ecstasy. 'I can't marry you,' she husked, and to Sir Pitt's horror and the audible delight of the person listening outside the door, she added, 'because I'm already married.'

17

Becky left Sir Pitt gobsmacked and stupefied on the sofa so she could waylay Briggs and prevent him from going upstairs.

'Oh my! *Quelle scandale!*' he said, his arms wrapped around his tubby body as if he couldn't quite contain himself. 'Who knew? How thrilling!'

Becky grabbed hold of his arm and frog-marched him down the hall and into the kitchen. 'Not a word of this to anyone,' she warned. 'Or you won't like the consequences.'

Briggs made a big show of rubbing his arm. 'So butch,' he complained. 'I don't know why you're being so mean to me. Though you were much meaner to Sir Pitt.'

There was no point in trying to talk any sense into Briggs, so with a firm order to get rid of Sir Pitt by any means necessary, Becky made for the stairs. She must see Dame Matilda before Briggs got there first.

Her steps were heavy as she ascended, as if she were wading through treacle in gumboots. It wasn't often that Becky felt nervous, but her mouth was dry, all the moisture in her mouth having migrated to her forehead and her upper lip, which were suddenly sweating. Not that there was anything to be nervous about. It was all going to be fine. Better than fine.

She knocked on Dame Matilda's door and

opened it to find the lady herself sitting up in bed in her favourite pale-blue satin bedjacket, with a welcoming smile on her face. Suddenly Becky wasn't nervous any more — her friendship with Matilda could survive anything.

'I hear Pitt's been sniffing about,' Mattie said brightly. 'Thank God, you managed to head him off. What did he want anyway?'

Becky took her time tidying away the pile of newspapers and magazines and a half-eaten box of Fortnum & Mason chocolates, so she could sit down on the bed. 'You're going to love this,' she said confidently. 'He . . . well, he asked me to marry him!'

'He did *what?*' Dame Matilda threw her head back and let out a peal of delighted laughter. She laughed so long and so hard that the bed shook and tears leaked from her eyes. Becky wondered if she might be having a relapse after all.

'I'm going to get you a glass of water,' she decided, but Dame Matilda's hand shot out and gripped her wrist.

'You'll do no such thing! This is the most hilarious joke I've heard in years.' And she was off again with the shaking and the tears, until finally she subsided with a couple of hiccups and patted Becky's hand instead of clutching it in a death grip. 'I hope you let the old goat down gently.'

Becky took a deep breath. 'Quite gently.' She exhaled. 'You see, I can't marry him when, well, I'm already married.'

Dame Matilda widened her eyes and silently 'oooh'ed. 'Are you? You kept that quiet, you

181

sneaky little thing. Was it some teenage act of bravado?'

'No, not really. I mean, I'm not really a teenager any more. I'm *almost* twenty-one.'

'I'm not quite sure I follow you.' Dame Matilda had become very still, like the Dowager Countess in *Lyndon Place* before she'd been killed off in her prime. 'And who exactly is the lucky man?'

Never before had Becky looked so innocent, so unworldly. 'Well, it's Rawdon, of course,' she said.

There was a moment of silence that seemed to last for an eternity yet was over far, far too soon as Dame Matilda made a strange, choked sound at the back of her throat. She spluttered for a few seconds — perhaps this time she really was having a relapse. But Becky didn't offer to fetch a glass of water, instead staring at the dame with the same calm expression on her face.

'Are you *pregnant?*' Matilda finally gasped once she'd regained the power of speech. 'Is that how you trapped him?'

Becky felt herself go clammy but forced herself to remain poised, to not give her agitation away by so much as a twitch of her fingers. 'I'm not pregnant . . .'

'Then why on earth did he marry *you*?'

'We're in love,' Becky persevered, though the word 'love' felt strange as she said it. It left a bad taste in her mouth. 'Just like you wanted.'

'*Like I wanted?*' Dame Matilda echoed incredulously. 'Why would you think this clandestine marriage is what I wanted?'

Becky patted Matilda's clawed hand just the once before the other woman yanked it away as if Becky had just given her an electric shock. Becky couldn't help but sigh. 'Mattie, I appreciate this might be a surprise, but you were the one who constantly threw Rawdon and I together, and what can I say?' She shrugged helplessly. 'Love blossomed.'

'*Love blossomed*, my arse! You didn't have to get married after knowing each other all of five minutes. I thought you'd have a fling, a brief affair, and he'd have his heart broken a little, which would be the making of him. Not this!' The dame's eyes narrowed. 'There's only one reason why you'd want to get married so young, and that's because you thought you were on to a good thing.'

'You're being very unfair, Mattie. Is it really so strange that I might want to spend the rest of my life with Rawdon, when he's funny and handsome and kind and . . . ?'

'Weak and gullible and easily led, and you, Miss Becky Sharp, amusing as you are to have about the place, are cunning, conniving and cruel. I'll concede that life has made you that way, and I pity you for that, but I know that instead of just breaking his heart a little, you'll break *him*. You won't be able to stop yourself,' Matilda said and there was real fear in her voice, in the shadowed look in her rheumy blue eyes. Foolish to be fearful, really. Becky had no intention of breaking Rawdon. He'd be no good to her if he was broken.

'I wouldn't say I was cruel. Was I cruel when I

was nursing you around the clock and waiting on you hand and foot?' Becky reminded her softly. Yes, her reasons for nursing Mattie round the clock might not have been entirely selfless, but she'd really gone above and beyond in her performance as a dutiful, caring companion. 'Really, I don't know why you can't be happy for us.'

Matilda thumped one of her Pratesi pillows. 'Because there's something rotten in the state of Denmark,' she quoted, though Becky looked at her blankly, because what had Denmark got to do with anything? She'd never got as far as Shakespeare in school. 'You're after my money. Of course you are! Why else did you conduct this so-called romance behind my back? Didn't even ask for my blessing. Oh no! You thought you'd present me with a *fait accompli* and pass it off as true love. I don't believe you love anyone but yourself!' She scooped up a handful of chocolates and threw them at Becky, who didn't flinch, didn't so much as blink, even when a violet cream bounced off nose. 'Get out and don't come back! And you can tell Rawdon that he's not getting a single penny out of me. I'm calling my solicitor today to have my will changed.'

Becky stood up far too slowly for Dame Crawley's liking. She was still outwardly placid but if Matilda hadn't turned her face away in a fit of pique, she'd have seen the positively feral glint in Becky's green eyes.

'Shall we talk about this when you've calmed down?' Becky asked in a soothing, level voice

184

that didn't waver or indicate how close she was to hitting the dame over her head with a copy of *Grazia*.

'I WILL NEVER BE CALM ABOUT THIS! GET OUT! GO ON, GET OUT!' She paused to rally her strength and Becky lingered by the door to see if, this time, please God, she really was going to relapse. A short, sharp, fatal heart attack to put them all out of her misery, but no. 'BRIGGS!'

Briggs came bustling in immediately as, of course, he'd been listening at the door. As Becky brushed past him, he was actually rubbing his thighs in glee. 'Mattie, dear,' he gasped. 'The nerve of that girl. I always thought there was something untrustworthy about her.'

'Yes! Yes!' Dame Matilda agreed, her cheeks stained a mottled purple, her voice thin and reedy. 'Something about her eyes and the set of her mouth, as if she was secretly laughing at me but I was too much of a silly old woman to see it.'

'You're not silly or old!' Briggs cried, though actually the pair of them were both of those things. 'You've gone a strange colour.'

'My pills . . . ' She clawed at her throat with a crabbed hand as Briggs froze in horror. Then the moment passed and she glared at him. 'I'm not dying, you silly bugger. I wouldn't give that girl the satisfaction.'

That girl was packing her bags. Or rather packing two vintage Louis Vuitton cases that had been shoved in the back of a cupboard, and which Dame Matilda would never miss because

185

she couldn't even remember buying them, along with the gold cigarette case, hip flask and powder compact that Becky had found in a drawer while the old lady was on her sickbed. It wasn't as if the dame had ever once offered to pay Becky for the hours and hours that she'd nursed her, so who could blame Becky for taking a few items in lieu? She also packed every last piece of clothing lent to her by her former benefactor, called an Uber to Rawdon's account and then slipped out of the front door, slamming it so hard behind her that one of the adjacent window boxes came tumbling to the ground in a mess of earth and crushed scarlet geraniums.

Upstairs, Dame Matilda heard the slam and crash and shuddered.

'Like a ghost walking over my grave,' she murmured quietly and though he'd said that he'd never trusted her (it seemed the right thing to say), Briggs was already missing Becky Sharp. He'd never been any good at dealing with the more mercurial aspects of Matilda Crawley's personality.

'Fan letters,' he said a little desperately, holding out a pile of post he'd been clutching, his excuse for lurking outside the door while the women fought. 'That will cheer you up.'

'Why would I be cheered up by the ravings of a bunch of fawning sycophants?' the dame demanded. 'They seem to think my career began and ended in that dreadful Sunday-night soap opera.'

'I'm sure they've written very lovely things about you,' Briggs persisted, wishing he had his

186

own tablets to hand. He was a slave to his beta blockers. 'And look! Here's a parcel. It's all soft and squishy. I wonder what it could be?'

'Who cares?' Dame Matilda lay sprawled on her pillows for all of five seconds, then held out her hand imperiously. 'Still, if someone's gone to all the trouble of sending me something then I suppose it wouldn't hurt to take a look.'

'Of course it wouldn't,' Briggs agreed, passing over the parcel, which was wrapped in brown paper and fastened with novelty tape adorned with little red hearts.

Inside was a misshapen, red, moulting, woollen *thing* that rendered Dame Matilda quite speechless.

'There's a card,' Briggs pointed out. 'Maybe it explains what it is. Shall I read it out?'

Dear Dame Matilda

I'm sure you don't remember me, but I'm Jane, Pitt Junior's life partner. I was at Queen's Crawley last Christmas though sadly we didn't get a chance to speak.

I heard that you weren't well so I knitted you a bedjacket. I had to guess the measurements and if it doesn't fit or you're thinking, 'Yikes, who is this scary woman and what is this scary garment she's sent me?' (I'm still struggling a bit with figuring out sleeves) then please just send it to the nearest charity shop.

Anyway, I hope you are feeling much better.

Yours truly

Jane

PS: Pitt Junior sends his love.
PPS: I thought you were awfully good in the
Lyndon Place Christmas special.

'Jane?' queried Dame Matilda in the same way
that Lady Bracknell once enquired about a
handbag. 'That lumpen creature living with Pitt
Junior?'

'Quite lumpen but quite sweet too,' Briggs
said. 'I mentioned in passing that the green
triangles were my favourite Quality Street and
she let me weed them out of the tin.'

'Jane . . . ' Dame Matilda said again. 'A very
plain girl. You know where you are with someone
who's never had to rely on their looks. And Pitt's
always been a good-natured boy. Can't write for
toffee, of course, but God loves a trier, don't he?'

'He does, he does,' Briggs came in for the
chorus though he wasn't altogether sure why
Mattie was suddenly so taken with two people
that she'd never had any interest in before.

'Yes, we'll invite them round for lunch,' the
dame decided. She shot a confused Briggs a
smile that was all teeth. 'I've always said that it's
important to have your family around you.'

18

Apart from his father, all his life Rawdon Crawley had been surrounded by people who thought he was wonderful.

As a baby, his sweet nature and cherubic good looks, as if he'd been sent from central casting rather than arriving in the usual way, had melted even his notoriously cold mother's icy heart.

It set a pattern that had continued throughout his life. His beauty and easy charm ensnared everyone who came into contact with him, from his doting elder brother, Pitt Junior, and indulgent Aunt Matilda to schoolfriends, drama coaches, casting agents and more recently, a Victoria's Secret model.

Then he'd met Becky Sharp.

'Nobody has ever been this mean to me,' he told her on their first date as they walked back to the car that Christmas Eve after he'd treated his five half-siblings to a trolley dash in a toy superstore and a McDonalds Happy Meal each.

She'd given him a sideways look. 'Well that explains a lot,' she said and Rawdon thought it was then that he fell in love with her. Of course, Becky insisted that it hadn't been a first date and rolled her eyes at every Happy Meal toy he brought her, even though it was the most thoughtful and romantic gesture that Rawdon had ever managed to come up with.

Treat 'em mean, keep 'em keen. The

engagement ring he'd put on Becky's fingers, and which she'd immediately taken off, was proof of how effective that old cliché was. Rawdon had to work like a Trojan for each smile, every vaguely kind word that Becky threw at him. When she'd first let him take her hand, it was as good as winning his first lead role. The certain liberties they'd enjoyed in her bedroom at his aunt's house — she stopped him long before either of them could reach the dizzy heights of passion — were like stepping out onstage on opening night.

And once they were married in a quick ceremony at St Pancras Town Hall ('Just nipping out to chase up one of Mattie's prescriptions,' Becky had told Briggs); with a cleaner and one of the ushers from the previous wedding as their only witnesses, the two hours they then spent in a junior suite at the Charlotte Street Hotel were better than applause. Better than a standing ovation. Better than curtain call after curtain call.

'You know you're my first,' Becky whispered as she let him peel off her clothes — the simple white dress she'd been married in, and the positively indecent black things she was wearing underneath it. 'Your father, Sir Pitt, he was absolutely desperate to go where you're about to, but I wouldn't let him. He tried, though. Had his hands all over me.' She took Rawdon's hand and placed it on her thigh. 'Here. And here. Oh yes, and here.'

Rawdon wanted to tell her that there was never a good time to talk about his father, especially not now, when she was spread naked — all pale, willowy limbs, impossibly fragile — on the bed. But when he thought about his father's grubby hands, with blackened fingernails, sliding up the soft flesh of his new bride's thigh, Rawdon had never been so hard, had never ached quite so much to be . . .

'Here. And here, but oh, definitely *not* here,' Becky purred and then she arched her back and cried out, as for the first time Rawdon wasn't following in his father's footsteps, but carving out new territory.

And later, when his manager, his agent and his best friend shouted at him for not bothering with a pre-nup, Rawdon didn't even care.

Love didn't come with contracts and clauses.

★ ★ ★

Until Rawdon Crawley, Becky had spent her life surrounded by people who treated her as a temporary hindrance.

Nobody had ever tried to win her, to woo her, to work so hard to make her smile and think about what might please her. Even those stupid McDonalds Happy Meal toys — of course, she'd much rather have had jewellery — were the romantic gesture of a man who was ready to risk rejection and ridicule if there was an outside chance that Becky might return his feelings.

Of course, there was also the small matter of her virginity. Which was a trifle. Barely important. There had never been any chance for Becky to be rid of it in Bournemouth, though

191

the good vicar would have been delighted to have done the honours. Then once she was in the *Big Brother* house, there was absolutely no way that she was going to give it up to any of those Neanderthals, and certainly not under a duvet tent and on camera too.

Once she'd left the house, her virginity was currency — about her only liquid asset. It would have been wasted on Jos Sedley. She might have surrendered it to Sir Pitt if the circumstances had been different, if he hadn't been 'married', if he'd been more generous with his baubles, but Becky was glad that it had been Rawdon.

He was pretty, he was on the way up and he'd do absolutely anything she asked of him. He'd given up all his bad habits because Becky had told him all about her parents — well, maybe not everything, but enough that she could say quite truthfully, 'So you see, Rawdy, the booze and the pills and the powders, they're a deal breaker for me. Same with the gambling. Did I ever tell you about the time that my father lost our rent money and all our other money in a poker game?'

But the best thing about Rawdon, God help him, was his kindness. He could kill a girl with kindness, so it was just as well that Becky Sharp was made of stronger stuff when she turned up on the doorstep of Rawdon's little pink mews house in Camden and told him that his doting aunt hadn't taken the news of their nuptials particularly well.

Rawdon took her in his arms and kissed away every tear that she'd managed to squeeze out during the short taxi ride over. 'It doesn't matter if Matilda cuts me out of her will,' Rawdon said without even a trace of anger. 'I have my own money.'

Rawdon did have his own money, but what Becky hadn't yet realised was that he wasn't guaranteed box office yet. He also insisted on choosing interesting roles, which stretched his talent and won him critical acclaim, but critical acclaim didn't come with a big pay cheque, and what money Rawdon had, slipped through his fingers. In the past, he'd lavished it on his friends, on partying, on gambling, but lately he'd lavished it on Becky. Furthermore, what money he did have was spare change down the back of a sofa compared to all of Matilda's millions, but he didn't seem at all worried about his aunt's fire and fury.

'She'll come round,' he told Becky as he took hold of her cases. 'Even if she doesn't, we'll be fine. I'll look after you.'

If he had a little more brain, I might make something of him, Becky thought to herself as she followed Rawdon up the stairs and into the little galleried bedroom.

Yet what Rawdon lacked, he made up for by having his own people. Who naturally became Becky's people. Agent, publicist and two whole marketing teams from the film he'd just wrapped and the film he was about to start shooting.

None of them were exactly pleased about the news that the devastatingly handsome actor that they'd positioned as a brooding and sexually potent hell-raiser was now a happily married man. But it was a done deal and as Rawdon's agent, Mike Cutt, said grimly when they all met for a council of war at the film company's offices in Greek Street, 'We'll just have to make the best of it.'

Becky gazed out of the window of the conference room, situated in a luxury office suite right in the middle of her old stomping grounds. Across the road had been the building where she'd once lived in two damp rooms with her parents on the third floor. They'd shared a bathroom with two Eastern European girls who'd worked out of the two rooms on the other side of the hall, and the men who'd come to visit them at all hours of the day and night. Just twenty metres and a whole world away from where she now sat in air-conditioned splendour . . .

' . . . And we won't announce anything to the press for now, just a few well-placed rumours to a couple of trusted sources. Then we'll go official on the red carpet at the film premiere,' said Rawdon's publicist, a gum-snapping man in dark glasses called Knuckles, who was incapable of sitting still and was nervously pacing the room. 'Gotta love a bit of synergy, right?'

'We also won't mention *Big Brother*,' Mike Cutt said firmly. 'We'll pretend that it never existed. Fake news.'

'Yeah, totally. I mean, we're living in the post-fact era. You really can fool all of the people most of the time,' one of the marketeers noted, while everyone nodded sagely. 'We'll focus on her being young, beautiful . . . ' She peered at

Becky with an assessing gaze. 'A blank slate. We can do what we want with her. A bit of modelling, a couple of brand ambassadorships, really build her up as a social influencer.'

'Don't talk about Becky like she's not even here,' Rawdon said, taking her hand, but Becky shushed him.

After all, she was a blank slate and all these people were gathered here with the sole purpose of making her somebody. Her heart pounded, in a way that no man had ever made it pound. To be lifted up, after years of having to claw her own way through . . . Besides, every hustler needed a side-hustle, especially if Mattie did make good on her promise to excommunicate Rawdon.

'And we'll have all the social media up and running before the premiere.' Knuckles came to a halt and took off his shades so Becky could see his perplexed expression. 'But I don't get it. How can you not have a social media footprint?'

'She's not even on Facebook,' Rawdon said proudly as if Becky's need not to leave a trail — another life lesson learned from her father — was just another adorable quirk of this beguiling creature that he couldn't quite believe he'd married.

But seriously, what would be the point of Becky tweeting about what she had for breakfast? Why would she want to connect with old school friends on Facebook when she'd stopped going to school by the time she was thirteen? Anyway, the fewer ties she had, the less need there was to crush any fools who had the nerve to say that they used to know her.

'Let's just do Instagram,' one of the marketing team was saying now. 'But we'll do Instagram really well.'

'We'll smash Instagram. Totally own it,' someone else said with great feeling. 'We'll create her own custom hashtag.'

'Instagram won't even know what to do with itself,' Knuckles yelped and he punched the air, and it seemed as if they were done here.

Operation Crush Instagram started a week later. Clothes were called in, hair and make-up were booked, a quirky apartment carved out of an old grain warehouse in Kings Cross was hired, and an up-and-coming fashion photographer spent two days shooting Becky for the Instagram account that she now had.

Staring adoringly at the rails and rails of clothes in a walk-in wardrobe that didn't belong to her. #LifeOfBecky #FashionInsider

Cuddling up to a pug puppy that belonged to the up-and-coming fashion photographer's assistant. #LifeofBecky #Puglife

She and Rawdon posing candidly on a battered leather chesterfield sofa, his head in her lap, her fingers in his hair. #LifeOfBecky #YoungLove #PowerCouple

Buying armfuls of flowers at Columbia Road Market. #LifeOfBecky #BloomingLovely

Shooting her own reflection in the mirror on her own newly acquired next-gen, state-of-the-art smartphone as she had her hair permanently tamed with a keratin treatment because Rawdon's team said that loose waves sent a more media-friendly message than riotous curls.

#LifeofBecky #FashionInsider #HairStory

Leaping over puddles in Regent's Park in wellies and a flouncy polka-dot dress just off the Paris runway. #LifeOf Becky #YesToTheDress #FashionInsider

And so it went on and on. As well as the Instagram takeover and a crash course in hashtags, there was media training, meet-and-greets with fashion and beauty publicists, and she and Rawdon welcoming a team from *Hello* into their 'beautiful home'. Again, the industrial-chic Kings Cross apartment Rawdon's agent had hired for the week, where they gave an exclusive about their romance, wedding and married life. The piece would run the day after they walked down the red carpet at Rawdon's premiere.

'I'm so sorry about all this,' Rawdon said on the day of the premiere, as they sat in the back of their limo in a long queue of other limos, waiting to be dropped off at the agreed spot at the bottom of the red carpet. 'All the phoney social media and publicity bullshit. I have to do it because it's good for my career but I never expected you to get dragged into it too.'

Becky was perched right at the very edge of the seat, her spine rigid, because her dress was so tight that she could really only walk in it. Luckily, they didn't even need to sit and watch the film, but could go straight to the after party. She couldn't turn her head either because it might destroy the carefully tousled red waves, which had taken hours and a vast array of products and tools to achieve. 'It's all right, Rawdy,' she said, reaching out blindly with her hand to pat where she thought his leg might be. 'This is all about you. You're the star, I'm just in a supporting role.'

'No, you're my leading lady,' Rawdon insisted and he really was very sweet.

'Everyone's here to see you,' she insisted as the car rolled slowly forwards. 'Nobody will be interested in taking my picture. Just you wait and see.'

AND THE BRIDE WORE . . . SAFETY PINS!
Rawdon Crawley shows off his beautiful young wife on the red carpet

(And his beautiful young wife shows
a whole lot of flesh!)

Hollywood heart-throb Rawdon Crawley is a hell-raiser no more. At the premiere of his new film, *Sentimental and Otherwise*, he proudly showed off his beautiful new wife, Rebecca, and his new role as devoted husband.

The son of Sir Pitt Crawley couldn't take his eyes off his glamorous bride, and who could blame him when Rebecca, 20, was flaunting her curves in a daring designer dress of slashed white lace held together with Swarovski-encrusted safety pins.

'She's absolutely gorgeous, isn't she?' Rawdon, 31, announced as he presented sexy Rebecca to his adoring fans and assembled photographers.

Not much is known about the woman who stole Rawdon's heart, but his publicist, Rory 'Knuckles' McGee, said that Rebecca was a family friend and that love bloomed for the glamorous couple after they spent Christmas together. 'They had a very quiet, very private wedding ceremony, which was all about their love for each other rather than turning such a special occasion into a media circus.'

It's not known if Rawdon's famous father, Sir Pitt, attended and his equally famous aunt, Dame Matilda Crawley, recently killed off in *Lyndon Place*, has been recovering from a bout of ill health. But McGee insisted that the Crawley family is delighted that Rawdon is putting his bad-boy ways behind him, 'and it's all down to the love of a good woman.'

It's certainly proving to be quite the year for Rawdon who's shooting back-to-back films in London. First up is a murder mystery, *Who Played on the Piano?*, then a WW2 spy drama, *The Girl I Left Behind Me*, which is good news for his blushing bride.

'We can't bear to be parted,' revealed radiant Rebecca, whose stunning slender legs were showcased in a pair of Christian Louboutin shoes also decorated with Swarovski crystals. 'We're still very much in the honeymoon phase.'

The lovebirds haven't yet had an official honeymoon but handsome Rawdon and Rebecca, whose Instagram profile describes her as an 'influencer and fashion insider', couldn't keep their hands off each other, even on the red carpet!

19

One fat tear landed on the picture of Becky and Rawdon, hand in hand on the red carpet. Then another tear dropped right in the centre of Becky's face. And another. And another.

Amelia Sedley tried to tell herself that they were happy tears. She was so pleased for Becky. Of course she was! In fact, when she'd seen Becky and Rawdon Crawley together in February, which was only four months ago but now seemed like several centuries, Amelia was sure that there was something going on between them.

It wasn't anything that Becky had said or done, although Becky had never smiled at Jos the way that she smiled at Rawdon. No, it had been the way that Rawdon had looked at Becky. As if she was his reason for living. Even when George had been unkind about Becky, Rawdon had stood his ground, and Amelia had been very cross with George afterwards.

Just thinking about that night brought a fresh flood of tears so that the picture of Becky and Rawdon was now completely saturated. Not only had George never once looked at Amelia the way that Rawdon gazed so adoringly at Becky, but Amelia had barely seen George since that February evening.

She'd tried not to be a nuisance because she knew he was very busy with his work, his very important work, and also the upcoming by-election, so she'd rationed the number of text messages she'd sent him. The same with emails, not even forwarding him funny cartoons or quotes that he might find inspiring. But still, he'd sent her quite a terse email the night before:

Sorry Emmy. With everything that's going on at the moment, probably better if we maintain radio silence. Sure you understand. Best. George.

And she did understand, because Becky and Rawdon weren't the only familiar faces in the papers that morning. With a shaking hand, Amelia steeled herself to turn the soggy page, and there was a man she knew only too well: her father. Although now it seemed like she hardly knew him at all. He'd been so distant lately. Off-hand. On a few occasions, he'd even snapped at her, but Mummy had said that she wasn't to worry and that was just the way that men were sometimes. But now it was very clear that there was a lot to worry about it. And also, why Daddy had been so determined that Amelia should stick to a monthly budget and become financially mature.

Amelia turned her attention back to the damp newspaper in front of her though it was hard to read when her vision was so blurred with tears.

SHARES IN FREEFALL AFTER SUCCESSFUL INVESTMENT BANK ASKS FOR BAILOUT

The City suffered huge losses yesterday afternoon after the collapse of private bank

Sedleys and its successful hedge fund.

Founder and chairman Charles Sedley resigned last night from the board after a series of investments, which he personally oversaw, failed to show a profit. It's feared that some leading high-street chains, several pension funds and a raft of personal, blue-chip clients are set to lose billions of pounds.

Now the Fraud Squad have been called in while the Bank of England have said that Sedley's shouldn't expect a bailout, even though thousands of workers who had their pensions invested in Sedley's funds look set to lose their retirement incomes.

Charles Sedley was unavailable for comment, though friends say that he is devastated. A classic rags-to-riches story, Sedley, 63, left school at 16 and worked his way up from the trading floor to running his own funds, then founded his own bank in 2005. He weathered the global crash of 2008 and earned a reputation for being a cautious but shrewd player. A popular City figure, he and his wife Caroline sit on the board of several charities and own a house in Kensington, said to be worth £15 million, a house in Oxfordshire, and several other properties around the world.

His son, Joseph, 33, lives in LA, where he operates a successful health-food and lifestyle company, while his daughter, Amelia, 22, is in her final year of an Art History degree at Durham University. She also took part in the reality-TV show, *Big Brother*, last year, which she won. She's rumoured to be dating George Wylie, who's currently standing for the safe Conservative seat of Squashmore in Cheshire.

Whether Charles Sedley will face criminal charges isn't yet clear.

Authorities have directed anyone with funds invested with Sedley to contact their financial advisor.

It was hard not to unleash a huge volley of sobs but Amelia vowed to be strong and just cry *silently*. When Daddy had come home the night before and told them the news, Mummy had clutched a hand to her heart and then collapsed. They'd had to call a doctor, who'd sedated her, so now Mummy was dead to the world and Daddy was closeted in his study with his lawyers, and there were journalists and photographers, and even TV crews, outside.

Obviously, it was all a terrible mistake. Amelia wasn't sure how these things worked, not really. But maybe if the pound suddenly rallied, then Daddy's funds would pick up, and all the people who'd invested in them would get their money back?

It could happen, couldn't it?

If it didn't, Daddy had said that they were ruined. They'd have to sell everything.

'Everything,' he'd kept saying the night before. The yacht. ('I should never have let your mother talk me into that one.') All the art. ('Never liked it anyway.') The wine. ('Must be worth a few million at least and it all tasted like cat's piss to me.') The horses . . .

'Not Pianoforte!' Amelia had gasped because Pianoforte might have cost a hundred and fifty thousand pounds, but he wasn't an asset. He was a pet. Her beloved childhood friend.

'You haven't ridden him in months and meanwhile I'm getting clobbered for stabling fees and God knows what else. And I don't know how I'm going to break it to your mother, but all her jewellery has to go too.'

It was terrible. Everything that Amelia knew, everything that she'd believed in, all ripped out from under her.

But the very worst thing of all was that George hadn't even texted her to see if she was all right — just sent that rather cold email . . .

★ ★ ★

'This is bad news. Very bad news. I've a good mind to call up the editor of the *Globe* and have him print a retraction. We were at Eton together, it's the least he could do,' Sir John Wylie thundered. 'Our George was *never* rumoured to be dating *that* Sedley girl. Just happened to be at school with her brother, though everyone knows that the Sedleys bought their way in everywhere. What do I say, eh? Never can trust trade.'

'Father, you're not helping,' George said, pinching the bridge of his nose between thumb and forefinger. His father was always delighted to find someone whose money was newer than his own and now George prayed the baronet wasn't

205

going to launch into his usual rant about arrivistes. Something about how most of them were foreigners who didn't wash their hands after they'd been to the bathroom.

'That's what they call it! A bathroom! A bathroom is where you bathe. A loo is where you piss . . . '

George, Dobbin and George's campaign manager, Michael O'Dowd, a smooth, slicked-back veteran of many other political campaigns, all shared an exasperated look.

'He'll be wittering on about foreigners for hours now,' George noted quietly. 'In fact, we could all leave the room and he wouldn't even notice.'

'Can't leave until we've come up with a plan of action,' O'Dowd said, holding up a copy of the *Daily Mail*. 'Your father does have a point. Not about the foreigners — I love a foreigner if they're here legally and pay their taxes — but about the Sedley girl.'

'Her name's Amelia,' Dobbin said sharply. 'Emmy. Have you called her?' he asked George.

'Of course I haven't. Don't be silly!' With an effort, George dialled down the impatient look on his face for something more benign, more voter-friendly, some people might even say more statesman-like. 'I feel for Emmy, of course I do.' His hand settled on the breast pocket of his navy-blue pinstripe suit. 'My heart goes out to her, but you have to see how it would look, Dobbin, if I was to . . . to . . . extend the hand of friendship to her, *now*.'

'You're already friends with her,' Dobbin

206

pointed out coolly, though his always prominent ears were such a deep shade of red that they looked painful. 'And you know the poor girl thinks — hopes — that you're more than friends. You said yourself that you were planning on marrying her.'

'WHAT?'

'What?'

'What?'

Dobbin's assertion, which he'd heard from George's own mouth, was met with apoplectic rage from the Baronet, disbelief from O'Dowd and blank denial from George himself.

'I don't think so,' George insisted. 'I may have, at one time, posited the theory that Emm — Amelia Sedley might at some point in the future make a good politician's wife and you must have misunderstood my intentions.'

'I misunderstood nothing,' Dobbin pointed out, but George just smiled blandly at his old friend. He'd been practising a bland smile in front of the mirror for weeks now, all ready for when he had his official picture taken as the new Conservative MP for Squashmore.

'You marry that chit and I'll cut you off faster than you can blink, my boy!' shouted the Baronet. If they'd been at the country estate and in his study, where he preferred to issue bollockings to his nearest and dearest, this would have been the point where he yanked an antique blunderbuss out of his desk drawer and brandished it at the source of his wrath. Alas, they were in a small airless room at Conservative Central Office so he had to make do with brandishing a water bottle, which didn't really have the same effect. 'Cut you off without a penny. See how far you get then, eh? Eh?'

'George, *George*,' O'Dowd remonstrated, though George didn't need to be remonstrated with. They were all singing from the same hymn sheet, as far as he was concerned. Running the same idea up the same flagpole. Looking at the same blips on the radar screen. But now O'Dowd had an avuncular arm around George's shoulders. 'You have to call things off with this Amelia chick. Those poor blighters who have lost their pensions . . . '

'It's terrible,' George said and Dobbin shot him a surprised but pleased look. 'My heart goes out to them too.'

'And you know what else those poor blighters are? They're going to be in all the papers with sad faces going, 'Boo hoo, that nasty, greedy banker, Charles Sedley, has taken away the pensions we've worked all our lives for.'' O'Dowd was getting so worked up about the plight of the common man that he was spraying George and Dobbin with a fine mist of spittle. 'Not exactly a confidence booster for the electorate if they think your father-in-law is going to diddle them out of their pensions.'

'But he's not my father-in-law,' George said through clenched teeth, ignoring the fact that the man who wasn't his father-in-law had still contributed generously to his campaign funds. 'Amelia and I aren't even engaged. We've never even been out on a date. I haven't so much as held her hand in public.'

Dobbin's ears were now a shade of red not even found in the Pantone book. George ignored Dobbin's look of disappointment, because he'd seen it so many times before that he was inured to it.

'Right, so we'll just issue a statement saying that the Sedleys are distant acquaintances, nothing more, and that if you get elected, you'll be keen to work with the appropriate agencies to see if there's anything to be done about reuniting those poor buggers with their pensions.' O'Dowd had already picked up his iPad to draft said statement.

'Perfect,' George murmured, adjusting his tie. 'Now that we've sorted that out, I must get back to my constituency. I mean, my *prospective* constituency.' He grimaced. Didn't want to tempt fate and all that. Squashmore was a former rotten borough, which had elected a Conservative MP for the three hundred and forty-seven years that it had existed, though God knows, it was a horrid little place. 'I'm sure there are some babies I haven't yet kissed.' He picked up some of the day's newspapers, which were heaped on the table. 'I'll take these for the journey up. You coming, Dobster?'

But once they were settled in a first-class carriage, Dobbin still fulminating, George wasn't at all concerned with the news about Sedleys or the fall-out for his prospective constituents. Not when Becky Sharp was on the front pages of all the tabs in a dress slashed to here and hiked to *there*.

And married to Rawdon Crawley, of all

people. George had known Rawdon since Eton and he'd hardly been at the front of the queue when they were handing out brains. On the contrary, he'd been languishing somewhere at the back.

'Look who scrubbed up all right in the end. Scrubber being the operative word,' he said, holding up *The Sun* so Dobbin could also get an eyeful of the Sharp girl. But Dobbin was still in a sulk with him and merely grunted.

It was funny, George reflected, as he stared at the faint outline of Becky Sharp's nipples, barely hidden by white lace, that he'd never really appreciated just how pretty she was. He'd been more interested in putting her in her place.

He still wouldn't mind taking her down a peg or two. And then, after checking that Dobbin was staring fixedly out of the window at the countryside rolling by, George discreetly adjusted his crotch.

* * *

'This is a very good shot of you, Rawdy,' Becky cooed, holding up *The Sun* for her husband's inspection. 'I look a fright. Who even knew that my dress was *that* see-through? But you look very handsome.'

'Not sure I like the world being able to see my girl's breasts,' Rawdon said, leaning over to nuzzle one of the items in question, Becky absent-mindedly petting his head as he did so.

The film company had put them up in quite a nice suite at the Ham Yard Hotel, though it was only a junior suite, which was now cluttered with the bouquets of flowers and presents that had been arriving all morning. Most of them for Becky, because what was it that the *Daily Mail* had said about her?

Oh yes, that was right.

'The beautiful Becky Crawley is the newest, hottest It Girl In Town.'

They hadn't even mentioned poor Rawdy's little movie.

To be supportive, Becky would hunt through the papers until she found someone saying something lovely about Rawdy's performance. But she'd do it in a minute because she was exhausted and . . .

'You know the Sedleys, right?' Rawdon suddenly asked. 'I was at Eton with Jos and we met his sister at that premiere we went to with Mattie.' He sighed, his breath ghosting Becky's breast, at the thought of his currently estranged aunt.

'She'll come round,' Becky said, as she always did. 'Nobody can resist you for long, Rawdy.' He was looking pained now, brow furrowed, bottom lip jutting out in a sad little pout, but one of the good things about Rawdon was that he was easily distracted. Though it seemed that, for once, her breasts weren't up to the job. 'What was that you were saying about the Sedleys?' Becky asked, though she didn't much care.

Rawdon waved one of the newspapers at her. 'Looks like they're having a really bad day. The worst day ever.'

211

'Not like us,' Becky said with some satisfaction, as she took the paper from Rawdon and pushed his head off her lap so she could smooth out the page. As she caught the headline, then looked down at the photo of a haunted, haggard Mr Sedley in a crumpled grey suit emerging from the offices of Sedley's Bank, her eyes widened.

'Looks like they've lost everything,' Rawdon said. 'Jos was a year above me and he was fat and awkward so we didn't hang out much, but Amelia seemed sweet when we met her.'

'Hmmm,' Becky murmured as if Amelia's sweetness was vastly over-estimated. She tapped a finger over the headline: GREEDY BANKING BOSS FLEECES HONEST WORKERS OUT OF THEIR PENSIONS. 'I always thought there was something dodgy about her father, so this serves them right for being mean to me.'

'They were mean to you?' Rawdon asked in surprise.

'Yes.' Becky put so much venom into that three-letter, one-syllable word that Rawdon made a mental note to never incur the wrath of his newly minted bride. And that was even without knowing the circumstances. How Jos Sedley had led her on, then dumped her. Worse! Dumped her via George Wylie and a text message to his sister. Then Amelia had made it all about her even as Babs Pinkerton had been summoned to remove Becky from the premises like she was a wilful puppy who kept soiling Mrs Sedley's newly renovated floors. 'Anyway, they'll be fine. Their sort always is. Bet they have millions all squirrelled away in secret offshore funds. He won't even go to prison.'

She sighed. It was the way of the world. The likes of Mr Sedley would walk free with just a slap on his wrist and maybe not so many invites to gala dinners. Whereas the likes of Mr Sharp, who had only ever taken money from other crooks or companies that had insurance against break-ins anyway, had been sent down.

'Still, it's not your friend Amelia's fault,' Rawdon suggested softly as there was a strange, hard look in Becky's eyes that he'd never seen before. Then she blinked, smiled and she was back to being the girl he'd married, the woman he didn't think he'd ever get enough of.

'You're right. It's not poor Emmy's fault.' Becky leaned over to grab her phone from the nightstand. 'I should probably text her to make sure that she's OK. See if there's anything I can do to help.'

And while Rawdon gazed at her tenderly, approvingly, Becky fired off a quick text to her former BFF:

Oh, Emmy! Just seen news. Cant believe ur pa would do such a thing. All those poor people. Anyway hope ur ok. Let me know if u need anything. Though v.busy at the moment. Ur dad not the only one in the papers! Luv u. Becky xxx

20

The treachery of Rawdon, her darling boy, marrying that scheming little trollop Becky Sharp, had sent Dame Matilda Crawley into a worrying decline.

She took to her bed, complaining of aches in her arms, pains in her legs, and a vicious fluttering in her heart that had poor Briggs into conniptions and Dame Crawley's three doctors into confusion.

'Her heart sounds fine,' her cardiac consultant reported to her GP. 'Though she says she's far too ill to leave her bed to have an MRI.'

'She's not running a temperature, though her blood pressure is a little on the low side, but that's only to be expected when she refuses to get out of bed,' her GP reported to her oncologist, who had seen the dame before her recent relapse and had been pleased to inform her that all her scans and tests had come back clear.

'Normally I wouldn't condone this kind of treatment, but I'm sure Dame Crawley will feel much better once she's out and about and able to take her 3 p.m. glass of champagne,' her oncologist said drily to the two other specialists, who both agreed with him.

Maybe once Matilda Crawley had processed the news, felt a softening in her temperamental heart and returned one of Rawdon's calls, then she would begin to rally. But before that could happen, Martha Crawley arrived in Primrose Hill with two suitcases and a pugnacious, determined look on her pinched face, which brooked no denial.

When Briggs tried to bodily prevent her from gaining access to his mistress's suite, Martha swept him out of the way as if he was a mere slip of a thing and not a portly fifty-something.

'Not now, Briggs,' she snapped. 'I'm here on a mission of mercy.'

Then Martha flung open Mattie's bedroom door and though her cardiac consultant had sworn there was nothing wrong with her heart, Dame Matilda very nearly did have a cardiac incident at the sight of her sister-in-law standing there.

'I'm not to be disturbed,' she said querulously but Martha was already stalking towards her, her body quivering in anticipation, from her clod-hopping size-eight feet, to her huge buttress-like bosom, to the tip of her pointy nose. And in her hand, she clutched the fateful, spiteful letter from Barbara Pinkerton.

'Oh, dear Mattie!' she cried. 'I come to you in your hour of need. I can't even imagine how you must feel at Rawdon's betrayal after *everything* that you've done for him. And as for that Becky Sharp! Well, no one can blame you for being taken in by that . . . I hate to be uncharitable, you know me, I don't have a bad bone in my body, but I'm *amazed* that she's married to Rawdon rather than serving time in Holloway. After all, her father was a hardened criminal. Look!'

215

She thrust the letter at the dame, who'd insisted on having the curtains drawn ('The light hurts my poor eyes') to shut out the brilliant July sunshine trying to stream in through the windows. But now she clicked her fingers at Martha.

'Can't see a bloody thing. Open the drapes and fetch me my reading glasses.'

Then she pored over the letter while Martha stood over her, hands clasped in glee, as the dame read out choice snippets.

'*She preyed on a weak, elderly lady! . . . Several items of jewellery, including my late mother's wedding ring, which went missing . . . I urge you to pluck out this thorn as soon as you are able, or you may live to regret it.*'

When she was done, Dame Matilda collapsed back on her Pratesi pillows, the letter fluttering to the ground as she clasped a hand to her heart, which was beating out quite a steady rhythm, all things considered.

'Oh my,' the much-celebrated actress whimpered. 'It's a wonder Becky Sharp didn't murder us all in our beds.' She tried to lift herself up then fell back with a weak cry. 'I'm sure I can't have a single piece of jewellery left. That creature will have stolen it all and hocked it to one of her lowlife associates. Oh, Rawdon! My boy! My foolish boy! What have you done?'

Then she fell to one side as Martha gasped in genuine alarm. It was a bravura performance, especially as later on Briggs couldn't find a single valuable missing, despite checking three times over. (Fortunately for Becky, Matilda had completely forgotten about the gold set of hip flask, cigarette lighter and compact, which, to her credit, Becky hadn't hocked to one of her lowlife associates but had hidden in a compartment of one of the Louis Vuitton suitcases, which Matilda had also forgotten about.)

Still, there wasn't much time for Matilda to dwell on such matters. Instead of railing against Becky (though she could hardly bring herself to utter that creature's name), she now had a more immediate figure to despise: Martha Crawley.

The woman had taken advantage of Matilda's frailty and Briggs's ineffectualness to move herself into the guest suite (recently vacated by Becky) but spent most of her time installed in the dame's bedroom.

Matilda didn't have a moment's peace. Considering her precarious state of health (how she regretted complaining about her ailments; now she wished that she'd been a silent martyr), it seemed as if her sister-in-law was determined to cosset her into an early grave.

Despite the heat of the London summer, the curtains and windows were firmly closed and Martha would have no truck with turning on the air conditioning. 'Full of toxins,' she insisted on the one occasion when Matilda was able to get out of bed undetected and turn it on herself.

She couldn't read or watch television or even sleep because Martha was a constant presence at her bedside, trying to stuff foul-tasting juices and mysterious pills down her gullet. Not that her doctors were allowed admittance either. 'The only reason they want to see you is so they can take your temperature and charge you a small fortune for the privilege. No, Mattie dear, what you need is tender loving care from your own flesh and blood. Well, flesh and blood by marriage, but you know what I mean.'

Normally Matilda loved someone who'd indulge her forays into ill health (Briggs was particularly obliging and always happy to work The Netflix Thing so Matilda could watch the show with the drag queens, or pop to the patisserie on Regents Park Road to buy a box of cakes to tempt her appetite) but Martha treated her like such an infirm invalid that Matilda feared that her limbs would actually start atrophying.

'No, Mattie dear, you're not to get out of bed. I'll get the bedpan I ordered from Amazon Prime and then I'll give you a blanket bath,' she'd insist with a determined look on her face. 'And I'll just take your phone away because we don't want you being bothered about anything except getting better. If there's someone that you need to talk to, you can tell me and I'll decide if they're likely to upset you.'

Then there was the talking. The woman did — not — stop — talking. If she wasn't trying to convince Matilda that Mr Death was all but hammering at the door, she was constantly carping on about Becky Sharp and how Rawdon had never had a lick of common sense anyway. That's when she wasn't promoting wretched Bute (who was currently as happy as a pig in muck that his domineering domina was staying indefinitely with his sister) and her own agenda.

218

'You know me, Mattie dear, I'm not one to cast aspersions, but Bute and I have enjoyed a very different standard of living to you and Sir Pitt. I say enjoyed, but what I really mean is endured. Bute has just as much acting talent as the rest of the family, though he's been cruelly overlooked by the industry, not that I begrudge you your success and what with Sir Pitt being the eldest, of course he was going to inherit Queen's Crawley, but you have to admit that Bute has rather drawn the short straw. It would be very easy for him to become bitter, but he's not like that, Mattie dear, as you know. He's always been your biggest fan, your greatest champion . . . '

If Matilda had been willing, or subsequently allowed, to leave her bed to have an MRI scan, it would have been discovered that she had developed a slight heart murmur, and that her weakened state after Rawdon's sudden marriage wasn't just a case of theatrics. But there was nothing like a heady dose of hatred to strengthen both resolve and a dodgy ticker, and the longer Martha stayed, the more Matilda hated her and the more she rallied. Compared to Martha Crawley, Becky Sharp was practically Mother Teresa . . .

★ ★ ★

Martha Crawley's hostile takeover lasted nearly a month, but even Martha had to nap occasionally. And so came that fateful afternoon in early August when the interfering busybody woke to

219

find that her place in Matilda's bedroom had been usurped.

As Martha ambled down the corridor to dear aunt Mattie's room, her thoughts resting happily on the tea and cake that she'd order Firkin to bring up, she heard a bright, perky voice say, 'Oh my goodness, you need some fresh air in here!'

A hand to her heart, Martha rushed down the hall to find a cuckoo in her nest! Or rather young Pitt's dreary girlfriend, Jane, flinging open curtains and windows. 'I got you some of those yogurts from M&S that you like, Mattie, and a thriller that all of my book group loved.'

'What is the meaning of this?' Martha demanded from the doorway, her body shaking with fury.

'Hello, Martha,' Jane said with some surprise. 'Are you joining Mattie and I?'

'Joining you?' Martha echoed, looking around the room for her patient but Dame Matilda was nowhere to be seen.

'For our girly date,' Jane explained with a kind smile that Martha wanted to rip off her face. 'Once a month we meet up for high tea, though it usually ends up involving champagne rather than a pot of Lapsang Souchong.' She giggled, guiltily.

'But Dame Matilda isn't well enough to go anywhere, let alone drink champagne,' Martha declared, looking about the room in case Dame Matilda was hiding under her dressing table. 'You're not welcome here, Jane. Dame Matilda needs me — '

'No, I don't,' said a cutting voice from the

doorway. Dame Crawley was standing upright, fully dressed, with a sweating Briggs cringing behind her. 'And if you're not gone in ten minutes then I'm calling the police and having you arrested for a false imprisonment.'

'Oh dear,' Jane murmured with an anxious glance at the tableau before her. 'I think I'll just pop downstairs and put the yogurts in the fridge.'

She darted out of the room, and Martha clasped a hand to her quivering bosoms.

'Mattie dear, what are you saying? You're not well, my love. Why are you up? Why are you wearing clothes? Should we get you assessed for Alzheimer's, because . . . OH!' Martha ended on an alarmed squeak as Firkin had appeared in that silent way of hers and suddenly had Martha's wrist in an uncompromising grip.

'Time for you to leave,' she hissed, applying pressure to Martha's arm.

'Don't you 'Mattie dear' me any more! There's nothing wrong with my mind and I'm wearing clothes because I'm going out with darling Jane. A little afternoon tea, though actually I could murder a glass of champagne,' Matilda said, as if a little afternoon tea was no big deal after being bedridden for weeks.

'A glass of champagne will do you the world of good,' Briggs ventured, still sweating like a furnace stoker in a heatwave. He hated confrontations.

'Yes, I think so too,' Matilda agreed crisply. 'Some fresh air, convivial company, a little Louis Roederor and then once we've said goodbye to darling Jane, Briggs and I are off to a screening at BAFTA.'

'But Mattie dear, this woman is manhandling me!' Martha tried to shake Firkin off, but the diminutive yet deceptively strong housekeeper refused to relinquish her grip.

Dame Crawley and Briggs exchanged a surprised look. 'Do you see anyone being manhandled, Briggs?'

Briggs licked his top lip nervously. 'I d-d-don't.'

'Neither do I.' Matilda turned away from the scene of the alleged crime. 'Now, do come on, Briggs, dear, the car is waiting and Firkin, do make sure that our uninvited guest leaves with all her belongings.' Then the dame swept away, only to reappear a second later. 'And none of *my* belongings, because I'm still convinced Becky Sharp didn't leave empty-handed.'

⋆ ⋆ ⋆

Dame Matilda clung on to Briggs as she climbed out of the car at the foot of the red carpet. Her legs were a little wobbly — no wonder, when she'd been forcibly detained in her own bed for so long. But the show must go on and her mind was once again on Becky Sharp, though she swore that she'd never say that name out loud again.

Whatever her faults or her intentions, that girl had nursed her through a nasty chest infection and even when Matilda had been feeling rotten, Becky had always been able to make her smile by impersonating Briggs at his shrillest or providing a very bitchy and entertaining commentary about what people were wearing in the *Heat* magazine.

Then as Dame Matilda and Briggs turned a corner so they were within sight of the entrance, there she was.

Becky Sharp.

That girl and Rawdon were facing a big bank of photographers and while Rawdon stood there with his trademark scowl and slouch, she was posing like a pro. Shifting her position slightly every few seconds, tilting her head first this way, then that, but always, always leaning into Rawdon, so he was eclipsed by his wife who was dressed all in white again and positively oozing that indefinable something that people called star quality.

'Well, the nerve of her!' Briggs breathed. 'That is some grade-A limelight-hogging.'

'The very nerve,' Matilda echoed and her murmuring heart hardened. In a moment of weakness, she might have missed the girl, but Rebecca Sharp (she would *never* be a Crawley) cared only for herself and Mattie would never forgive herself for being taken in by the little baggage. Never forgive Rawdon, either, for thinking with his privates rather than his head. For being just like his father.

'Dame Matilda! Over here!'

'You feeling better, Dame Crawley?'

The photographers had, *finally*, noticed Dame Matilda Crawley because so-called star quality was no match for a career that had spanned over

223

fifty years, thank you very much.

A couple of black-clad wranglers began to usher Dame Matilda forward so she could take her turn on the red carpet, and Becky was still smiling that simpering smile and Rawdon had turned to see his aunt approaching.

He took off his shades and smiled, oh, that heartbreaking, crooked smile of his, but then he and that girl were already being led away.

Matilda liked to think that she was graceful and yet stately, as befitted the greatest actress of her generation, as she posed for the cameras.

'Dame Matilda, can we get a group shot with Rawdon and Becky?' called out one of the photographers and the others took up the cry so that Becky and Rawdon, who were waiting at the entrance, were called back by one of the wranglers.

'Mattie,' she saw Rawdon shape the word, because she couldn't hear him over the roar of the crowd. Then that creature came trailing after him with a hopeful smile on her face, which Matilda wasn't buying.

'Lovely jubbly, let's have one all together for the family album,' shouted out the nice photographer from the *Daily Mirror*, who Matilda used to have a lot of time for as she'd known him since he was a bumbling seventeen-year-old assistant. Now, she could quite happily have killed him.

'Mattie,' Rawdon said again as he reached her side and then that girl was there, in front of her.

'It's *so* lovely to see you, Matilda,' she breathed. 'I've missed you and I feel *wretched*

about the argument we had. This unpleasantness, it's so *silly*. Can't we be friends again?'

'Come on. All together!'

'Can you give the dame a kiss? One on each
cheek.'

'Come on, Rawdy, it would be wonderful to
have a picture of the three of us together again.'
Becky moved to stand on the other side of the
dame, and as she passed in front of her, she gave
Mattie just a hint of a twinkle, a look that said,
'What *larks!*'

'Well, Rebecca, it isn't at all lovely to See you.
In fact, it's quite a nasty shock,' Matilda said
coldly, even inch the *grande dame*, though that
twinkle gave her such a pang of loss over the fun
they'd once shared. But had it really been fun or
had it actually been a girl on the make,
humouring a silly old woman? Besides, it had
never really been the three of them; it had been
Rebecca reeling Rawdon in, and Matilda had
just been the means to that end. What a fool
she'd been!

The dame took a step back from the pair of
them. Oh, she couldn't even *bear* to look at
Rawdon, so crushing was her disappointment,
her worry, at his choice of a first wife. Becky
Sharp was far too clever for her own good and
far, far too clever for poor Rawdon. Matilda took
another step. Then another.

Despite her wobbly legs and aching back, with
head held high, she cut them dead on the red
carpet in front of the entire press corps.

'I think she just broke my heart,' Rawdon
muttered, his shoulders slumping. 'She's never

going to come round, is she?'

'She will. It's only been a few weeks. For God's sake, *smile*,' Becky hissed, because *that* woman might just have humiliated them in front of photographers from every major British news outlet, but Becky was damned if they were going to catch her looking sad about it. 'Even I know that you should show a united front in public, and I was raised by wolves.'

But as she and Rawdon slowly sauntered back up the red carpet towards the entrance of the restaurant where the reception was taking place, Becky felt as if her heart was breaking too.

When she was on top form, even with a chest infection, Mattie had been wicked fun. It was so rare for Becky to ever find someone she could be wicked with and she . . . well, it was possible that she missed the demanding old witch. But that wasn't the only reason why Becky's heart was in a sorry state. If Matilda was going to cut Rawdon off from all her millions, then Becky was going to have to rely solely on Rawdon's acting ability to keep her in a style that she could only dream of.

And based on tonight's performance, his acting abilities needed a huge amount of work.

21

It seemed to Amelia that it took no time at all her for entire life to be dismantled.

All their property was sold, for a lot less than market value, according to Mummy, with the house in Kensington the last asset to go. Two quite terrifying men from the Official Receiver's office, not much older than Amelia, had supervised as the Sedleys had chosen what they wanted to keep from a meagre selection of their former possessions before everything else was sold at auction. The paintings, the jewellery, the beautiful hand-painted bedroom set Amelia had been given for her fifteenth birthday, which had always made her feel like a princess. Even Pianoforte had been put up for sale.

It was ghastly.

The papers had gleefully picked over all their things and though Amelia had kept away from the auction — everyone from the lawyers to dear old Dobbin had said that it was pointless to put herself through such a horrid ordeal — Mrs Blenkinsop had gone and had come back practically bursting with news and a face full of smiles. Which was odd because Mrs Blenkinsop had been quite bitter ever since Daddy had had to let her go. She'd also been furious when the forensic accountants had queried why a monthly Ocado delivery was being made to an address in Leytonstone where Mrs Blenkinsop's sister lived.

'The Royal Doulton dinner service went to a cruel-looking lottery winner. He's been in all the papers,' she reported when Amelia met her for coffee in a Starbucks around the corner from the auction house. 'He also bought all your mother's furs.'

'The good thing is that no one really needs to wear fur,' Amelia pointed out because she was trying so hard to find some good in this far-from-good, left-good-several-months-ago-with-no-hope-of-returning situation. 'What with global warming.' She peered at Mrs Blenkinsop. 'You know, those look a lot like the earrings Daddy got Mummy for her fortieth birthday.'

'Do they?' Mrs Blenkinsop touched the three strings of what looked like diamonds dangling from her left ear. 'They're from Elizabeth Duke at Argos. I couldn't afford your mother's jewellery. Despite what the accountant said. Implying that I'd been skimming off the housekeeping for years. The cheek!'

'Of course, of course,' Amelia said quickly, because it was so nice to have someone to sit and drink coffee with, even if it were Mrs Blenkinsop. All her other friends had dropped her like she was made of radioactive waste. Some of her former *Big Brother* housemates had given interviews to the papers where they'd said some very unkind, very untrue things about her and when Amelia had tried to defend herself on Twitter, it had all got rather ugly. Then it had transpired that Durham University had some of its pension fund invested with Sedley's Bank, so it was suggested in the strongest possible terms that she didn't return, even though she was due to sit her finals in a few weeks.

And George? Amelia hadn't seen hide nor hair of him, though it wasn't his fault. Campaigning to become an MP must have taken up an awful lot of his time and Dobbin had come round and said that he was there on George's behalf.

'He wants to see you, Emmy,' he'd explained, sitting on one of the uncomfortable hardback chairs, which were one of the few things they'd been allowed to keep, his long legs tucked awkwardly beneath him. 'But it's a very delicate time for George. What with the by-election looming.'

'Oh, I absolutely understand,' Amelia had said, because she did. Sort of. Although she personally hadn't made any bad investments and it wasn't as if Daddy had made the bad investments on purpose.

'I knew you would because you have such a kind, sweet heart,' Dobbin had said and his ears had turned as red as Amelia's cheeks (it was rather nice to know someone who had the same maddening, reddening complexion). 'Anyway, George would want you to know that you're constantly in his thoughts but he can't do anything, can't be seen to, er, have associations with . . . with . . . '

'Me and my family,' Amelia supplied sadly. 'Because people are very, very angry about that nasty business with the pensions, and some of those people live in the constituency where George is hoping to become MP.'

'Well, that's about the long and the short of it.'

Dobbin had gulped nervously, grateful that Amelia had voiced the words that he couldn't quite spit out himself. 'But he is thinking of you and I'm sure when everything has settled, he'll reach out to you.'

Everything was settled now, though. George had been elected as the new MP for Squashmore with a very comfortable majority and yet he *still* hadn't 'reached out' to Amelia.

In fact, the only other person from her old life who had been in touch had been Becky who'd sent Amelia a text as soon as the news had broken. It had been quite a strange text and she hadn't heard a word from Becky since, but then she knew Becky was very busy too. Busy being married to the man she loved, who loved her back, and as well as being in the papers *all the time*, Becky was using her powers for good and was fronting an anti-bullying campaign and . . .

' . . . that girl, Becky Sharp? Emmy! Are you listening to me? You and your family never listened to me, just treated me like I was a piece of furniture.'

Amelia turned her attention back to Mrs Blenkinsop. 'I'm so sorry. It's just with everything that's happened, I'm all over the place. You were saying something about Becky?'

'She was there at the auction.' Mrs Blenkinsop leaned closer so the earrings, which *really* did look remarkably like the ones Mrs Sedley used to have, twinkled in the overhead lights. 'With that film-star husband of hers. They bought your old bedroom set.'

'Oh, did they?' The pain was swift and

immediate and it burned like acid. Becky had loved that bedroom set.

'You *are* lucky, Emmy,' she'd said, as she'd stroked a hand over the carved wooden headboard, which had been painted cream and padded with the most extravagant dusky-blue velvet, like something from a French chateau. 'When I was fifteen, I don't think anyone even knew it was my birthday.'

Amelia swallowed the pain away. It was only fitting that Becky should have it and knowing Becky, she probably thought that in some small way she was helping out by buying some of their possessions. But it was all so awkward and embarrassing: it wasn't surprising that she hadn't been in touch.

'I'm actually glad that something I loved has gone to someone I love,' she said to Mrs Blenkinsop, who looked disappointed that her news had been received so calmly. Then she cackled.

'If you say so, love.' Then she stared down at her phone. 'I made a list. What else?'

'My horse. Pianoforte?' Amelia asked hopefully, though she almost couldn't bear to know what had happened to her dear old four-legged friend — if he'd been bought by a cruel-looking lottery winner too, then she wouldn't know what to do with herself.

'Withdrawn from sale due to ill health.' Mrs Blenkinsop's face softened and she tried to discreetly arrange her hair to cover the diamonds dangling from her ears. 'Sorry, Emmy.'

'It's all right.' Amelia tried to swallow past the lump in her throat. 'He is twenty and I suppose

231

that's *quite* old for a horse.'

'Maybe they'll put him out to grass and he'll have a nice, gentle retirement?'

'Yes, maybe . . . ' Amelia agreed and never before had her smile been so forced. 'All the oats he can eat and lots of scritches behind his ears. He loves scritches. I'm sorry, Blenky, I have to go now. Just remembered an urgent appointment.'

Amelia's throat was tight and her nose prickled as she scraped her chair back as if she really did have to be somewhere else: the truth was, she had no urgent appointments these days. There was no one who was that desperate to see her. With a feeble waggle of her fingers she said goodbye to her old housekeeper and rushed out of Starbucks to hit the street just as the first sob tore its way out of her throat.

Although she used to cry all the time, these past few months, Amelia had been resolutely dry-eyed. She liked to think that this was because she had inner reserves that she'd never noticed before. She'd even taken the Eleanor Roosevelt quote, 'A woman is like a teabag. You don't know how strong she is until you put her in hot water', and adopted it as her own personal mantra.

But now she wasn't dry-eyed or strong but weeping, really noisily and with so much snot, on a street in broad daylight in the middle of the lunchtime rush while people hurried past or tutted loudly because she was blocking their way.

She started walking, her progress hampered by the fact that she was blinded by tears, until in the end she sank down on a bench with her head in her hands so she could cry it out. Grieve for her old life because yes, she had liked being rich and being able to have whatever she wanted whenever she wanted it. Had loved living in a lovely house surrounded by lovely things, and though Daddy worked hard and Mummy stressed out about what the women at her tennis club would think of each new major purchase, they were what Amelia knew now to be First-World problems.

Home was now a horrid little ex-council house Jos had bought them in Burnt Oak, which was right at the northern end of the Northern Line. He'd wanted to buy them somewhere much nicer but the lawyers said that if they were seen living somewhere nice, people would get angry. Even angrier than they already were, which was really quite awfully angry. So the poky little house that smelt of damp and the hostile neighbours (who all looked down on the Sedleys for being a bunch of wrong 'uns in much the same way that their neighbours in Kensington used to look down on them for being new money) would have to do.

Everything was awful. And though Amelia tried to tell herself that it could be worse — that she or Mummy and Daddy might have some dreadful incurable disease or live in the actual Third World — it was small comfort right now, so she carried on crying, until the homeless man she happened to be sharing the bench with felt moved enough to offer her a sip from his can of Tennent's Extra. And well, she didn't want to offend him by refusing, and hopefully the alcohol would sterilise any germs.

SEDLEY GIRL ON SUICIDE WATCH!!!
Big Brother's Amelia in booze and breakdown hell!!!

Friends and family of Amelia Sedley, *Big Brother* winner and daughter of disgraced banker, Charles Sedley, spoke of their concern for the 23-year-old, after seeing our shocking photos taken yesterday afternoon.

Passers-by were stunned to see the former socialite staggering about in broad daylight, weeping in public, than sharing a can of lager with a homeless friend of hers.

'It was clear that she had both mental-health and substance-abuse issues,' said office worker Natalie Slingstone, who recognised last year's *Big Brother* winner immediately.

It has been quite a comedown for golden girl Amelia, who used to live in a £15 million mansion in Kensington and had several exotic holidays a year. Now she and her family are living in a house on a run-down council estate in north London and have seen the trappings of their extravagant lifestyle auctioned off to pay their creditors.

Friends of the ex-reality star are concerned that she's heading for a complete mental breakdown. 'Poor Emmy has always been a fragile soul,' said Rebecca Sharp, 21, beautiful wife of Hollywood heart-throb Rawdon Crawley. 'I'm very worried that this will send her over the edge. I'd love to see her do some volunteer work with On The

Streets, the homeless charity I work with, so she can see that there are people who really do have nothing.'

When we approached Amelia for a comment, lawyers acting for the Sedleys issued a statement saying that this was a family matter and asked for privacy at such a difficult time.

VOTE IN OUR POLL
Do you feel sorry for Amelia Sedley?
Yes? Text 18101
No? Text 18102

22

'Poor Emmy,' George Wylie said when William Dobbin slapped a copy of *The Globe* down on his desk in his office in the Houses of Parliament. 'But, Dobs, do you really think she's become one of those awful people who sit on park benches in the middle of the day, swigging cheap lager?'

It was a small desk in a small office that George shared with another newly minted MP, but everyone had to start somewhere. He was already sniffing around for a couple of select committees that might need a man of his calibre, and the PM's speechwriter, whose younger brother had been at Eton with George, had offered to help him with his maiden speech. George didn't envisage having to share office space for long, particularly not with a lower-middle-class, middle-aged woman from Essex who'd spent years working her way up through local politics before she was finally selected as a candidate.

'No, I don't,' Dobbin bit out and he wanted to say something cutting about how MPs sat in the House of Commons bars in the middle of the day drinking alcohol that was heavily subsidised by the tax-paying public, but he managed to restrain himself. 'You know how the press makes things up. They doctor photos, that sort of thing.'

'True. They said I was chair of the Oxford

Debating Society when *everyone* knows that to be chair of the Debating Society isn't anything that one would aspire to.' He allowed himself a small, congratulatory smile. 'Though I did excel in more than a couple of debates.'

'George!' Dobbin slammed the paper down again. 'What about Emmy? I said that you'd reach out to her once the dust has settled.'

'I don't know why you'd say that,' George muttered and it might have been because the office was small and Dobbin was very large and he did tend to loom, but George felt uncomfortably hot, so much so that he even had to loosen his tie. 'What Charles did . . . well, it's not the sort of thing that will ever settle, is it? Doesn't look good for anyone associated with him either. The whiff of impropriety and all that.'

'But it's Emmy,' Dobbin said through gritted teeth. He rather wished himself back in Helmand Province having to clear out Taliban insurgents from rugged terrain liberally set with landmines, than wrestle with the perhaps-non-existent conscience of one of his oldest, and at this moment, undearest friends. 'Poor, lovely Emmy.'

George sat up straighter. 'Did you just call her lovely?'

Dobbin put a hand to each of his burning cheeks. 'Little. I said 'Poor, little Emmy.' George, she's living in a shoebox in Burnt Oak. Luckily Jos has come through for them, though the Official Receiver is being very sniffy about how much he's allowed to contribute, but Emmy gets laughed out of every job she interviews for and she doesn't qualify for benefits.'

Finally, Dobbin had George's attention. 'Emmy, get a job? Are things really that bad?' He glanced around the cluttered office then leaned in closer. 'Surely Charles has a few mill tucked away in an off-shore account or two?'

'He declared everything,' Dobbin said.

'Well, more fool him.' George picked up the paper and peered at the girl who adored him without rhyme or reason. She'd been caught mid-sob. Amelia had never been a pretty crier but apart from that, misery and destitution rather agreed with her. She'd lost an awful lot of weight. Had quite the figure now, George thought as he looked at Amelia's legs, clad in shorts and trainers. Not a patch on the legs of Becky Sharp, but still, nice legs. And though Charles's fall from grace had been very unfortunate, especially as George had hoped to rely on him for further contributions, at least he wouldn't be beholden to him any more and Emmy would be very grateful if . . . 'I wonder what the results of this poll are?'

'You what?' Dobbin grunted as George slammed the paper back at him.

'This poll asking the public if they feel sorry for Amelia? God, where's a junior researcher when you need one? I'll do it myself,' George said, looking up the newspaper website on his phone to discover that, as he suspected, the tide was turning: 52 per cent of the readership felt sorry for Amelia. Which wasn't a clear majority but what was good enough for a hard Brexit was surely good enough in this case. 'You're right, Dobbin. Poor Emmy. And I am elected now, aren't I? It's not as if they can suddenly unelect me for getting in touch with an old friend?'

Just when Dobbin wondered why he was still friends with George Wylie, George always managed to surprise him by doing the right thing.

'So, you'll reach out to her?' he clarified.

George groaned. 'Don't use that awful expression 'reach out', Dobs. You really do spend too much time hanging out with the lower orders. But yes, I'll get in touch with Emmy. I'll arrange to see her. Not in Burnt Oak though.' George wasn't sure exactly where Burnt Oak was but he had a strong suspicion that he wouldn't like it very much. 'I'll call her, take her out to dinner maybe.'

'Good man,' Dobbin said; clapping George enthusiastically on the shoulder and earning himself a furious look.

'Don't ever do that again. You nearly punctured my lung. I hope you're more gentle with any terrorists that you round up.'

In that moment, Dobbin didn't know whether he wanted to hug or punch his oldest friend. As usual, he decided that it was probably a combination of both. Of course, what he really wanted was to hug Amelia, to take her away from Burnt Oak, to make all her problems disappear and give her the life she deserved. But Amelia didn't want that from Dobbin. She loved George and always would, so Dobbin would give her George instead. That was how much he loved her.

★ ★ ★

For weeks, *months*, all Amelia had wanted was some small sign to show that, no matter how far she'd fallen, George would be there to catch her.

But it turned out that signs from George Wylie were like buses, a mode of transport which Amelia had become very familiar with. You waited and waited and waited and then two came along at once.

It was a hot, sticky, late-summer afternoon and Amelia couldn't even sit in the concreted patch of yard that she tried to pretend was a back garden. Mrs Bawler next door, who'd come round on the Sedleys' first day in their new house to say, 'Your sort aren't welcome here,' would stare angrily at Amelia from her bedroom window and elderly Mr Binny on the other side was a staunch member of the Revolutionary Communist Party and liked to lecture Amelia over the fence about the dangers of capitalism.

So, she'd been sweltering indoors, without even a fan on, because it simply ate through the money in the electricity meter. Mummy was upstairs with one of her heads, Daddy was in town for yet another meeting with his lawyers and Amelia was going through job ads in the local free sheet when her phone rang.

The only people who ever seemed to ring her were journalists, especially after the silly story in *The Globe*, where they'd made it seem as if she was one can of super-strong lager away from suicide. She steeled herself not to answer it — who knew that the day would ever come when Amelia Sedley could ignore her ringing phone? — but then she looked down and saw George's number and his lovely face flashing on the screen.

She answered in an instant. 'Oh, George,' she murmured brokenly and through sheer force of will, managed not to burst into tears.

'Emmy, little Emmy, how the devil are you?' George drawled as if the horrid, horrid months since he'd last spoken to her hadn't happened and they were just picking up from where they'd left off.

'I'm fine,' Amelia said. 'Well, not fine, not exactly. I've been better, but then I've been worse too.'

'Well, let's concentrate on the being better part,' George said smoothly and actually, to have George be George, not smothering her with uncharacteristic kindness, but being as flippant as he ever was, felt very comforting. 'It's been an age since I last saw you,' he added as if the terse email he'd sent, practically severing all ties, had never happened.

'You've been busy,' Amelia noted. 'Congratulations on winning your seat, by the way.'

'You sweet girl, always thinking of others before yourself. Now, let's go out to celebrate my rise to power and we can drown your sorrows at the same time. Champagne I thought, unless you'd prefer Tennent's Extra,' he said with a laugh, and Amelia couldn't believe that George was joking about *that* at a time like this, but she was laughing too.

Gosh, she couldn't remember the last time she'd laughed. 'I'd much rather have champagne,' she said firmly. 'And the story, it twisted *everything*. I'm not on suicide watch, not at all.'

'Glad to hear it, because I'd rather miss you if you did top yourself,' George murmured and then he made arrangements for dinner the next week, even said he'd send a car all the way to Burnt Oak, and asked if she would mind if they dined somewhere quiet and out of the way. 'Obviously I don't give a hoot what people think, but I'm in the public eye now, and all that rot.'

Amelia didn't mind at all. She was floating on air as George said goodbye then she floated all the way to the front door when the doorbell rang, not even tensing in case it was another bailiff (who were awfully persistent even though all claims were meant to be going through the lawyers).

It wasn't a bailiff or one of the neighbours popping round to tell Mr Sedley that he wanted shooting. It was a courier with an envelope addressed to Amelia, which she rashly signed for even though it was most probably a court summons or something equally ghastly.

It wasn't though. It was something perfectly lovely. Three photos of a roan pony with a dark mane and tail and a roguish look in his eye, not looking the least bit like a horse that had been withdrawn from auction due to ill health. And there was a card too.

Dear Emmy,

Dictating this to you, as my hooves make it quite difficult to hold a pen or deal with a computer keyboard.

Rumours of my condition have been greatly exaggerated. I am quite well. A little tear in the cruciate ligament, which will heal quite nicely with rest and physio, but scuppered any chances of being sold to the highest bidder at auction.

Instead a very nice young man arranged for me to move to a riding school where I'll be nursed back to health then earn my keep by being ridden by pony-mad youngsters. Apparently, I'll get lots of hugs, all the apples I can eat and will never have to do anything more vigorous than a canter.

The best news is that my new digs are in Totteridge, which isn't far from you. Being a horse, I've never taken a bus but I understand you can catch the 251 from the top of your road and it will take you door to door. That is, if you fancy hanging out with . . .

Your old friend
Pianoforte

Amelia had stopped floating in favour of crying. But they were happy tears. Rather than being sold to a cruel-looking lottery winner or sent off to the knacker's yard, Pianoforte would have a lovely retirement just a bus ride away.

And it was George (so like him to mockingly describe himself as 'a very nice young man') who had made it happen, even going so far as to forge Pianoforte's 'signature'. Yes, he could be careless and selfish sometimes, but underneath it all, he was the kindest, most caring, most wonderful man that Amelia had ever met, and she couldn't wait to show him how grateful she was.

23

A year later

The sun beat down and the flags on the promenade fluttered gently in the Mediterranean breeze as Becky and Rawdon enjoyed a leisurely *al fresco* breakfast on the terrace of a fancy restaurant on the Croisette.

She'd have been perfectly happy to have her spinach-and-egg-white omelette and a revolting green juice on the yacht, where there was a team of handsome young men in tight white T-shirts and shorts all ready to satisfy her every wish, but Rawdon had put his foot down.

'I want to see more of Cannes than one of the guest suites of a super-yacht, then red carpet, photo call, champagne reception, repeat to fade,' he'd complained as if those were all very terrible things to endure.

So, now they were eating a €50 breakfast, though neither of them were doing carbs, and Rawdon could rub shoulders with the common man and woman. Becky didn't have the heart to point out that it was the common man and woman who had made his breakfast, served his coffee and would do the washing up afterwards.

So much had changed in a year. For one thing, the honeymoon was well and truly over. Rawdon had been shooting movies back to back and reacquiring all his bad habits, so it was just as well that Becky's side-hustle as an Instagram influencer and spokesmodel was proving lucrative. She really couldn't rely on Rawdon for anything much, but thank God, he *finally* had a new film coming out, so Becky's red-carpet appearances and increased media profile would lead to even more endorsements and opportunities. A girl always had to have a plan B, after all.

'Let's go for a stroll,' Rawdon said now, leaning over to take Becky's hand. 'See the real Cannes.' Becky moved her hand away, apparently to adjust her enormous sunglasses, which didn't prevent her from seeing the crestfallen look on her husband's face.

As long as the real Cannes involved popping into the boutiques that Becky had seen on their walk from the yacht — Chanel, Prada, maybe Gucci — she was perfectly happy to spend an hour letting Rawdon buy things for her. 'Then I have to start getting ready for tonight,' she said, already thinking of the hairdresser, the make-up artist, the stylist with rails full of dresses, who would all be heading to the yacht to get Becky ready for yet another red-carpet appearance and yet another premiere and one more champagne reception. Perhaps Rawdon did have a point — it did get a little boring after a while. But Becky would much rather be bored in a designer dress with a glass of vintage champagne in her hand, surrounded by movie stars and millionaires, than how she used to be bored: standing on a freezing Soho street corner waiting for the convenience store to open at seven so she could charge up the meter key and buy a Pot Noodle with the money she'd scrounged up from going through Frank Sharp's pockets while he'd passed out in a drunken stupor. Fun times.

'It used to be a fishermen's village,' Rawdon was saying. 'Maybe we could find some fishermen.'

Becky pushed up her sunglasses so her most withering look wouldn't be wasted. 'Why would we want to do that?' Then her attention was caught by a curious sight. 'At your three o'clock . . . oh, for fuck's sake, do be discreet, Rawdy . . . is that . . . is that Jos Sedley?'

Rawdon swivelled around — he was getting worse and worse at taking direction — then stood up and waved. 'Hey! Sedders! Over here!'

It *was* Jos Sedley, scuttling along the cobbles with that strange top-heavy gait of his. No other man on earth could be that particular shade of mahogany or quite that triangular. He was wearing white knee-length shorts and a tight, *tight*, white T-shirt as if no one had thought to tell him that that was what all the best-dressed super-yacht deckhands were wearing that season. Considering it had been nearly two years since Becky had last clapped eyes on him, he also had much more hair than he used to.

He waved back enthusiastically.

'Oh God, now he's coming over,' Becky hissed, because Jos was scurrying towards them, a wide smile on his face to show off all that expensive Californian orthodontistry, which dimmed as he saw who his old school friend was with.

'Crawley,' he managed to say in a strangulated

voice. 'Won't disturb you.'

'Don't be a dick,' Rawdon said, still standing up, so it wasn't as if Becky could kick him under the table. 'Join us. You know Becky, don't you? Used to be friends with your sister.'

One of the most irritating and yet, at the same time, endearing qualities about Rawdon Crawley was his absolute inability to retain information. Learning lines was a nightmare, but it was very useful when it came to changing the narrative (he was surprised anew every time Becky's *Big Brother* appearance reared its ugly head), and now he obviously couldn't remember that ridiculous front-page story after Jos had humiliated Becky outside that stupid nightclub.

'Yes, yes, of course,' Jos muttered, eyes fixed on his feet, which were clad in an extraordinary pair of backless, sky-blue Gucci loafers. 'Talking of my sister . . . '

Jos stepped aside and hiding behind his bulk was . . . 'Emmy?' Becky said, pushing up her sunglasses again to confirm that yes, there was Amelia Sedley beaming at her toothily and clutching the hand of . . . George Wylie.

'*Une autre table et trois chaises, s'il vous plaît,*' Rawdon was saying to the maître d' in a perfect French accent, which always made Becky quiver a little (she was only human, after all), even though she was also absolutely furious with him right now. Not just for inviting Jos to join them — that was the very least of his crimes. Last night, so coked up to the eyeballs that he could barely stand, Rawdon had begged Becky not to 'make such a fuss about it' when the studio head who'd invited them to stay on the super-yacht had tried to do something unspeakable to her in the hot tub with a champagne bottle.

'Come on, you'll join us for breakfast.'

'Bit late for breakfast,' George pointed out. Unlike Jos, he was the perfect sartorial representation of an Englishman in the South of France. He was wearing a cream, summer-weight wool suit, a pink shirt and aviator shades, his usually pale skin toasted to an exquisite shade of light caramel, thanks to a distant ancestor from Martinique.

'Brunch, then,' Rawdon decided, pulling Amelia in for a hug, then a kiss on each cheek, while she tried (and failed) not to look thrilled. '*Garçon! Champagne!*'

Becky stood up, pasting on her best 'delighted' face.

'Emmy!' she said again, holding out her arms so Amelia had to awkwardly squeeze through the tiny gap between table and railing to be very lightly hugged by Becky and kissed on the cheek. Amelia went in for the second kiss but Becky was already sitting down. 'It's so good to see you. Come and sit next to me . . . there's loads of room if you just breathe in and we can share the big parasol. You are *awfully* red. Do you need some sunblock? I get mine specially blended from a lovely woman who has a little salon in Mayfair.'

'I'm fine,' Amelia said, as a waiter followed Becky's directions and placed a chair next to her.

Then Amelia squeezed through the tiny gap again, which made her redder. 'Maybe a glass of water.'

'Oh, we can do better than a glass of water.' Becky put her hand over Amelia's and leaned in so she could whisper and riot embarrass her poor friend. 'Don't worry about not being able to afford breakfast. Honestly, I nearly fainted when I saw the prices too, but it's my treat. How funny that now I'm the one that's treating you and not the other way round.'

'I suppose it is funny.'

'I mean, not funny ha ha, funny peculiar,' Becky said, running a hand through her hair, which was so much sleeker, straighter and shinier than it used to be. 'So, you and Gorgeous George, what gives?'

Across the table, Rawdon and Jos were deep in conversation about Jos's interminable protein balls, while George sat slightly apart, eyes glued to his phone.

'Not that much,' Amelia said a little sadly. 'We've been seeing each other since last year. But not officially seeing each other . . . you won't say anything to anyone?'

'Cross my heart and hope to die,' Becky said, drawing a little cross over her heart so Amelia couldn't help but glance at the plunging neckline of Becky's white sundress. Then she couldn't help but notice that George's eyes had strayed in the same direction.

He smiled blandly at Amelia then went back to his phone. 'Even on holiday, George never stops working,' Amelia said. Could the girl not manage one whole sentence without sounding a little sad when she spoke?

'And are you working?' Becky asked, not that she was interested but it seemed the polite thing to do, as Amelia hadn't even bothered to ask one question about what Becky had been up to lately.

'Oh yes! I'm working at a riding stables in Totteridge.' It was the first thing that Amelia hadn't said sadly. On the contrary, her eyes were now gleaming with an evangelical zeal, like she was about to tap Becky for funds for Riding For The Disabled or a Pit Pony Refuge. 'It's quite a funny story really and it's all down to George . . .'

Listening to Amelia's story, Becky doubted that George Wylie would do anything altruistic unless there was something in it for him. She allowed herself a little sniff and George looked up from his phone, looked at Becky appreciatively (a far cry from how he used to look at her, like she was dog shit that an underling had tracked into the carpet), then glanced over at Amelia who was coming to the end of her long, meandering rant about her minimum-wage job mucking out stables.

' . . . and so fulfilling, you know.' Amelia was done at last and reached for her glass of water. As she'd barely stopped for breath she must have been parched, Becky thought, as her former BFF gratefully gulped down the mineral water at €12 a bottle. 'And of course you're well. I see you in all the papers and magazines.'

Becky waved a dismissive hand. 'I can't imagine why they're so interested in me,' she said, even though she now had her own agent, publicist and social-media intern who were all paid handsomely (apart from the social-media intern who just got her travel expenses) to ensure that the whole world was interested in Becky Sharp.

Amelia's brow furrowed. 'But what exactly is it that you *do*?' she asked so artlessly that George was forced to put down his phone.

'Quite rude,' he opined gently, but enough to make Amelia blush on top of the ruddy glow she already had. ' "What do you do?" works just as well.'

'It wasn't rude at all,' Becky said, because George Wylie was the very last person who should ever lecture someone on rudeness. 'Anyway I'm a spokesmodel for two charities, one that helps homeless teens and another that helps the victims of bullying. Isn't bullying the worst, Emmy?'

'The absolute worst,' Emmy agreed, thinking not of the woman sitting next to her, who could always be relied upon for a spot of timely undermining, but how horrid the press and their Burnt Oak neighbours had been.

'I never asked to be thrust into the public eye,' the former *Big Brother* contestant continued. 'And I never asked my Rawdy to fall in love with me.' The object of her affection left off from his conversation with Jos about squats versus lunges to shoot Becky a doting smile tinged with relief that she didn't seem to be furious with him any longer. 'But he did fall in love with me, and being married to a very famous actor has given

251

me a platform, so I want to use it for the greater good. Give something back, you know?'

'Oh yes, I'd do exactly the same thing,' Amelia assured her quickly. 'It's why I spent those two weeks in Niger hugging those poor orphans.'

Becky waved a dismissive hand at the mention of the poor orphans of Niger. 'So, anyway, my charity work is very important but then I'm also a brand ambassador for a fashion label and a high-street chain, and I'm hoping to get a beauty client on board because that's where the real money is,' Becky said, raising her eyes to the heavens because some divine intervention would really help on that score. 'And then companies pay me to feature their products on my Instagram. Not tat either. You wouldn't even believe how much I got for being all hashtag bliss over an Italian coffee maker. It does actually make really good coffee but Rawdy and I haven't got the first clue how it works.'

'It all sounds wonderful,' Amelia said sadly because she was back to saying things sadly again. 'Do you remember how, after *Big Brother*, I got sent all those things?'

Becky nodded. 'Though me being on *Big Brother* has been officially purged from my record. Didn't happen.'

'But . . . but you *were* on *Big Brother*. I was right there with you!'

'Fake news, Emmy!'

Becky smiled, all pink, healthy gums and newly veneered teeth. Not the little half smile that she'd perfected over the last two years, but something more natural and unaffected so that

Amelia couldn't help but smile back and remember how Becky Sharp could make you feel as if you were the only person in the world that truly mattered to her.

A big bottle of champagne had arrived, a Jeroboam, carried aloft with some ceremony by a waiter. 'A glass for everyone,' Rawdon said with a magnanimous sweep of his hand like it was fizzy pop and not hideously expensive vintage Taittinger.

'It's funny, but when you have nothing, everything costs more,' Amelia mused. 'You have no bank credit so you have to have your electricity supplied on a meter, which is more expensive than paying by bill. Same with pay-as-you-go mobiles. And now I'll walk an extra ten minutes and go to two different supermarkets just to save a couple of pounds, because those two pounds matter.'

'But when you have everything, people are *literally* queuing up to give you free stuff,' Becky said. 'Not just clothes and accessories and beauty products, but sending cars and arranging for you to spend a day at a polo match so you can be photographed drinking a certain brand of champagne, when I can buy my own clothes and toddle off to the polo under my own steam, if I wanted.'

'Supply and demand,' said George loftily, finally able to find a way into their conversation. He was at Cannes on a little work jolly, a so-called 'fact-finding mission' sponsored by the British Film Foundation, though he too could have gone to Cannes on his own dime, if so inclined. 'Anyway, Becky, having everything obviously agrees with you.' He raised his espresso cup in a toast to the girl he once despised, as the girl who loved him wilted at the gesture. 'What is it they say? 'I've been poor and I've been rich and rich is always better.''

'*You*'ve never been poor, so how the hell would you know?' Becky asked sweetly and George was about to tell her about some of the utter horror shows that came to his ghastly monthly constituency surgeries, but she was already looking past him. 'Jos! You haven't even said hello to me. How rude! Tell me, how are your balls?'

Jos immediately tipped his decaff soy latte down his immaculately white T-shirt. 'Beg pardon?' he spluttered.

'Your protein balls,' Becky clarified as Rawdon laughed because he always found it funny when his wife had someone in her sights, especially if it wasn't him. 'What other balls would I be talking about? So, are you now the *number-one* seller of protein balls on the West Coast?'

'You remembered?' Jos said as he ineffectually mopped at the coffee stain.

'Becky never forgets anything,' Rawdon said. '*Frailty, thy name is woman.*'

Behind her shades, Becky's eyes narrowed because she didn't like it when Rawdon was perceptive. Not that it happened very often. And he was a fine one to accuse her of being weak when he was completely spineless. Not that Becky had any intention of letting the assembled company know that there was trouble in paradise.

'I do love it when you quote Shakespeare. Sends shivers down my spine.' And she wriggled very slightly where she sat so that Jos immediately squirmed in his chair and ran a stubby finger around the collar of his T-shirt and Rawdon smiled at the thought of what Becky might let him do to her if they went back to the yacht instead of trying to find the real fishermen of the real Cannes. Even George Wylie had to put his copy of that day's *Times* on his lap. What with the wonderful things that delightful shudder had done to her breasts and the way Becky Sharp's foot had been caressing his leg for the last half an hour, he was quite undone.

★ ★ ★

Despite the dangerous undercurrents at brunch, the five of them were nevertheless reunited the following evening at a benefit gala at Le Mirage. The fashion company who were sponsoring the event had sent Becky a delicate tight tulle sheath almost the same colour as her skin, so she'd have looked quite naked if the dress hadn't been scattered with crystals that matched the mischievous glint in her eyes.

The proceeds of the silent auction, the climax of the gala, would be going to the anti-bullying charity that Becky represented, though even she was unaware that most of the money would be siphoned off by the husband and wife who'd founded the charity as a way of increasing their tax exemptions.

Being involved in charitable causes — the

right kind of charitable causes — was such a good way of meeting the right kind of people. Climbing up that greasy pole so that Becky was *practically* A-list by association. Only the other month, she'd been at a charity lunch and had been seated two tables away from an HRH.

But there was no point in being *practically* A-list if there was no one present to witness how far Becky Sharp had come. People who had once treated her like she was some kind of charity case herself, and then grown tired of her. People like Amelia Sedley, for instance, or her brother, Jos, who'd thought that he and his protein balls were too good for the likes of her. Becky hated to give him even faint praise but at least George Wylie had never pitied her.

'That's about the only point in his favour,' she remarked to Rawdon once she'd sent one of the designer deckhands off with three handwritten invitations to the benefit to be delivered to the hotel where George and the Sedleys were staying. It wasn't even that nice a hotel because at this time of year, bona fide movie stars and Hollywood executives trumped the Member of Parliament for Squashmore, even if he was heir to a baronetcy. Not like the luxurious guest suite of the super-yacht, where Rawdon was currently sprawled on the bed recovering from the night before. 'I still hate him though.'

'Poor Wylie. He did seem quite smitten with you at breakfast the other morning,' Rawdon noted lazily, relieved that it was someone else's turn to be the target of her wrath. 'Couldn't take his eyes off your tits.'

'These old things,' Becky said mockingly, lightly touching the articles in question. As she'd learnt from their wedding night, few things stoked Rawdon's ardour like the thought of other men wanting to fuck his wife (even though lately his ardour had been impeded by the substances that he smoked or snorted). She imagined that it was something to do with having gone to public school. 'I might have to get your initials tattooed on them. Just so George knows who they belong to.'

Rawdon pricked up his ears, as well as other parts. 'You'd do that?'

'Maybe.' Becky would never do any such thing but she might consent to having a small *R* on her wrist or something. It was her own initial, after all. 'We're getting sidetracked here, Rawdy. Now, do you promise that you'll behave yourself tonight?'

His lazy good mood instantly evaporated. 'I'm not a child,' he snapped. 'And you're not a nanny any more.'

'I might just as well be,' Becky reminded him. 'All five of the bratty little Crawleys were better behaved than you. Even Thisbe.'

Rawdon scrabbled for his shades and put them on so he wouldn't have to look her in the eye. Then he lounged back on the bed, the effort to appear nonchalant testing every single skill that he'd been taught at RADA. 'You knew I was a hell-raiser when you married me,' he drawled, having conveniently forgotten that he'd vowed on his dead mother's grave to go straight before Becky would even let him kiss her.

'But you don't raise hell, Rawdy. That might be quite exciting,' Becky said with a sniff. 'You just get coked up, talk bollocks for hours and what money you haven't spent on drugs, you manage to lose at the casino. Why do you gamble when you're terrible at it? At least my father knew how to count the cards.'

'You know what they say? Unlucky at cards, lucky in love.'

'I'm certainly not lucky in love,' Becky said so savagely that Rawdon quaked behind his dark glasses. 'If you really loved me, you'd have done more than tell me not to make a scene when that brute tried to shove a champagne bottle up me.'

'You were the one who said I should hustle more, network more, schmooze more. That's what I was trying to do with him in the hot tub before you arrived,' Rawdon protested in a very whiny voice, which always made Becky want to slap him.

'Oh, really? Because it looked to me like you were just hoovering up huge lines of coke . . . '

'Everyone does coke and anyway, Becks, he said it was an accident and that he just slipped, so there was no need to stab his hand with a lobster fork,' Rawdon said sulkily.

'*I* slipped. What *I* did was an accident,' Becky parroted Rawdon's own words back at him, then she turned away as she couldn't bear to look at his ridiculous adolescent pout. The super-yacht was being rented from a Russian oligarch and their guest suite was decorated in black marble with gold trim and mirrors everywhere, so it looked a lot like the loos of a fancy suburban nightclub in the late eighties. Becky stared at her own reflection, which was usually so pleasing to her. But not today, when she had an unattractive furrow between her eyebrows, a petulant droop to her mouth, so that she could see exactly what she'd look like five years down the line if she and Rawdon were still together. Which, at this moment, seemed highly unlikely unless Matilda softened and he became a much more . . . attractive proposition than he was currently.

She closed her eyes so she wouldn't have to see Rawdon in the mirror, still spread-eagled on the bed with his mouth hanging open.

'Baby, I'm sorry.' She heard him get up and pad towards her. Then he was nuzzling the back of her neck. 'Don't be cross with your Rawdy. I promise to be a good boy.'

Both the nuzzling and the baby talk reminded her of Sir Pitt and she shuddered, though Rawdon seemed to think it was a shiver of anticipation because he doubled down on the nuzzling.

'Only if you promise not to do any more drugs,' Becky said in a vaguely conciliatory tone. And when Rawdon caught her gaze in the mirror, she even managed a smile. 'You've seen what I can do with a lobster fork.'

He stopped nuzzling and — Becky wanted to throw her head back and scream — he was pouting again.

'No drugs, no gambling, no fun.' He touched the side of his head in a mocking salute. 'Got it!'

It was going to be a very long, very dreary night if Rawdon was in a sulk. Becky summoned up a naughty, conspiratorial smile that would have made Rawdon's eyes gleam if he didn't still have his bloody shades on.

'I said no drugs but we can still have fun,' she purred, reaching up to pat his cheek. 'We can even do a little bit of gambling, if you fancy it?'

'At one of the casinos?' Rawdon asked hopefully.

'Ha! Nice try. We're broke after your last visit to Les Princes,' Becky scoffed, patting his cheek again. 'But that doesn't mean we can't have a little wager between us.'

'A bet?' Rawdon couldn't hide his interest. Not even Frank Sharp had been such an inveterate gambler — he knew to quit when he was ahead, whereas Rawdon would never fold; not even when the odds were stacked against him. 'What are we betting on?'

'We're betting on how well you know your old friend George Wylie,' Becky said and suddenly the night ahead, the gala, was no longer going to be dreary. Not with what she had planned. 'When faced with unbearable temptation.'

'It's not much of a bet. Wylie likes to keep his nose clean,' Rawdon said, not even acknowledging the irony that his own nasal passages were constantly sullied by the finest Peruvian marching powder. 'Always has.'

'What was that you said before about him staring at my breasts?' Becky asked idly, her gaze dropping to her cleavage. 'You don't even want to know what he was doing under the table.'

'What was he doing?' Rawdon tried to sound angry, territorial even, but he couldn't hide the lust in his voice at the thought of his old school adversary, superior, supercilious George Wylie, trying it on with Becky, when she was his. 'Was he trying to feel you up? He wouldn't dare!'

'Wouldn't he?' Becky took her breasts in her hands as if she was offering them up to the gods. 'Care to make a bet on it?'

Both breasts and bet were an offer that Rawdon couldn't refuse.

'I'm in. I'm all in.'

24

Amelia Sedley was wearing her nicest dress. The grey chiffon number, studded with little sparkly stones, that she once hadn't been able to get into and now fitted like a glove, though it was still a little tight under the armpits. It was also the dress that she'd lent Becky Sharp two years before to wear on that fateful night when Jos had got terribly drunk and ended up kissing Becky and tearing the dress, but Amelia had painstakingly mended all the rips and it was almost impossible to see that the dress had ever been damaged.

And now George Wylie had the delicate chiffon in a death grip as he pumped into Amelia, bending her over the sink in the tiny en suite of the worst room in the not-great hotel that was all they'd been able to book.

George had taken one look at her when she'd stepped out of the bathroom in the dress and his eyes had darkened, causing Amelia to feel that delicious ache start deep in her belly.

'Emmy, that dress . . . you look absolutely fuckable,' he'd said in that precise voice of his. A voice that Emmy had always dreamed would one day murmur sweet nothings into her ear. 'Knickers off, there's a good girl.'

'B-b-b-but we'll be late for the benefit,' Amelia said uncertainly even as she reached under her dress to slide off her M&S white cotton briefs.

'Well, that will be all your fault for making me want you,' George had said and he hadn't even kissed her, just marched her into the bathroom and told her to bend over.

He'd been absolutely insatiable for the last two days and Amelia couldn't think what had got into him, though she was really very pleased with what had got into her.

They were late down to the lobby to meet Jos and lovely Dobbin, who'd worked as an advisor on a documentary about post-Taliban Afghanistan and had flown in to be on a post-screening panel.

Dobbin, dashing in a black evening suit, stepped forward as Amelia tripped out of the lift.

'You look lovely, Emmy,' he said gravely. 'Quite glowing.'

She *was* glowing and still slightly sore *down there*, and George, Gorgeous George, shot her a naughty, knowing look, so all she could do was giggle.

They piled into a taxi, Amelia sandwiched between Dobbin and George. 'A rose between two thorns,' Dobbin said and George cuffed the back of his head and told him not to be so clichéd, but Amelia wouldn't let anything prick her happiness tonight. Not when George's thigh was pressed against hers, his hand beneath her dress, under the cover of darkness.

It was so different to how things had been in London. Snatched dates in out-of-the way restaurants whenever George could find space in his very busy schedule. He'd kissed her a few times but they'd seemed like polite, perfunctory kisses and she wondered if he was just being polite and perfunctory in taking her out.

Then she'd remember how he'd rescued Pianoforte from being bought by a cruel-faced lottery winner, which surely was something that a man would only do if he had proper feelings for a girl.

It had all been very confusing until that night when they'd had dinner at a small Italian restaurant in Stanmore and Amelia had mentioned that Becky Sharp was in *Hello!* In fact, she still had the magazine in her bag.

She'd pulled it out so that George could see her dear, though quite absent, friend on the cover in a white-and-gold bikini. 'It Girl, Becky Sharp, talks about her charity work and life as Mrs Rawdon Crawley while modelling her exclusive swimwear range for ASOS.'

'She's made very little go a long, long way,' George had noted with an odd look on his face, which Amelia had put down to the flickering candle stuck in a wax-encrusted chianti bottle. Then he'd put his hand over hers where it rested on the table. 'You know, Emmy, you're looking very pretty tonight. Very pretty indeed.'

Amelia was sun-kissed, her hair lightened by all the hours spent outdoors. And yes, she'd lost weight, which was due to a combination of grief for her old life and her days spent doing manual labour. But she wasn't sure that she looked *pretty* without the eyelash extensions and the carefully applied fake tan, the manicures and pedicures, and the huge amount of products she used to apply to her face. These days, Amelia's look was rather too homely for her liking.

'I'm sure I just look weather-beaten and straw-haired,' she'd mumbled but hoped the appreciative gleam in George's eyes was all for her and wasn't just another trick of the flickering candlelight.

'All that time you spend riding,' he'd mused.

'Oh George, I wouldn't spend so much time riding if you hadn't rescued Pianoforte,' Amelia had said, as she did at least once every time she and George met.

And as ever, George had frowned and pretended that he didn't know what she was talking about. Amelia was sure that she was the only person who ever got to see this modest, unassuming side to George Wylie.

'No need to mention it, I'd rather talk about all the things you can do with your thighs after sitting on a horse all day. I bet you've got muscles that I haven't even dreamed about.' Then, unbelievably, he'd taken Amelia's hand and dragged it down, under the table, to rest in his lap. 'Feel that? I'm hard just thinking about it. Thinking about you.'

It had all been so sudden, so unexpected. Of course, Amelia had dreamed that one day George would think of her with, even a fraction of the affection she had for him, and now here he was, telling her that he was dying to be inside her.

They couldn't go back to Burnt Oak — not with her parents living there and besides, George could no sooner go to Burnt Oak than he could fly to the moon. His pied-à-terre in Victoria was *miles* away too, so their first time, Amelia's first time, was in a motel called The Spider's Web on the A41 Watford Bypass, though it had been no less romantic for that.

Since then, they'd done it half a dozen times and since they'd been in Cannes, they'd done it loads and loads. Amelia was pretty sure that the cranberry juice she guzzled with every meal wasn't going to be enough to stave off a UTI, but she didn't care.

What she cared about was that when she walked into the ballroom of Le Mirage, and felt the nerves kick her in the stomach like Trixie, the most skittish of the riding school's ponies, she was on George's arm. When you were with a man as commanding and as capable as George Wylie, there was no need to be nervous.

Jos, predictably, had wedged himself into a white dinner jacket, which meant within five minutes of arriving, three people had mistaken him for a waiter and had asked him for more champagne. He never learned his lesson about the perils of wearing a white tuxedo. 'Everyone wears a white DJ in LA,' he kept muttering under his breath and even Dobbin, who had faced down the Taliban, Al Qaeda *and* ISIS, was sweating and discomfited.

'Champagne for my lovely lady,' George said suavely, lifting two glasses from a passing waiter's tray and presenting Amelia with one.

Once Amelia felt the champagne bubbles fizzing on her tongue, the nerves mellowed out and she could take in her surroundings. The elegant ballroom had been designed in the art nouveau style, and its decorative flourishes could be seen in the fretwork of the sweeping staircase, the delicate pillars and the painted friezes on the balconies that overlooked the scene.

And the scene consisted of four hundred mostly beautiful people. Amelia stared at women poured into dresses she'd seen in the windows of the exclusive boutiques that lined the Croisette. Their faces were as expensive as their clothes; skin stretched tight over preternaturally smooth foreheads, lips and cheeks plumped with the very latest in-fillers, framed by hair as glossy as liquid silk.

In her dress, that really was so very three years ago, and silver sandals that had already given her blisters, Amelia felt quite the poor relation, but George was still at her side and every now and again he'd smile at her, and Amelia wouldn't have swapped places with any other woman in the room.

Not even Becky Sharp, who was moving towards them with a fluid grace, the crowd separating to allow her free passage, just like God had parted the Red Sea for the Israelites. In a room full of beautiful, beautifully-dressed women, Becky was easily the most beautiful and the most beautifully dressed.

Amelia suddenly thought back to the first time she'd met Becky on that first night in the *Big Brother* house when Becky had stuck salt-and-vinegar crisps between two slices of heavily buttered white bread and said mournfully, 'All the other girls in here are so sophisticated. I'm glad you're not like that.'

Now Becky looked like she lived on a diet of vintage champagne, gulls' eggs and nectar. She'd acquired an iridescent, untouchable patina that only the truly famous seem to have, so Amelia wouldn't have been surprised if she'd glided right past them. But Becky didn't. She stopped in front of the foursome and held out her slender white arms in greeting.

'I'm so glad you could all come. And Captain Dobbin too. What a lovely surprise,' she said in the slightly breathy voice that now sounded as if she'd been born and bred somewhere in the Royal Borough of Kensington and Chelsea. 'Emmy, you look absolutely adorable. So brave to wear a cocktail dress when everyone else is in a gown. Good for you.'

Was it possible that Becky didn't even remember the dress? Amelia was gathered up in a fragile embrace as if she might break Becky if she hugged her too hard.

Mind you, Becky had probably worn so many designer gowns in the last year or so that who could blame her if she forgot a frock or two? 'You look lovely, Becky. Um, is that er . . . Gucci?'

Becky looked down at the blush-coloured tulle sheath dress that clung lovingly and glimmeringly to her. 'Not Gucci, silly Emmy. It doesn't look anything like a Gucci. It was custom-made for me. Unless you're familiar with haute couture, you wouldn't have heard of the designer,' she revealed almost apologetically. Then she looked beyond Amelia to smile brilliantly at the three men she'd come with.

'Now, let's find some fascinating people for you to talk to. Come! Follow me!'

So Amelia, the Member of Parliament for Squashmore, a celebrated war hero, and the founder of the most successful protein ball company on the West Coast, obediently and meekly followed Becky Sharp, as the glittering masses parted for her once more.

Becky's hips undulated sensuously, which made Amelia feel as if her own hips were made of Lego, as they slowly climbed the sweeping staircase to the galleries above. In an alcove was a table littered with mostly empty bottles of champagne, and sitting around the table were a variety of people in various stages of inebriation.

Becky beckoned to a wizened old man who looked as if he'd wandered in off the street and pulled Dobbin forwards. 'Do you know Sam?' she asked expectantly, as if most people did.

'I'm afraid not,' Dobbin said, wondering why on earth he should.

'He's a very famous film director,' Becky scolded. 'Aren't you, Sam?'

The gnome-like figure shrugged impassively.

'Modest too. Anyway, he's making a film about the war in Syria and you must have been to Syria doing soldier stuff, so I've decided that Sam absolutely has to talk to you.' Becky nudged Dobbin further forwards. 'Go on, he doesn't bite, but I don't think he's turned on his hearing aid.' She tapped Sam, the famous director, on the shoulder and gestured at his ear, while the old man smiled and put a proprietorial and liver-spotted hand on her bottom.

Becky didn't even flinch, just calmly removed the hand and turned her attention to Jos. 'I have someone all lined up for you too,' she said, tucking her arm into Jos's as she used to do during those few heady weeks when Jos had been the happiest man in London. 'He helped to finance Rawdy's last film and apparently his family own a chain of gyms in the Midwest and he's very curious about your balls.'

'Protein balls,' Jos corrected as Becky dragged him over to the next table where Rawdon was holding court, in sunglasses and a leather jacket, while surrounded by a bunch of perma-tanned men, whose white teeth glowed in the dim light, and their female companions who all looked as if they'd come straight off a conveyor belt in a factory that made Victoria's Secret models.

'Becky seems to know everyone,' Amelia said to George but he just grunted as if knowing everyone wasn't such an impressive feat. Then when she took his arm to console herself that even though she was two stone heavier and six inches shorter than all the other women in their immediate vicinity, she was still worthy of George Wylie, he tensed and shook her free.

'Don't cling, Emmy,' he admonished as Becky came towards them with a beautiful elegant woman in tow. He puffed out his chest, stood a little taller, a little straighter and Amelia steeled herself for Becky to introduce George to her stunning friend, but it was Amelia she reached for.

'Emmy,' Becky said, taking Amelia's hand and pulling her out of George's orbit. 'This is Claire.

It turns out that she was at university with the brother of one of the M's.'

Amelia had recognised Claire immediately but could hardly bring herself to look at her, in case Claire's otherworldly beauty sapped the life right out of her. 'I've seen all your films,' she breathed, while next to her George made the tiny, hissing sound which always meant that he was embarrassed by her latest display of gaucheness. Still, Amelia couldn't help herself. 'And I thought you were terribly good in that TV adaptation of *Where Angels Fear To Tread.*'

Claire inclined her head, which rested on a swan-like neck. 'Thank you,' she said gravely. 'And of course I loved you in *Big Brother*. I wish I could cry on cue like that and not have to rely on glycerine drops.'

'No, she really does cry that much,' Becky said and Amelia wanted to point out that that wasn't entirely true, certainly not lately, but Becky's grip on her hand tightened. 'Claire has to ride a horse in her next film and she's absolutely terrified. I knew that you would be the perfect person to put her at ease. Why don't you two go and have a chat?' She pointed out a distant corner. 'There's an empty table over there.'

'*Will* you?' Claire asked earnestly, because her drama coach had told her that she lacked sincerity and now she over-compensated so no one would think that she was shallow. 'I have *so* many questions. I'm *particularly* worried about what it will do to my *thighs*. Will it make them *bigger*? Those girls who do *dressage* at the *Olympics* all have *thunder* thighs.'

Amelia could feel her own thighs expanding under her dress as Claire led her away, nattering in her ear, so she didn't even have a chance to look back at George to see if he minded.

And it was probably just as well, because Amelia Sedley and her thighs were the very last thing on George's mind. Becky Sharp looked to her left and then her right, and once she'd established that she and George were the last two standing, she stepped closer to him. Close enough that he could smell the heavy, exotic tang of her perfume, like lilies a day away from decay. Close enough that George could see the gentle rise and fall of her breasts as she took a couple of deep breaths as if she were nervous. Close enough that not even a whisper could come between them.

'Gorgeous George,' she purred. 'Alone at last.'

And when he walked her backwards into the dimmest, darkest corner, she didn't even make a token protest.

25

Amelia was lost.

Claire had talked earnestly about her *fear* of horse riding and what it would do to her *body* for well over *half an hour* before Amelia could escape her clutches. She hadn't even had a chance to give the woman a few pointers on technique.

She'd wandered over to the table where she'd last seen Becky and George but they were nowhere to be found. Dobbin was deep in conversation with the funny little man who Amelia still couldn't believe was a film director. There were glasses and champagne bottles laid out in formation on the table in front of them, which meant that Dobbin was describing a particular battle or airstrike or some such. He looked up as Amelia hovered and smiled at her but she didn't want to get in the way of what looked like such an interesting (and also quite dull) discussion, so she smiled and backed away.

Jos had been welcomed into the fold of the perma-tanned clique, whose biceps were all straining against their handmade shirt sleeves, so he'd obviously found his people. Amelia didn't have the heart to disturb him and anyway, it was George that she wanted to see. He'd been so different, so attentive, since they'd been in Cannes, and she wanted to soak up every second before they had to go back to London and the spell would be broken. But he was nowhere to be found.

Amelia had done three complete circuits of the ballroom and the upper balconies trying to find George. She had even texted him to see if he'd got bored and gone back to the hotel, but there was no reply. Nor when she texted him again to ask if he was at the bar. Not even a reply to her third text message to see if he was on the terrace at the back of the ballroom looking out at the twinkling lights of the harbour.

She was on her fourth sweep of the upper floor when she finally caught a glimpse of him. He suddenly stepped out of the shadows, adjusting his bow tie, which was crooked, then glanced over his shoulder. Said something to someone and laughed as *Becky* stepped out of the shadows too, her hair loose, when before it had been pinned up.

Amelia felt the exact moment that her heart broke.

Becky placed a hand on George's sleeve and curved her body into his, he said something to her, and she threw her head back and laughed. There was an easy intimacy between them as if they'd been lovers for a long time, rather than snatching a hurried half hour at a crowded party.

Her pain, her agony, must have screamed at the pair of them, because they both noticed Amelia at the exact same moment. George turned away, guilt written all over his face, from the shifty look in his eyes to the way he gnawed on his bottom lip. But Becky Sharp didn't turn away. Although a faint hint of colour rose on her

274

cheeks — perhaps the first time Amelia had ever seen her blush genuinely — she nevertheless held Amelia's gaze steadily, with an expression on her face that was impossible to read. Then she lifted a hand and gestured at Amelia to come forward.

All that Amelia wanted to do was run and maybe hurl herself into the sea so she could be mown down by a super-yacht but her feet obeyed Becky, even if the rest of her didn't want to.

'Emmy! There you are,' Becky exclaimed and then she had the audacity to pull Amelia into a hug so that Amelia could smell George on her. The citrus tang of his aftershave mingling with the heavy, cloying scent that Becky now wore. The olfactory assault made Amelia's stomach roil and she thought she might be sick on Becky's Louboutins. Almost wished that she was, but Becky was already thrusting her away.

'You're so red-faced,' she said, placing a cool hand on Amelia's blazing cheek. 'Next time we go out, I'll lend you my make-up artist — my treat. I'm sure he can do something with your complexion.'

'George,' Amelia said in a low voice, even as she had to fight the urge to scrub her face to get rid of the phantom touch of Becky's hand. 'I've been looking for you everywhere. What have you been doing? I texted you.'

'I wondered why my phone was going off like a rocket,' George said and he smiled blandly. Much as she loved him, even still, that bland smile of his always set Amelia's teeth on edge. 'I

275

was doing what people do at these sorts of things. Having a drink, catching up with an old friend . . . '

'Talking of drinks, I'm absolutely parched,' Becky cut in smoothly. Her hand was back on George's arm as if it belonged there. 'Be a darling and fetch me some champagne, will you?'

'Of course,' George said and he trotted off quite happily to do Becky's bidding, not even asking Amelia if she wanted anything. In fact, he didn't deign to look at her as he brushed past.

'God, these parties are boring,' Becky complained, brushing past Amelia too so she could sink down on an over-stuffed pink-velvet-and-gilt opera chair. 'My shoes are killing me. I'm thinking of having Botox in the balls of my feet so I won't even feel the pain any more.'

'I don't think you feel anything,' Amelia said bitterly. 'Not anything good, like kindness or decency . . . '

Becky widened her big green eyes then blinked slowly. 'What a horrible thing to say,' she gasped, a hand to her heart as if Amelia had mortally wounded her. 'I've looked after you, introduced you to Claire so you'd have someone to talk to, and I paid the £2,000 a head for the three of you out of my own pocket. Not that I minded, because this charity is so important to me. And you have the nerve to say that I'm unkind?'

'You always do this! You twist everything. And you say the most horrible things but you say them in such a way that they never stick to you.' Amelia gave a groan of pure frustration. 'What have I ever done to you that you have to make me feel so ugly, so small?'

'Only you are responsible for the way you feel,' Becky said calmly. 'I've never said one horrible thing to you ever. Not one! I just offered to treat you to a session with my make-up artist. Oh my goodness! What a colossal bitch I am!'

'You're twisting things again,' Amelia complained. 'I don't want a session with your make-up artist so he can fix all the things that are wrong with my face.'

'I knew it.' Becky shook her head sadly as if all her worst suspicions had just been confirmed. 'I know what this is all about. You're jealous, aren't you? Because now I'm the one with everything and you have nothing.'

'I am not jealous.' It was true. Amelia didn't envy Becky any of it. Not the material things, anyway. The dresses and the shoes that looked heavenly but pinched like hell. She didn't even envy the glamorous friends that Becky had acquired or even her handsome husband, but oh! how she wished that she had Becky's self-belief, her confidence, her ease in whatever world she found herself in.

Even when Amelia had been rich, she'd never had that. And now the one thing that she did have, the one thing that made her happy, Becky was intent on taking away.

'You can have any man you want, you're *married*, so why would you try and take George, when you know what he means to me?' she pleaded in a low, urgent voice.

'Take George?' Becky laughed. 'I wouldn't

have him gift-wrapped.' She crossed her exquisite legs and slowly rotated an ankle. 'And even if I were to take him, you wouldn't do anything about it, would you?'

'What would you want me to do?' Amelia asked hopelessly, her hands clenched into futile fists. She knew only too well that when Becky Sharp set her sights on something there was no weapon forged that could defeat her.

'You could slap me round the face,' Becky suggested. 'Then call me a bitch and say that no one was going to come, between you and your man. Or you could even thank me for showing you what a rat he is. Then you could dump Gorgeous George because why would you want to be made a fool of by someone who's very clearly eager to get into my La Perla undies?'

'You're disgusting!' Amelia gasped, blinking back the inevitable tears.

Becky put a hand to her mouth as she yawned theatrically. 'I'd have a lot more respect for you, Emmy, if you grew a pair instead of just letting life happen to you and then crying when it doesn't go the way you were expecting.'

'I don't cry all the time any more,' Amelia sobbed and then she made a valiant effort to get the tears under control. She took a deep breath in, then exhaled slowly. Tipped her head back and blinked her eyes. 'And I don't let life just happen, but I do believe that when life gives you lemons then . . . you should ruddy well try to make lemonade.'

'No, Emmy,' Becky said wearily as if Amelia was a particularly stupid child. 'When life gives you lemons, you throw the lemons right back in life's face.' She straightened up. 'I'm serious. *You* should dump him. He doesn't care about anyone but himself.'

'You'd know all about that,' Amelia snapped and Becky laughed delightedly.

'That's more like it,' she said and then she looked past Amelia and doled out one of her utterly hateful yet absolutely dazzling smiles. 'Ah, talk of the devil.'

George was back with a bottle of champagne, two glasses and an eager expression on his face. 'You were talking about me? Good things, I hope.'

'Wouldn't you like to know?' Becky asked in an awful, purring voice that made a mockery of Amelia's feelings.

'We should go and find the others,' Amelia insisted weakly, though she wished she had the guts and the upper body strength to physically haul George away to a place of safety. 'Last time I saw Dobbin, he looked like he was getting carried away with his war stories. He was using actual props.'

'How boring,' George said, presenting Becky with a glass of champagne, which she received with another glittering smile. Then he poured out the other glass and Amelia waited for him to hand it to her but he kept it for himself. 'Be a good girl then and liberate our Captain Dobbin before he recreates the Battle of Kamdesh.'

'I thought you'd come with me;' Amelia said and George made the little hissing sound she dreaded and a look of exasperation flashed across his face. He even tensed his jaw as if he was grinding his teeth.

'We're not joined at the hip, Emmy,' he said quite evenly, even as his face still said something different. 'You're not going to be much good at political functions if you're too scared to leave my side.'

It was the carrot and the stick. The promise that there would come a day when, instead of furtive dates in the outer suburbs, George would let her back into his world, and the threat that he might not, because he doubted that Amelia had what it took to be a dutiful political plus one.

'Anyway, George, I wanted to pick your brains about government policy and my homeless teenagers,' Becky said and she patted the over-stuffed chair next to her so George would sit down. Three became two, and one was the loneliest number.

Amelia had no choice but to stumble away, retracing her steps back to where Dobbin was now having a very boring talk about military-issue helicopters with the gnomic director. He smiled distractedly at her as she sat down next to him so she could have a ringside view of Becky and George, her George, heads together as they talked and laughed and kept touching each other. His hand on her thigh, her hand coming to rest on his — God, they didn't even have the decency to sneak back into the shadows.

'Emmy, you don't look very happy.'

'That's because I'm not happy,' she said, turning to Dobbin who was now able to give Amelia his full attention, the decrepit director retiring for the night. 'George has forgotten that I even exist.'

Dobbin followed her gaze back to where Becky and George were doing a very good impersonation of two people who only had eyes for each other. 'I wouldn't worry about that,' he said. 'Your friend, Rebecca . . . '

'It turns out that she absolutely isn't a friend of mine,' Amelia said.

'Well, you're much better off without her,' Dobbin insisted because he had a lot of experience of dealing with insurgents, enemy agents and snipers, and as far as he was concerned, Becky Sharp was a dangerous mixture of all three. 'George won't be the first man or the last to be taken in by her, but you know it's you he loves.'

He actually crossed his fingers behind his back as Amelia sighed. 'Will you take me back to the hotel, please?'

'Far better to sit here and pretend that you're having a wonderful time without him.' Dobbin dared to touch Amelia's bare arm with his clumsy fingers. 'If it would help, I could tell you a joke. Though it might not necessarily be a funny joke.'

Amelia's smile was completely genuine even if it did sag at the corners. 'Dear Dobbin, if only more men were like you. But I really don't want to stay here a second longer . . . Oh! He's coming back . . . '

George was striding towards them and Amelia lifted her head, her foolish heart lifting in unison, but he wasn't stopping. 'Becky's cold. Said I'd get her wrap,' he explained as he passed them by, walking over to the table where Rawdon Crawley had removed his shades and was trying to rustle up a posse to decamp to the Casino Barriere.

Amelia watched as George said something to him and Rawdon shrugged, looked around helplessly, even patting his pockets. Finally he had a lightbulb moment and from the back of his chair produced a filmy piece of fabric that wouldn't have kept anything warm. Not that it was cold in the ballroom — on the contrary, it was steaming hot, especially on the upper levels, even with all the doors thrown open.

Again, George spoke to Rawdon and again there was the same exaggerated pantomime from the actor that the New York Times had described as 'one of the most gifted and subtle proponents of his craft', until Rawdon produced a pen. Amelia watched as George walked away, this time to an empty table where he picked up a canapé menu and began to write on the back of it. It took him a good five minutes to compose his thoughts and the note. Amelia's silly heart lifted again. It was an apology, of course. A little love letter asking for her forgiveness.

But it was nothing of the sort. George was on the move, walking past Amelia with a vague, polite smile as if they were distant acquaintances and he wasn't the man who'd bent her over her bathroom sink not two hours before.

She could hardly bear to watch him hand Becky her wrap, the note concealed in its folds. George probably thought he was being stealthy, not realising that wherever he was in a room,

Amelia would always stare longingly at him. Or maybe he did realise but he just didn't care and her heart, which had had quite the workout this evening, sank and broke all over again.

'I really do want to go back to the hotel, Dobbin,' she said in such a fractured, frigid voice that Dobbin didn't try to persuade her to stay and style it out.

★   ★   ★

It took ages to get rid of George Wylie, like a particularly stubborn case of nits. Even after Becky kept her hands to herself and dimmed her smile by several megawatts, George persisted in outstaying his welcome.

'Not now, Dobs,' he said when his huge-footed, jug-eared friend came over and pointedly told him that Amelia was leaving because she had a headache. 'Probably drank too much champagne. She just needs to take a couple of aspirin and sleep it off.'

'George!' Dobbin said sharply. 'You mustn't monopolise *Mrs* Crawley.'

Becky laughed at that; Dobbin was about as subtle as one of the tanks he commanded when he was blowing up the innocent inhabitants of some poor village that were standing between him and the Taliban.

Dobbin had shot Becky a look of pure dislike, which had made her laugh again. The captain was of absolutely no use to her so who cared what he thought? And though she was desperate for George to leave, she turned to him and

283

moistened her lips with a slow sweep of her tongue. 'Now, where were we?'

Dobbin flounced off, in his fury almost colliding with a waiter and his tray of lobster rolls, and Becky had to suffer George banging on about his wonderful career and how people had compared his maiden speech in the House to Winston Churchill's.

Finally, Rawdon realised that his wife had been missing for a good hour and came over to claim his bride.

Behind his shades, his eyes flashed furiously at the sight of their bodies perched so comfortably close together.

'You touch Becky one more time on the leg and I'll break every finger on that hand,' he said menacingly and in a very un-Rawdy-like voice. It was just as well that he was fresh from rehearsals for his role as a drug-running gangster in the Parisian slums.

'Now, now, Crawley, Becky and I were just catching up,' George blustered, shrinking back slightly as he remembered the time at Eton when Rawdon had beaten the living daylights out of a much older boy when he found out that he'd tried to bugger one of the new intake of F-blockers. 'You're hardly newlyweds any more. You'll have to learn to share the most beautiful woman in the room.'

Becky simpered at George's gallantry and Rawdon scowled then growled, actually growled, 'She's mine and I don't fucking share.'

George scuttled off pretty sharpish after that, looking over his shoulder at Becky and mouthing, 'Read the note.'

Becky sank back in her chair. 'Jesus Christ, I thought he'd never go.'

Rawdon held out his hand to haul her up. 'You did want him to go, didn't you?' he checked, doubt creeping into his voice because he and Becky had had a bitter row just before they'd left the yacht when she'd discovered him hoovering up a couple of lines on her Chanel mirrored box clutch. Though Rawdon still wasn't sure if she was angry about the coke when he'd promised to stay clean tonight, or if she was angry because he'd done it on her Chanel bag.

And though Becky was still angry with Rawdon, both for doing coke and doing it on the mirrored box clutch that she'd been waitlisted for, she hadn't been even the slightest bit tempted to linger in the arms of George Wylie. As it was, she'd had to suffer a couple of his very amateurish attempts to kiss her. 'I was *desperate* for him to leave,' she said, letting Rawdon pull her up and fit her against his body. He'd been working with a trainer because the Parisian gangster he was going to play spent most of the film in a tight, white wife-beater and Becky could feel all the newly defined musculature hard against her.

'He had his hands all over me,' she said in a shocked whisper. 'Not the way you expect a Member of Parliament to behave.'

Rawdon, bless him, was so predictable. His eyes and his voice darkened and his abdominal muscles weren't the only hard thing digging into Becky. 'Where did he touch you?'

'I'll tell you later,' she promised. 'When we're on the plane. How long do you think it will take to fly to Paris?'

They both shuddered in anticipation. Rawdon, at the thought of taking his wife in mid-air after she'd shown him the places on her delectably naked body that George Wylie had dared to touch. Becky was giddy simply at the thought of flying on a private jet.

There had been a time when she couldn't even imagine that she might one day travel on one of the planes she saw leaving vapour trails across the London skyline. Then, once she'd been on enough planes to resent the fact that the sybaritic luxury of first class was denied to her, she'd dreamed of turning left, not right.

And now, private jet pissed on first class's chips every time.

'About an hour,' Rawdon answered.

'That's long enough for you to do all sorts of depraved things to my poor, innocent body,' Becky decided and the furious rows were all forgotten as Rawdon stared down at the perfect beauty of his wife's face and how it was improved by her filthy smile, the arch of her eyebrow. 'If you can still get it up after all that coke.'

'Don't Becky,' Rawdon murmured. 'Don't ruin it.'

'I won't, I'm sorry,' Becky said meekly and she tucked her hand in his. 'Come on, take me away from all this. Take me to Paris.'

They were halfway down the sweeping staircase, heads turning to watch them depart because they really were the most striking pair, when Becky remembered that she was still holding George's note.

All the better to tap Rawdon on the hand with it. 'I told you that gullible fool would put it in writing,' she said triumphantly. 'You owe me a thousand quid.'

CRAWLEY CRASHES AND BURNS

Though it premiered in Cannes amid great fanfare, *The Girl I Left Behind* had the lowest opening box-office weekend of any film released so far this year.

The London-set, World War Two spy drama, considered to be a breakout vehicle for Rawdon Crawley, son of Sir Pitt Crawley, was widely panned by critics for its 'lumpen script, heavy-handed direction and soulless performance from the hotly tipped Crawley,' as Thomas Coffin wrote in a particularly savage one-star review in the *Guardian*.

The bad news doesn't end there for Rawdon Crawley. Filming on his latest project, *How to Live Well on Nothing a Year*, was temporarily suspended due to a dispute between director, Archie Auteur, and production company, Chopper Films, over costs spiralling out of control.

No sooner had filming resumed when it stopped again after Crawley sustained lacerations to his face and a broken nose in what his publicist described as 'a bad case of being in the wrong place at the wrong time.'

However, on-set gossip is that Crawley, living up to his hell-raiser reputation, was involved in a bar fight.

Happily for the troubled production, Auteur felt that the actor's facial injuries added piquancy to his role as a gangster involved in a turf war between rival Parisian gangs, and filming resumed.

Is *How to Live Well on Nothing a Year* doomed before it's even wrapped? Watch this space!

26

When Rawdon called and begged for her help, Becky was determined to let him stew in his own drug-addled juices. He'd promised not to gamble. He'd promised to keep his nose clean, literally, after the incident a few weeks ago when he'd had said nose broken after losing a fortune in a poker game and not having the funds to pay what he owed because he'd spent all his money on coke.

But he'd been lying. Again. Instead, he'd carried on doing just what he damn well pleased: cocaine and playing poker very badly, and now he owed even more money and was being held captive until he honoured his debts. Or rather, until Becky bailed him out.

'They're not messing around, Becks,' he whispered. 'They say they're going to start with my fingers. I *need* my fingers.'

'You can manage perfectly well without a couple of fingers. Might shock some sense into your thick, fucking head.'

She put the phone down on Rawdon's inarticulate pleas. She wasn't going to spend a second worrying about him. He was big enough and ugly enough to take care of himself.

But as she sat there, biting her nails and contemplating whether to have a hopefully relaxing bath in the huge claw-foot tub or not, she began to feel uneasy. Rawdon wasn't ugly.

He was pretty. Those soulful eyes, framed with dark, sooty lashes that Becky couldn't hope to replicate, not even with the most expensive lash extensions. Perfect, pouty lips that had launched a thousand teen-girl crushes, cheekbones that could have been carved by Michelangelo himself and photographed so well. As did every other inch of Rawdon Crawley, which was why his face was his fortune. It was Becky's fortune too and God knows what would become of her if the thugs that Rawdon had got involved with did irreparable damage to her meal ticket.

But really, this wasn't her problem. This was Rawdon's agent, Mike's problem. After all, he took 15 per cent of everything Rawdon earned so he could damn well sort this out.

Mike begged to differ when Becky phoned him. Said it was Rawdon's publicist, Knuckle's problem. But when Becky finally managed to get in touch with Knuckles, he said that Rawdon hadn't paid him in *months* but she could try the unit publicist for the film Rawdon was meant to be shooting when he wasn't getting himself into all sorts of trouble.

Becky didn't appreciate being given the runaround like she was some annoying problem that wouldn't go away. It reminded her of the bad old days when she was passed around like an unwanted parcel between different case workers. By the time she'd been given the brush-off by the unit publicist, the producer and finally the producer's *second* assistant, Spooney, she'd completely ruined her expensive manicure by chewing her nails down to the quick.

'It's not that I don't care, Becky, my angel,' Spooney shouted down the phone, while in the background it sounded like he was at a raucous party. 'It's just at this point, it would be cheaper to fire Rawdon and reshoot the movie with an actor who actually shows up on set each day at his allotted call time without any facial injuries.'

'Spooney,' Becky cooed, though her seductive tone of voice was wasted because Spooney shouted at her to speak up. 'Come on, $50,000 is loose change. You could just write it off as expenses. I'd be ever so grateful.'

'No can do. You and Rawdon have already blown through half our budget with your demands. And our liability insurance has already gone through the roof,' Spooney bellowed cheerfully. 'Afraid you're on your own. Though if you need some ready cash, then I know a guy who knows a guy who knows a guy. I'll get someone to give you a call.'

It wasn't at all what Becky wanted to hear but she had to pretend that she was grateful, though Spooney cut her gratitude off after five seconds.

'Laters! And Rawdon better be on set at 7 a.m. or he'll wish his new friends had killed him.'

Becky paced the floors of the €10,000-a-week apartment in the third arrondissement, waiting for the phone call. They owed €40,000 back rent because the production company had slashed costs. Said that they could stay in a crummy hotel out in Beaugrenelle like the rest of the cast and crew. Rawdon would have agreed to that but Becky had insisted that no one would treat him like a star if he didn't act like a star, so they'd stayed put. They'd probably have to do a runner as soon as filming finished.

Then her phone rang. It was someone who spoke French with a guttural foreign accent and didn't bother with any social niceties. Just issued a series of instructions and gave Becky an address. A part of her, quite a large part, was tempted to call it quits and leave Rawdon to his own grisly fate but the smaller, somewhat kinder, part of her won out. She packed a bag and ran down to the street to find a cab to take her to a little man who operated out of the back of a Turkish restaurant in a quiet corner of the Place D'Italie.

Then she was in the back of another cab trying really hard not to cry. The fat-fingered bastard had ripped her off and there was nothing she could do but take the three bundles of US dollars that were all he would give her. Everything that she'd worked so hard for was gone now. All the jewellery from Jemima Pinkerton, which hardly compensated for all the bedpans and incontinence pants and wiping the ailing woman's arse. The items she'd got from the Sedleys, who had suffered her presence with gritted teeth, treated her like a charity case, then threw her out because she wasn't good enough for their precious Jos. The art deco brooch, which had belonged to Rawdon's mother, given to her by Sir Pitt because he hoped it would prise her legs open. The gold hip flask, cigarette case and compact from Matilda Crawley, which had been her reward for nursing that ungrateful woman back from the brink of death.

She asked the driver to stop at an ATM and then — she was properly crying by now — she withdrew pretty much everything she had in the bank. All the money she'd earned from endorsing products that she didn't need or want. Cosying up to agents and publicists and all those businessmen in their suits and aftershave. Smiling, smiling, smiling every time their hands lingered in places that they shouldn't have been touching in the first place. Smiling again when they made lewd remarks and improper suggestions.

Becky Sharp had started with absolutely nothing. Everything she'd acquired had been hard won, hard fought for, and yet it all fitted into one of the leather bags she'd been given for letting a happily married man twice her age stick his hand up her dress. She wasn't crying because she was sad or even because she couldn't bear to part with the sum total of her life's work, but because she was so angry that she wanted to break the cab's windows with her fists and scream her rage into the night.

She did neither of those things, though, but held herself very still and didn't even argue with the driver when they got to Saint-Denis and he pulled into the kerb and said that he wouldn't go any further.

'Then I'm not going to pay you a single euro,' she said and there was something in her voice, in the grim, set expression on her face that the man didn't argue with, though he called her a bitch when she got out of the car.

There was a man called Raoul waiting for her on the corner, though he couldn't have been more than fourteen. He escorted her through the back alleys of a Paris far away from the pretty Haussmann boulevards or the twinkling lights that reflected on the inky-black water of the Seine. Here it was all boarded-up windows and doors, daubed with gang tags and racist epithets. Hard-faced girls worked each corner and further into the shadows, there were mounds of skin and bones sleeping on sodden cardboard, shaking for a fix or a drink or because their demons wouldn't let go.

Becky held her breath. She was better than this, she'd done everything she could to escape this and yet, here she was again.

Eventually, they came to what looked like another derelict doorway. Her escort banged on the corrugated iron, a door opened and Becky stood her ground and spoke in the expletive-laden French she'd learnt at her mother's knee. No, she wasn't going inside. What was going to happen was that they'd bring Rawdon to her and she'd give them the money. No Rawdon, no cash. And no, she didn't care if they did break one of his fingers for each minute she wasted, she was staying right here.

It took three minutes for Rawdon to appear in the doorway, all his fingers sadly intact, accompanied by three heavies that could have found more honest work as extras on his film. 'I'm all right,' he said, like Becky even cared. 'I think I might have a broken rib, though.'

'Good thing broken ribs don't show up on

camera then, isn't it?'

Becky handed over the cash and for one heart-stopping, gut-clenching moment, the fat man with a bullet tattooed on his forehead, his tracksuit stretched grotesquely over his elephantine limbs, said it wasn't enough.

'*Soixante*,' he said and he spat on the ground, phlegm landing on the toe of one of Becky's limited-edition Prada sneakers. No point in wearing heels if you might have to run for it.

'We agreed fifty, you fat fuck.' Then she spat back because Rawdon was just a poor little rich boy, a slum tourist, dipping a toe in the filth and the fury of the back alleys, knowing that it would wash off.

But Becky knew these streets. Knew that some things would never wash off even if you scrubbed yourself red raw trying.

'*Cinquante*,' she said again. 'Not one cent more.'

The three men talked among themselves about whether they should take the money and break Rawdon's fingers, maybe kneecap him too, while they made Becky watch. Becky's hand didn't even shake as she brought it to her mouth to cover her yawn.

'I haven't got all night,' she snapped. 'And I've got a driver two streets away who's going to call some people if I'm not back in five minutes. Says his brother knows a guy called Ali, maybe you know him too?'

The man who'd bought her jewels for a tenth of what they were worth had told her that the neighbourhood was controlled by two gangs.

This bunch of hoodlums in hoodies from the Côte d'Ivoire were deadly rivals of a Muslim faction run by an old guy from Algiers who had a glass eye, one ball and went by the name of Ali.

'Fuck you then,' the fat guy hissed and he snatched the bag out of Becky's hold, ripping one of her nails as he did so, then Rawdon was thrust towards her.

'What did he say?' Rawdon asked, as thank God, the door was slammed in their faces. His knowledge of French was only sufficient to order a round of drinks. 'What did you say?'

Becky said nothing but started walking, trying to remember the way out of the maze of tiny streets. Rawdon hobbled after her, hissing slightly, hampered by unseen injuries sustained during his abduction.

'Becky?' he bleated. 'I'm sorry. Don't be mad at me. I hate it when you're angry at me. Come on! Say you forgive your little Rawdy.'

She turned another corner and they were out of the darkness and on to a main road. It was still the worst neighbourhood in Paris, but there were streetlights that worked, cafes and bars, shops selling everything from exotic produce to wigs. It was safety of a sort, though everyone turned to look at Becky and Rawdon as if they were from another planet. In Saint-Denis, the third arrondissement was another planet.

'Becky! You have to speak to me sooner or later. It's OK. I'm good. We're good. No bones broken, apart from maybe a rib. Did I mention that they took away my phone but . . . '

'SHUT THE FUCK UP! SHUT UP! SHUT

UP! SHUT UP! I WISH THEY'D BROKEN EVERY FUCKING BONE IN YOUR USE- LESS BODY!' She was shouting, hitting Rawdon, raining her fists down on whatever part of him she could reach. Not his face, but everywhere else including his suspected broken rib, and she was glad when he cried out.

People stopped looking at them, because here fights were nothing special, nothing remarkable.

'Becky! Stop it! I'm sorry,' Rawdon cried and he managed to grab her wrist as she kept pounding on him with her other hand closed into a fist. 'I'm sorry!'

One last blow to the side of his head, enough to make his ear ring, and Becky stopped, wrenched herself free from Rawdon's grip. She let her arms hang down, tried to slow her ragged breaths even as she stared up at him with a savage expression that would be the last thing Rawdon Crawley would remember, many years later, when he was on his deathbed.

'You promised to look after me, then you promised that at least you'd look after yourself, and you can't even do that,' she reminded him in a voice that was murderous and low. 'You're a dirty, lying bastard. It makes me sick how weak you are.'

'I'm sorry,' Rawdon repeated. If he could say it enough times, maybe it would wipe out everything: his debts, his weakness, his betrayal.

'I should leave you,' Becky threatened even though she currently had nowhere else to go. That face of his, healing up nicely, just one fresh cut above his eyebrow, was the only liquid asset she still had. 'Give me one good reason why I shouldn't.'

'Because . . . because I love you!' Rawdon said with the air of a man pulling a rabbit out of a hat on his third attempt.

'You're going to have to do better than that,' Becky said and she turned away, started walking again, slower this time, all energy spent.

Rawdon sighed as if she were being unreasonable, impossible, then in a few quick strides, caught up with her. 'I'm not going to do it any more,' he promised *yet again*. 'Not any of it. The drugs, the poker games.' He dared to nudge her arm so when she glanced across at him, he was smiling in that way that he thought she found irresistible because she was a much, much better actor than he would ever be. 'You do still love your Rawdy, don't you?'

That dark, viscous rage boiled in her veins again. 'If my lousy father taught me one lousy thing it's that you only gamble when you have nothing to lose. You had *everything* and now it's all gone.'

'But we still have each other, right?' He actually dared to bat his eyelashes at her, so Becky felt justified in elbowing him in his suspected broken rib again.

'Did you hear me? We have nothing. No money, nothing to fall back on, no plan B, and this is all on you. You've spoilt it all.'

'I'll unspoil it. I'll make it better,' Rawdon said and he stepped in front of his wife, blocked her path so he could put his hands on her shoulders, lean his forehead against hers. 'Look, I'll get in

298

touch with Mattie. Make things up with her and we'll all be friends again. You'd like that, wouldn't you?'

Rage gave way to the faintest flicker of hope. 'Do you think she'll listen? She's still very angry with you,' Becky reminded Rawdon.

'Yeah, but unlike you, she can't stay mad at me for long.'

27

It was late October and Becky and Rawdon were huddled outside a dingy club in Montmartre, a chill wind whistling around them. It was four weeks since Becky had bailed Rawdon out, and they were at the wrap party for *How to Live Well on Nothing a Year*; never had a film been more aptly titled. Rawdon was chain-smoking Gauloises and Becky had come out with him because the production accountant kept trying to talk to her about the rent demands on the apartment.

'The film is *way* over budget, so I don't see what difference our rent is going to make,' she complained to Rawdon. 'It's so petty.'

'I'd have been perfectly happy to stay in the cheap hotel in Beaugrenelle,' Rawdon said, blowing out a stream of smoke so he looked like a very louche dragon. Along with all his other bad habits, he was meant to have stopped smoking too, but there were only so many things that Becky could ride him for without him calling her a nagging bitch and without that deeply unflattering furrow appearing between her eyebrows. She wasn't ready for Botox quite yet so she counted to ten and contented herself with pointedly fanning the air. 'Nobody's forcing you to stand here and watch me smoke.'

'If I go inside and talk to other people, then you sulk about me ignoring you. You get so needy when you're not the centre of attention,'

Becky complained and she could *feel* her brows knitting together.

'Ha! That's rich coming from you,' Rawdon said with a sneer, as deep within the breast pocket of his leather jacket, his phone started to ring. 'Saved by the bell.' He retrieved his mobile. 'It's Mattie. Very late for her to be calling.'

In the end, it had only taken a week for Dame Matilda to come round, which left Becky fuming for all the lost time they'd burned through since parting. Perhaps it was because the last few years had made her frailer and more aware of the end of her mortal coil, but Mattie was now taking Rawdon's calls and when they got back to London (which couldn't come soon enough) he would have to redouble his efforts. It was the very least he could do, especially as his previous film had bombed and everything indicated that this one was going to go straight to streaming release if it was ever released at all. Despite Becky's ambitions to be a kept woman, they were existing on whatever funds she could scrounge up endorsing any old tat on her Instagram, from waxing strips to carb-free, dairy-free, sugar-free chocolate, which had been banned in the US for giving people chronic diarrhoea.

'But she is calling, so that's something,' Becky said, her irritation fading, not even minding the cigarette smoke as she moved closer to Rawdon so she could try and hear what his aunt was saying. Maybe this was the call where the dame finally moved on from referring to Becky as '*that girl*'.

'Mattie? Mattie! Is everything . . . Briggs! Why are you calling me on Mattie's phone?' Rawdon raised his eyebrows at Becky, who couldn't make out a single word, just what sounded like sobbing on the other end of the line.

Then Rawdon staggered down the five steps that took him to the kerb so he could sit down heavily, legs splayed out. 'I can't believe it,' he muttered brokenly. 'But she was fine when I spoke to her yesterday. Hang on.' He put his hand over the mouthpiece so he could turn to Becky, who was standing expectantly behind him. 'God, Becky . . . Mattie's dead. Died in her sleep.'

Something cold slithered its way down her spine. 'Oh?' Becky stood frozen to the spot. Then she looked up to the navy-blue sky, tried in vain to find a star, and lifted up her glass of cheap cava in a silent salute to the demanding old cow of whom she'd actually been quite fond. She'd even had a grudging respect for the way Mattie had seen right through her. She swallowed past the lump in her throat. 'I'm so sorry, Rawdy.'

But she was already forgotten. Rawdon was talking to Briggs again, asking with choked emotion about the arrangements for the funeral, then suddenly the phone clattered from his slack fingers into the road and he let out an eldritch howl that made every hair on Becky's body that hadn't been lasered away stand to attention.

'What? What is it?' she asked but Rawdon slumped, head in his hands, and started to cry.

It was left to Becky to retrieve his phone. 'Briggs? It's Becky.' She looked up again at the sombre sky. 'Will you please stop making that awful noise? I can't hear what you're saying.'

Briggs swallowed snottily a couple of times. 'Becky . . . oh, Becky. It's terrible.'

'I'm sure you must be devastated. I know I am. I was convinced that she'd eventually summon me round to Primrose Hill and we'd say a few more horrible things to each other, then finally make up. But Mattie hadn't been well and at least she went peacefully,' Becky said delicately. Oh, so very delicately. She was shocked at the news, even sad about it, but was it too soon to broach the subject of whether Mattie had been to see her solicitor lately? 'Had she been out and about much recently?'

'And Sir Pitt. When all's said and done, I suppose he must have loved her in his own way . . . oh! Oh . . . ' It was no use. Briggs had descended into incoherent weeping all over again.

Becky had no choice but to hang up the phone, and tug on Rawdon's hair until he lifted his tear-swollen face up to hers.

'It's very sad,' Becky said and she hoped that she sounded as if she meant it. She didn't have that much experience when it came to expressing her true feelings. Feelings were best tucked out of sight where they couldn't get in anyone's way. 'But you have to stop crying because I can't get any sense out of Briggs. He said something about your father . . . ?'

'He's dead,' Rawdon burst out.

Becky stared at him in confusion. 'What? Who's dead?'

'Dad's dead too. Briggs said . . . ' Rawdon's face — his patrician, perfect features — collapsed in on itself. Becky chewed the inside of her cheeks and waited for him to gather himself, as Mattie would have said.

'How can Sir Pitt be dead?' Becky shook her head. 'You must have misunderstood.'

'Briggs . . . ' Rawdon tensed his muscles, to hold the tears back. 'Briggs said that when he called Dad this morning to tell him the news, he — literally — dropped down dead. Massive heart attack.' Rawdon's bottom lip was wobbling like a kite on a windy day. 'I always thought I hated the bastard, but knowing that I'm never going to get the chance to tell him how much I hated him breaks my heart.'

With a silent apology to the Marc Jacobs dress she was wearing, Becky sank down on the kerb next to Rawdon so she could take his hand and wind her fingers through his. 'You might have hated him, but you loved him too,' she said softly. 'That's the deal with fathers, no matter what bastards they are, and no matter how much the hate feels like love and the love feels like hate.'

'Yeah, it's exactly like that,' Rawdon agreed. 'You always understand. You know me better than anyone ever has.'

'That's because I love you,' Becky said, which was a lie. Really it was because Rawdon wasn't a very complex character, and had nothing in the way of layers. 'I know right now that it feels like the world is ending but you still have me. Everything will be fine.'

Though Becky had been feeling quite upset about Mattie and fairly ambivalent about Sir Pitt, now she dared to feel a little optimistic.

Between Rawdon's aunt and his father, at least one of them (but please, please, please let it be both) had to have left Rawdon something in their will.

MEET BRITAIN'S NEWEST MILLIONAIRE!
Sir Pitt Crawley's eldest son inherits two fortunes on the same day . . .

While a nation mourns the passing of two of Britain's greatest actors, Dame Matilda Crawley and her younger brother, Sir Pitt Crawley, one member of the Crawley family has every reason to celebrate.

Pitt Junior, Sir Pitt's son, has been named the sole beneficiary of both his aunt's and his father's wills. Dame Matilda left over £25 million to her nephew as well as her six-bedroom house in London's trendy Primrose Hill, a chateau in the South of France and a stunning villa in Palm Springs, California.

As eldest son of Sir Pitt, the lucky lad will also inherit Queen's Crawley, a palatial Georgian mansion in forty acres in rural Hampshire, a Chelsea townhouse and a personal fortune estimated at around £10 million, despite the legendary thespian claiming to be broke.

So, while the luvvies of London get ready to say goodbye to Dame Matilda, who died peacefully in her sleep last week, and Sir Pitt who died suddenly of a heart attack on hearing the news, we're sure Pitt Junior has the champagne on ice.

It's quite the rags-to-riches story for the newly minted millionaire. While his more famous younger brother, Rawdon, inherited his father's and aunt's acting talent, poor

Pitt Junior is a struggling writer whose greatest claim to fame is a collection of short stories that sold only two hundred copies.

Now Pitt Junior has star billing and Rawdon, whose last film, *The Girl I Left Behind*, bombed at the box office, and was recently involved in a bar fight, is rumoured to have been cut off without a penny. At least Rawdon has his wife of one year, ravishing Rebecca Sharp, model and Instagram queen, to dry his tears, but it must be small consolation.

Meanwhile Pitt Junior, who was living in a grotty flat in Finchley, has been seeing Jane Sheepshanks, a marketing executive, for the last five years. A close friend of the late Dame Matilda claims that it was her affection for Jane, who'd been devoted to the ailing *Lyndon Place* star, that was behind her decision to leave all her dosh to Pitt Junior. What are the odds that gentle Jane now makes Pitt put a ring on it? She certainly deserves it and lucky Pitt can certainly afford it!

28

'That fucking bastard!' Rawdon held up his iPad so that Becky could see the *Daily Mail* article he'd been reading, then flung the device on the floor of the room in the Novotel on the outskirts of Paris where he and Becky had decamped after they'd done a moonlight flit from the fancy apartment.

'Which fucking bastard are you talking about? Your father, your aunt or your brother?' Becky asked calmly. Outwardly she was serene, but on the inside she was screaming like a wolverine.

'My fucking father, he always hated me. Couldn't stand that I might be better than him. A better actor, better looking . . . fuck him!' The croissants that Becky had stolen from next door's breakfast tray (served them right for leaving it outside their room) were Rawdon's next victims as he hurled them out of the window. Then he went back to pacing. And ranting. Something about Pitt Junior and how he'd always broken Rawdon's toys when they were little. 'And Matilda. I loved her, Becky, I *fucking* loved her but what a vindictive bitch. She always said that she was going to leave her money to me. When someone makes a promise like that, you live your life in a certain way, with certain expectations. God, I'd have signed on for the big-bucks Hollywood blockbusters if she hadn't said I was going to inherit her millions . . . '

Becky didn't point out that Rawdon had said that he didn't care about inheriting Matilda's millions. After all, he'd said it when he'd married Becky, and yet, she was the one person that Rawdon hadn't blamed for his current predicament. Which, really, was very generous of him.

'Rawdy, darling, it can't be good for you to charge around like that,' Becky cooed, as she tapped his brother's email address into her phone. 'Why don't you go and have a cigarette, clear your head.'

'Fucking bastards!' Rawdon snarled one final time, then he gathered up his Gauloises (an affectation that he still wasn't in any hurry to drop) and headed for the door. 'I'll be back in ten.'

'Take your time,' Becky said sweetly and as the door slammed behind him, she let out a heartfelt sigh then turned back to her phone.

It would probably be better to send a handwritten letter, but her handwriting hadn't progressed far beyond the childish block letters that she'd somehow managed to learn during her occasional visits to the primary school on Great Windmill Street, and her phone had spellcheck. Also, she wasn't trusting this message to the postal service. It would take too long and time absolutely wasn't on her side.

Dear Pitt

I hope you don't mind that Briggs gave me your email address, but I wanted to write to offer you my condolences.

I am so sorry for your loss, both your losses. I

309

know how fond you were both of Sir Pitt and Dame Matilda and I can't begin to imagine how wretched you must feel.

How lucky you are to have Jane as your partner. I'll never forget how she stayed up into the night on Christmas Eve to make me that lovely red wool corsage so I'd feel like one of the family, rather than the hired help. And you too, Pitt, went out of your way to treat me kindly that Christmas at Queen's Crawley.

So, I'm pleased that your kindness and your good heart has been rewarded. Rawdon is too. Honestly, he couldn't be happier for you. His career is going from strength to strength (those stories in the paper are just malicious gossip) and I have my own very successful career as a social influencer and brand ambassador, so neither of us want for much.

I would really hate if any of this inheritance business came between you and Rawdy. Family is so important and Rawdon and the Crawleys are the only family I have, so it would break my heart if the two of you were to fall out over some imagined grievance.

With that in mind, would it be a terrible impo-sition if we came to see you and Jane at Queen's Crawley? (Briggs mentioned that you'd decided to live there for the time being and give up your London flat.) I really think you and Rawdon should spend time together, to heal after the tragic deaths of Pitt and Mattie. But more than that, I would love to see the children. The poor poppets! They are the real victims in this, practically orphans since Rosa ran off with that masseur.

I hope that, in some small way, I might be able to offer them some comfort. It might sound unprofessional but I did grow to care for them very deeply when I was their nanny — so would love to be there for them in their hour of need.

We're due to leave Paris any day now to travel to Mudbury for the funerals and, if at all convenient, would love to stay at Queen's Crawley for a while. Not long enough to get on your nerves, I promise!

It will be so lovely to see you and Jane, get to know you properly, become a real family. That's worth more than all that money.

Your loving sister
Becky xxx

29

As Becky and Rawdon left Paris — and a series of unpaid bills — behind them, Amelia Sedley was peeing on a stick and praying that the two blue lines wouldn't appear. Or was she praying that they *would* be there, just like they'd been there on the five other pregnancy tests she'd done?

She'd always wanted children. In her dreams, they had always been George's children, though ever since they'd returned from Cannes, Amelia was sure that she still hated him.

When he'd finally got back to the hotel on the night of the charity gala, after abandoning her for Becky (*even though Becky was married and didn't even like George and actually Becky was a horrible, horrible person and always had been but Amelia had been too stupid to realise it but she couldn't help being kind-hearted even though it meant people walked all over her and she absolutely wasn't going to get over the whole Becky thing anytime soon and if Becky tried to contact her to say sorry then Amelia planned to be icy and dignified and say that as far as she was concerned she and Becky were no longer friends because friends didn't treat people the way that Becky had treated her*), Amelia had pretended that she was asleep.

'Emmy, don't be cross with me,' he'd had the nerve to say. 'I'm sorry. I'd had too much to drink. In the normal way, I wouldn't even look at that Sharp creature . . . '

'She's not Sharp. Not any more. She's a Crawley,' Amelia had said furiously, abandoning any pretence of sleep so she could sit up and glare at George. Normally the sight of him looking contrite — he did this thing with his eyes that was particularly affecting — was enough to make Amelia melt, but not this time. 'She's *married*. Not that that stopped you. You obviously don't care a thing for me.'

'I was wrong. Behaved like a complete cad and anyway, you're twice the woman she'll ever be,' George had said silkily and then, unbelievably, he'd tugged at his bow tie as if he was about to get undressed. 'Let me make it up to you.'

Amelia would always love George. At times she felt as if loving George Wylie was imprinted into her mitochondrial DNA, but on this particular occasion, she found that she didn't love him one little bit. Or maybe she did love him just a little bit but Becky's words had hit home. She really did let bad things, and bad people, happen to her without ever attempting to stand up for herself. Well, now she was going to be a new, improved Amelia Sedley who didn't let people walk all over her.

George's betrayal with Becky Sharp of all people had devastated her and devastation could make even the quietest of mice roar. Though in Amelia Sedley's case, the roar was more of a very squeaky voice that said, 'I'd stop taking your clothes off if I were you, because there is absolutely no way that I'm having with sex with you tonight.' She'd paused. 'Or for the foreseeable future.'

That had been that. George had sent her one text since they got back to London. 'You really are being very immature, Emmy. Let's sit down and talk about this like grown-ups.'

The old Amelia would have immediately capitulated but the new Amelia didn't deign to reply. She had a father whose trial date was coming up and a mother who spent more days in bed with a migraine than she did out of bed. She also had a physically demanding job and colleagues who were very firm and forthright and would never let their boyfriends treat them the way George had treated her. In fact, he'd never once even referred to her as his girlfriend!

But now it turned out that she was pregnant and maybe she wasn't *quite* so angry with George any more. He'd done a terrible thing but then Amelia would go to work and she'd stroke the tangles out of Pianoforte's unruly mane and feed him carrots and remember the one wonderful thing that George had done when he'd rescued her childhood friend from an uncertain future of either a cruel-faced lottery-winner owner or the glue factory. He had to love her to have done that.

Even so, it was quite hard to remember that she did still love George in the face of his cold, condemning anger when she presented him with the five positive pregnancy tests.

'How on *earth* can you be pregnant? Why the hell weren't you on the pill? For God's sake,

Emmy, how could you have been so stupid? It is mine, I take it?'

'Of course it's yours,' she snapped. 'And I got pregnant the usual way and yes, I was on the pill but it's only 98 per cent effective and I haven't been stupid, just unfortunate to get pregnant by a man who would be horrid enough to accuse me of sleeping around,' she said in that squeaky but furious voice that she'd found in Cannes.

They both blinked in surprise. George had agreed to meet her in a McDonalds on Whitehall because he reasoned that no one he knew would ever go to a McDonalds but he'd still be able to get back to Parliament to vote within eight minutes if he got a text from the Whip's Office. Even so, he kept looking over his shoulder as if he expected to suddenly see the Minister for Agriculture queuing up for a quarter-pounder and large fries.

'I'm sorry,' George said, eyes narrowed because Amelia was quite the unknown quantity lately. 'It's just a bit of a shock, Emmy.'

'How do you think I feel then?' Amelia said and the smell of fast food kept warm under heat lamps was making her feel queasy (not throwing up in the mornings was quite the challenge when she was on mucking-out duties). 'It's hardly ideal.'

George's eyes narrowed again. 'So, you're not happy about it?' He could hardly keep the relief out of his voice. 'I could . . . make a few discreet enquiries. There's no reason why this has to be a problem.'

Amelia retched then, eyes watering with the

315

effort not to vomit, while George watched her fearfully, edging back as far as the seat, which was bolted to the table, would allow.

'I'm not going to be sick and I'm not going to get rid of it,' she said eventually and it was George's turn to wonder if he might throw up. Or cry. One of the two. 'This isn't a problem. It's a baby. *Our* baby.'

As soon as she said that, the first sentence icy cold and the final one all warm and melting, George Wylie knew that there was no getting rid of it.

No getting rid of Amelia either: he'd have to marry her now. There was absolutely no way that a man in his position, with his potential, could afford to have an illegitimate child tucked away in Burnt Oak. He'd also have to use his influence (which wasn't yet as great as George would have liked it to be) to keep her father out of jail, and as for her mother . . .

Then there was Amelia herself. Not quite the wet little fool that she'd once been, but she wasn't as malleable as she'd used to be either. That was no bad thing — she'd need a bit of backbone to be an MP's wife, but this was the second occasion when Amelia had acted quite out of character. It was a side to her, one that he didn't think even Amelia was aware of, which quite frankly terrified George.

Still, what was done was done. She'd always be grateful to him and gratitude could be awfully useful.

'Our baby,' George repeated and he tried to sound pleased rather than resigned. His father would kill him. Or at the very least, have him horsewhipped. 'You know, now that the shock is wearing off, I'm starting to get used to the idea. Even pleased.' He pretended to consider the many joys of impending fatherhood. 'Yes, pleased.'

Amelia still looked as if she might projectile vomit if he made any sudden movements. 'Really?' she asked doubtfully, hope (and nausea) written all over her face. 'Pleased?'

'It's not every day that a man discovers that he's going to be a father and a husband, is it?' George summoned up a smile from the very depths of his being.

Hope won out over nausea and Amelia smiled tremulously. 'A husband?'

There was no way that George was getting down on one knee. Not in his Richard James suit and not in a McDonalds where any one of the ferret-faced clientele could whip out a phone and make the proposal go viral. He settled for another tight smile and gingerly reached out (there was a dried smear of red sauce on the table) to take Amelia's hand. 'Amelia Sedley, would you do me the utmost pleasure of agreeing to become my wife?'

30

The funeral service of Sir Pitt Crawley and Dame Matilda Crawley was held at the Actors' Church in Covent Garden, and most of those present, who had fallen foul of one of the deceased at some point or other, took a silent delight that in death the two were forced to share joint billing.

Then the coffins were transported to Hampshire for a private burial, family only, in the graveyard at St Simeon the Holy in Mudbury, where generation after generation of Crawleys had become worm food.

It was a grey October day, rain slashing down, so the walk back to the house through the overgrown grounds was wet and muddy. Pitt had stayed behind to talk to the vicar so Becky walked with Jane, each of them holding a child's hand. They'd had an excruciatingly earnest conversation about whether the five children should attend the burial, Becky's opinion highly sought as she had personal experience of such matters. Although, there hadn't been a funeral for either her mother or her father — they'd been cremated courtesy of Westminster Council and HM Prison Service respectively and as far as Becky knew, their ashes were sitting on the shelves in a municipal storeroom somewhere.

'I can't see that it would do any harm,' she'd told Jane when she and Rawdon had arrived at

Queen's Crawley that morning. 'It may even help the poor mites come to terms with what's happened.'

Truthfully, she didn't care either way but Martha Crawley had very strong opinions that the children should be spared all talk of death. She kept banging on about how Pitt and Matilda had gone to sleep in God's spare room, which was reason enough for Becky to take the opposing view. Briggs, absolutely paralytic on champagne, had told Becky about the letter that Martha had shown Mattie, after getting that bitch Babs Pinkerton to dish the dirt. So Becky would now make it her life's work to ensure that Martha Crawley never knew another happy moment.

As it was, Martha and Bute were walking behind Becky and Jane and positively seething that there hadn't been room for them in the front pew. Bringing up the rear was Rawdon, who'd been in a massive sulk ever since Becky had told him that Pitt had invited them both to stay. He was with Thisbe, who was as vile and snot-encrusted as Becky remembered him. Whatever riches she managed to claw out of the estate by the time she and Rawdon left Queen's Crawley would be well deserved for having to put up with his godforsaken family.

Becky had forgotten how cold and forbidding the house was — Pitt and Jane were welcome to it, she thought as she unwillingly shrugged out of her coat and went to join the company in the drawing room.

At least the fire was lit. 'I know that Sir Pitt

had some funny ideas: no fires until the clocks went back! But it's so cold,' Jane said to Becky. 'Pitt and I are agreed that the house needs a completely new central heating system as soon as probate is granted.'

'And a new roof and windows that aren't rotting in the frames,' Becky suggested helpfully. She put a hand on Jane's arm, her expression concerned, sincere. 'I feel so sorry for you and Pitt. It's quite the poisoned chalice you've inherited.'

'Isn't it?' Jane agreed. For someone who'd just inherited millions and millions, not to mention at least five houses spread over three continents, she didn't look very happy. Her mousy hair looked lank, though that probably had every-thing to do with Queen's Crawley's antiquated plumbing system (another thing that Pitt would have to throw thousands of pounds at) and its brackish water. She had dark shadows under her eyes and an angry red spot on her chin — Becky suspected that since she'd become lady of the manor, she'd been comfort eating.

Not that she was officially lady of the manor. It wasn't as if Jane and Pitt Junior were married but even if they had been hitched, marriages ended in divorce all the time. It would be quite the scandal though, ditching Rawdon for his older, much, much, much richer brother . . . Becky's reverie was interrupted by Pitt himself entering the room, nervously fussing with the few strands of hair that were all he had left. Just the thought of what it might be like to be touched by those lily-white, fleshy, soft hands sent a shudder through Becky from tip to toe. Besides, the money was one thing, but Pitt the Younger wielded absolutely no influence and now had sole custody of his five half-siblings.

No, Jane was welcome to him.

'Honestly, we don't know where to start.' Jane was still lamenting, without pause, the sorry state of Queen's Crawley. 'Also, you have to believe me, Becky, Pitt had no idea that everything would come to him.' She gestured to the threadbare sofa by the draughty window where they couldn't be overheard and Becky, ears pricked, gladly followed. 'Martha and Bute, but mostly Martha, have been thoroughly unpleasant.'

'Oh?' It almost killed Becky not to seize Jane by the lapels of the frumpy brocade blazer she was wearing and demand all the gossip. 'I thought Martha was looking a little out of sorts but I put it down to grief.'

'Huh!' Jane snorted and though she was a thoroughly decent sort, who still abided by the Brownie Guide Law and her old school motto of *Beati mundo corde* (Blessed are the pure in heart), Martha Crawley could alienate anyone. If Oprah Winfrey ever came into contact with Martha Crawley, then even Oprah would have wanted to slap her. 'She's said some very unkind, hurtful things. Implied that I ingratiated myself with Aunt Matilda and put pressure on her to change the will. Which I didn't. I really didn't.' Jane went quite white at the very suggestion, which made her spot look even redder and angrier.

'Of course you didn't,' Becky said soothingly, though she'd thought exactly the same thing. But now that she'd been forced to spend quality time with Jane, it was obvious that the woman didn't have a bad bone in her body. That probably explained why she was so dull. 'Mattie was very much her own woman, wasn't she? Once she got an idea in her head, then she wasn't for turning.' Though Becky was still furious that Dame Matilda had been as good as her word and had left her and Rawdon high and dry, she felt a momentary pang. How she wished that Matilda were here to liven up this dreary gathering by being rude to everyone.

'Is Rawdon very angry with us?' Jane asked with an anxious glance at her brother-in-law who was slouched next to a portrait of one of his ancestors done by a pupil of Gainsborough, puffing on one of his stupid Gauloises (even though Bute had lectured him at length about the evils of passive smoking), and sipping from a glass of his father's most expensive whisky. 'He's barely said a word to either of us.'

'Oh, never mind Rawdy,' Becky assured her. 'He's almost mute with grief. Too frightened to speak, in case he breaks down. You know, he *adored* Mattie . . . '

'Again, we're really so sorry that Auntie disinherited him . . . '

'I don't blame you.' Becky's voice trembled with emotion. 'I blame myself, but Jane, we can't help who we fall in love with, can we? Both of us were powerless to resist it.'

Jane didn't think she'd ever seen a sight more

beautiful, more heart-tugging, than Becky's face as she talked about hers and Rawdon's love. She and Pitt rubbed together well enough but gosh, it wasn't like she'd had a long line of men queuing up to date her before she'd met Pitt at a rock choir they'd both joined. How she longed to experience the passionate love that Becky was describing. 'Yes, I absolutely understand.'

'Strictly between us girls, I blame Martha: she went running to Mattie with all sort of lies she'd dug up from a vile old drunk who used to know my parents. The things she said about my mother . . . ' Becky sniffed, then pulled out a lace-trimmed hankie from her Chanel clutch so she could dab her eyes. 'My mother died when I was eight and just being here, seeing the children, it brings it all back . . . '

'Oh, Becky,' Jane sighed, gathering Becky into her arms so she could hug her and making a vow that Martha (who'd been angling for her and Bute to move into the lodge house after Pitt had spent money renovating it) would never experience any kindness from her. 'I know that we've only met a couple of times, but I feel . . . I think . . . I would very much like us to be friends.'

'I'd like that too, more than anything,' Becky said, her voice muffled from where her face had been smooshed into Jane's bosom. She struggled to free herself and just in case Jane had failed to notice it (though she'd have to be blind not to), she lightly touched the red wool corsage, which had been moulting fluff all over her black Celine dress. 'I've wanted to be friends with you ever since you gave me this, but you seemed so together, so sophisticated, and I was just a twenty-year-old nanny that . . . '

'No, not another word!' Jane insisted, quite ecstatic at Becky's description of herself as sophisticated when she'd been in awe of the younger girl's beauty, her self-possession, the way that Rawdon had looked at her even then. 'We're friends and I couldn't be happier about it. End of.'

One down, one to go.

31

Pitt Junior scurried along the corridors of Queen's Crawley with stooped shoulders and a haunted expression on his face. Each corner he turned brought him face to face with more problems, from dry rot in the Long Gallery to water damage in the attics due to the missing shingles on the roof.

Heavy was the head that wore the crown and Becky could swear that the sparse strands of hair that Pitt clung to had been seriously depleted in the last five days. Only that morning, Bute — no longer able to contain his fury at being left only £10,000 by his brother and some actually very profitable shares by his sister — had demanded that Pitt gift him at least one of Matilda Crawley's properties *and* the Lodge House.

Pitt was already pretty bloody cross with Martha for upsetting Jane, and Bute had chosen his moment very badly indeed as Pitt had just seen off a structural surveyor who'd told him that he'd be better off burning Queen's Crawley to the ground, claiming on the insurance and starting all over again rather than trying to rebuild and repair.

There had been words. Many shouted words. 'Swear words mostly,' the children had reported gleefully. 'Three fucks, two buggers and we lost count of all the shits and bastards.'

Pitt Junior hadn't shouted or sworn in all the

years that Jane had known him, but the querulous Crawley genes hadn't missed him out entirely. They were buried deep and his uncle had brought them up to the surface.

'Get out! Take your evil wife with you and never come back,' Pitt had shouted as Jane had wept on Becky's shoulder, while Becky had kept herself very still so she didn't wriggle in sheer delight. It was so rare that someone else did the heavy lifting for her and, thanks to Pitt, she no longer had to wreak vengeance on Martha Crawley all by herself.

Becky waited until dinner that evening before she made her move and gently placed her hand on Pitt's arm, because now that Martha and Bute had disappeared in a puff of sulphurous smoke (or their Ford Mondeo, to be more accurate), Becky was sitting on Pitt's right.

'I just wanted to say . . . ' she paused delicately and Pitt steeled himself for yet more demands. What everyone failed to understand was that until probate had been granted, he couldn't do anything with all the money he was starting to wish he'd never inherited. This afternoon his accountant, who was more used to dealing with Pitt's pitiful personal tax return, had calculated the amount of death duties Pitt would have to pay, and Pitt had wanted to cry like a baby.

'Yes?' he asked warily, because much as he disliked Martha, she'd had plenty to say about his sister-in-law, and none of it good. Also, like a lot of unremarkable men, Pitt had an innate distrust of beautiful women, mostly because they never wanted to sleep with him.

'If you want Rawdy and I to clear out, if you feel that we're imposing on you in any way, then you really must tell us,' Becky said, shrinking back in her chair as if she simply couldn't bear it if Pitt thought that his younger brother and his wife were a pair of opportunistic freeloaders.

'We could go back to London,' Rawdon said hopefully from further down the table where he was sitting with the children. About the only time that he wasn't in a colossal sulk was when he spent time with his half-siblings, intent on cheering them up, though they didn't seem that upset about the passing of their father. Probably because he was a distant, shouty figure who'd deprived them of all their creature comforts such as heating, sugar and television.

'No, no, you're fine,' Pitt said hurriedly, staring down at his hands. He could hardly bring himself to look Rawdon in the eye. Being the eldest son, he'd expected to inherit Queen's Crawley because, although his father didn't seem to like him very much, his resentment of Rawdon was verging on biblical and it had barely seemed to register that he had five other children. So Pitt had assumed that whatever assets Pitt Senior possessed might come his way, and Rawdon would inherit their aunt's estate in due course, as she delighted in reminding them all. And yet here they were. He'd never imagined that Sir Pitt's assets would be so vast or that his Aunt Matilda would take so violently against Rawdon's wife. 'Absolutely fine. Lovely to have you both.'

'And despite the sad circumstances, it's

wonderful to be here,' Becky said, glancing down the table fondly at her former charges. 'To be reunited with my darling little Crawleys.'

Jane blinked rapidly. She was determined not to cry again and even Pitt marvelled silently at how one woman could be so beautiful but kind.

'We weren't your darling little Crawleys when you were our nanny,' an accusing little voice piped up from the other end of the table and Thisbe (who else?) dared to smirk at Becky. 'You used to pinch us if we didn't behave and call us terrible names.'

How Becky wished that she were sitting next to the little bastard so she could pinch him now. Instead she smiled sweetly at him. 'Acting out,' she murmured. 'It's to be expected after everything they've been through.'

'Becky only used to pinch *you*,' Calliope reminded her brother in equally piercing tones. 'Because she said that you were the only one of us who should have been drowned at birth.'

There was a moment's shocked silence. Jane and Pitt both looked horrified, Becky scrambled to find something to say and Rawdon — Rawdon put down his knife and fork and started to laugh. He laughed so hard and for so long that, in the end, he rested his arms on the table and his head in his hands as he shook with mirth.

If Rawdon was laughing, then it was all right for Jane to smile, even giggle, because the children were absolutely impossible. Then Pitt, giddy with relief that his younger brother was no longer sulking, started to laugh too. The children joined in because the grown-ups had been so sad

328

and silent and had expected them to be sad and silent too, even though they were actually quite happy because Mrs Tinker let them have chicken nuggets every day and Jane let them watch television whenever they wanted.

Only Thisbe and Becky were tight-lipped and absolutely not laughing. In fact, Becky took advantage of the fact that everyone else around the table was yakking it up like a bunch of hyenas, to hold Thisbe's insolent gaze and draw a line across her neck in an unmistakable threat.

In reply, Thisbe gave her the finger.

'Children really do say the most silly things,' Becky said at last. She covered Pitt's hand where it rested on the table as his laughter simmered down to the occasional chuckle. 'They're such a comfort in bad times.'

★　★　★

It was another two weeks — a long, long, long two weeks, where it seemed to rain incessantly so that the creaky old house rang out to the resonant sound of water dripping into countless containers to catch the leaks — before Becky decided it was time.

Time to make poor Pitt pay the piper. Twice he'd caught Becky with her head bent over the slim volume of short stories that was the only fiction he'd had published. Quite frankly, she was amazed that Pitt had found anyone deluded enough to want to publish them. Every story seemed to centre round a male writer, estranged from his father, whose girlfriend didn't understand him.

The first time Becky had been disturbed by Pitt as she struggled through his turgid prose stylings, she'd acted startled ('Oh goodness, how embarrassing! I hope you don't mind') and the second time, as if she was quite overcome with emotion. 'You have such a way with words,' she sniffed, dabbing at her dry eyes with a tissue. 'You do such beautiful things with them.'

Now, it was her turn to startle Pitt as she came into his father's study where he liked to disappear of an evening. He was bent over his ancient laptop, face puckered into a frown, which instantly transformed into a smile of pure pleasure as he saw Becky at the door.

'Am I disturbing you?' she asked.

'No, no, no.' Pitt slammed shut the laptop where he'd been working on a story where a male writer, estranged from his father who had recently died, found himself with a *tendresse* for his sister-in-law, who seemed unaware of his affection. *Oh, cruel woman!* as his last desperate line read. 'I'm very happy to be disturbed.'

He expected Becky to sit in one of the chairs on the other side of the desk but she came closer, swung herself up on the desk in front of him and invaded his space with the heady, intoxicating scent of her perfume, the shadowy cleft of her breasts, her legs. She tilted her head and regarded him with a look on her face that he would struggle to put into words.

'Were you writing, Pitt?'

'Something and nothing,' he mumbled. 'Nothing mostly. Nonsense.'

'I'm sure it wasn't,' Becky said warmly. 'Not if

330

what I've already read of yours is anything to go by.'

'Please, you flatter me too much,' Pitt said, ducking his head as Becky marvelled that he shared the same gene pool as his late father and Rawdon, and yet those wonderfully patrician Crawley good looks had eluded him entirely. 'I'm just an old hack.'

'I'm glad you're writing again,' Becky said, though Pitt was a little peeved that she didn't immediately rush to refute his claims of being just an old hack. 'I know that you've had all this extra responsibility thrust on you; the children, the houses, the inheritance tax . . . '

With each item that she listed, Pitt's head hung lower and lower.

' . . . the staff, the lawyers, surveyors, accountants. Honestly, Pitt, no one would blame you if you'd run away, but you're stronger than that.' Becky's gaze travelled to the portrait of Sir Pitt, which hung over the fireplace and featured him as Hamlet, in edgy black leather, clutching Yorick's skull. 'I see so much of your father in you.'

'I'm not sure how,' Pitt said, because for all of his father's charisma and magnetic good looks, he'd also been a complete bastard.

'But you have something your father never had,' Becky continued, her eyes fixed firmly on Pitt now, so he hardly dared to blink. 'You have the soul of a poet, so I'm glad that you're writing again. That even though you're now the head of the family, you won't forget what makes you special and sets you apart.'

She held his gaze so Pitt couldn't doubt the sincerity in her words and for a moment, as he lost himself in the fathomless green depths of her eyes, all his immediate worries were forgotten. Then Becky blinked and sniffed loudly (all of them were suffering with colds), and the moment was gone and already Pitt was bereft.

'Anyway, I've come to say goodbye,' Becky said briskly and suddenly Pitt felt colder than the grave where they'd recently deposited his father.

'You're leaving?'

''Fraid so.' She sounded positively jaunty. 'We've just heard, Rawdy's been offered the title role in a production of *Coriolanus* at the National and rehearsals are starting immediately.'

Pitt couldn't help but pull a face. '*Coriolanus?* Not my favourite Shakespeare. There's a reason why it's one of his least popular plays.'

'I know,' Becky agreed then smiled impishly. 'For God's sake, don't get commissioned to write a review, not when you and Rawdon have been getting on so well.'

'I'm pretty sure it would be a conflict of interest,' Pitt said, although he'd never been in the top tier of writers who were commissioned to review big opening nights at the National Theatre. Also, Rawdon had got over his sulk and was back to his usual affable, slightly vacant self and Pitt didn't want to jeopardise their rapprochement. Rawdon had even said that if he'd inherited Matilda's millions, it would have done him no good.

'I'd have probably pissed them all away in a

game of poker,' he'd said heavily. 'Or wound up dead from an overdose before the end of the year.'

Pitt had always planned to do the right thing by his younger brother, but since that conversation he worried that perhaps Rawdon would go off the rails if he had access to too much money. Now he wondered if it might be better to give Rawdon an allowance, rather than a lump sum, administered through Becky, who despite her youth seemed to be a woman of good sense.

'But when Rawdon tells you his news, can you be enthusiastic? It will be our little secret.' Becky smiled conspiratorially and Pitt smiled back, delighted that the two of them were united, and that really, when you thought about it, they had so much in common. 'Anyway, I must go and pack now, as he wants to head back to London in the morning.'

'So soon?' Pitt asked a little mournfully, but Becky was already jumping up from the desk, as if she had a million and one items to cross off her to-do list.

'Yes, though there hasn't been time to organise anything,' she said, leaning back against the edge of the desk as if she was inclined to linger. 'We don't even have anywhere to stay. We gave up the place we were renting when we went to France.' She sighed and drooped a little, like a flower deprived of sunlight. 'So much to sort out, not to mention a deposit, three months' rent in advance and all sorts of hidden fees . . . I bet you're glad you've left the rental market behind.'

With all his new worries, Pitt thought fondly

back to the days when his biggest source of anxiety was whether he'd get his security deposit back. 'But Rawdon gets paid well for his films, doesn't he? And this new role at the National?'

Becky sighed heavily, her face suddenly tense and drawn. She shook her head as if she was willing away whatever dark thoughts had overtaken her. 'It's not your problem, Pitt. Rawdon and I can take care of ourselves,' she said. 'I'd hate you to think that we were spongers like Bute and Martha. I want to be a help to you, not a burden.'

Typical Rawdon! Pitt could just imagine what he'd done with his film money. At Eton, famously, he'd lost his entire term's allowance by betting on the outcome of two raindrops trickling down the window of the Upper Fourth common room.

'Talking of being a help, while we're back in London, do you want me to look in on Mattie's house in Primrose Hill?' Becky asked because she really was a sweet girl. 'It's just when I was staying with Mattie, there were so many burglaries in the neighbourhood and the house is just sitting there empty. I could, I don't know, set the lights on a timer . . . '

'I've got a better idea . . . ' Pitt exclaimed, as he suddenly saw a way to take care of Becky, because Rawdon was obviously doing a lousy job of it, and solve yet another problem that he hadn't even been aware of. 'You see, Mattie's housekeeper is still living there, and Briggs . . . '

'Oh! Of course they are.' Becky smiled at him forlornly. 'That's so kind of you, Pitt. Otherwise they'd have nowhere to live . . . '

'But they're just rattling round the house with nothing to do, not that I begrudge them a roof over their heads and a salary — '

'Bute and Martha would have had them out in the blink of an eye,' Becky pointed out. 'Mattie wouldn't have wanted that.'

'Would you . . . that is . . . do you think you and Rawdon might move in there?' Pitt asked and flinched as Becky bristled, folding her arms so her breasts jutted out delightfully.

'We don't need charity, Pitt,' she said coldly, and it was he who took her hand, her frozen little hand, in his.

'I'm not saying you do, but you did say that you wanted to be a help and it would be doing me a huge favour if you stayed at the house in Primrose Hill and kept an eye on that housekeeper.' He patted the back of her hand awkwardly. 'Briggs said that some of Mattie's things had gone missing.'

'Oh?'

'A solid-gold cigarette lighter and a couple of other bits. Mattie's been dead not even a month,' he said, and though Pitt had been frightened of his aunt, her sharp tongue and even sharper gaze, as if she constantly found him wanting, he was struck by her loss. And any loss always reminded him of the greater loss of his mother, which hadn't dissipated over time but was now a dull ache in the background instead of a constant piercing pain. 'The estate is all tied up in probate. Will be for a couple of months at least, but I want you and Rawdon to have the house in Primrose Hill,' he added rashly. 'Mattie would have wanted you to have the house if she hadn't been so bloody minded about everything.'

'Pitt, no . . . ' Becky covered her face in her hands and her shoulders shook with the force of her silent sobs. 'It's too much.'

'It's hardly anything. The very least I can do.'

Becky uncovered her stricken face. 'It's the kindest, loveliest gesture but Rawdon and I couldn't afford to take on a house of that size and in that condition. It's pretty much falling down and the bits that aren't falling down haven't been touched since the fashion in interiors was seventies shag palace.' She tried to laugh at her own joke but it came out as a sob. 'You must think I'm so ungrateful.'

'Not at all, but there is money. That is, there will be money for you and Rawdon too, and in the meantime, you can do whatever you need to with the house to make it somewhere that you want to live. Just send me the bills,' Pitt said impulsively and Becky's look of incredulity was replaced with a brilliant smile so that Pitt felt like she was the sun and he was a lowly planet happy to satellite around her all day. (The line needed work but he took a mental note to fine-tune it at a later date.)

Forget the latest hip nightclub or trendy bar, the hottest ticket in town is Sausage Sundays at the Primrose Hill home of London's It couple, Rebecca and Rawdon Crawley. Billed as a 'sausage 'n' mash salon', and strictly by invitation only, supermodels, royalty, politicians, pop stars and YouTubers who'd usually eschew carbs, are desperate for an invite so they can chow down on a plate of sausage and mash. Of course, the sausages are supplied by gourmet butchers, The Happy Pig, and the mash is whipped up by whichever celebrity chef is in attendance, while cocktails are provided by a featured bartender every week.

There's plenty of entertainment too as attendees are expected to sing for their supper. Guests spill out into the Crawleys' sprawling back garden to sit on cushions while Zadie Smith might read an excerpt from her latest novel or Harry Styles provides an acoustic set.

The low-key, high-glam salon is the brainchild of Rebecca Crawley, model, charity spokesperson and social influencer, though *Vogue* describes her as 'simply the wittiest, prettiest woman in London.'

'Sunday evenings are my least favourite time of the week, I always get that awful back-to-school feeling,' Becky explained in a break from entertaining her guests. 'I invited a few friends and neighbours over one

Sunday, though I did the cooking and burned the sausages to charcoal, but we had such a great time that I decided to do it the next Sunday too, and it took off from there.'

Of course, when your friends happen to be models like Cara Delevingne and Georgia May Jagger and your neighbours include Benedict Cumberbatch, Claudia Winkleman and Ed Sheeran, then having friends over for supper is always going to be a star-studded affair. And with the added draw of handsome husband Rawdon Crawley (fresh from his triumphant return to the London stage in a sell-out run of *Coriolanus* at the National Theatre), there is more than a healthy sprinkling of Hollywood glamour too. Last week, salon regulars were astounded to see none other than Kanye West and Kim Kardashian wolfing down some vegan artisan sausages and it's rumoured that Beyonce's people have already been in touch to lock down an invite next time Queen Bey is in town.

'I expected people to get bored with bangers and mash, but the other week we had to turn away two Victoria's Secret models,' said Becky with an embarrassed laugh. 'I was absolutely mortified but I really couldn't have squeezed in even one more person.'

With a cookbook and a TV show in the works and plans to take the humble banger to pop-up sausage salons in New York and Paris, it looks like Becky will have to start employing a bouncer to turn more people away.

You can catch a glimpse of the sausage 'n' mash salon on Becky's Instagram Stories and Facebook Live, every other Sunday at 6 p.m.

32

Becky gazed out of the second-floor window of her bedroom (which had once been Matilda's but someone had come in and burned lots of sage to get rid of any malevolent spirits) down at the throngs of beautiful people gathered in her garden. If they weren't beautiful, then they were powerful and well connected, which was far more important than simply being easy on the eye.

It was a sultry Sunday evening at the end of June and the sausage 'n' mash salon was in full swing. The whole affair was now sponsored by a gin company who had paid for everything from a new kitchen, to the garden re-design, to the wait staff milling about with gin-based cocktails and, of course, a generous monthly stipend for Becky.

There was a celebrity chef, whose manager had paid handsomely for the privilege, barbecuing sausages — chorizo and red onion, Old Spot pork and Bramley apple, and merguez and harissa — at a special grilling station that had been set up in the garden, because Becky had only just finished doing up the house and the smell of grilled meat clung to everything.

Every week poor Briggs had to field calls and emails from publicists desperate to get their clients an invite. Becky had been determined to lose Briggs and Firkin, out with the old and all that, but they had refused to go.

340

'You need me,' Briggs had kept bleating when Becky had tried to evict him from the Louis XIV-inspired suite on the first floor where he'd lived for the last twenty or so years. 'And I need to be needed. Without Matilda here, I just don't know what to do with myself.'

'Well, it's about time you found out. Why should I let you stay? You practically came in your pants when Matilda called me all those vile names and threw me out,' Becky had reminded him because Briggs was on her list and she was itching to score his name through.

'I tried to stick up for you. Dear heart, you know that I adore you,' he'd insisted, on the verge of tears. 'You won't even have to pay me. Mattie left me very comfortably provided for.'

It turned out that Briggs had been left £60,000 a year for the rest of his life, and after a week Becky realised why Matilda had kept him around for so long. He was awfully good at organising things, from the building works to rustling up invites to parties and restaurant openings and first nights and any other event that Becky wanted to go to. While Rawdy was busy with his dreary Shakespeare, Briggs was also an excellent plus one. 'A walker,' he called it. He made sure that she always had a drink in her hand and someone fascinating to talk to and that she never, ever had to linger on the pavement waiting for a car to take her home.

Then once they'd started the sausage and mash thing, he'd really come into his own. But to keep Briggs on his toes, and because he still had to be punished for his former crimes, she'd

341

refused to sack Firkin.

'But she stole from Mattie!' Briggs kept reminding her. While this was quite untrue, divide and rule meant there was no harm in letting Briggs continue to think that and letting Firkin hate Briggs for casting aspersions about her good character.

Becky's so-called kindness also ensured the taciturn Firkin's unswerving loyalty, even managing to crack a smile when she brought Becky breakfast in bed every morning, and with Briggs and Firkin hating each other, it meant that they didn't turn on her. Really, everything had worked out so well, Becky thought, as she waved down at Pitt who'd been searching high and low for a glimpse of her.

He always stayed with them when he needed to come down to London, even though he'd inherited Sir Pitt's Chelsea house, which apparently needed a lot of work done before it was habitable. Even though probate had been granted and Pitt had signed over the deeds of the house to her (because they agreed that Rawdon, bless his heart, couldn't be trusted), it still paid to keep Pitt sweet.

For instance, she'd invited him and Jane this evening, and later on she'd introduce Pitt to Salman Rushdie while Jane could babysit Rawdon, who was the only person in London who really didn't want to attend an ironic bangers-and-mash salon on a Sunday evening.

Pitt, on the other hand, was very grateful and he showed his gratitude by being very free with the Crawley family jewellery. 'It's just as much yours and Rawdon's as it is mine and Jane's,' he'd pointed out last month when he'd handed over a pair of diamond earrings, a necklace and two dress clips. They'd agreed that they wouldn't tell Rawdon. Becky had told Pitt exactly what had happened in Paris — under duress, of course, and with a lot of very pretty crying. Then she'd confessed her suspicions that Rawdon was gambling again, so she and Pitt had also decided that it was best that the generous monthly allowance he wanted to give them should go straight to Becky.

It was funny the difference a year made, Becky reflected as she turned away from the window. A year ago they were on their uppers and now Rawdon was a hot property once again and she was the toast of London.

Becky looked at herself in the cheval mirror. The salon invite said 'Sunday casual', which sometimes meant she wore a tiny pair of shorts with trainers and a faded seventies rock-band T-shirt, but tonight she was wearing a floaty chiffon vintage Celia Birtwell dress and a pair of flip-flops. She planned to drift through her guests like an elusive butterfly, never lingering too long, disappearing in the middle of a conversation with a vague smile. Sometimes you had to leave people wanting more . . .

Her gameplan for the evening was interrupted by a sharp knock on the door, which opened before Becky had a chance to answer the summons.

'Briggs! We've talked about this,' she snapped, when he poked his head around the door.

'I know, but I have a party of six people who *have* to come in,' he garbled. 'Security are having none of it because they're not on the list.'

Having security on the door really didn't go with the ad hoc, free-form vibe of the salon but Camden Council had got very sniffy and had even tried to make them apply for some kind of licence, and had only been mollified by the promise of two burly bouncers. Anyway, without security, anyone might walk in off the street. Like this party of six, for instance.

'You know the rules; if they're not on the list, then they're not coming in,' Becky sing-songed, as she twirled in front of the mirror. There was a slip that went under the dress, which she'd discarded so that if anyone wanted to look hard enough, they'd be rewarded with a glimpse of her nipples.

'You wouldn't say that if you knew who was getting very cross on your doorstep,' Briggs said, his voice getting shriller with each syllable. 'You *have* to come down and sort it out. The bouncers won't listen to me.'

'It had better be someone very important,' Becky grumbled. Then when Briggs gave a wordless, desperate moan she stopped zhuzhuing her hair and tore herself away from her own very pleasing reflection. 'Royalty at least. Though if it's either of those beasts from St James's Palace, they can fuck right off. I don't care if they are princesses by blood, they're still practically D-list.'

'It's hard to imagine they're royalty when the bucktoothed one has such thick ankles,' Briggs sniped in a whisper as he followed Becky down the stairs. When he wasn't having conniptions, he was full of amusing, acidic asides, another reason why Becky was quite happy to keep him around. 'Or is it the other one, with the googly eyes?'

'Sending that pair packing would be my finest moment,' Becky decided but when she got to the front door, there were no sartorially challenged princesses to be seen. Just an old man in a blue-and-white striped seersucker suit with two younger men and three bland, blonde women, all teeth, tans and tits. 'You dragged me down two flights of stairs for this?' she hissed at Briggs, not caring if her voice carried.

'It's Lord Steyne,' Briggs hissed back, a fine film of sweat coating his face. '*The* Lord Steyne.'

How many other Lord Steynes were there? None. The Hackney-born media mogul was in a class of his own. Tom Steyne had started his career in the post room of the *Daily Herald* when he was fourteen. Had got his first scoop at sixteen when he'd happened upon a victim of the Krays bleeding to death outside The Hat and Fan pub in Mile End and, instead of calling the police, had taken down the man's dying words to be splashed across the front page the next morning. At twenty, he was editor of the failing *Daily Witness*, the youngest newspaper editor Fleet Street had ever known.

By twenty-five, he owned the *Daily Witness* and a dozen regional papers and now, some fifty years later, he pretty much ran Britain and America with his newspapers and his movie studios and his TV channels. If Steyne decided that the UK was going to Brexit, then Brexit it would. If he wanted a narcissistic, yellow-haired, orange-skinned reality-TV star in the White House, then the American voters were there to do his bidding.

With a friend like Lord Steyne, the world was yours for the taking.

'You're not on the list,' Becky said, tapping the clipboard that one of the bouncers was holding. 'If you're not on the list, then you're not coming in.'

She was addressing all six of them but her gaze kept returning to Lord Steyne who was watching her with a slight smile. He was old, like proper old. Liver-spotted old. Stooped old. Completely-bald old. The two men he was with, his sons, were strapping and tall and had all the arrogance that a life of privilege brings, but it was Steyne who radiated real power, like a fierce gravitational pull. So it didn't matter that he was old *old*, when he had a metric fuckton of charisma.

'Are you sure we're not on the list, sweetheart?' he asked Becky. 'Because if we're not then I'll have to sack all six of my assistants.'

Becky shook her head. 'Sucks to be one of your six assistants then,' she said even as Briggs moaned faintly somewhere behind her. Steyne barked out a laugh.

'I'll send you a picture tomorrow of them carrying their possessions out of the building in cardboard boxes,' he promised and it had been a long, long time since she'd met anyone who knew how to play this game. Mattie had, of course, but she was gone. Maybe Rawdon in the first few weeks, but he'd just been playing a part. Tom Steyne was the real deal.

'Still, I'd hate to be personally responsible for a bump in the unemployment figures,' Becky demurred and she stepped aside. 'You can come in . . . just this once.'

The sons and the blondes swept past her with tight smiles, a couple of murmured thank-yous, but Steyne stopped in front of her. Even though she was wearing flats, they were practically eye to eye.

'And to whom do I owe the pleasure?' he asked. Despite the wealth and the peerage, he'd made absolutely no attempt to lose the East End accent, which roughened his words.

He knew exactly who she was. Men like Steyne made it their business to know everything.

'There hasn't been any pleasure, has there? Not yet. And I'm Becky Sharp,' she said. 'Or Mrs Rebecca Crawley, if you prefer.'

'Mrs Crawley it is, then,' Steyne said and he didn't tell her his name because he knew he didn't have to. Then he gave her a perfunctory smile and proceeded to walk into her house as if he owned it, lock, stock and barrel.

★ ★ ★

Steyne sent flowers the next day White, tightly furled roses with a card that read, 'To the most beautiful woman in London.'

Becky put him on the list for the next salon, with no plus five this time. Not even a plus one, in case he fancied bringing along his third wife, a Ukrainian woman half his age with a fierce reputation that was all her own.

Of course, he turned up. And of course Becky ignored him, until right at the end of the evening when she came to perch on the arm of the garden sofa he was sitting on, with a little circle of acolytes (among them a newspaper editor, an Oscar-nominated film director and the owner of a chain of very successful high-street fashion boutiques) gathered around him.

'Are we having fun?' she asked and everyone assured her that yes, they were having fun, the sausage and mash had been beyond compare ('better than me old Ma used to make,' said the film director, because he liked to play up his Irish heritage, even though his old Ma's family owned most of County Kildare) and they couldn't wait for the next salon.

Then when they went back to their own conversations, Steyne's hand grazed Becky's hip. 'Have dinner with me.' He didn't make it a question or a suggestion. 'Just the two of us.'

'That would be lovely, but I don't think so,' Becky said, rising from her perch and walking off without looking back.

The next day, there were more white roses.

And Steyne was at the next salon and so it went on, this game of theirs, until she agreed to have dinner with him. It wasn't a hole-in-the-corner dinner either, because Steyne was no George Wylie. He did what he wanted, when he wanted, with whom he wanted and anyway, the formidable Lady Steyne was in Kiev visiting family and Rawdon was away filming for a week on the Irish director's new film. He'd only be in it for five minutes but apparently it would be a pivotal, career-defining five minutes.

'That's what Declan said, anyway,' Becky explained to Steyne as they sat at the best table in a newly opened restaurant, which had once been a Shoreditch police station and had a three-month waiting list.

'You can thank me afterwards,' Steyne said, as he put on his glasses to look at the wine menu, even though he always ordered the most expensive bottle of champagne for whatever woman he was with, while he had a beer.

'Thank you for what? Dinner? Like those teenage boyfriends that expected me to give them a blow job for a cheeky Nando's?' Becky asked, though she'd never had a teenage boyfriend, but she wanted to see how Steyne would react.

Nothing. Nada. Zip. Which was interesting. Quite annoying too. The Pitts, Younger and Elder, Rawdon, and all those other men had been very predictable when it came to Becky getting what she wanted.

'Thought that you might be grateful I sent your beloved husband away for a week,' Steyne said, turning a page and casting his eye down the list. 'I had a word with Declan. Perks of owning a film studio. Cristal for the lady and I'll have a beer, and it better not be chilled, or I'll have your knackers for afters.'

The restaurant didn't actually serve beer but for Lord Steyne, the sommelier (the bus boys

349

weren't to be trusted) would go to the pub across the road for a room-temperature pint of London Pride.

'Well, of course, I'm grateful for that but I'm not sure how grateful I am,' Becky said, because. Rawdon was definitely gambling again, definitely imbibing things he shouldn't again. Hanging out with his old friends, even though they were a motley collection of almost-made-its and never-weres. They were yesterday's news, whereas Becky had all sorts of interesting and useful new friends, and Steyne was the most interesting and useful of them all.

She didn't kiss him to thank him for the dinner, though she'd ordered the most expensive things on the menu and ate them with gusto because it was obvious that Steyne hadn't had dinner with a woman who ate anything with gusto since he'd left Hackney as a teenager and come Up West to make his fortune.

She patted him on the cheek before she gracefully climbed out of the back of his Bentley. 'Thank you for dinner. We really must do it again some time.'

Eventually Steyne stopped coming to the salon, but instead would take Becky out for dinner at least once a week when he was in town. Sometimes to a new restaurant and sometimes to a very old restaurant (he was particularly fond of Simpsons on the Strand). Sometimes it was even dinner with other people — say, the Foreign Secretary and the leader writer of *The Times*. As if having dinner with a married woman, when neither of their spouses were anywhere to be found, wasn't anything to be secretive about.

'Hiding in plain sight, sweetheart,' Steyne said and he laughed when Becky asked him exactly what he thought they were hiding when they were simply good friends.

By now, the flowers had been replaced with gifts of a higher monetary value. A diamond tennis bracelet, though Becky didn't play tennis, a matte-alligator Hermes Birkin almost the same shade of green as her eyes, and, best of all, a weekly lifestyle column in *The Globe*, the UK broadsheet he owned. In return, Becky now pressed a kiss to Steyne's wrinkled cheek when she got out of his Bentley, but she hadn't given him any more than that, and why should she? She hadn't asked him to buy her fancy presents, not even hinted that he should. Hadn't even pretended that she found him attractive, which made a welcome change.

She knew, however, not to drop her guard with Steyne because a man like him didn't do anything merely out of the goodness of his withered old heart or simply for the pleasure of the company of a beautiful woman.

It took Steyne a good three months before he made his counter-move.

'You seem to think I'm a patient man, sweetheart, but I'm not,' he said on the night that he took her to a charity dinner at the National History Museum where they'd dined on sturgeon eggs under the blue whale. He held onto her wrist after she kissed his cheek. 'I don't intend to wait for ever.'

Becky held his gaze, though he wasn't wearing

his glasses so she worried that her brazen stare wasn't as effective as she'd like it to be. 'Wait for what?' she asked coolly.

'Don't play games with me, Mrs Crawley,' he said, tugging her closer and whispering right in her ear. 'I invented the game, you see, so you're always going to lose.'

'Who says I'm playing by your rules, though?' Becky flexed her fingers and that was all it took for Steyne to release her. She did wonder if she'd overstepped but the next day, there weren't flowers or a delivery from Net-a-Porter or even a box from Garrard's, but a stiff-backed envelope from Buckingham fucking Palace, thank you very much, inviting her and Rawdon to a gala evening in aid of a mental health charity, which enjoyed the patronage of the Duke and Duchess of Cambridge.

'As special guests of Lord Steyne,' some palace flunky had written in a perfect copperplate script in navy-blue ink on the invitation.

Even Rawdon dropped the studied cool that was as stale as his breath after one of his nights out with his phone turned off. 'Buckingham Palace? Us? Me?' he gabbled when Becky flashed him the invitation. Then his eyes narrowed. 'What's Steyne got to do with anything?'

'He's been to a few salons while you were away filming,' Becky said, reaching forward to wipe away an imaginary spot of dirt from Rawdon's pretty face. Then she turned away from him to take something, anything, out of the huge fridge that had been installed in their deconstructed kitchen, as if talking about Steyne didn't even warrant her full attention. 'We support some of the same charities, so I suppose it has something to do with that.'

There was no point in making Rawdon suspicious, not that he had anything to be suspicious about. Yet. Also making Rawdon suspicious usually meant that he'd want to have sex with her — it was the only way to get a rise out of him these days — and Becky really didn't want to have sex with Rawdon. It would serve absolutely no purpose and rarely gave Becky any kind of pleasure.

She couldn't help but feel that this thing with Rawdon had run its course. Still, it wouldn't hurt to wait it out. Since his run in *Coriolanus* and since she'd introduced him to all sorts of influential people at the salon, Rawdon was up for all sorts of tantalising projects. If one of them catapulted Rawdon right up to the upper rungs of the A-list and with a pay packet commensurate with that, then Becky could only benefit too. Especially as a good divorce lawyer would get her at least half of it.

Becky turned back from the fridge and smiled. 'We haven't had a date night for ages, have we? And it doesn't get much better than a date night at Buck House with Kate and Wills.'

As an avowed republican who was quite adamant that the monarchy should be abolished and forced to live in a static caravan park in Hull, Rawdon all but swooned. 'Do you think the Queen will be there?' He tugged at his hair, which needed a good wash. 'Jesus, Becks, I haven't got a fucking thing to wear. Can you blag me a decent evening suit? Dior Homme, ideally.'

'For you, anything.' Being on good terms with Rawdon was so much better than being irritated by every single thing he said and did.

Besides, an evening spent rubbing shoulders with royalty was one in the eye for all those people who never thought she'd amount to anything. How she'd rub it in their faces. Becky had been thinking about how she was going to take down Barbara Pinkerton — grassing her up to HMRC just hadn't been satisfying enough, not even when she was ordered to pay hundreds of thousands of pounds in back taxes. Maybe she'd send her a photo of little Becky Sharp deep in earnest conversation with the Queen and flirting with Prince Philip.

Becky also planned to casually mention it to Pitt and Jane next time she saw them, but Jane beat her to it by calling Becky to gush about how she and Pitt had been invited to Buckingham Palace too.

'It must be because I persuaded Pitt to give 10 per cent of the inheritance to the Prince's Trust to distribute as they saw fit — it was the Christian thing to do, Becky.'

That was how the four of them ended up together in the back of an S-Class Mercedes crawling up the Mall.

'We're very lucky, eh, Rawdon, to be in the company of such beautiful women,' Pitt said gallantly, though his eyes kept straying to Becky and not to Jane, who was starting to despair that Pitt would ever pop the question.

'You look lovely, Jane,' Rawdon said in the

sultry, drawly voice he used when he was trying to soft-soap Becky, though Jane was wearing a strapless mustard satin gown that did nothing for her complexion or her flabby upper arms.

'And I don't?' Becky asked waspishly as Jane tittered and mumbled inarticulate words about how she didn't and Rawdon was mean to tease her.

'You always look lovely,' Rawdon said wearily as if to suggest that Becky's loveliness bored him. He cast a cursory glance at his wife and his eyes narrowed. 'Where did you get the earrings and necklace from?'

It was just as well that Becky wasn't the blushing sort. 'These?' she queried, touching the earrings in question, which had belonged to Rawdon's late mother and had been gifted to her by Pitt after she invited him to be her plus one at a little lunch thrown by Hatchards, where he'd been seated next to Hilary Mantel. The necklace had belonged to Rawdon's grandmother and Pitt had handed that over after Becky had introduced him to the MD of Penguin at one of her salons.

Now Pitt cringed where he sat.

'They're not real, Rawdy,' Becky snapped like he was a fool for thinking otherwise. 'It's not like you can afford to buy me proper diamonds, is it? These are on loan from a high-end costume jewellery boutique in Bond Street as long as I do a sponsored Instagram post.'

'They look real,' Rawdon muttered because he had a distant and yet distinct memory of watching his mother getting ready to go out when he was little, of her clipping the earrings into place, then turning from the looking glass to smile at him.

'Since when are you an expert?' Becky said and she sniffed. Eager to break the tension, Jane leaned forward.

'Your dress is beautiful too, Becky,' she said eagerly, almost daring to touch the deep-red georgette satin that spilled across the expanse of seat between them. The bodice was beautifully draped and the skirt fell in a series of tiny, knife-edge pleats. Jane frowned. 'It's odd. I had a dress just like it, which seems to have disappeared off the face of the earth. Where did you get it from?'

Opposite, Rawdon audibly sucked in a breath. Early on in their relationship, he'd thought it funny when Becky relieved him of his mobile phone and wallet, without him even feeling her fingers investigating his pockets. Now he didn't think it was at all funny, even as Becky assumed a vague expression.

'I can't even remember. Fashion companies give me clothes all the time.' She fixed Jane with a glacial look, which made the other woman wilt. 'And not to be funny or anything, but it's hardly like we take the same size, is it?'

'Oh, of course not, I wasn't implying anything,' Jane quickly said though she'd bought the dress in question in a moment of madness after she'd got a huge bonus at work. And that was after six months on Atkins and a bout of norovirus had whittled her figure down to proportions that she'd never managed to replicate again. Still, Becky had had the dress altered and taken in by a little Russian tailor that all the *Vogue* girls used for their alterations. 'The dress really does look beautiful. You look beautiful.'

Becky simply sniffed and stared fixedly out of the window while her three companions stared down at their laps, and somehow all the giddy joy of attending a party at Buckingham Palace had been sucked out of them.

THE TIMES
Birth announcements

WYLIE On May 2nd at the Lindo Wing, St Mary's Hospital, London to Amelia (nee Sedley) and George, a son, George John Archibald.

33

Little George was the most perfect, most beautiful baby that anyone had ever seen.

No woman on the planet had ever given birth to a child blessed with such soft, downy cheeks or such adorable tiny toes that made Amelia want to weep when she looked at them. Though the private maternity nurse said that although little George's cheeks and toes were very nice, it was likely that Amelia had 'a slight case of the baby blues'.

But Amelia wasn't blue at all, she was happier than she'd ever been. She realised now that she'd never experienced love until a squalling little George, covered in blood and vernix, was placed on her chest and immediately latched on to her swollen nipple.

Of course, she was still a little cross that big George hadn't been at the birth but he'd had to vote on a very important bill to privatise huge swathes of the NHS, so he'd missed the moment when his son was born.

'But you are a very, very clever girl giving me a son and heir at the first attempt,' he said warmly, when he eventually turned up at the Lindo Wing. 'Should smooth things over nicely with my Pa too.' He'd even bought her a beautiful platinum charm bracelet as a push present and said that he'd add to it with every new Wylie that Amelia produced.

Terrified that little George's physical, mental and emotional development would be blunted if she'd had an epidural or even gas and air, Amelia had had a completely natural birth. She was still high from the endorphins that the bossy woman at her NCT class swore her body would release, and high from the fierce and frightening force of love she had for little George. But she didn't mind sharing that love with big George. He might not have done any of the heavy lifting, but he'd done his bit to bring this wonderful new life into the world. 'Would you like to hold your son?' Amelia asked, holding the tiny miracle towards her husband.

George stared down at the red-faced and wrinkly baby that was still smeared with gunk and couldn't prevent the shudder that rippled through him. It was splendid that the family name and genes had been secured for another generation but until the infant was old enough to be put on a pony, then George had absolutely no use for him.

'Thanks awfully, Emmy, but I won't. New suit,' he explained and when Amelia's face darkened, he backtracked. 'Anyway, don't want to get in the way of your first few precious hours with young George. Don't all your baby books say that you should spend the first forty-eight hours skin-to-skin?'

Amelia had bought and read so many books on pregnancy, birth and childrearing that it wasn't at all surprising that George had managed to acquire some of that conflicting knowledge, even if it was by osmosis. Or maybe it was because Amelia had been banging on about it for months and months.

She sniffed. 'I suppose you're right,' she said and George leaned down to kiss her cheek, holding his breath at the raw animal scent, the milkiness of her. Now probably wasn't the time to suggest that she take a shower or do something with her hair. And it definitely wasn't the time to ask when and how she planned to lose the baby weight, he knew that much. 'Look, I'll leave you to get some sleep. You can ring for a nurse to take him away so he doesn't keep you up by screaming his head off.' He couldn't help but shudder again. 'My younger sister did nothing but howl for the first year of her life. She and Nanny had to go and sleep in the East Wing so she didn't disturb us.'

It wasn't the most auspicious start to George's relationship with his son but they had all the time in the world to get to know each other. Though perhaps it would be helpful if George would stay for longer than fifteen minutes when he came to visit.

Apart from George senior's intermittent appearances, there was a steady stream of visitors. Amelia's mother and father, of course, though they'd had to go almost as soon as they arrived as the soft mood lighting in Amelia's private room made her mother's head throb. The last specialist Mrs Sedley had been to, paid for by Amelia from the allowance that George gave her, had opined that Mrs Sedley's migraines were psychosomatic and suggested that she saw a psychotherapist. That suggestion had gone down like the *Titanic*. Meanwhile Mr Sedley had developed a nervous twitch and an obsession with clearing his name, which mostly involved studying the stock-market reports going back twenty years or so and writing detailed reports on his findings which he'd send to everyone from the Governor of the Bank of England to his local branch manager at Barclays. The pair of them were shadows, an echo of the people they used to be before they'd been ruined.

However, marriage to the most handsome MP on the Conservative backbenches and the subsequent securing of the Wylie baronetcy had finally restored Amelia's reputation. To that end, she'd been visited by the wives of some of George's parliamentary colleagues — he was particularly pleased that the life partner of the Minister for Social Justice had popped in for five minutes — as well as her old friends from school and university, including every single one of the five M's. She'd even entertained a couple of her *Big Brother* housemates because there was nothing like forcing a human being out of your vagina to let bygones be bygones.

Only one person from Amelia's past and her quite recent present was absent — Becky Sharp. She had sent a beautiful gift basket full of exquisite things for the baby, though every single item was pink despite the announcement in *The Times* stating very clearly that Amelia had had a boy. Amelia didn't like to think it was a deliberate slight, but then she didn't like to think much about Becky at all. Of course, little Georgy didn't know they were pink and, according to many independent studies, had no concept of gender constructs, but George senior did, so Amelia asked one of the nurses to distribute the pink contents to the mothers in the NHS bit of the hospital.

In fact, there had been so many people in and out of the room and interfering with the bonding process that Amelia was quite pleased that on a quiet evening six days after Georgy had arrived, it was just the two of them.

She was just settling down for a much-needed nap, Georgy fed and changed and tucked into his darling little sleepsuit, when there was a quiet knock on the door. She pushed herself up, brushing her hair back and pinching her cheeks with the hand not clutching Georgy — how like George senior to drop in so late!

The door opened, revealing Captain Dobbin of Her Majesty's Royal Regiment. He came timidly into the room, then promptly skidded on the water dripping from the absolutely massive bouquet of mixed blooms he was clutching in one hand, and careered into the bassinet, which thankfully was empty. Amelia had no intention of placing little George in it; why, it would be like putting him in a cage!

As it was, Georgy woke up from where he'd been slumbering on his mama's breast and let out an ear-piercing cry.

'Sorry, so sorry, Emmy. What a clumsy oaf I am,' Dobbin stuttered. 'Two left feet. I'm a bloody liability . . . Oh, Emmy . . . he's a wonder, isn't he? What a splendid little chap you've made,' he added, his voice husky with emotion.

Amelia, who'd been about to tell Dobbin off for swearing in front of Georgy, simply smiled beatifically at him. She was exhausted and grey, her hair still sweat-tangled and limp, but Dobbin thought she'd never looked more beautiful. 'He is rather wonderful,' she agreed. 'He's already my very favourite person in the world. Are those for us?'

As well as the flowers, Dobbin was holding a huge helium balloon with 'It's a boy!' printed on it, which ordinarily he'd have considered common, as well as a plush blue elephant which was twice the size of Georgy, who'd weighed in at an impressive nine pounds and six ounces.

Then, tenderly and carefully, when Amelia proudly showed off Georgy's ten toes, Dobbin bent down and kissed his perfect, perfect feet, so that if it weren't so battered, Amelia's uterus would probably have clenched in delight. If only George had shown a fraction of Dobbin's delight, she thought, as he straightened up and perched warily on the side of the bed.

'So, that's you and George settled then,' he said, as though that wasn't already the case. They were married, after all, and despite George having a lovely little flat in Victoria, he'd bought a house in Leakington, a village in his constituency, and had intimated very strongly that Amelia might like to spend most of her time down there 'doing mum things. London is no place for a baby. All the pollution.'

'Well, yes,' she said gently, because she had

come to realise — had always known, really — that Dobbin had feelings for her, which was very sweet of him, but George had always been the heir to her heart. Even when he was beastly, Amelia would always remind herself of how he'd rescued Pianoforte (who was now enjoying retirement in Leakington because the house came with fifteen acres and a stable) for her at a time when the rest of her friends and acquaintances had spurned her. 'But you always knew that George was the only man for me.'

Dobbin sighed, his earlier joy gone. 'I can't stay,' he said heavily.

'Oh, that's a shame. I suppose visiting hours are almost over.'

'I mean, I'm leaving London. Britain. Signed up for another tour.'

And despite her assertions about George, Amelia felt an icy dread settle over her.

'But I thought you were done with active duty.' Amelia shifted the baby at her breast so she could sit up properly, wincing as she did so, while Dobbin tactfully averted his gaze from her pendulous, blue-veined breast and straining nipple. 'Your focus is training new officers and ceremonial duties, isn't it?'

Dobbin placed the tips of his huge fingers on Georgy's downy head. 'Things change. I'm not needed here and so it's best to go where I am needed.'

'Maybe not needed, but valued and liked very much,' Amelia protested, though it was a weak argument and her heart was so suffused with joy and love for a little being that had only existed for a few days, that already she had a little less love for the other people in her life. Even so, the thought of dear old Dobbin back on active duty, where all sorts of wrong 'uns would try to kill him, cast a dark shadow over her newfound bliss. 'You will come back to us, won't you, Dobbin? I'll be furious if you don't.'

This time, Dobbin placed his hand on Amelia's cheek, the backs of his fingers caressing her hot, flushed skin. 'I'll always come back to you, Emmy,' he said throatily, but the baby was fussing and Amelia turned to her son, and by the time she lifted her head, Dobbin was gone.

34

Only two miles away but a world apart, Becky was being carefully lowered, then sewn into an intricate black lace dress which had been hand-stitched by nuns in a cloistered convent to the west of Paris.

When the last satin-covered pearl button had been fastened and her dressers stepped back, there wasn't a single person in the room who was more beautiful than Rebecca Crawley. There were several models present, two of them household names, who would have sworn that they were, but they would have been wrong.

In contrast to the finely worked black lace, Becky's skin was alabaster white apart from the delicate flush of colour in her cheeks. Her hair, no longer at the mercy of a monthly keratin blow-dry, was a riotous, red tumble of curls and her green eyes glittered like the emerald earrings which had been Steyne's latest gift.

As well as being at the peak of her pulchritude, Becky Sharp decided that, at this moment, in this room, with these people, she was at the height of her powers.

She'd been profiled in the *Sunday Times* and *Vogue* (both the UK and US editions), she'd made the *Evening Standard's* 'Thirty Power Players Under the Age of Thirty' list and the 'Most Fascinating People' lists in both *Tatler* and *US Weekly*. She'd been on *Newsnight* and

Loose Women and had made a scene-stealing appearance on *Have I Got News For You* when she called Jeremy Clarkson out for a sexist remark. She had been awarded plaques, trophies and a quite hideous crystal bowl for her charity work. She had ten million followers on Instagram, roughly the same amount on Twitter and her inspirational TED talk on how she'd turned a red-carpet moment into a global brand had been watched five million times.

There were people — mostly white, middle-aged men who wrote peevish opinion columns in the broadsheets — who asked, 'What does Mrs Rawdon Crawley actually do?' But as Becky said in her most liked Instagram post ever, they were just the death rattles of an almost extinct patriarchy.

Apart from those blowhards, she was lauded, applauded, sponsored, branded and had the ear (and anything else she wanted) of one of the most influential men in the world.

Not bad for a girl who'd come from absolutely nothing.

Now, she was about to walk in a fashion show which was being live streamed around the world in aid of Sister4Sister, a global campaign to encourage women to encourage other women. 'Good luck with that,' Becky had thought when she'd first been approached.

Each haute couture dress had been specially created by a different fashion house and worn by women who personified the campaign's core ethos of Compassion, Independence and Strength. Though it was quite the coincidence that all of the twenty women chosen were thin, beautiful and mostly Caucasian.

Becky was closing the show because she was the only woman who was tiny enough to fit into the black lace dress, but also because Lord Steyne had called in a few favours. 'About time I called in a favour of my own,' he'd said with heavy emphasis, which Becky would worry about later . . .

Right now, she could only worry about negotiating a fifty-metre catwalk in dangerously high heels and a dress with an impossibly restrictive fishtail hem and a twenty-foot train, with two supermodels who had a reputation for elbowing their rivals right off the runway.

She stood in the wings, waiting for her cue as people pulled at her hair, her dress, patted her face with powder to ensure that she couldn't look any more perfect.

'One, two, three, go!' said the show producer and there wasn't even time to take a deep breath when she was shoved forward.

It was a blur of light and flashes and faces as she stepped out and she'd thought that she might be nervous, but once she was bathed in the warm glow of all that attention, all that adulation, Becky felt her heart rise and her head lift — she was right at home, where she was always destined to be. She didn't walk so much as glide down the long white expanse of runway, the long train of her dress undulating after her.

Over the shouting of the photographers, she could hear another sound getting louder and louder. People were clapping, cheering, their

cries and the smack of their hands reaching a
crescendo simply because she was young and
beautiful and she could put one foot in front of
the other.

It was easy to take so much when most people
were happy with so little, she thought as she
reached the end of the catwalk, held her pose,
and allowed a small, triumphant smile to break
through.

★ ★ ★

For better or for worse, he'd married her, and
when Rawdon Crawley watched his wife walk
down the runway, the many complicated reasons
why he both loved and hated her in equal
measure were all contained in her triumphant
smile.

Rawdon had never expected to play second
billing when he'd plucked his half-siblings'
twenty-year-old nanny from obscurity to a life of
fame and fortune. OK, there had been a couple
of glitches with the whole fame and fortune
thing, but before him, Becky had been nothing
and now Rawdon worried that without Becky, it
would be he who had nothing.

He told himself that the potential film roles
that were stacking up like the stiff invitation
cards on their mantelpiece were all due to his
talent, but when your wife was a close, personal
friend of Lord Steyne, who happened to own the
film studio behind all those film roles, talent
didn't have much to do with it.

In the long, dark evenings of the soul when his

wife was nowhere to be found and Rawdon was teetering on the brink of a comedown after hours of hoovering up white lines, he wished that he'd never met her. Before Becky, he'd been motoring along quite happily, critically acclaimed but with enough box-office draw to satisfy both his artistic temperament and his agent.

Now, he felt as if his whole life was an illusion. He lived in a house gifted to him by his brother, though by rights it should have been Rawdon's in the first place. His career was at the whim of a man who wanted to sleep with his wife. And his wife . . . Rawdon couldn't even get close to her to say hello, slide his arm around her waist, smile for the photographers so at least he might get some press from attending this celebrity-infested charity clusterfuck.

Rawdon exchanged his empty glass of champagne for a full one as he grimly and determinedly fought his way across the huge marquee that had been erected in Hyde Park, right next to the Serpentine Gallery.

'Rawdon, so lovely to see you! Wasn't Becky *wonderful?* You must be *so* proud of her!'

'Ah, it's Mr Becky Sharp, as I live and breathe!'

'Rawdon! Rawdon! Can you get Becky to call me? Been trying to reach out to her for weeks.'

He ignored all the people who tried to talk to him, because they only wanted to talk about *her*. Over their heads, he could see his wife's red curls and he imagined tangling his fingers in them until it hurt her, tipping her head back so she'd have to look him in the eye.

371

'Without you, I'm nothing, Rawdy,' she'd say, he decided with a grunt. Then he sniffed hard, so that the last few crumbs of coke hit the back of his throat and like a truth serum, he knew that Becky would say no such thing. 'Without me, you'd be lucky to get a bit part in *Hollyoaks*, you fucking loser,' she'd be more likely to say.

Becky was on the move, a couple of black-clad, thickset men separating her from the hordes so she could take a moment, have a sip of champagne to ease her dry throat from all the air-kissing and 'Darling, you're too sweet, all I did was manage to walk without going arse over tit.'

'She's *my wife*,' Rawdon hissed, as another couple of all-in-black flunkies tried to stop him from following Becky into a cordoned-off area and into the perfectly proper and polite embrace of Lord Steyne, who kissed her on both cheeks and said something that Rawdon couldn't quite catch because he was still too far away.

'It's a wedding dress,' he heard Becky say as he drew nearer. 'The wedding dress always closes the show.'

'Looks more like widow's weeds,' Steyne laughed. 'Which is appropriate.'

For five heart-pounding, fist-clenching seconds, Rawdon was set to storm over and punch Steyne so hard that it knocked his head clean off his frail, geriatric neck.

'I don't want Rawdy dead,' Becky said thoughtfully. She looked at Steyne from under her lashes in a way that Rawdon knew only too well. 'He's very good-looking. He's much better-looking than *you*. He has a lot more hair than you too.'

Steyne laughed again and Rawdon turned away, disgusted, down-hearted, dejected. He pushed his way back through the crowd so he could get out, breathe fresh air that wasn't polluted by expensive perfume and hypocrisy.

An hour later, he sat at a table in a Park Lane casino and tried to decide if Becky was a sociopath or a psychopath. Or if he should feel sorry for his hard-hearted wife who could never be happy with what she had but was always searching for her next mark, her next conquest, her next . . . victim.

'Place your bets.'

Rawdon came to with a start. The pile of chips he'd started with had almost gone though he couldn't remember losing them. He'd been mesmerised by the spin of the roulette wheel and distracted by thoughts of Becky and how she'd never really been his, not even when she was lying in his arms.

'Sir? Do you want to place a bet?' Rawdon blinked bleary eyes at the croupier.

'Yeah. I want to place a bet.' With unsteady hands, he pushed his little pile of chips forward. 'Put it all on twenty-three.'

The twenty-third of January was her birthday and she'd currently spent twenty-three years on this earth. They'd been married twenty-three months. (It was actually thirty-three months, but Rawdon had done so many lines of coke by now, he could be forgiven for getting his dates muddled up.)

If she'd ever loved him, even a little, then twenty-three would come up.

'No more bets.'

The croupier spun the wheel. The breath hitched in Rawdon's throat as he watched the ball clatter.

He clung to the faint hope that she had loved him once, before they'd gone to Paris and everything had been ruined. No, *he'd* ruined everything.

Twenty-three had to come up, because for a few sweet months, Becky had loved him and he'd loved her too.

The ball spun closer to twenty-three to taunt Rawdon, to tease him. As the wheel started to slow, his vision became blurred but then, as the ball rattled between twenty-three and the ten that was next to it, it became crystal clear. Then just as the wheel stopped, the ball gave a quicksilver leap and landed on five.

'Fuck this!'

In accordance with gambling law, alcoholic drinks weren't served on the casino floor, but Rawdon picked up his glass containing the dregs of the Coca-Cola he'd been drinking and flung it across the room.

'Fuck it all!'

There was a scream as the glass glanced off the back of someone's chair then shattered.

'Sir! I'm going to have to ask you to leave,' the croupier said, her fingers scrabbling for the panic button under the table, but already suited security men were hurrying from all directions, Rawdon their target.

He dived across the table to grab a handful of chips and throw them high in the air so they rained down like hailstones, until a hand suddenly wedged into his armpit. 'Let's not have any trouble, sir!'

'There's already trouble,' Rawdon snarled. 'I'm choking on trouble.' With his free arm he tried to take a swing at the man, who captured his flailing limb with an insulting ease so he could pin both of Rawdon's arms behind his back.

Rawdon wasn't going down without a fight. He bucked and he kicked as two more goons arrived to force him down to the floor. They carried him off like that, through a set of doors marked 'private', then down a flight of stairs, his forehead smacking against concrete as they descended.

And throughout it all, Rawdon cried like a baby.

At the police station, he was booked in, fingerprinted and photographed. They asked him if he wanted a lawyer but all Rawdon wanted was his one phone call.

It went straight to voicemail. 'This is Becky. I'm so sorry I can't take your call. Leave a message and I absolutely promise to get straight back to you.'

'It's me. I still love you. I wish I didn't. I wish I never had. Also, I've been arrested. I'm at Charing Cross Police Station. Can you call me back, Becky? Please.'

But Rawdon knew better than anyone that Becky's promises never amounted to anything but a handful of dust. Even once he'd sobered up, Rawdon kept banging on his cell door to ask the custody sergeant if his wife had rung. But she never did.

He was in court the next afternoon, still in his dinner jacket and blood-stained white shirt with cuts on his face and two black eyes, much to the delight of the pack of photographers waiting for him as he exited the police van.

Rawdon stated his name then pleaded guilty to criminal damage and common assault, because he was guilty. Guilty of so many other things that weren't even on his charge street. His bail was set at £10,000 and when they got back to the police station, he called Becky again, though she couldn't have failed to see his battered face plastered all over social media. Not to mention the front covers of all the daily papers, because of course a couple of casino employees had tipped off the press, so they'd been there to see him escorted off the premises in handcuffs.

'Never mind, my son,' said the custody sergeant. 'We'll put you in a cell, get you a cup of tea and some toast, and I bet by the time you're finished, the missus will have called back.'

'Do you think?' Rawdon asked. He couldn't stop his traitorous heart giving a thud of hope, though he'd kept telling himself all the way through his long, sleepless night that he never wanted to see or speak to Becky Sharp ever again.

'I've been married for thirty years. She's angry with you for being such a silly bugger — got to give her time to come round.'

Rawdon had just taken his last bite of toast when the custody sergeant lifted up the hatch in the cell door. 'I'm sorry, mate. Your good lady did call but she says she's not well and she can't do anything to help you right now.'

'Yeah, of course, she did,' Rawdon said, sinking back down on the rubber mattress, because he'd been a fool to expect anything else from her.

'Anyone else you know who might have a spare ten thousand tucked away?'

★　★　★

'Oh, Rawdon, your poor, poor face,' Jane said, four hours later as she spirited Rawdon into the back of a cab. Luckily, she'd been in town anyway buying new school clothes for the five Crawley children who were no longer feral, thanks to regular meals, enrolment at the local primary school, ten hours' sleep a night and the love of a good woman. 'Does it hurt very much? Should we take you to a doctor?'

'It's fine. I'm fine,' Rawdon said, though his cuts and bruises stung like a bitch and he was pretty sure that he'd broken a couple of fingers. 'Thanks for bailing me out.'

'It's quite all right,' Jane assured him, her plump, homely features creased with concern. 'You know, it was actually quite exciting, like being in a film or something.' She pulled an apologetic face. 'Sorry, probably not quite so exciting for you.'

'I've had worse nights,' Rawdon said, though he hadn't, not even when he'd been roughed up by those gangsters in Saint-Denis. At least that time, Becky had rescued him, but then, she'd given him fair warning that she wouldn't do it again.

'Where do you want to go?' Jane asked as the taxi driver obligingly did another circuit of Trafalgar Square. 'Our place in Chelsea or . . . let me take you home, back to Queen's Crawley.'

'Queen's Crawley isn't home,' Rawdon said, blinking bloodshot eyes at his sister-in-law. 'My home is meant to be with Becky . . . '

'Rawdon, I don't think that's a very good idea,' Jane said. But, ignoring her advice, Rawdon leaned forward to slide back the glass panel.

'Primrose Hill, please, mate.'

35

It was just gone eleven when the taxi dropped him off in Gloucester Crescent, the full moon staring impassively down at Rawdon as he climbed the steps up to the house.

Normally Firkin was at your side as soon as you walked in, ready to take jackets and bags and silently do your bidding, but there was no one there to greet Rawdon as he came through the door.

The ground-floor rooms were empty but there was music coming from above and as he climbed the stairs, he could hear a man speaking, then Becky laughing. The rippling cadence of her mirth seemed to have a mocking tone.

There was no longer any cocaine in his bloodstream so Rawdon didn't take the stairs two at a time. Didn't send the door to Becky's bedroom crashing back on its hinges. Didn't shout and scream and swear, but just stood quietly taking in the scene afforded to him by the door left ajar.

That filthy Steyne was lounging awkwardly on the bed, Becky's bed, their *marital* bed — though there'd been precious little marital anything in it lately. Steyne wasn't the lounging sort and it wasn't the most flattering angle for an elderly man. His paunch, usually hidden in a well-cut suit, strained against his shirt and his trouser legs were hitched up, showing spindly legs and pale-blue socks that were a perfect colour match for the veins that snaked up his skin.

The thought of Becky being touched by Steyne's hands, paper-skinned and liver-spotted, kissing his thin lips, reaching past the paunch to undo his trousers, didn't make Rawdon hard. It made him want to throw up a mouthful of bile. Made him want to punch someone or something.

'You really are the most beautiful woman I've ever seen, Mrs Crawley,' Steyne said, rubbing his hands together delightedly. 'And I've had two Miss Worlds, you know.'

'Oh, I'm sure you say that to all the girls,' trilled Rawdon's wife from her en suite bathroom, and then she was there in the doorway. They'd obviously just got in from one of the dull parties that Becky loved to go to, for she was wearing a little black dress, emphasis on the little, and she was glowing, sparkling, from the jewels around her wrists, neck, in her ears, even threaded through her hair. 'But you're not going to have me, are you?'

'Nothing, and I mean *nothing* would delight me more,' Steyne wheezed, his wrinkled hands clawing in anticipation.

'You misunderstood me. I said that you're *not* going to have me.' Becky ran a hand down her delectable body lovingly showcased in black silk. 'You can look but that's all you're ever going to do.'

'Mrs Crawley, you never fail to amuse me, but let's get down to business, shall we? It's time for you to pay the piper, sweetheart.' Steyne was still smiling but it was the kind of smile that the wolf gave to the lamb before it ripped the lamb's head off.

'What exactly am I meant to be paying the piper for?' Becky didn't flinch, her own smile didn't falter, and as much as he hated the sight of her, Rawdon had to admire her sheer audacity.

'Services rendered,' Steyne reminded her tightly.

'I thought those services were freely given.'

'Really? I never took you for a fool, Mrs Crawley. Seems I was wrong.' Steyne tutted and shook his head. 'Let me spell it out. You owe me and so I own you. I can do whatever I like with you. And what I'd like to do and what I shall do is fuck you.'

'I thought we were friends, Tom,' Becky said reproachfully. 'You're not being very friendly. All this talk of owning me. Nobody owns me.'

'Beg to differ. I own you, I all but created you, and I could destroy you with just a couple of phone calls.' He smiled again, showing yellowed teeth. 'Did you really think that I was going to let you have everything you wanted without taking something for myself?'

Rawdon couldn't bear it any longer. He shouldered open the door. 'My wife isn't yours for the taking, you disgusting old goat!'

Becky's mouth fell open so that in that second she looked almost ugly. 'Oh God, Rawdy what the fuck are you doing here?' she gasped, irritation flashing across her face.

'Well, this is awkward,' Steyne said, struggling

381

to sit up straight from his reclined position.

He wasn't even embarrassed, though Becky had the good grace to cringe where she stood, arms wrapped tightly around her now. 'Shut up,' she hissed at Steyne. 'You're making things worse.'

'Things are already worse,' Rawdon rasped in a rusty voice like he'd swallowed a bucketful of metal shavings. 'How could you?'

'How could I what? What exactly am I meant to have done?' Becky asked, suddenly cool again with her hands on her hips.

'It's obvious,' Rawdon said dully, because in the face of her irritation and Steyne's amusement, he wasn't angry any more. Instead it was as if he was the one that was intruding, though he had every right to be there. But this . . . this battle of wills he'd just witnessed — an irresistible force meeting an immovable object — wasn't at all what he'd expected to find when he'd climbed the stairs. 'Wait, so you're really not sleeping with him?'

'No! Not everything is about sex.' She had the nerve to roll her eyes.

'But it's the only currency you have,' Steyne reminded her silkily. 'I certainly haven't stuck around this long because of your conversational skills. Not that they aren't delightful.'

'Do you swear that you haven't slept with him?' Rawdon asked again. 'Not even once?' He realised his mistake as soon as the words left his mouth and hung in the air with nowhere to go. Becky hated to be doubted and to repeat the question made her visibly furious: she strode towards him so that they were nose to nose.

'I don't mind you hating me for the things I have done, but I won't have you hating me for the things I haven't done.' She stared Rawdon down, so he didn't even dare to blink. 'I'm sick to the back teeth of people underestimating me, thinking I'm *that* predictable.' She flicked an insolent glance towards Steyne, paused and then lifted her chin. 'And you might think I'm a whore but you're the one who has to pay for sex, so what does that make you?'

Steyne sucked a breath in. 'You treacherous little bitch. You were nothing, a nobody, before you met me. Just another social media wannabe with no talent, no substance. And by the time I'm done with you, you'll be less than nothing.'

Becky's eyes flashed in a way that Rawdon knew only too well, because it always led to his downfall. 'Maybe I've already taken out some insurance on *you*,' she suggested. 'Maybe I have the means to destroy *you*.'

'Don't bullshit a bullshitter. You're clever, I'll give you that, but you're also a whore and every whore has their price . . . '

She fluttered a hand, swatting Steyne's words away. 'I certainly won't be your whore. I didn't mind people thinking that we were sleeping together because where's the harm? But no, you couldn't be happy with that. I don't even care that you just tried to blackmail me into bed; I've been expecting it for weeks. But how dare you try to take all the credit for who I am, what I've become, when it was my own bloody hard work and sacrifice that got me here?'

Steyne was rendered speechless. His mouth opened, spittle clinging to the edge of his dry, thin lips, but no words came out. Becky turned away from him to set her husband back in her sights. 'Anyway, Rawdy, what gives you the right to charge in here acting like the wronged husband. I've done nothing, I'm innocent — '

'Innocent?' Steyne finally exclaimed, hoisting himself to his feet. 'You're about as innocent as your slut of a mother and the conman she claimed was your father.' His face was almost purple with rage, eyes bulging, a vein pulsing at his temple. 'And you, boy?' He turned to Rawdon. 'You were quite happy to pimp out your wife, weren't you, for the sake of your career, but believe me, she wasn't worth the bother.' He tried to snap rheumatic fingers at Becky, who shook her head in denial, her mouth a thin, tight line. 'I will have my pound of flesh, Mrs Crawley. I didn't give you all those diamonds you wear so prettily out of the goodness of my heart. You might have acquired expensive tastes but you're still a common little tart who likely only exists because your mother would forgo a johnny for an extra fiver.'

'You impotent old bastard! You've got absolutely nothing on me.' Becky pointed an imperious finger in the direction of the exit. 'Get out!'

'Gladly, my dear.' Steyne picked up his jacket, the panama hat he wore in summer in the city, and walked casually towards the door where Rawdon was still motionless. 'Out of my way, boy,' he purred, utterly at ease, confident that the man he'd tried to cuckold would step aside.

But Rawdon sprang to life, seizing the other man by his collar, until Steyne writhed under his arm, forcing him towards to the floor.

'For God's sake Rawdy, don't kill him, you idiot! Aren't you in enough trouble?' Becky screamed, and suddenly she was on Rawdon's back, pulling him away from the choking Steyne with a strength that Rawdon wouldn't have believed possible. But it was still easy enough to fling her away.

'Take them off! Take off every last thing he gave you!' Rawdon demanded. Becky sighed and shook her head as if he was being ridiculous, tiresome, but when Rawdon took a step towards her she began to remove Steyne's sordid gifts until all that was left was the pear-drop diamond round her neck. She struggled with the clasp until Rawdon wrenched it free himself so he could fling the necklace at the prostrate Steyne, striking him on his bald forehead and cutting the skin, a scar he'd carry to his dying day. 'What else? What else did he give you?'

'God, Rawdy, don't kill *me*,' Becky said with a spluttery little laugh as if it were possible to turn his heartbreak, her betrayal, into a joke. But her hands were shaking,as she tried to touch Rawdon's face, press a gentle finger to the cut above his left eyebrow. 'What a mess they've made of you.'

He tore himself out of her grip. 'You've done this,' he said in a low voice. 'You've made a mess of me, of our marriage . . . '

She stepped back again, cold once more,

folding her arms. 'Actually, Rawdon, I think you'll find that you did that all by yourself.'

From behind them, Steyne gave a groan, but Rawdon ignored him and instead took hold of his wife, fingers gripping her upper arms hard enough to leave bruises so he could haul her close in a parody of a lover's embrace. She'd betrayed him for the last time.

'He's right, you know, you were a nobody when I met you. I should have told Mattie to leave you to rot in Mudbury.'

Becky stared Rawdon down, her face a perfect blank. He couldn't tell what she was thinking. Though he now realised that in all the time they'd been acquainted, he'd never once understood what really went on in her head.

'That's not true, Rawdy, and it's actually rather hurtful,' she said calmly and she only squeaked when his grip on her arms tightened and he began to walk her backwards. 'What are you doing?'

He steered her across the room and threw her down on the pink chaise longue that had belonged to his aunt.

'What else did he give you?' he asked, not waiting for a reply but striding over to her dressing table and pulling out the drawers so he could rifle through the stack of velvet jewellery boxes. She'd accumulated quite a collection. 'You'll be telling me these are all fakes too? Out on loan, are they? Well, these prove you a liar, don't they?' He waved a handful of certificates of authentication that were in one of the drawers.

There was a movement behind him and

Rawdon turned in time to see Steyne limp out of the door. Once they'd heard his unsteady tread on the stairs, Becky clasped her hands together. 'Who can blame me for taking advantage of his vanity? It doesn't make me a whore; it makes me smart, and him a fool. Anyway, you weren't exactly complaining when you got to benefit from the fact that Steyne had the hots for me.'

'You might not have fucked him but you still sold yourself to the highest bidder,' Rawdon said bitterly, holding up a huge stack of £20 notes. It didn't even look like real money, more like a prop from one of his films. 'About time people found out what you really are.'

'You're just being silly now, Rawdy.' Becky stood up with as much ease and assurance as if she were wearing a suit, not a flimsy black dress that revealed more than it concealed. She walked over to where he was still going through her ill-gotten gains: a banker's draft from Steyne made out for £50,000; the deeds to the house that Pitt had said he'd signed over to both of them, though only Becky's name was on them; and come to think of it, some of that jewellery really did look like the glittery things he remembered his mother wearing.

Rawdon rounded on her again, seizing hold of her. 'Did you sleep with Pitt? My own brother?'

'You've always been obsessed with the idea of other men fucking me, haven't you?' she asked with a smile. All it took was a shift of her hips and she was pressed against him. And — just like that, Rawdon was hard and he hated himself for it. Then she pushed him away with the tips of her fingers. 'No, I didn't sleep with your brother. Or your father. Or any of the other men who thought they were using me when I was using them. If you'd looked after me like you promised you would, I wouldn't have had to do any of this. So, really, when you think about it, Rawdy, this is your fault.'

'What? No, it isn't,' he protested weakly, because he no longer had the courage of his convictions. She always managed to tie him up in knots of his own making. 'I was fine before I met you. And we were fine when we first got married. But you always wanted more . . . '

In his clenched fist was a flash drive. Becky uncurled each one of his fingers so she could take it from him.

'What I wanted was a husband who didn't do drugs, didn't gamble, didn't think only of himself,' Becky said sadly. She shook her head. 'No wonder I've had to hustle so hard. Without me, we'd have been destitute. I've been destitute before. Believe me, Rawdy, you wouldn't like it.'

'You're twisting everything,' Rawdon insisted and he knew he was right, but when Becky looked at him in confusion, again he wasn't sure of anything. 'Even if I hadn't gone off the rails in Paris, even if a couple of my films hadn't bombed, if we'd kept living the sweet life, it wouldn't have been enough for you. You always want more. Christ, you're insatiable.'

'This is getting boring now, Rawdy.' Becky drew herself up and pointed an imperious finger towards the door. 'You have to leave.'

'I don't have to do anything,' Rawdon said and

he reached for her, because his wife could be scary, she could be a regular bitch goddess, but she was still his wife and she wasn't going to order him out of his own . . . her own . . .

'I really don't want to call the police, especially when I'm *covered* in bruises, and aren't you out on bail? I mean, it is still a criminal offence for a man to beat his wife, isn't it?' Becky pondered, holding out her arms so Rawdon could see the patterns his bruising fingers had made on her pale skin.

'You're a bitch,' he told her as he slunk towards the door.

'Well, I suppose that makes a nice change from you calling me a whore,' Becky decided with a sniff, and though it just about killed him, Rawdon had to let her have the last word, then left the house that would have been his if she hadn't stolen it out from under him.

He didn't even have the money for a bus fare, let alone a taxi, so he walked across town to Pitt and Jane's London residence, his father's old house in Chelsea. Bought for a pittance with the money from Sir Pitt's first lead role back in the seventies and now worth a king's ransom.

'You can stay here as long as you like, Rawdon,' Pitt said awkwardly and held out his arms as if he wanted to hug his wayward younger brother, then dropped them. Rawdon could hardly bring himself to look at Pitt. Not just because of the liberties that Pitt might have taken with his wife. But because he hated to think that he was just as weak as his brother, had been just as blinded by Becky Sharp.

'It's only a short stay. I'm going to be arrested in the morning,' Rawdon said as Jane gasped in dismay from behind Pitt. 'Or maybe even later tonight. I assaulted Steyne, though what I really wanted to do was wring his fucking neck. And Becky . . . '

'Rawdon, you didn't,' Jane said sadly and with a disappointed expression that — despite all the other indignities that had been heaped on poor Rawdon Crawley in the last forty-eight hours — made him fall to his knees and cry like a little boy.

⋆　⋆　⋆

In the morning, on Jane and Pitt's advice, Rawdon waited for the Crawleys' family lawyer to arrive so they could go back to Charing Cross Police Station and he could turn himself in.

But when a lawyer turned up on the doorstep in sombre suit and sombre expression, it turned out that he was on retainer to Lord Steyne.

'You've had a wasted trip, I'm afraid,' Rawdon told him, as he pulled on his leather jacket. 'I'm just waiting for my man to come so I can go and confess my crimes.' He held out his wrists as if they were already cuffed. 'It's a fair cop and all that.'

'I'm Mr William from William, Makepeace and Thackeray. Is there somewhere we can talk?' the man asked, his voice smooth and unhurried, but with a pointed look at Jane who was lurking in the hall. He ushered Rawdon into the drawing room on his left and firmly shut the door with all the confidence of a man who charged £2,000 an hour. 'You misunderstand my intentions, Mr Crawley. Lord Steyne has no intention of pressing charges.'

'Say what?' Rawdon grunted incredulously as he collapsed into a chair.

'A very unfortunate set of circumstances,' said Mr William, placing his briefcase on an end table and opening it. 'Nothing more than a misunderstanding, and to show that he bears you no ill will, I've been instructed to give you this.'

He handed over the bulky, familiar pages of a script and the less bulky pages of a contract, which Rawdon took with nerveless fingers. He tried to read the top sheet of the contract but the words swam in front of his eyes.

'If I may précis?'

Rawdon nodded dumbly.

'It just so happens that the creative team at Lord Steyne's company, Gaunt Productions, think you'd be perfect for the lead role in a new film franchise. Quite an exciting project, as I understand it . . . '

The lawyer went on to name the box-office darlings already signed on and the director, who had an unimpeachable track record when it came to critically acclaimed but commercially successful movies. He had won more Best Picture Oscars than any other director, 'Except Spielberg, so I'm led to believe. Of course, you'd have to commit to making all three movies back to back and you'd be shooting in New Zealand — well, quite a remote island off New Zealand — but your fee more than makes up for that inconvenience. Plus, there'll be a percentage of box office and all manner of product tie-ins. You'll want to get your agent to take a look at it, but he's already spoken to Lord Steyne and assured him that you'll do it.'

'I'm sorry, what?' Rawdon hadn't taken in half of what the man had said but he'd picked up the highlights. Like a particularly stinky, slimy piece of rubbish, he was being ruthlessly disposed of — sent as far away as it was possible to send someone without shooting them off into outer space.

But if and when he came back, everything would be different. He'd be different. He'd be rich. He'd be famous. A household name. Men would want to be him, women would want to have him, everyone would want to know him. It would show that worthless wife of his that actually, he could manage perfectly well without her. Even if it was thanks to the largesse of the man who had been pulling all their strings these last few months. But Rawdon found that he didn't care very much about that any more.

'Where do I sign?' he asked hoarsely.

'There are tabs on the contract showing you where,' the lawyer said helpfully. 'You'll want a pen. Here, you can borrow mine.'

He held out a fountain pen that cost the same as a small two-door hatchback, then whisked it away before Rawdon could take it.

'Just one thing before you sign,' he said. 'Lord Steyne wonders if you might do him a personal favour? The smallest of favours? A mere trifle, if you will.'

SUNDAY HERALD
'MY MARRIAGE IS OVER!'

Heartbroken Hollywood hell-raiser Rawdon Crawley reveals his shock split from reality-TV star Becky Sharp, after she bedded countless other men and her out-of-control spending left him millions of pounds in debt.

SUNDAY NEWS
'BECKY SHARP STOLE FROM MY DYING AUNT!'

Agent to the stars Barbara Pinkerton on how a teenage Becky Sharp preyed on her beloved aunt and national treasure, Jemima . . .

NEWS OF THE PEOPLE
BECKY THE BULLY!

Finally! *Big Brother* housemates break their silence to reveal what really happened in that swimming pool — the truth will shock you!

GLOBE ON SUNDAY
HAS THE BECKY BUBBLE BURST?

From con artist to reality TV to queen of Instagram: how Becky Sharp fooled the world, ten million Instagram followers and a Parisian couture house . . .

36

They say that revenge is a dish best served cold, and how patiently Becky's enemies had waited with their stories on ice until Lord Steyne's lackeys came calling.

The only person that Becky could forgive was Rawdon because his revenge wasn't cold. It was the fiery-hot act of someone recently betrayed and Rawdon always did have very poor impulse control. But what she couldn't forgive Rawdon for was serving divorce papers on her and naming some man she didn't even know as her lover. Not when he was using the same firm of lawyers who did all of Steyne's dirty work.

It wasn't just Steyne's newspapers. The rest of the fourth estate couldn't wait to line up and give her a kicking too. They were all there outside the house. Ringing on the doorbell, banging on the windows. Her phone was ringing off the hook with everyone from *The Times* and *Access Hollywood* desperate for the inside scoop while Phillip and Holly wanted Becky live on the *This Morning* sofa so that their viewers could phone up and call her terrible names.

The *Sunday Sport* had even found a troupe of stripper dwarves called The Seven Inchers who claimed that they'd all had her during one riotous, chemsex-fuelled night in a Blackpool Travelodge. She'd never even been to Blackpool!

Only the *Guardian* had come to her defence in

some long-winded opinion piece about social mobility and how there weren't many routes open to working-class girls from broken homes, and so who could blame Becky for weaponising her sexuality?

Becky pushed the papers off the bed with her bare feet because she couldn't stand to see her downfall spelt out in black and white and 72 point on all those front pages. Even as a little consoling voice in her head said, 'Still, you made the front pages. At least you didn't end up on page seven or worse!'

It wasn't that much of a comforting thought and Becky burst into tears again. She'd cried so much over the last three days that she expected Amelia Sedley (about the only spectre who hadn't drawn up a seat at the feast) to sue her for copyright.

In seventy-two hours, Steyne had destroyed everything that Becky had achieved in the last four years. Her reputation, her carefully constructed image and those lovely, lucrative sources of income — all gone!

She'd been fired by every single one of the companies that had kept her little gravy train chug-chug-chugging along. One of them had even sent round a couple of recovery agents to repossess all the clothes they'd given her.

Becky's publicist had blocked her number, her agent had put on an Eastern European accent when Becky had got through then pretended to be the cleaner, and her business manager had said, 'No offence, sweetheart, but right now I'd rather deal with an incurable case of herpes than with you.'

And all because she wouldn't sleep with Tom Steyne, though she doubted the evil old gnome could even get it up. For one tiny moment, Becky even wondered if she should have just let him have his way with her, but the thought of Steyne thinking he'd conquered her, *owned* her, would have been more than she could bear. Even when she'd had nothing, she'd still had her pride. Though even her pride had taken a beating over the last three days.

'How could I have been so stupid?' she wept and she was still weeping when Briggs, with the help of Firkin and a video they'd watched on YouTube, took her bedroom door off its hinges so they could finally gain admittance.

It had been three days since Briggs had taken up the papers in trembling hands, and the only reason they knew Becky hadn't killed herself was that they could hear her crying at all hours of the day and night.

They found their mistress a snivelling, snuffling, forlorn heap on the bathroom floor. Her glorious red curls tangled and matted, the face that had launched a thousand #spon #ads swollen and blotchy from crying so long.

'Oh, Becky, this will all blow over,' Briggs said consolingly but not at all truthfully as he met Firkin's eyes over Becky's sobbing figure. Firkin made the sign of the cross so that they wouldn't be struck down for such a wicked lie. The former foes were now united once more — the only people in the world prepared to stand by Becky Sharp, because hadn't she done the right thing by them?

So, they would be Becky's staunch defenders and willing supporters, until such a time as she could no longer afford to pay them.

'Mrs Crawley, don't cry. Sadness wrecks the complexion,' Firkin said. She patted Becky's shoulder. 'Have a shower, wash your hair, because it smells like old socks, and I'll make you a nice cup of tea.'

They shared another helpless look as Becky wailed and writhed on the bathroom tiles.

'Honestly, Becky, I understand that you're grief-stricken but . . . Oh!' Briggs scooched back from his kneeling position as Becky unfolded herself and he could finally see her face.

It wasn't the blotches or the puffiness which stood out, though they were both impressive, but the wild, raging pools of her eyes.

'I'm not grief-stricken,' she spat. 'I'm *fucking* furious! How dare he! And Rawdon can go fuck himself too! As for Babs and Martha and that whole other parade of losers and sad-sack wankers, I will destroy them. I'm going to make what's left of their sorry lives an endless round of misery and pain.'

'That's the spirit,' Briggs said. He'd heard a similar refrain from Dame Matilda when she'd seen some of her opening-night notices. 'You get it all out of your system.'

'I'm going to buy anthrax on the dark net,' Becky vowed, as Briggs and Firkin helped her slowly to her feet. 'I'm going to frame Babs Pinkerton for child sex trafficking. I'm going to make sure Martha Crawley gets syphilis and . . . '

They pushed Becky into the shower as she promised a great and terrible retribution on those who had wronged her, and when she emerged from the bathroom half an hour later, she was calm and composed.

Briggs looked enviously at her smooth, pale face. Not a sign of the traumas and trials of the last three days left.

'I'm not really going to do any of those things,' she told Briggs as she sipped on the green tea that Firkin had made her. 'What must you think of me?'

'Oh, we all say and do silly things when we're racked with grief. When my mother died, I tried to kill myself by sticking my head in the oven,' Briggs recalled fondly. 'I'd completely forgotten that we had an electric cooker.'

'I mean, why waste all that time and energy on finding ways to bring them down?' Becky mused. 'I should be focusing on myself.'

'It's all lies in the papers,' Briggs said stoutly, though he did wonder about the dwarves. He'd heard from a friend who'd had an uncle who'd worked on *The Wizard of Oz* that the male munchkins were all hung like horses. Who could blame a girl if that were the case? 'You've never been anything but kindness itself to me.'

'Dear, sweet Briggs,' Becky sighed, clasping her faithful retainer's hand. 'I'm going to have some time out, I think. Take a dip in Lake Me. Decide what I really want from the rest of my life. Like, spiritually and stuff.'

'That's my girl,' Briggs said. Hopefully Becky wasn't planning to go to an ashram, expecting him to accompany her. Vegan food went straight through him.

'Yes, I'm going to dedicate myself to enlightenment and self-improvement,' Becky said, her eyes shut as if she was already on a higher plane of being. Then her eyes snapped open. 'But first, I'm going to make that limp-dicked fucker Steyne wish that he'd never been born.'

★ ★ ★

Becky had haemorrhaged Instagram followers over the last three days. The comments on her last picture, of her arranging some flowers in a vase with a beatific smile on her face (due to the huge endorsement fee she was getting from an internet florist), could be summarised with a pithy 'Die u whore!'

But the followers that she had left, and anyone curious to know what you posted on social media when your entire world had crumbled to dust, were delighted to see a new post from Becky.

There was a 'play' symbol to indicate that a clip had been uploaded. But there was no film, just an audio recording of an old man with a cockney accent barking orders at someone who was clearly David Smirk, editor of the *Herald*, the UK's biggest-selling daily newspaper:

'Dave? Tom here. Was just wondering if someone had cut your balls off? Yes, it's very sad that all those poor little kiddies got mown down by some retarded fucker in an articulated lorry just because their teacher once turned him down for a date. Boo fucking hoo. But I don't give a fuck that you and your little editor mates have agreed to spare their families at such a difficult time. I want to know which grieving mother is having an affair. I want to know which gutted father has been done for domestic assault. What? They've already suffered enough? Good! Suffering sells! Now get into their phones, listen to their voicemails, hack their email accounts. I want every stringer in the North-East on their doorsteps to get me a week's worth of front-page scoops. Christ, you useless fucker, do I have to think of everything? Hang on . . . Mrs Crawley, I hope you're not eavesdropping, I'll have to spank you if you are . . . Dave? Are we clear? Doorstep 'em. Hack 'em. Hound 'em. Or I'll cut off your balls myself.'

And then Becky Sharp disappeared off the face of the earth. Or at least off the face of social media, which was pretty much the same thing.

A year later

BLOOD STEYNES ON HIS HANDS!
Evil media tycoon due to give evidence to Parliamentary Select Committee on Press Ethics today . . .

37

The elderly man who limped into the conference room at the Palace of Westminster looked so frail that George Wylie wondered if the breeze coming in from an open window might knock him over.

After Becky Sharp's spectacular takedown of the most powerful media mogul in the world, the headlines had written themselves, and although the press (including some of the papers he used to own, which had been sold off after they had lost most of their advertising revenue) depicted him as a despicable despot, it was an apparently broken man appearing before the Select Committee today.

Steyne was accompanied by a bevy of dark-suited lawyers and his three eldest children — Lady Steyne having been granted a quickie divorce on the grounds of emotional cruelty. The two forty-something sons were shifty-eyed and pale, and only his daughter, Laura, the heir-apparent to a now-tarnished crown, walked into the room with a confident stride and an easy smile.

George was happy to take a back seat as a chippy Labour MP, whose Midlands accent grated on his nerves, was desperate to have her fifteen minutes.

'So, Lord Steyne, do you accept responsibility for the campaign of harassment against the grieving parents of the children murdered at Fairlands Primary School? Harassment that contributed to the suicide of Alison Hall, who had waved two children off on that fateful Friday morning, never to see them alive again?'

'I accept nothing of the kind!' Lord Steyne barked, tapping his cane on the floor for emphasis. 'That recording were faked . . . '

'It's been verified by several forensic audiologists . . . '

'I won't have it!' Lord Steyne barked again, but since his stroke his bark was much worse than his bite, and his bark sounded a lot like the yapping of a tiny Chihuahua that had had all its teeth removed. 'That bloody Crawley woman.'

'I'm sorry.' Laura Steyne — elegant, poised and married to the founder of a powerhouse blue-chip public-relations company — leaned forward. 'Could we take a break for ten minutes?'

After the break, Laura Steyne came back into the room. 'If I may, I'd like to read a short statement,' she said. Saying no evidently wasn't an option.

''Owing to ill health, Lord Steyne will resign as chairman of Gaunt News, Gaunt Entertainment and all affiliated companies, effective immediately. His daughter, Laura, will serve as chairperson in the interim.

''And while Gaunt News is not admitting liability in any way, we personally want to offer our sincere apologies to all the families who lost loved ones at Fairlands Primary School for any distress they may have suffered.

' 'Going forward, Gaunt News welcomes any recommendations from this committee in respect to better working practice, but would stress in the strongest terms possible that freedom of the press is the cornerstone of democracy.' Thank you.'

There was a moment's silence and the member for Wolverhampton West clicked the lid of her pen on and off several times.

'Your sincere apologies won't bring back Alison Hall,' she said at last, fury unabated.

'What my right honourable colleague is forgetting is that Alison Hall's tragic suicide wasn't solely due to the misguided and unfortunate tactics of the press,' George said smoothly, because what his mouthy colleague was also forgetting was that he was chair of this committee, and God knows he'd had to do a lot of dreary drinking with dull backbenchers to make that happen. 'As a devoted father myself, I couldn't begin to imagine how devastating the loss of her two children must have been. However, this committee looks forward to working *closely* with Ms Steyne on implementing a code of conduct for the media, without hampering press freedom. Now, it's nearly four on a Friday afternoon. I suggest we reconvene on Monday morning when we'll be hearing from a panel representing the news agencies. Agreed?'

Afterwards, as George made to hurry away before he could be buttonholed by any coarse-voiced Labour MPs, or, God forbid, anyone from the SNP, Laura Steyne fell into step beside him.

'I just wanted to thank you for your adept chairing of the committee,' she said, with a little sideways look at George. She was very pretty in a corporate kind of way. Quite a strong jaw, though.

'Congratulations on your new role, by the way,' George said. 'I can't imagine your father or your brothers are too happy about it.'

By mutual and silent agreement, they came to a halt behind an ornate pillar where they couldn't be seen.

Laura Steyne grinned. 'I do love a bloodless coup,' she said. 'Less messy, I always find. And if I ever meet that bloody Crawley woman, I'd like to buy her a drink. Several drinks.'

'You really wouldn't want to meet her,' George said with a shudder because every now and again, when he least expected it, he'd suddenly remember that night in Cannes and how Becky Sharp had promised him everything and then laughed in his face, and feel fiery hot and then as icy cold as the grave. 'She's an evil bitch.'

'George . . . can I call you George?' Laura Steyne seemed undaunted by the granite look on George's face.

'All my *friends* do,' George said with what he hoped was a subtle emphasis. Under Laura Steyne's steerage, there was no reason why Gaunt Media wouldn't claw back their advertisers and their readers.

'People tell me you're one to watch,' Laura said, staring George right in the eye. 'That you're a man who's going places. So I'd think twice before you start labelling women as evil bitches. I get called that a lot, or words to that effect.'

'But you've never met the woman. If you had, then — '

'I've met enough strong, ambitious women who'd be admired and promoted a hell of a lot quicker if they were men. But because they have tits and two X chromosomes, they get called bitches instead,' Laura said and George felt himself wilt inside, as if he was being given a dressing down by one of the Dames at Eton. Or Becky Sharp herself, for that matter. 'Just a friendly warning, because I do hope that you and I are going to have a mutually beneficial *friendship*.'

'I hope so too,' George agreed. The sad and infuriating truth was that he needed Laura Steyne a lot more than she needed him. For now. To show that he wasn't completely whipped, he ostentatiously checked the time on his watch. No flashy Rolex for him, how common, but a watch that had belonged to his great-grandfather and still kept perfect time. 'I'm afraid that right now the only place I'm going is back home. My wife and child have hardly seen me all week.'

It was worth reminding Laura Steyne that he was a happily married man and a father too. Perfect credentials for a politician who photographed *extremely* well and was already tipped for a ministerial post in the next Cabinet reshuffle.

⋆　⋆　⋆

Usually the thought of going home, or rather going to the house in Leakington where Amelia and young George spent most of their time, filled George with a dull sort of dread.

There wasn't much to do down there but play golf with members of the local Rotary Club who were all Conservative councillors with very strong opinions on immigrants (terrorists), single mothers (feckless tarts who didn't deserve government handouts) and building on conservation areas (perfectly reasonable unless it was going to encroach on the unspoiled vistas from their own houses). But if he wasn't playing golf or opening a jumble sale, then George had to spend time with Amelia.

'There you are!' Amelia said when he got home, as if she'd asked him to pop out to get nappies on Monday morning and he'd only just returned at seven fifteen on Friday night. 'You almost missed bedtime.'

Amelia was in the nursery with the boy attached to her breast — did the boy spend all of his waking hours with his mouth firmly clamped around Amelia's nipple? Though he had a perfectly lovely nursery and a cot where he'd quite happily sleep, drunk on his mother's milk, Amelia insisted that he sleep with them when she and George came up to bed.

'I told you right from the start that I was very strongly drawn to attachment parenting,' she reminded him whenever George pointedly remarked that it would be nice to sleep with his wife without his child getting in the way.

Not that he had much desire to sleep with Amelia when she smelt of milk all the time and she *still* hadn't lost the baby weight though the child was over a year old now.

George cast a jaundiced eye around the nursery, where there were haphazard piles of terry-towelling nappies and baby clothes and all manner of paraphernalia adorned with teddy bears and ducks.

'Has the housekeeper quit?' he asked. Amelia absolutely refused to have a nanny but George had put his foot down and insisted on a daily cleaner because he wasn't having any of the local busybodies saying that the Wylies couldn't afford help.

'No. But now that Georgy is crawling, he pulls everything out as soon as I put it away,' Amelia said, as Georgy released her bulbous red nipple with a little pop. She gently placed him on her shoulder and began to rub his back. 'Haven't you got a kiss for us?'

George dutifully came closer to kiss Amelia's cheek and pat his son on his downy head. It was just as well that he got his needs seen to Monday to Thursday by the latest in a long line of very comely research assistants. Still, he wouldn't say no to a little bunk up with missus. When they weren't oozing milk, her tits were quite spectacular and she still rode that old nag of hers that George spent a fortune stabling, so when she squeezed her muscles, sometimes he thought he saw God.

About time Amelia remembered that she was married to a very powerful man, who kept her in a style to which she certainly wasn't accustomed when she'd been living in Burnt Oak. 'I've actually had quite a busy week. Did you see me on *Newsnight* on Tuesday?'

Amelia giggled. 'I'm in bed long before *Newsnight*. Being a mum is much more exhausting than being a politician.'

'Oh, don't exaggerate, Emmy,' George said, watching on tenterhooks as Amelia laid the baby down, on his back, in the cot. Go *straight to sleep, you pint-sized fucker.*

With a tired murmur — he really was quite a decent little chap — young Georgy clutched his cuddly Winston Churchill and drifted off to dreamland.

George hovered impatiently for another five minutes while Amelia stared at her slumbering son (though surely she was sick to death of looking at him by now), before finally retreating.

'Let's have a drink. A large one,' George said as he followed her down the stairs. Despite the housekeeper, there seemed to be more piles of stuff all over the house. How many toys and clothes did one very small child need?

'You know I can't, George, not while I'm breastfeeding,' Amelia said. 'But you have one and tell me all about your very busy week.'

Rather than hanging on to his every word as she used to do, George had the impression lately that Amelia was merely humouring him, but he managed to cajole her into having a very small glass of Chardonnay as he took her through the triumphs of his week in the corridors of power.

'And everyone agreed that I was an excellent chair of the committee,' he said when he got to the events of that afternoon. 'Not that I like to brag.'

'Of course you don't,' Emmy agreed. She was standing in front of the Aga stirring what she promised was a Thai curry. She was quite a good, if hearty, cook. George didn't dare even look at a carb from Monday to Thursday, otherwise he'd have to ask his tailor to let out the fat straps in all his suits. 'By the way, I was wondering how you voted on that bill to cut nursery funding?'

Why? Well, at least she was taking an interest in his career, and after he'd wowed her with tales of his parliamentary acumen and persuaded her to have another couple of glasses of Chardonnay, then maybe she'd let him bend her over the kitchen table. She did used to like it when he bent her over things.

'I voted for the cuts, of course,' he said. 'Our party position is that the poor have to help themselves. If you can't afford to have children then, QED, don't have children.'

Amelia snorted. George couldn't be sure because she was half in profile, but there might have been an eye roll too. 'If only people who could afford to had children, then the human race would die out pretty quickly,' she said tartly. 'Besides, the children of the poor will still grow up to pay taxes and contribute to society, though they'll struggle to achieve anything when you and your colleagues have closed libraries, underfunded schools and done just about everything they can to eradicate social mobility.'

'What has got into you?' George was appalled. It was like being in the Commons bar, stuck next to a table of shouty, rabble-rousing Labour backbenchers. 'We *personally* didn't close any libraries or underfund schools. You want to take that up with your local council.'

'Your golfing buddies, you mean,' Amelia sniffed. George had thought it was safe to leave her down here in the country, mouldering away as she hand-washed organic cotton nappies and experimented with baby-led weaning, but she'd obviously been mixing with some undesirable elements.

'What do you do all day and who do you do it with?' he asked suspiciously.

'Unlike you, I mix with all sorts of different people when I take Georgy to baby yoga or the music-makers' session at what should have been the local library, but it closed down. Which is fine, we can drive two towns over, but that's not an option when you don't drive or you can't afford the bus fare . . . '

George wished that he'd decided to spend the weekend in London. 'Oh, please, Emmy, *everyone* can afford the bus fare,' he said with the confident air of a man who'd never actually been on a bus in his life, which Amelia pointed out with a lot of aggressive gesturing with a wooden spoon.

He couldn't help but remember those little flashes of this Amelia — harder, stronger, not so docile or biddable — that he'd seen when he'd proposed. He'd actually thought that motherhood and a very generous allowance would make that different Amelia disappear.

'You know what? I should stand for the council myself,' she was now saying and sounding as if she meant it.

'Don't be ridiculous,' George snapped. 'You'd be bored to tears. It's all planning applications and people moaning about rubbish collections.'

Amelia paused to taste her sauce. 'I suppose you're right,' she mumbled and George let out a sigh of relief. Best to quash any signs of rebellion as soon as they appeared.

'Have another glass of wine,' he said solicitously because Amelia's cheeks were red in a way that had nothing to do with slaving over a hot stove. 'And shall we have a quick bunk-up before dinner? About time we gave dear little Georgy a brother or sis — '

'This is a bigger problem than just our council,' Amelia said as if she hadn't heard one word of George's very magnanimous offer. 'It's nationwide. I bet there are a million women, mothers, who've been affected by these cuts . . . '

'Enough, Emmy!' George barked, standing up all the better to loom over her. 'Not another word. You have a baby, a successful husband and a lovely home, what more could you possibly want? I won't stand for you having ideas. In fact, I forbid it!'

Amelia had the audacity to snort again. How George missed the young, empty-headed little Emmy who had unquestioningly adored him!

'Oh, well, if you forbid it . . . ' she said and let the sentence hang with, yes, a definite eye roll this time that made George shudder. Not just because Amelia was definitely having ideas but because, in that moment, she reminded him of none other than Becky Sharp.

412

Six months later

THE MARCH OF A MILLION MUMS
We're mad as hell and we're not going to take it anymore!

8th March — On International Women's Day we call for a day of action against government cuts that impact on our children's emotional, physical and mental well-being.

STRIKE! We call on all Mums to stop work on this day. No child-rearing, no household chores, no emotional labour.

MARCH! Take part in one of the fifty-seven marches happening in cities and towns across the UK to protest against government cuts.

DONATE! We need your time, support and money to help ALL mothers and children fulfil their potential.

For more details of how to take part, visit www.amillionmums.org.co.uk

Proudly sponsored by Mumsnet, the Women's Institute, M&S and the Crawley Family Foundation.

38

'Amelia, enough! Enough of all this nonsense. I absolutely forbid you from going on television.' George was a tinny voice on her mobile phone, forbidding her from doing something that she absolutely intended to do, much as he'd been doing for the last six months.

'Really, George, you said in the House of Commons that you were very proud of me,' Amelia reminded him as a make-up girl finished doing something to her face that actually gave her cheekbones. 'That it was about time someone showed the caring side of the Conservative Party.'

George spluttered inarticulately — he'd been doing a lot of that lately too — and Amelia terminated the call. She needed to focus. She was being interviewed by Jon Snow, who she'd always had a crush on, and she needed to be on point.

She needn't have worried, Jon Snow was perfectly lovely, though the battle-axe they'd dredged up from the Christian Wives' Association to provide a counter-argument was perfectly horrible. She didn't even smile when they showed footage of that day's march and a close-up of Georgy holding a placard that said, 'I might need a nap, but I'm still woke.'

'So, Amelia, six months ago you started the Million Mums campaign on your kitchen table and today over a million mothers across the country downed tools and marched to protest against government cuts. How does that make you feel?' Jon (he'd said that she could call him Jon) asked.

'I feel very proud and humbled by each and every mother who took part in today's protests,' Amelia said. 'Who realised that together we're powerful. Instead of sitting back and passively allowing government policy to adversely affect the lives of our children, we've become a movement for change. Today, I've talked to so many women who want to be represented, to have their voices heard, whether that means standing for election to their local council or becoming a school governor. We're taking back control for our children.'

'And Anne Vere-Vane, chairperson of the Christian Wives' Association, I take it you didn't march?'

'I did not,' the middle-aged woman said censoriously. 'A woman's place, a *mother's* place, is in the home, at the heart of her family, not on the streets.'

'We took *to* the streets to fight for our families,' Amelia said, though everything in her longed to backtrack and apologise in the face of the older woman's disapproval. She asked herself, as she often did these days, what would Becky Sharp do? Becky Sharp, without a question of doubt, would take this bitch down and do it with a smile on her face. 'Let's not forget that there were a lot of mothers who'd have loved to march today but they had to work to provide for their families. Although, what with the cost of childcare and the drastic cuts to the Sure Start scheme . . . '

'I've always thought that mothers who work can't love their children very much,' the gorgon on the other side of the table said, and though lovely Jon Snow was meant to be impartial, even he looked pretty shocked.

'Then I pity you for having absolutely no Christian compassion,' Amelia said calmly. 'Because I've met a lot of mothers over the last six months, from all sorts of backgrounds. Mothers who are trying to survive on benefits and mothers who have three nannies, some who work because they want to but more often because they have to and some who are stay-at-home mums. But what they all have in common is their love for their children.'

Jon Snow commented, 'It's been said today by Conservative MP, Quentin Quadroon — a colleague of your husband George, Amelia — and I quote, 'What these women don't seem to understand is that politics is a very complicated business.''

'Not that complicated. And I've seen better behaviour at a two-year-old's birthday party than I have in the Chamber,' Amelia said drily and she couldn't help it, even though darling Jane Sheepshanks-Crawley had begged her not to because it was very unprofessional, she rolled her eyes. 'And what they all seem to be forgetting is that the hand that rocks the cradle is the hand that rules the world.'

'I'm afraid that's all we have time for,' said Jon

416

Snow. 'Amelia Wylie, Anne Vere-Vane, thank you very much.'

After the cameras stopped rolling, Anne Vere-Vane wouldn't even shake Amelia's hand, but Jon Snow was happy to pose for a selfie and tell her that she'd done a great job. Glowing from the praise and the hot studio lights, Amelia switched on her phone so she could post the selfie on Instagram. She saw that she had fifteen text messages from her husband, each one more irate than the last.

'OMG George,' she texted back, quite irate herself. 'Stop oppressing me. B part of the solution, not part of the problem. And make your own sodding dinner.'

★　★　★

The next few months were a happy blur of marches and meetings, lobbying and campaigning, which coincided with a snap General Election. It was quite a bloodbath for the Conservatives, who lost a significant number of seats, while three first-time candidates, all of them members of their local Million Mums chapters, were elected to Parliament. George's majority had decreased considerably and he'd been in a foul mood ever since.

Of course Amelia wanted to get her marriage back on track but, as she'd confided to her dear, new friend Jane Sheepshanks-Crawley, she wasn't sure if their marriage had ever been on track. 'I just went along with whatever George wanted because I was so grateful to him for loving me and supporting me, even after all that unpleasantness with daddy's bank.'

'Maybe another baby?' Jane had suggested wistfully, because she and Pitt were on their third round of IVF, in spite of the fact that they had so many little Crawleys to look after.

'If you want another baby, then you'll have to stop with all this radicalism,' George had said. 'It's not exactly a turn-on to have you shrieking about mothers' rights every time I switch on the television.'

Sometimes it was very hard to love George Wylie. But then Amelia would look out of the window of her study and see Pianoforte trotting happily in the lower paddock, and she'd remember why she loved George. Though truthfully, she didn't like him very much lately.

He'd also been extremely gloating when she'd had to admit that she needed help with Georgy. He was now a rambunctious toddler who couldn't be put to her breast and then fall asleep for an hour while she took a meeting or did an interview. In fact, much to Amelia's dismay, Georgy had decided that he no longer wanted 'booby' and would much prefer a packet of Pom-Bears.

George had been quite smug about that too, though the smile had been wiped off his face when he saw who was going to pick up the slack when it came to childcare.

'There has to be someone else,' he complained when Mrs Sedley turned up to stay for the weekend so Amelia could go to Paris for the first French *Un Million de Mamans* day of action.

'I thought you were all about family values,' Amelia said as Mrs Sedley caught sight of Georgy, squealed in delight ('he looks so much like Jossy did at that age') and covered her protesting grandson in kisses.

Mrs Sedley was quite recovered from her migraines, which had turned out (to no one's surprise) to be psychosomatic after all. It had inspired her to train as a counsellor and she'd now launched an offshoot movement of the Million Mums. Great Grannies was a global volunteer network of older retired ladies who provided babysitting and childcare so that mothers could go off and protest or stand for political office.

'Well, it gets me out of the house,' she'd said to Amelia, because she and Amelia's father were still tied to the poky little house in Burnt Oak, though Mrs Sedley was now a stalwart member of the local residents' association and commanded a certain amount of respect on the estate. 'Leaves your father free to write his letters and really, he's been much better since the residents' association agreed that he could be their treasurer.' She'd sniffed, because a contemptuous sniff was something that had been handed down the maternal line. 'I'm not sure I'd trust him with the raffle money, but there you go.'

Mrs Sedley had been drafted in to look after George this weekend too. Amelia had been invited to Pumpernickel, a German spa town, for a global conference on children and women's rights. Not just invited, she was going to speak on a panel about digital activism.

Apart from the round of media interviews when she'd won *Big Brother* (which now seemed as if it had happened several lifetimes ago and to someone else), Amelia had never done any public speaking. Even a year ago, the prospect of talking to a room full of important people would have terrified her, but now Amelia felt as if she could do anything if she set her mind to it. In the last six months she'd found her voice.

She was waiting quite happily in the departure lounge of Heathrow Airport reviewing her talking points, when her attention was caught by one of the TV screens directly in her line of vision.

It was a news report on the terrible conditions in one of the refugee camps on the Syrian border. Amelia sighed. Those poor children. Still, one couldn't help *all* the children in the world . . . Hang on! That wasn't . . . It couldn't be . . .

'Becky Sharp!' she gasped out loud, because it was Becky in that dusty refugee camp, swathed in something loose-flowing and impossibly snowy-white, given the conditions. Her head was covered by a black headscarf, which really showed off her porcelain skin and green eyes to their best advantage. She looked more beautiful than ever as she cradled a very skinny baby and . . . No! That wasn't . . . It couldn't be . . .

It was Jos! There was Jos in the background, smiling proudly as Becky spoke to a reporter. Normally Amelia was a stickler for security and keeping a tight hold and an eagle eye on her luggage, but she leapt to her feet to get nearer to the TV so she could hear what the hell was going on.

' . . . and so I asked my lovely old friend Jos Sedley, who has the most successful protein ball company in the United States, if there was some way we could apply the same principles behind superfoods and protein snacks to feed starving people.' Becky smiled triumphantly. 'And it turned out there was.'

'It's an energy drink, then?' asked the reporter.

'Well, it's more of a high-calorie, special protein drink and the really great thing about it is that it has a very long shelf life and can be stored in any kind of temperature,' Becky said enthusiastically. 'Best of all, it's main ingredient is a very resilient natural plant protein that can be grown even in a very dry climate. We've been talking to the United Nations about establishing a micro-loans scheme so that communities will be able to grow their own food.'

'So, you've gone from the red carpet to literally eradicating world hunger?'

Becky laughed self-deprecatingly. 'I wouldn't say that. I had the initial idea but it was Jos and lots of very hard-working food scientists and climate specialists that did the heavy lifting . . . '

'Flight BA127 to Cologne now boarding at Gate Thirteen.'

They were calling her flight. In a daze, Amelia turned back to check that her luggage was still there and hadn't been infiltrated by any terrorists.

On the way to board the plane, she stopped at the newsagent to stock up on barley sugar so her ears wouldn't pop and to search the papers so she could find out what the *hell* was going on with Becky Sharp, who'd fallen off the face of the earth for nearly two years.

But Amelia didn't need to search very hard because as she entered the newsagent, there was a pile of glossy magazines with a familiar face wearing a familiar half-smile staring back at her.

VANITY FAIR
THE RISE AND FALL (AND RISE) OF BECKY SHARP

She's been a reality-TV star, a trophy wife, an Instagram sensation, a tabloid *cause célèbre* and now Becky Sharp is adding global philanthropist to her CV. Emily Swastz meets the woman who took on Lord Steyne and lived to tell the tale . . .

Free from both entourage and make-up, Becky Sharp strides into the garden terrace of the Beverly Hills Polo Lounge with a bright smile and her hand outstretched in greeting. Dressed in simple white blouse and black cigarette pants, red hair pulled back in a loose ponytail, her beauty is unadorned but no less radiant for it.

Over a large cappuccino ('I seem to be the only woman in LA who does caffeine and full-fat milk') and two croissants ('I also refuse to give up carbs') she's refreshingly candid about her rise to the top and her shocking tumble from grace.

'I've made mistakes, a lot of mistakes,' she says with a rueful grin and a graceful wiggle of her shoulders. 'But really, I only ever did three things that were unforgivable, and that was to be female, working class and ambitious . . . '

39

Pumpernickel was a horrible little *hole* of a place and Becky couldn't imagine why anyone had thought it was a good idea to hold a conference there. Any kind of conference, even one about office stationery products, let alone a global conference about children and women's rights, attended by all sorts of movers and shakers in the world of A-list philanthropy.

But she was the guest of honour so she had to show willing. She had been on her best behaviour a lot lately — it was quite dull. As was the plain, though beautifully cut, black dress she was wearing, accessorised with a pair of hot-pink heels, to give the keynote speech.

'As soon as I was in a position to make a difference, to have some influence, I've always worked with charities that are especially dear to my heart,' Becky said to a packed house and hundreds of thousands of people around the world who were having the speech live-streamed to their devices. 'In particular, charities who work with the most vulnerable in society: children.'

She swallowed hard, just as she'd rehearsed back in the presidential suite of her hotel. 'This won't come as any surprise because my entire life has been tabloid fodder, but I lost my mother when I was eight and my father went to prison when I was twelve, then died when I was fifteen.

I had to stand on my own two feet at a very young age and use whatever means necessary to survive. I won't apologise for that and I absolutely refuse to be condemned for it either.

'But compared to the children I've met in Syria, who've had their lives torn apart by war, or the two little boys, Munir and Rana, that I met in South Sudan who lost their family in the terrible famine, I realised that even at my very lowest moments, compared to these children, I had so much.

'And that's why I'm so humbled to be appointed a UN Ambassador for Children. In this role I'm determined to give a voice to the voiceless, to give power to the powerless, to lift up those who have sunk to the bottom through no fault of their own.'

It was a great speech, put together by one of Barack Obama's former speechwriters, who said that even Obama hadn't made as many changes as Becky had. But she knew exactly what she wanted to say and she didn't need any fancy four-syllable words to say it.

Of course, when she was done, she was given a standing ovation. It would have been pretty bloody rude if people had kept their arses on their seats. Once again, Becky was bathed in the warm glow of a hundred camera lenses and the sound of all those people clapping was like champagne corks popping.

Oh, how she'd missed this!

What she hadn't missed was the meet and greet. The mingling. Having to shake the clammy hands of people she didn't know and didn't care to know and make polite but meaningless conversation with them even though she hoped to God she'd never have to meet any of them again.

In particular, the Pumpernickel conference was full of dreary do-gooders. Not at all like the glamorous world of global philanthropy where Angelina Jolie, George and Amal Clooney and Colin and Livia Firth were now close, personal friends.

Then a name caught her attention.

'And this is Captain William Dobbin of Her Majesty's Royal Regiment who's here to have his humanitarian work recognised,' droned one of the publicists from the (slightly dodgy) investment bank that was sponsoring the conference. 'He *literally* rescued babies from a burning building.'

'Becky? Becky Crawley? What on *earth* are you doing here?'

Why couldn't the hapless Captain Dobbin have styled it out so they could both pretend they'd never met and merrily go their separate ways after a few seconds?

'It's Becky Sharp, as I'm very happily single these days, Dobbin,' Becky said sweetly, as the publicist melted away. 'And I'm here, I can't quite believe it's escaped your notice, because I've just been made a UN Ambassador — '

'Becky! Becky Sharp! I've been so cross with you for so long but gosh! It's so good to see you!'

A very hot, very red-faced Amelia Sedley threw her arms around Becky and hugged her like they were hugging friends who'd kept in

426

touch, their past grievances long forgotten.

'Amelia, how lovely to see you,' Becky said, removing Amelia's arms from their death grip around her neck and taking a step back. 'No George?' She angled an arch look at Amelia and then at Dobbin. 'Unless you and the good captain . . . '

'No, no, George and I are still very much together. Of course we are,' Amelia insisted manically and then she dared to glance shyly up at Dobbin who was the only person in the very crowded and stuffy reception room who was more red-faced than she. 'Dobbin . . . William, I had no idea you'd be here too. It's been so long. I'm so, so glad you're not dead!'

'I'm rather glad I'm not dead too,' Dobbin said gravely as Becky stifled a yawn. What a pair of utter imbeciles they both were. 'I did say that I'd come back . . . to you.'

'And you're not the sort of person who breaks his promises,' Amelia said sadly, thinking of all the thousands of promises that Gorgeous George Wylie had made to her and then broken.

'Do you want to get a room?' Becky asked with such a sincere expression that neither Dobbin nor Amelia could tell if she was joking. 'I mean, seriously, you two . . . '

'Gosh, I say! The old gang's back together!' said a braying voice from behind them and Jos Sedley lumbered up, his face aglow with genuine delight, followed by Briggs, laden down with Becky's coat, handbag, a bottle of mineral water and a box of press packs. 'Emmy! You got a hug for big bruv?'

'Jos!' The two Sedley siblings hugged. 'Though I'm very cross with you too because you didn't come home for Christmas and you never even told me that you and Becky were . . . With the protein drink and . . . What exactly *are* you and Becky?'

'She's the brains behind the brawn. My muse. My inspiration . . . ' Jos paused as he tried to sum up exactly what Becky Sharp was to him ever since she'd walked back into his life some eighteen months ago and turned it upside down.

'We're old friends,' Becky said firmly. 'Who work very well together.'

'So well,' Jos echoed and even Amelia, who loved her elder brother dearly, had to admit that he'd never looked better.

He was no longer triangular in shape and his neck was no longer the same circumference as his waist, now that he'd stopped bench pressing his own body weight and was taking a more holistic approach to his health and fitness.

Jos had also gone quite a few shades lighter (twenty, by a conservative estimate) on the fake tan and was now a light latte rather than a deep, deep mahogany.

It hadn't been the easiest transformation. There had even been tears when Becky had pointed out that no one would take Jos and his protein balls seriously in the world of global philanthropy if he looked like Buzz Light year on steroids. 'Nobody's going to give you any awards for having the most over-developed pecs and guns on the West Coast,' she'd said as Jos had fretted about losing his precious, precious muscle mass.

Jos would never be handsome but at least he no longer burst the seams of all his suits and . . .

'You look happy,' Amelia said in wonder. 'I don't think you've ever looked this happy, apart from that one Christmas when Daddy bought you a mini-Bentley.'

'I am happy,' Jos said and he looked at Becky in rapt admiration, then had to ease a stubby finger round the collar of his shirt, because some things never changed.

'And are you happy with Gorgeous George?' Becky asked and though that was Amelia's cue to bristle, for the tears to prick her eyes as she thought back to Becky's disgraceful behaviour in Cannes, she remained both bristle- and tear-free.

'I'm happy with little Georgy,' she said, whipping out her phone so Dobbin and Becky could admire how handsome he was. Becky had to clench her jaw to stop herself from yawning again. This much restraint couldn't be good for her blood pressure and what could one say about a toddler with something orange dribbling from its mouth?

'Charming,' Becky said. 'Very cute.'

'He has your eyes,' said Dobbin, who'd been silent all this time.

'Oh? You don't think he looks like George?' Amelia asked in surprise because George's family always said that there was absolutely nothing of Amelia in Georgy, apart from a propensity to whine, and that he was a Wylie through and through.

'He has a sweetness to his face which is all you,' Dobbin said and Becky really wanted to put a finger to her mouth and make gagging noises or at least say something very cutting. Being a UN Goodwill Ambassador was really cramping her style.

'I'm not quite as sweet as I used to be,' Amelia said and she didn't finish the sentence with a self-deprecating giggle or flush bright red. Becky looked at her former BFF with genuine interest for maybe the first time in all the years that they'd known each other.

There was a determined focus to Amelia's blue eyes, a certain, uncompromising set to her mouth and she had a new habit of raising her chin as if she was expecting an argument and planned to give as good as she got. How ironic that being married to George Wylie had been the making of her, and not in a way that either Amelia or George had expected.

'You've grown up, Emmy,' Becky decided. 'Got a backbone. Good for you.'

'For God's sake Becky, Emmy's always had a backbone,' Dobbin said, rounding on Becky, who raised her eyebrows, not giving an inch, even though Dobbin was a good foot taller and much, much, much angrier than her. 'She was a lovely girl and she's become a lovely woman.'

'Calm down, dear. I hope you have a bit more self-control when you're commanding your soldiers,' Becky said, and she took a step to the side so she no longer had to be confronted by the furious, huffing Dobbin, and so she was face to face with Amelia, who was definitely easier on

Becky's eye and ear, for that matter.

'Well, we should catch up properly,' Becky said, as she really didn't relish having to spend the evening in Pumpernickel, having to socialise with dull people who wanted to talk about dull things like education and period poverty. 'Tonight. We'll have dinner.'

'I'd love to,' Amelia said. Becky was now a UN Goodwill Ambassador and surely the UN wouldn't have given her the gig if she were lacking in goodwill? And Becky was still the most funny, fascinating person Amelia had ever met, even if she still hadn't forgiven her for all the wrongs she'd done. And yet . . . 'I'm meant to be having dinner with some women who want to set up Million Mum organisations in Germany and Holland.'

'I'm not going to beg, Emmy, but having dinner with me is going to be heaps more fun than with some downtrodden mothers,' Becky said firmly because she hadn't lost the art of saying something crushing about a cause close to Amelia's heart, whether it was George Wylie back in the day or the grassroots movement that had politicised an entire generation of women. It was quite reassuring in such a topsy-turvy world.

'I did want to catch up with Dobbin too,' Amelia said hesitantly, as the good captain looked as if he were about to cry happy tears.

'Fine, Dobbin can join us,' Becky said wearily as if she was talking about being booked in for root-canal surgery. 'Jos, you'll want to come too, I suppose.'

'You know I do,' Jos assured Becky eagerly.

'Every second we're apart is tort — Ow!' A malevolent glare from Becky shut Jos up so abruptly that he bit his tongue.

'Because you haven't seen your sister in *years*,' Becky reminded him. The publicist was suddenly at her side and nervously looking at Becky's arm as if she was wondering if she might dare take it and usher the newest UN Goodwill Ambassador over to a delegation from the World Health Forum.

'I hope I'm not interrupting anything,' she said with a cringing smile. 'I'm going to have to whisk Ms Sharp away.'

'I'm not having dinner in Pumpernickel,' Becky called over her shoulder as they left. 'Briggs! Book a private room in the nicest restaurant in Cologne. Make sure it has at least one Michelin star!'

40

That evening, in a private room in one of only two restaurants in Cologne that had a Michelin star, Amelia and Dobbin nursed a mineral water each and tried to make polite conversation as they waited for Becky and Jos to arrive.

There had been a time when Amelia wouldn't have thought anything of spending half an hour in Dobbin's company. They'd have talked about everything under the stars. Or rather they'd have talked about horses or George Wylie, as those two topics had been all Amelia ever thought about and Dobbin had only ever wanted to make her happy.

Now George was the very last person that Amelia wanted to talk to Dobbin about. Horses didn't have the same fascination for her either and besides, Dobbin was uncharacteristically monosyllabic. Amelia questioned him about what he'd been doing since they'd last seen each other in a hospital room a few days after Georgy was born. Where had he done his latest tour? Was it very awful? Did he feel as if he was making a difference and gosh, *literally* pulling orphans out of a burning building must have been very scary, but Dobbin gave her nothing to work with other than a few polite grunts.

Amelia couldn't imagine why he was brooding. It was a relief when her phone pinged with a message from Jos to let her know that Becky was running late — she'd had to take a phone call from her dear friend, the president of Iceland — and they'd be there as soon as possible.

'Imagine Becky being dear friends with the president of Iceland,' she remarked to Dobbin with a conspiratorial giggle, which he didn't return. 'Though really I don't know why I'm surprised at anything Becky does.'

'Quite,' Dobbin said.

'The only thing I'm surprised about is how pleased I am to see her again,' Amelia persisted in the face of Dobbin's utter lack of enthusiasm. 'Of course, I'm under no illusions as to what she's really like.'

'Are you though, Emmy?' Dobbin suddenly sat up from his slumped position, which would have had his old sergeant major making him do laps around the barracks as penance. 'Because I don't care if she is a UN Goodwill Ambassador and that she's managed to fool the world into thinking that she's a decent, honourable person. She hasn't fooled me and she's not the sort of person you should welcome back into your life.'

'I'm not a child, Dobbin,' Amelia snapped instantly, because that was now her automatic response to any man giving her his unsolicited advice. 'And I won't be told what I can and can't do. You're not my father and you're certainly not my husband, thank God . . . '

They both flushed for different reasons. Lately, when Amelia thought of George, her insides constricted and she had an odd sense of impending doom. And Dobbin was carmine of complexion because his old friend, George

Wylie, now felt like his bitterest foe.

'I understand why you married him,' he said rashly, because any fool could do the maths on Georgy's conception, 'but I don't understand why you *stay* married to him. I always looked up to George when we were younger: he was amusing and confident, everything I wasn't. But now it pains me to see that he's gone down the wrong path and is intent on dragging you with him.'

'He's not dragging me anywhere,' Amelia said. She and George led two very separate lives these days. As she so often did, she asked herself why she was still married to a man with whom she no longer shared any values, and she came back to the same reason that she always did. 'Deep down, George is a good, kind man.'

'Well, that's certainly not reflected in his voting record,' Dobbin muttered darkly. 'I see very little goodness and kindness there.'

'He was good and kind when it really mattered. When everyone had turned their backs on me, George stayed true,' Amelia insisted, and sometimes she wished that George hadn't stood by her, because then it would be so much easier not to love him now.

'That's not quite how I remember it,' Dobbin said, thinking back to the meeting with George's father and his campaign manager and how they'd all unanimously agreed that Amelia Sedley should be quickly disposed of.

'Well, it's how I remember it,' Amelia said, her hand on her foolish heart. 'He bought back Pianoforte for me . . . '

There was a clatter as Dobbin's glass crashed to the floor, blood streaming from the wound where he'd crushed it in his big, meaty hand.

'Oh, Dobbin! You haven't changed a bit!' Amelia said, and she tried to smile because Dobbin was still as clumsy as ever, and it was still endearing, but then she saw the stricken look on his face.

He turned away from Amelia's gaze. 'How is Pianoforte?' he asked in a choked voice.

'He's splendid,' Amelia said with a frown. What had made Dobbin look like that, as if his world had stopped turning? And why was there suddenly such tension between them, as taut and as tight as a tourniquet? 'Apart from little Georgy, I've never loved anyone or anything as much as I love that horse. Not even George, and that's why it still means the world to me that George saved him and gave him back to me.'

'Forgive me,' Dobbin said, resting his blood-smeared hand on his forehead, and finally Amelia understood why her old friend was in such despair.

'Did . . . *did* George save him?'

'There was a note. I wrote a note . . . purportedly written by the horse, which I hoped was a piece of whimsy you might like . . . ' Dobbin shook his head. 'But I thought . . . '

'What did you think?' Amelia's voice was thick with tears. Not the tears that she used to be able to summon so easily. These felt as if they were being dredged up from the very depths of her soul.

The last three years of her life — her marriage,

436

even the existence of Georgy — were all due to a misunderstanding, a miscommunication. And all this time she'd clung to her shaky belief that George loved her.

'Why would you do that, Dobbin?' she asked, though she already knew the answer. 'Why did you rescue Pianoforte?'

'Because — because I love you.' The words were wrenched out of him. 'I've loved you since the first moment I saw you at a school open day and I thought you were the most beautiful girl I'd ever seen. I've loved you all this time and I tried to tell you before I went away, but you didn't care . . . '

'Dobbin! I'd just had a baby, George's baby!' Amelia protested. 'It wasn't that I was ungrateful . . . ' But she had been ungrateful. She'd always known that Dobbin had a crush on her and though she'd been flattered, she'd hardly ever given either Dobbin or his feelings much thought. Worse, Amelia admitted to herself with a guilty start, she'd so often used Dobbin as a means to one end: George. Everything had always come back to George.

'You were indifferent,' Dobbin spelt out harshly and Amelia hung her head. Dobbin had every right to be harsh with her. 'I don't know why I thought anything would change in telling you this. My constancy and devotion mean nothing, because you'd still rather give your time and your love to people who don't deserve it. George, that awful Sharp woman, but not me. Never me!'

'You should have said something! At Cannes,

when you saw how he treated me, you should have told me then,' Amelia said because it was easier to be furious at Dobbin for his deception when really she was furious with herself for squandering her own constancy and devotion on George Wylie.

'It wouldn't have been any use,' Dobbin said bitterly. 'I know what your heart is capable of: it can cling faithfully to a recollection and cherish a fancy, but it's not worthy of the love I've given you. You couldn't — you wouldn't be able to comprehend, or even begin to return the sheer weight of the love I'd have given you, and which another woman might have been happy to have. Well, I'm done, Emmy! It ends here.'

He scraped back his chair with such force that it toppled over but Amelia didn't giggle at yet another display of Dobbin's legendary clumsiness. Instead, she stood too, scared and silent and ashamed. Deeply ashamed because what Dobbin had just said was true. He had placed himself at her feet and she had trampled all over him. She didn't want him, but she wanted him with her. She'd given him nothing over the years, but had taken everything that he had to give her.

She wasn't worthy of his love, and it broke her heart in a way that would have made Dobbin dare to hope, if he only knew.

'You're not going away, are you, William?' He was finally William to her. Not Dobbin, the fool. But it was all too late.

'I can't stay. I've wasted enough of my life on this nonsense,' he said, and he was gone before Amelia could even beg him to stay, brushing past

Becky Sharp, who'd been stood in the doorway for quite some time. It would have been rude to interrupt the highly charged scene in front of her and besides, she couldn't remember the last time she'd been so entertained.

41

Amelia wasn't crying, which had to be some sort of miracle, but was standing there looking as if she'd been slapped around the face with a kipper.

'The reason we're so late has nothing to do with the president of Iceland and everything to do with your brother coming down wearing such a ridiculous suit, a pink-and-grey houndstooth, that I had to send him back to his room to change,' Becky said airily, and oh yes, here were the inevitable tears, trickling down Amelia's cheeks like raindrops. She sighed. 'You haven't grown up at all, have you? You're still a very silly girl.'

'Don't, Becky,' Amelia snapped, because she really wasn't a silly girl at all. She was actually a very silly woman. 'What do you know about love?'

'Not a fucking thing, but I do know that if I had a man like that Dobbin, with brains and a heart, I wouldn't even care about his huge ears and feet.' Becky paused. 'Or I wouldn't care too much.'

'He doesn't love me any more and I can't blame him!' Amelia burst out, the tears flowing thick and fast now. 'He's right, I don't deserve his love and anyway, I love George. Or I thought I did, when really it was just a silly adolescent crush that should have run its course. It's all such a mess!'

Amelia's tearful soliloquy was, thankfully,

interrupted by a waiter who appeared in the doorway to inform them that Mr Sedley had just collided with another gentleman and a passing sommelier carrying a bottle of red wine and that Mr Sedley was going to be further detained because he had to go back to his hotel and change again.

'Oh God,' Becky groaned. 'Bring me a glass of champagne, and what do you want, Emmy? Though maybe not any alcohol, because it will just make you cry even more than you normally do.'

'I don't cry all the time.' Amelia raised a tear-soaked face to the waiter who was clearly wishing that he hadn't drawn the short straw when it came to being the bearer of bad tidings. 'The man Mr Sedley collided with — was he very tall?'

'Quite tall.'

'And was he wearing — '

'Very tall, very red of face with absolutely huge ears and feet, yes?' Becky stepped in, otherwise this would take up even more time that it already had.

'Yes,' the hapless man agreed. 'He was in a rush because he'd just ordered a car to the airport.'

'The airport!' Emmy wailed. 'But he was meant to be staying for another day so he could attend a panel on landmines.'

'What do you care?' Becky asked, waving the man away because that champagne wasn't going to get itself. 'He made his feelings perfectly clear, and anyway, you just said you didn't deserve his love.'

Amelia tried to glare and cry at the same time, failing to do either effectively. 'George . . . ' she sighed. 'He might not have bought Pianoforte, but he still reached out to me and we were . . . We were *intimate*, it was why we were in Cannes, so he does . . . did love me.'

'Ah, Cannes.' It was Becky's turn to sigh. 'I won't say I did it out of the goodness of my heart, because I didn't. I did it because George had earned some payback from me, but for goodness' sake, Emmy, I told you at the time that a man in love doesn't behave the way he did in Cannes.'

'You led him on,' said the feminist campaigner who was always banging on about the solidarity of the sisterhood.

'Believe me, I didn't have to lead him very far.' Becky started scrolling through her phone. 'This was all George,' she added, holding up the screen so that Amelia could see the note George had written on the back of a canapé menu. Becky had photographed it (because who knew when it might come in handy?) before she'd tossed it out of the back of her limo on the way to catch a private jet to Paris.

Darling, delicious Becky

As if you could ever imagine that Emmy means anything to me. She's a stupid little girl while you're all woman. As for Rawdon, he's too dumb to appreciate what he has. Why did you have to marry him when if you'd waited, you could have had me?

Together we would have been magnificent,

unstoppable, so at least let us have this one night.
I ache to possess you.
Your Gorgeous George XXX

'Judging by the date of the birth announcement, you must have already been pregnant when George was aching to possess me,' Becky said with a grateful smile at a new waiter who'd been persuaded to bring her a glass of champagne.

'Georgy . . . ' Amelia moaned faintly. 'I have to think of little Georgy.'

'Because big George is such a hands-on parent, is he?' Never had Becky so eagerly awaited the arrival of Jos Sedley because this conversation with Amelia was torturous. In fact, water-boarding had to be preferable to this. 'Oh, Emmy, we both know what you really want, so can we just stop all the amateur dramatics and tedious soul-searching?'

'I'm sorry if my pain and confusion is boring you,' Amelia sniffed, but she couldn't help but take the bait. 'What do I want, then? I wish you'd tell me because I'm sure I don't know.'

Becky leaned back in her chair and took a long sip of her drink. 'You want to race out of the restaurant just as a cab will inevitably pull up, and before its passengers can get out, you'll have already jumped in so you can scream, 'To the airport!' Although by now you're a good half an hour behind old Dobbin — all the better, so that when you do get there, you can see that his flight is about to depart and you jump the barriers and there's police and guards running after you

— though maybe they might just shoot you in the back because we are living in times of heightened security — and then you jump on to one of those airport buggies and you get to the gate just as Dobbin goes through and you call out his name and then . . . '

Becky took another long, long, *loooonnnnggggg* sip of her drink.

Amelia was in a torment. 'And then . . . and then what?' she begged.

'He turns around and sees you. He wants to be angry with you, wants to flounce away and cut off his huge nose to spite his big, red face, but he's loved you for so many years that he doesn't know how not to love you. And you've made this big, romantic gesture so maybe, just maybe, you do love him a fraction as much as he loves you, and even though he has important work to do — more orphans to drag out of burning buildings, no doubt — he has to take this chance. By now, you're thinking that you've blown it because Dobbin is just standing there with a gormless look on his face. You say his name again, falteringly, sadly, and he springs to life, fighting his way through the people still trying to board, falling over bits of hand luggage for comic effect . . . '

'Becky!' Amelia admonished. 'Don't be mean. Then what happens?'

'You run over to him, he holds out his arms and you jump into them and you kiss . . . '

'And everyone claps and cheers and I say that I've loved him, that I've always loved him . . . '

'And then the police arrive and they arrest you

for half a dozen crimes relating to terrorism and they send you off to Guantanamo Bay, never to be seen again,' Becky said with some relish.

'They *closed* Guantanamo Bay,' Amelia said, but her eyes were sparkling and full of hope. 'Oh! It's so romantic, like something out of a film. If I go now, I'd only be about fifteen minutes behind Dobbin.' She was already gathering up bag and pashmina shawl. 'I have to give it a shot. I have to show Dobbin that I do deserve his love.'

She was already halfway out of the room so Becky could finally yawn, then had to snap her mouth shut as Amelia's head popped round the door. 'But what about George's political career? He's tipped to be Prime Minister one day.'

'Ha! I very much doubt that,' Becky said. She'd just taken on a PA who'd been a junior researcher for the MP who had the office next door to George at Westminster. She'd had plenty to say about Gorgeous George and his extra-curricular activities with half the research staff of the House of Commons. Becky already had a lunch booked in with Laura Steyne, who owed her a huge favour now that she was running her father's empire. 'Go on! You only get one chance at love!'

'Becky, you're the best,' Amelia yelped and she was gone.

Becky Sharp smiled to herself. 'I know.'

THE *DAILY GLOBE* EXCLUSIVE! DISGRACED MP GEORGE WYLIE RESIGNS!

Scotland Yard launch an investigation as five more women accuse him of sexual harassment

The ambitious Minister for Environmental Affairs, who many tipped as a potential leader of the Conservative Party, today offered his resignation to the Prime Minister.

Epilogue

And so the great and good gathered to heap praise on each other at a five-hundred-quid-a-head gala dinner.

Jos Sedley, in a perfectly cut suit at last and quite dazed at the number of people who stopped by his table to talk to him about how the superfood technology behind his protein balls was eradicating world hunger.

Rawdon Crawley, due to be honoured for his tireless efforts to publicise the plight of the endangered New Zealand southern elephant seal, as he filmed what had turned out to be the most successful film franchise in motion-picture history. He'd begged to be seated at the very back of the room so he didn't run into any old friends. He was joined in social Siberia by his brother and sister-in-law, Pitt and Jane Sheepshanks-Crawley, who didn't realise they'd been seated on the worst table. On the contrary, they were simply thrilled to be invited and even happier to have a night away from their five young charges so they could discuss what to do with Thisbe (always Thisbe) now that he'd been expelled from his fifth school. 'It really isn't any reflection on our parenting skills or lack thereof,' Pitt assured Jane who smiled gratefully. 'I see a

447

lot of my late father in the boy.'

On a much better table sat Amelia and Dobbin, both glowing with happiness, which meant their faces were almost the exact same shade of red. Amelia was six months pregnant and as soon as her divorce was finalised, she and Dobbin planned to plight their troth and devote their lives to good causes.

George Wylie, of course, wasn't present. It was best not to show one's face when fifteen (and counting) very comely and very telegenic junior parliamentary researchers had all come forward to accuse one of taking liberties with them. George had retreated to his father's estate and was wondering if he could ever dare to show his face again. 'For God's sake, man,' the Chief Whip had said witheringly during the most humiliating ten minutes of George's life. 'We all do it, but the difference is, most of us are smart enough not to get caught doing it.'

Everything comes to she who waits, Becky Sharp thought as she lovingly caressed the Humanitarian of the Year award she'd just won for the benefit of the assembled photographers. Then she handed it over to Briggs, who was hovering dutifully behind her. 'Be a dear and stash this somewhere, will you? It's really ugly and I don't want to have to cart it around all night.'

'It is very eighties,' Briggs agreed with a shudder and disappeared to deposit the award in the green room and say hello to a couple of celebrities en route. No one was more relieved than Briggs that Becky's philanthropic endeavours now centred around black-tie dinners and they didn't have to go schlepping around any more refugee camps.

'Who'd have thought that we'd end up here,' Amelia gushed as Becky sat back down at their table. 'Six years ago we were on *Big Brother*.'

'Was I on *Big Brother*? I don't remember,' Becky drawled, lifting up a languid hand to wave at Bono who was a few metres away, hoping that he wouldn't come over. She'd sat next to him at one of Cindy Crawford and Rande Gerber's dinner parties and he really was the dullest man alive.

'Ooh! Is that Bono? Is he coming over?' Amelia asked excitedly, as Becky quickly stood up again.

'I have to go and say hello to the Duke and Duchess of Cambridge,' she muttered. 'It would be so rude if I didn't.'

She hurried off as fast as the tight skirt of her black gown allowed, shouldering Bono out of the way as if she hadn't seen him. It was so like Becky, Amelia thought. She herself had so many reasons to be grateful to Becky and so many reasons to still be furious with her that she could never decide if she liked or hated her.

Probably it was some complicated mixture of both, especially as Amelia suspected that very soon, she and Becky would be more than friends.

Very, very soon, because Jos sat down in the chair that Becky had just vacated and with shaking hands, pulled a little box from the inner pocket of his jacket. 'It's not like I can ask her father for her hand, on account of him being dead,' he said, trying to prise open the lid with fumbling fingers. 'But you know Becky better than anybody . . . '

'Does anyone really know that Sharp woman?' Dobbin asked, earning himself a fierce poke from Amelia, who'd asked him not to keep calling Becky that.

'She has many layers,' Jos agreed gravely. 'But she's given me reason to think that she'd quite like to become Mrs Sedley . . . she said that we could be the new Bill and Melinda Gates . . . '

'You're not *that* rich, Jos,' Amelia said drily.

'Almost that rich,' Jos said, because so many governments around the world had reserved parts of their aid budgets to purchase his famine-busting protein drink that he had more money than he knew what to do with. Even with Becky taking 25 per cent, like they'd agreed when she first came to him with the idea. But then Jos couldn't say no to her. His life without Becky Sharp in it had been a barren wasteland. 'Should have married her six years ago, as it goes, but was too much of a fool to realise it. Got your George to thank for that.'

'He's not my George,' Amelia said crossly, as Dobbin patted her hand, which rested on her bump. 'And he never really was.'

'But I have your blessing to marry Becky?' Jos asked nervously. 'I know she can be a bit tricksy, but the poor girl's had to fight her whole life.'

Amelia took her. brother's hand. 'You really love her and she really loves you?'

'I love her to the moon and back,' Jos declared instantly, though the second part of his sister's question took a little longer to answer. 'She did say that when she got married again, it would be forever.'

That wasn't exactly true. What Becky had said was, 'The first time I married for money, but now I'm very rich in my own right, so the second time I get married, it has to be for something better than being very rich.'

But Becky had just come out of a spin class and had been glistening with sweat and Jos had had her legs around his ears as he'd helped her stretch (Becky found it almost endearing just how much Jos hadn't changed over the years), so he hadn't been listening that closely.

Amelia stroked her bump meditatively. 'In that case, if she makes you happy, then you have my blessing.'

'And may God rest your soul,' Dobbin muttered under his breath, earning himself another poke in the ribs.

Meanwhile Becky was deep in conversation with the Duke and Duchess of Cambridge about how much work there was still to be done to eradicate world hunger, and also to finally finish the renovations to their private quarters at Kensington Palace.

'I know, underfloor heating is more trouble than it's worth,' she was saying when a tall man in a double-breasted suit greeted the Duke.

Another hanger-on, Becky thought, raising her eyes just as the Duke said, 'Rebecca, I don't believe you've met my father.'

The Prince of Wales, recently enough widowed that he was still wearing a black armband, but not so recently widowed that it was considered improper for him to attend a social function, smiled as Becky curtsied, which gave him a delightful view of her cleavage.

'Ms Sharp and I have met on several occasions,' the Prince said, taking Becky's hand as she straightened up. 'Though I'm sure you don't remember talking to an old bore like me.'

'That's not true,' Becky said, shooting the heir to the throne a little sideways look from under her lashes. 'We had an absolutely riveting conversation about Lady Hornblower's hat at a garden party a couple of years ago.'

'I was sure you'd have forgotten,' the Prince said, guffawing with delight. It was the first time he'd laughed since he'd been widowed. 'Those purple feathers.'

'You said that it looked like a gigantic feather duster and then I said how the hell do you even know what a feather duster is,' Becky recalled and they both laughed, but it was very bad manners to monopolise royalty, so Becky murmured something about having to talk to Bono and retreated.

Being a global philanthropist had become quite boring, Becky mused as once again she blanked Bono, otherwise she'd be stuck talking to him for *hours*. Yes, she'd restored her reputation and also saved hundreds of thousands of people from dying of hunger, but being a professional do-gooder was so tedious that the whole thing made her want to scream.

She really needed to find a new project. A new challenge. New heights to scale. So it was very serendipitous that a moment later, the Prince of

Wales's private secretary appeared at her side to ask if she might be free to dine at Clarence House later in the week. A private dinner. Just Becky and HRH, who was very keen, '*very keen indeed*', to become better acquainted with her.

'I'd love to,' Becky said. As she glided back to her table, she wondered if she'd still be allowed to take the title of Queen, what with her being divorced . . . ?

Enough! She was getting carried away. It would be a much better use of her time to rehearse what she'd say to Jos when she refused the absolutely hideous ring he'd bought a few weeks ago. Then she'd be free to devote all her time and energy to new projects. Happily, she was something of an expert when it came to old men and at least this one had more going for him than her previous conquests. Several palaces, quite a few duchies, not to mention the Crown Jewels . . .

But this was ridiculous: he wasn't the King yet! Although the current Queen couldn't live forever and when she did croak, HRH would need a lot of comforting, and Becky did look splendid in black . . .

'Which of us is happy in this world? Which of us has his desire? Or having it, is satisfied?'
Vanity Fair, W M. Thackeray

Acknowledgments

My most excellent editor, Martha Ashby, for asking me if I'd ever thought about writing a contemporary retelling of *Vanity Fair*, putting up with backchat in the comment boxes and saving me from several counts of libel. Thanks also to Kimberley Young and the team at HarperCollins.

My agent, Rebecca Ritchie, or The Other Becky as she's now known, for cheerleading me through a really tight deadline.

Simon Fox was a firm but fair copyeditor. My aunt Lesley Lawson seemed to be the only person in Britain who'd actually read *Vanity Fair* and could listen to me wondering aloud how to parse the Napoleonic Wars into the modern day. Eileen Coulter hadn't read *Vanity Fair* but she was still happy to listen to me banging on about it.

And to all the people who have ever wronged me, thank you. Every uncharitable thought that you've ever made me thunk, I channelled into Ms Becky Sharp. I couldn't have done it without you.

THE MARS ROOM

Rachel Kushner

Romy Hall is at the start of two consecutive life sentences at Stanville Women's Correctional Facility. Outside is the world from which she has been permanently severed: the San Francisco of her youth, changed almost beyond recognition; the Mars Room strip club, where she once gave lap dances for a living; and her seven-year-old son, Jackson, now in the care of Romy's estranged mother. Inside is a new reality to adapt to: thousands of women hustling for the bare essentials needed to survive, amid the deadpan absurdities of institutional living. Romy sees the future stretch out ahead of her in a long unwavering line — until news from outside brings a ferocious urgency to her existence, challenging her to escape her own destiny . . .

CALL OF THE CURLEW

Elizabeth Brooks

1939: Ten-year-old Virginia, an orphan, arrives to meet her new adoptive parents, Clem and Lorna Wrathmell. Their mysterious house, Salt Winds, sits on the edge of a vast marsh — a beautiful but dangerous place. It's the start of a new life for Virginia, but she quickly senses that all is not right between Clem and Lorna — in particular, the presence of their wealthy neighbour Max Deering, who takes an unhealthy interest in the family. When a German fighter plane crashes into the marsh, Clem ventures onto the deadly sands to rescue the airman - and sets in motion a fateful chain of events . . . 2015: Virginia, now eighty-six, has always known she will meet her death on the marsh. One snowy New Year's Eve, a sign arrives that the time has finally come . . .